Praise for *Singletini*

"Take one shot of shopaholic, one jigger of wedding planner, and one dash of pure fun, mix it all together and you've got *Singletini*, the coolest thing to hit chick-fic since cosmos and mojitos!"

—LAUREN BARATZ-LOGSTED,
author of *A Little Change of Face* and *The Thin Pink Line*

"Fresh, flirty, and oh-so-much fun, *Singletini* is a fantastic beach book. Amanda Trimble captures the zany highs and lows of the singles scene with pitch-perfect humor and style. A classic romantic comedy served up with a delicious twist."

—JOHANNA EDWARDS, national bestselling author of
The Next Big Thing and *Your Big Break*

"Tart yet sweet, Amanda Trimble's *Singletini* is a delicious read, the ultimate chick lit bonbon!"

—JOSIE BROWN, author of *True Hollywood Lies*

Singletini

A NOVEL

Amanda Trimble

THREE RIVERS PRESS • NEW YORK

Published in the United States by Three Rivers Press, an imprint of the Crown
Publishing Group, a division of Random House, Inc., New York.

www.crownpublishing.com

Three Rivers Press and the Tugboat design
are registered trademarks of Random House, Inc.

Library of Congress Cataloging-in-Publication Data
Trimble, Amanda, 1977–
    Singletini : a novel / Amanda Trimble.— 1st ed.
        p.   cm.
    1. Single women—Fiction. 2. Chicago—Fiction. 3. Dating services—
Fiction. 4. Female friendship—Fiction. 5. Weddings—Planning—Fiction. I. Title.
PS3620.R56S56 2006
813'.6—dc22   2005024347

ISBN-13: 978-0-307-23864-1
ISBN-10: 0-307-23864-4

Printed in the United States of America

Design by Chris Welch

10 9 8 7 6 5 4 3 2

First Edition

This is for the girls . . .

SIN•GLE•TI•NI

n   **1**: A curious type of female typically found living in urban settings; possessing an unusual, some would say deathly, fear of growing up and getting married **2**: *Informal* One who is single, having experienced her fair share of martini hangovers and painfully awkward what's-your-name-again conversations that tend to occur in the wee morning hours **3**: *Slang* Rare exotic butterfly, known to be highly social, with a select few even possessing talents in the ancient art form of matchmaking *syn:* MATCHER, MARRIAGE BROKER, SOCIAL ESCORT, LOVE LIAISON, GODDESS OF LOVE, CUPID, WINGWOMAN

Leo

Caution: tornado ahead. Your life is about to fly into a crazy whirlwind. Buckle up and hold on tight. Feeling lonely these days? Don't despair, little singletini. It's just a dating slump. You'll get your sparkle back soon. A hot new crush is right around the corner. Until then, keep your skirt on (literally) and enjoy the nightlife.

YOUR WEEK AT A GLANCE

STRENGTHS: Telling white lies
WEAKNESSES: Alarm clocks
CONQUESTS: Zero, nada, zip, zilch (Sorry, love. You've hit a dry spell.)
TO DO: Be prepared for big life changes. Don't freak out. We repeat. Don't freak out.

(Zero? Nada? Zip? Zilch?! Hmph. Stupid astrologers.)

In the Name of Love: Wingwoman Bares All

By Jay Schmidt

They're hip. They're hot. And they're for hire. Meet the wingwoman—the Chicago bachelor's new secret weapon. These single guys are saying if you want to score, you have to bring your game *and* your wingwoman. So I went undercover last night to test out this new generation of dating. And I quickly discovered my wingwoman would do whatever it took to hook me up with the girl of my dreams . . .

Chapter 1

OH. MY. GOD. What the . . . ?

My heart thumps wildly as I snatch a *City Girls* magazine off a Lincoln Park newsstand. I clutch the glossy little weekly in horror as my eyes zero in on the headline: WINGWOMAN BARES ALL.

Shitty! It can't be.

Chills prickle down my spine as I rip off my Diesel sunglasses to take a closer look. The mortifying picture just below the headline is every girl's worst *nightmare*. And it's right smack on the cover of the dishiest, most well-read social magazine in Chicago.

A butt photo.

Yep. There it is—a way-too-big snapshot of a girl's flouncy white miniskirt tucked into a lacy pink thong, her pearly white butt peeking out for the entire world to see.

I clap a hand over my gaping mouth. This can't be happening. It just can't be. I mean, that girl in the picture? It's . . . well . . . it's . . .

ME.

My cheeks flush feverishly as I inspect every inch of my high-resolution butt. Hands shaking. Head pounding. Panic. Panicky. Panicking. I mean, this is humiliating. This is a nightmare. This is . . .

Aaack! *Is that cellulite?* I squint hard, slowly turning the magazine right, then left. *It is!* I can't believe this. I close my eyes in pure torture.

Just then, a gaggle of girls struts past. They spot the picture from four feet away and immediately huddle around the newsstand. Their squeals of laughter hurt my ears.

"Look!" one girl shrieks, pointing. "That's hilarious. Can you imagine?"

"Eww!" another girl hisses. "Her ass is *droopy.*"

I whip around, shoving on my sunglasses and pulling up my puffy black North Face vest all the way to my ears. Tears well up as I glare down at the photo. At least you can't see my face. Someone is bound to find out, though. Aren't they? They'll recognize my outfit or my blond hair or something. I'll be discovered. I, Victoria Hart, will forever be known as the girl in the butt photo!

I need to get home—*fast.* Stuffing the magazine under my arm, I rush back to my apartment a few blocks away.

Damn my job.

Damn that reporter.

Damn last night.

Why do these things always happen to me? I mean, the night started off *sooo* wonderfully. You know . . . kind of. At least I thought so. (Okay. Okay. Maybe it was a tad shaky. But that's totally understandable. Right? It was my first night on the job!) Hmph. Maybe I should see what you think . . .

•

THERE WE ARE, flying down Lake Shore Drive in a sleek black SUV limo with the tinted windows rolled down, moonroof open, and our hair flipping all around. Just me, two other wingwomen, and a *City Girls* magazine reporter. It's a gorgeous April night. Crisp and cool. There are dark foamy waves from Lake Michigan crashing to the left and the Chicago skyline sparkling to the right. I gaze out the window at the Hancock Building as I nervously sip my bubbly champagne and try to remain calm.

Tonight I'm training to be a wingwoman. And I'll admit it, I'm freaking out. I have no clue what I'm doing. None. I mean, I went through wingwoman training and everything, but tonight is for real. Tonight I'm actually meeting clients and trying my best to hook them up with all the hot girls they're interested in.

I'm completely nervous. And it doesn't help that this stupid *City Girls* reporter is going undercover with us tonight to see if this new dating revolution actually works. I don't even know what I'm doing yet and he'll be analyzing my every move.

Oh God. I bite my lip. What if I screw up? What if . . .

Okay. I just need to relax. Everything will be fine. I take another sip of my champagne and glance over at the two other wingwomen. I barely even know them, but they seem nice enough, I guess.

There's Lexi, the Tyra Banks wannabe. She's a total diva—decked out in shiny gold everything and currently on her cell phone fighting with her agent in L.A. Something about a toothpaste ad? I don't know. Whatever it is, Lexi is livid and keeps screaming, "No fucking way! Tyra wouldn't be caught dead."

And then there's Redd, a strawberry blond babe in a skimpy red skirt and shockingly tall black boots. She's a self-proclaimed gold digger. Rough and tough in every way, with a set of pricey double Ds proudly stuffed into a black sequined top.

I eye my nonexistent cleavage self-consciously.

Anyway, I guess these two girls are the pros. They've been wingwomen since the very beginning, ever since Chicago Wingwoman opened its office down on State Street by Marshall Field's about a year ago. And they're supposed to be showing me the ropes tonight.

"Oh yeah? Well, fuck you!" Lexi suddenly shouts, snapping her cell phone shut and tossing it into her gold hobo bag. "Hmph. Minty fresh my ass!" she huffs as she steals a flute of champagne from the limo bar and downs the entire thing. "Look at me!" she bellows to no one in particular. "I have an amazing body. I should be doing Victoria's fucking Secret."

That's when Jay, the *City Girls* reporter, pulls out his spiral notebook and silver voice recorder. "Can I ask you girls a couple of questions before we get to the bar?" he asks.

"Shoot," Redd says, fluffing her strawberry blond hair.

Lexi gives Jay an evil stare, but shrugs. And I nod, trying my best to appear cool and confident like the other girls.

"Great." Jay grins, peeling off his suede sports coat. He clicks on the recorder. "Since we don't have a lot of time, let's get straight to it. Tell me. Why did you girls become wingwomen? Because it's fun? Because you get paid to party?"

"Screw that. I'm in it for a husband," Redd rasps, lighting a cigarette. "A rich one."

"Don't be stupid. You know we can't date clients," Lexi snaps, lowering her gold glittery eyelashes at Redd. "Talk about *desperate*."

"Speak for yourself, prissy pants." Redd laughs heartily, taking a long drag and blowing out a white puff of smoke. "I don't care what management says. They're crazy if they think I'd pass up an eligible bachelor with a fat wallet. Forget that! He's mine. Finders keepers."

Jay scribbles in his spiral notebook, then turns to me. "Okay. So. What about you? It's Victoria, right?"

I nod, shifting uncomfortably in the leather seats. "Um . . . I don't know. I guess I *like* being a matchmaker. I always have." I wrinkle my nose, realizing how naive and dreamy I must sound. But it's true! I've always played matchmaker for all my friends. First there was Julia and Kevin. Then Gwynn and Bryan. I mean, I'm really good at setting people up. And, well, that's what being a wingwoman is all about. Right? *I was born to do this job.*

"How cute." Lexi smirks, batting those eyelashes again.

"Oh Vicky, doll!" Redd coughs and slaps her knee. "You're cracking me up. I almost bought that bullshit. You're good. *Really good.*"

"Sounds like you're very dedicated." Jay smiles, ignoring the others. "How long have you been a wingwoman?"

"Um . . . actually it's my first night," I say. "These girls are showing me how it's done."

Redd yanks up her black sequined top and lets out a huge, "Hell yeah!" She holds up her champagne in cheers. "It's gonna be a real good night."

"To a good night!" Everyone whoops and clinks glasses. Well, everyone except Lexi. She's already on her cell phone again.

As we pull up to Fulton Lounge in the trendy West Loop meatpacking district, I can already hear the gyrating music thumping onto the streets. This is the city's new ultra-hip neighborhood, filled with cool brick lofts, art galleries, and loads of chic lounges, restaurants, and clubs. Our driver runs around and opens the limo door.

"Ready?" Redd grins, a fresh cigarette dangling from her lower lip.

"I think so," I say, taking a deep breath and dabbing on some sheer pink lip gloss.

Jay is already on the sidewalk, snapping photos as we climb out of the car. We squeeze our way through the designer crowd milling around outside, blue spotlights flickering all around our heads. I guess the clients are meeting us at the door. They have our pictures, so they'll find us. All we know is that they're businessmen from Texas with a lot of cash to throw around.

"I bet that's them," Lexi hisses, pointing a slick red fingertip at a pack of cowboys looking outrageously out of place among all the hipsters.

Redd stamps out her cigarette and nudges us toward them. "Hee-haw, ladies! Let's get after it."

Suddenly an arm sweeps around the four of us. It's attached to an enormous, red-cheeked man with a five-gallon cowboy hat and an expensive white suit.

"Howdy there!" he hollers. "I'm Max. Are you gals our wingladies for the night?"

"That's us," we say in unison.

"Boy, ya'll sure are a sight for sore eyes." Max tips his big white hat. "Meet the boys," he says, waving over the crew of cowboys. And suddenly we're surrounded by boots, blue jeans, and big ol' belt buckles. I can barely keep up with all their names. Billy, Clint, Austin, Luke, and . . . is it Dusty?

The girls decide they should take three clients each and I should stay with the reporter, so I can watch and learn while they do their thing. Lexi leads her Texans past the bouncer and into the glitzy crowd. And Redd flips her strawberry blond hair off her shoulders, hooks arms with Max, and flashes a big, dazzling smile.

"So tell me about your ranch," Redd purrs sweetly as she makes her way past the doorman. "Is it big?" Her other cowboy clients lag a few steps behind.

Jay turns to me, swinging his sports coat over his shoulder. "Should we grab a seat at the bar?"

We watch as Redd and Lexi work their magic. They flutter around the lounge like social butterflies, a brightly colored martini in one hand and a cowboy in the other. It looks effortless, how they work their way into conversations. How they flirt and laugh. How they casually introduce their clients. It all seems so easy. So natural.

And just look at how happy all the cowboys are! Max is beaming from ear to ear, chatting it up with a gorgeous brunette in a powder-blue slip dress. Lexi and Clint are working their game with a feisty redhead. And the rest of the cowboys are surrounded by six-foot blond models.

All of a sudden, I have an urge to give it a whirl myself. I mean, I can do this! *Totally.* I'm absolutely giddy with anticipation.

Just then, Redd struts up. "It's your turn, baby cakes. Show us what you've got."

"Awesome!" I hoot, leaping off the barstool.

Jay looks nervous. "Are you sure you're ready? Maybe I should go with Redd?"

"I can do it." I put my hands on my hips, slightly hurt. Why is Jay doubting me? How hard can this be?

"Go get 'em." Redd gives me a thumbs-up. "I'm gonna grab a drink. Yell if you need backup."

"Will do." I beam excitedly. I'm going to be fine, though. Better than fine. Brilliant!

"Let me take a closer look at you," I say to Jay.

He takes a few steps back, and I carefully eye him up and down. Cute enough. Very stereotypical writer. Tasseled loafers. Levi's. Rumpled blue oxford. That suede jacket thrown over his shoulder. Let's see . . .

My professional opinion: we're going to need someone a tad on the artsy side. Not funky, though. Very well read. Down-to-earth. *A nice girl.* Hmm . . . I scan the crowd.

Too high maintenance.

Too girlie girl.

Too porn star.

Ooh. Wait a minute . . . there! "What about her?" I point to a cute girl with rosy cheeks, tiny wire-frame glasses, and dark curls flowing all around her face.

Jay wrinkles his nose. "She's kind of nerdy. I can do better. Don't you think?"

What? Nerdy! She's cute. Adorable, actually. Doesn't Jay realize I'm a trained professional? Hmph. He should trust my judgment. That could be his soul mate! His entire reason for . . .

"What about one of *those* girls?" Jay points to a pack of Paris Hiltons, all skin and legs. In fact, as I look closer, I'm not entirely sure they even have clothes on.

Gulp.

"Um . . . yeah. Sure." I scratch my head, suddenly wishing I had downed more than one drink. A little liquid courage might be handy right about now. "Let me go feel out the scene. I'll be right back."

As I walk over to the Hiltons, my hands shake and my knees wobble. Okay. I just need to stay calm. Everything's fine. *This is my calling.* Get it together, Vic.

I plaster on my best glittery grin and prance right over.

"Hey!" I squeak. The flock of fake eyelashes, heavily lined lips, and big blond hair stares back at me.

Silence.

Um. Okay. This is awkward. Let's try again. "What's going on?" I say, a bit louder this time.

More silence.

They all frown.

Wow. Are you kidding me? No wonder guys need a wing-woman. These girls are like ice queens. "Don't you just love this place?" I say, even louder.

"We're trying to work," one girl snaps. "Do you mind?"

Thank God.

"ME TOO!" I yowl, practically throwing my arms around them. "This is my first night. Can I just tell you . . . I am *sooo* incredibly nervous."

The Hiltons eye me skeptically. Hmm. They're probably not used to running into other wingwomen, that's all.

"So where are your clients?" I smile, feeling totally relaxed now. I mean, I'm bonding with coworkers. This is so great! I wonder if they know Redd and Lexi? Ooh. Now that I think about it, I should really ask if these girls have pointers for me. They look like they've been around the block, um, a few times and . . . "Oh, I'm sorry. Were you saying something?"

"I said that's who we're looking for. Clients," one girl grumbles. "So if you could just . . ."

"You lost them?" I gasp. "I'm so sorry! Can I help? Maybe they're in the bathroom or something. How awful. Can you get fired for that?"

The Hiltons look at one another strangely and then burst out laughing.

"What's so funny?" I ask, my eyes growing wide. "Did I say something wrong?"

"Oh, sweetie! We're working girls."

•

RIGHT. OKAY. That didn't exactly go so well. It wasn't my fault, though. Jay picked out the prostitutes, not me. How could I have known? It was an honest mistake. The trouble is, things aren't getting any better. It's been one painfully awkward attempt after another.

"Oh my God. I love your shoes!"

"Um. You're blocking my view. Could you move?"

"Wow. Is that a Pucci scarf?"

"Yeah. So?"

"Your highlights are amazing."

"What? It's my natural color!"

"This is embarrassing. Do you have a tampon?"

"No."

"Don't you just love this place?"

"Vad? Förlåt? Jag förstår inte?"

"Tough night?" Redd asks Jay and me later in the evening.

"Awful." I sigh, my high hopes completely deflated by this point. "What's wrong with me? You and Lexi made it look so easy."

"Don't worry," Redd rasps. "You'll get the hang of it."

Jay jabs me in the ribs. "Hey! What about her? She's hot." He points to a gorgeous Asian girl in a white tank top, black miniskirt, and stilettos.

"Sure," I mumble. "Let me run to the bathroom real quick. Keep an eye on her."

I stumble into the restroom to regroup. I can't believe how hard this wingwoman stuff is! I thought it would be a snap. You know. Have a few drinks. Laugh. Chat it up with a few gorgeous people. Make an introduction or two. Easy breezy. But people just aren't interested in talking to random strangers. What am I going to do?

I grab a paper towel and dry my hands. I can't quit. No! Victoria Hart is not a quitter. I'm going to go out there and show everyone I can do this. Because I can! I just know it. I swing open the bathroom door and walk back into the shrieking laughter and thumping house music with newfound confidence.

As I march over to Jay, I suddenly become very aware that people are staring at me. Hmm? That's odd. Maybe I have toilet paper stuck to the bottom of my shoe? I stop and peer down at my silver strappy heels. Nope. Nothing.

Good God. People *really* are staring at me. How rude.

And look, is that girl pointing at me? My cheeks flush fever-ishly. What the . . . ?

Actually, she's laughing at me. Aaack! They are, too!

Wait. *Everyone is.*

I can feel tears pricking at my eyes. What's going on?

Redd suddenly comes bounding toward me. "YOUR __IRT!" she screeches.

"What?" I yelp. I can't hear her over the pulsating music.

Redd yanks the back of my skirt down. "Your skirt," she says breathlessly. "It was stuck in your thong!"

Oh my God. My heart stops. I whirl around and stare at all the howling faces in horror. People are doubled over in laugh-ter. (Which thong did I wear tonight?! Please let it be a cute one. *Please.*) The Hiltons are wiping tears away from their eyes. And that's when I see Jay . . . snapping pictures with his camera.

I can't believe him. I run over and rip the camera out of Jay's hands. "WHAT ARE YOU DOING?" I shriek.

"Hey! Give me that camera back!" Jay yells, dropping his spiral notepad and pencil. "I'm not going to print anything. Swear. What kind of guy do you think I am?"

"You're a jerk," Redd growls at Jay, then races after me. But I'm already pushing my way toward the door.

I'm MORTIFIED. (And really, *ree-eally* praying I didn't wear that grungy old blue thong with the hole in it.)

I clack down the stairs of Fulton Lounge, tears flooding down my cheeks. I just want to go home. I dump Jay's camera in a trash can and stumble into a cab. As we pull onto Halsted Street, I sink back into the dark sticky seats. And right as I'm about to shut my eyes, I pull up my white skirt just enough to see my thong. (Pink G-string. Calvin Klein. Very cutesy. Thank God.) My eyes flutter shut.

What a night. I have to be honest. I don't know about this

whole wingwoman thing. It's not how I imagined the job at all. I mean, I wasn't using any of my matchmaking skills.

How did I get myself into this?

I rest my head on the cool cab window and let my mind float back. I guess it all started about a week ago with that one phone call. THE NEWS THAT CHANGED EVERY-THING. I mean, I knew my friend's life was going to change forever. But little did I know mine would change, too. How could I have predicted that life as a singletini would never be the same?

Chapter 2

WHEN I GET THAT CALL, I know something's up. I just know it. Gwynn never calls late on a Sunday night. Ever.

"I'M ENGAGED!" she squeals as soon as I pick up my cell phone.

No hi.

No nothing.

I nearly drop the phone. "Are you kidding? Oh my God. *Tell me you're kidding.*" I can feel the blood rushing to my neck and cheeks. And I seriously think I might pass out.

I hear Gwynn laughing at the other end of the line.

"This isn't funny," I gasp, clutching my stomach. "I . . . I can't breathe. I mean, what? You're engaged? Are . . . are you sure?"

"Yes, I'm sure!" Gwynn shrieks. "Bryan proposed last night at Blackbird."

"Wow," I say, shaking my head in disbelief. I'm stunned. I mean, I know I set them up after college and everything, but I haven't been so sure about them lately. They've been fighting a lot. Mostly about Bryan's mom. She desperately wants him to move back to New York and Gwynn wants no part of it. None. And, well, I swore I wouldn't say a word, but Julia and Kimmie—our other two best friends—spotted Bryan getting cuddly with his old East Coast girlfriend, Kaitlyn, a few weeks ago. Yeah. I KNOW. And now he wants to marry Gwynn? I was expecting a breakup call, not this. It doesn't make any sense.

"Isn't this so super exciting?" Gwynn bubbles away. "Oh Vic—and the ring! It's amazing. You're going to die. I picked it out a few months ago. But . . . *shh*. Don't tell anyone. I want Bryan to get all the credit."

Wait a minute.

My ears perk up. Did she say ring? Gwynn never told me she went ring shopping!

"What does it look like?" I ask, my stomach suddenly fluttering with excitement. Don't get me wrong. I'm still not sure if this wedding thing is a good idea or not, but who doesn't want to hear about diamonds?

"I love, love, love it!" she squeals. "It's absolutely perfect. Super simple and super big!"

"It sounds amazing!" I gush, already wondering how much it was. It *had* to be ridiculously expensive if Gwynn picked it out. I mean, she grew up with an entire silver place setting in her mouth! Of course I'd never ask. That's so inappropriate. But . . .

Well? We *are* good friends . . .

(No. No. Don't do it.)

It's just a question. It's not like she has to tell me if she doesn't want to . . .

(Don't do it!)

"How much was it?" I blurt. Aaack! What's wrong with me? I'm terrible. Do I have no self-control?

"Mmm . . . I think it was, like, fifty or sixty? Something like that."

"Thousand?!" I cough. That's almost twice my yearly salary!

"Yeah. Hello! It's a Harry Winston."

"Oh. Right. Absolutely," I say, trying desperately not to show my surprise. I mean, seriously. Shut up! A Harry Winston? Isn't that the ring they give away on *The Bachelor*? Hollywood stars wear Harry Winston. And even they usually just borrow those sparkly boulders for Oscar night.

Gwynn keeps talking and talking—telling me all about how she really, *ree-eally* wants a September wedding and on, and on, and . . .

Wait . . . what? SEPTEMBER? That's not even five months away!

"Fall weddings are gorgeous. Don't you think?" Gwynn chatters. "It's still warm out. Not too hot. And it's so pretty with the leaves changing. I'm thinking the Lincoln Park Zoo. What do you think? Too overdone? I don't know about all those stinky animals, though. Eww. I'll have to think about it. Anyway." Gwynn sighs. "I'm so excited! Can you believe I'm actually engaged? I have a wedding to plan now. I have a *fiancé*!"

Once we hang up, I sit down on the corner of my bed in shock. This is not good. Not good at all. What if all those rumors are true? I'd feel terrible. *I set them up.* I'd be partially responsible.

I have such a bad feeling about this. And . . . okay, fine . . . it's not *only* because of Bryan.

I'll admit it. What . . . what does this mean for me? Gwynn is going to be a W-I-F-E. Part of a legally bound couple. Where will the rest of us girls fit in?

I know. I know. I sound incredibly selfish. I should be pelted with a thousand bags of that songbird-safe rice you toss at all the newlyweds. What's wrong with me? Don't I want Gwynn to live happily ever after?

I do. I really, really do. I want that for all four of us. But right now? We're having so much fun! Living it up in Chicago and being singletinis. We even made a pact.

It was our senior year at the University of Illinois. The night before we graduated. Gwynn, Kimmie, Julia, and I decided we had to go out big. We ended up at Kam's (where else?)—home of the drinking Illini and home to some of our best college memories. We danced and drank all night, and eventually made our way to the Quad around daybreak. It was so calm and peaceful. It felt like the entire campus was ours. We lay on our backs in the fresh-cut grass, gazing up at the lavender sky. We talked about everything that night. Our hopes. Our dreams. We were going to have it all when we moved to Chicago. The jobs. The money. The men. The martini parties. We'd be singletinis, someone said. "Long live the singletinis," we shouted over and over again, laughing into the sky. "Long live the singletinis . . ."

Ha! And I almost forgot. We even created a new martini the first night we moved to Chicago. (How fun is that?) We lugged home a couple bottles of SKYY and a bunch of ingredients and garnishes, and we mixed and experimented until we came up with the perfect drink. Our drink. The Singletini. Mmm. Speaking of, I could really use one right about now.

I mean, what is going on? What is Gwynn thinking? We've only had two years of bliss. (Crazy fun! Well . . . mostly. Everyone dates a few jerks. Right?) I mean, we're not ready to get engaged yet. Are we? We always said we'd get married later on, when we got older.

Oh dear God. Are we getting old?

"Arghh!" I shriek into a white ruffly bed pillow.

Okay. Calm down. Breathe. It's not like Gwynn's moving to

the suburbs or anything. (Oh no. *No way.* Gwynn would never do that. She has scoffed at the suburbs ever since I've known her. She always said she'd rather die than become one of those stuffy North Shore ladies.) Right. So getting engaged is not a big deal. People do it all the time. It was bound to happen. Nothing to get freaked out about. It doesn't mean we're getting old! Get a grip, Vic.

Armani, my chubby black cat, leaps onto my lap. The tiny silver bells on his collar *ting-ting-ting* as I scratch behind his ears.

Hmm. What time is it? I've got to talk to Kimmie! I dial her number, nervously biting my thumbnail.

Come on. Pick up.

Kimmie's answering machine flips on. *Hey, it's Kimmie. Leave a message.*

I call Julia and same thing. No answer.

Hmph. *Now what?*

I should take a bath. Relax. Clear my head. As I run the water, I examine my face in the vanity mirror above the sink. Are we really getting old? I lean in closer and tilt my chin up to get a better angle. There are faint lines at the edges of each eye. (What are those called? Crow's-feet?) I wrinkle my nose and watch as the annoying little lines deepen.

Eww.

I relax my face, stretch the skin back with my fingertips, and study the reflection. Better. But the lines are still there. *Great.* I'm prematurely aging. I'll probably have to get Botox before I'm thirty. And that stuff always looks so fake, anyway.

I step away from the mirror and sigh. At least the rest of my body is in decent shape. I lift up my T-shirt and tap my abs. Okay. Maybe I'm a tad bit softer than I was in college. But overall, not bad. I slowly turn and stand on my tippytoes to see my profile in the mirror. Suck in. Suck in.

At least my stomach is flat. Well, kind of . . .

I exhale sharply and watch in horror as a small (or not so small) pocket of skin forms under my belly button. Aaack!

I have a . . . oh my God.

I have a pooch.

How could I let myself go like this?

I throw myself onto the floor into a flurry of sit-ups. 1-2-3-4. Yes. Oh yes. 5-6-7-8. This is good. 9-10-11. I should do this every day. My abs will be back in shape in no time. 12–13–14. Yeah. I'm not getting old. Who cares if I have a friend who's engaged. 15–16. Woo. Okay. It's really starting to burn now. 17 . . . 18. Good God. Are you kidding me? This sucks.

I flop onto my back and groan. Pathetic attempt, Vic. Pathetic. Armani purrs and nudges his furry black head against my calf.

"Not now, Armani." I bat him out of the way, feeling tears spring to my eyes.

This is a crisis situation on *sooo* many levels. Why did Gwynn have to go and get engaged?

She's not ready for this.

I'm not ready for this.

Chapter 3

WHEN I WAKE UP the next morning, something is off. I can just feel it. My bedroom seems a little too warm. A little too bright . . .

I roll over and squint at the bedside alarm clock.

Shitty!

I rub my eyes, then check the fuzzy green numbers again.

IT'S TEN O'CLOCK. Oh my God. I was supposed to be at work—an hour ago!

This can't be happening. It can't be.

I leap out of bed, ripping off my T-shirt and boxers and flinging them on the floor. What's wrong with me? How is this happening to me—AGAIN? (Okay. Okay. I might have a teensy-weensy problem with being late. But now is *sooo* not the time to harp on it!)

What am I going to do?

I can't go in. Can I?

No. It's way too late. By the time I throw clothes on and race down to the office, it'll be almost eleven. Think, Vic. Think.

Should . . . should I call in sick?

No. No. I can't. I did that last Thursday. That's the day Kimmie got dumped by Jack the Ass and desperately had to go shopping. She *needed* me. And okay, Kenneth Cole was having one of their insane one-day sales and I really *needed* those black kitten-heel boots. I had to be a good friend to Kimmie. I couldn't let her go shopping alone. Right?

Okay. Okay. I need to focus. I'm standing here naked and I'm supposed to be at work this very instant.

Think.

Hmm. Doctor's appointment? (No. I used that excuse last Monday.) Grandma died? (Oh no—I don't have the nerve to bring Gramms into this.) Tell the truth? That I overslept? That I'm freaking out because my friend's engaged? Because her fiancé might be cheating on her? Because I'm getting old? (Hmm. I'm thinking no to those excuses, too.)

Ooh. Wait a minute.

I have an idea. (Yes. Yes. This is good.) What if I pretend that I marked today off as a vacation day? Pretend I told my boss, Krabby Karen, about it weeks ago? I mean, it's not my fault if it slipped her mind. (Perfect!) This means I don't have to call in *or* show up to work. After all, this was supposed to be my day off. I'll simply stroll in tomorrow as if everything is completely normal.

Ha! I'm brilliant. I can't believe I haven't thought of this plan before. I patter into the bathroom and turn on the shower. Do-do-do. I'm so pleased with myself I can hardly stand it. Honestly. Way to take a problem and really turn it into a positive. Well done, Vic. Well done. It's almost a shame I can't share this news with Krabby Karen. She's always saying I need to work on my problem-solving skills.

To be honest, I haven't learned much of anything else from my first postcollege gig. (Well, except how to shop online while making it appear as if I'm analyzing spreadsheets very, very diligently.) I work in computer sales and hate it. Despise it. I thought the professional world would be so different. Filled with expensive designer suits and briefcases. Schmoozy lunches. Super-important meetings with CEOs and head honchos. Me being that "go-to" person. Leading the team in do-or-die situations. Basically people handing me money and asking for my brilliant opinion all the time.

Yeah. Well. I'm definitely the "go-to" person. That is, Krabby Karen's "go-to" person for coffee, copies, and every other crap job.

"Victoria! Where's that fax? I need that fax."
"Victoria! Staple these. What? Yes. I mean ALL OF THEM."
"Victoria! Get in here. Are you checking e-mail again?"
"Victoria! Go on a Starbucks run. I need a tall skim latte. Now."
"Victoria! Get your nose out of that City Girls *magazine!"*
"Victoria! If I catch you on e-mail again, I swear . . ."

It's all I hear—Victoria! Victoria! Victoria! It's so annoying. Once, she actually accused me of putting whole milk in her latte to sabotage her diet. Yeah. I know. *The nerve.* (Of course, it's totally true. I *did* order her whole milk at Starbucks that day. But can you believe she actually called me on it?)

Wait a minute. Why am I wasting my precious day off thinking about Krabby Karen? I should be thinking about something fun. Like what I'm going to do today. Go shopping? Ooh. Grab a mani-pedi over at Maxine? (Ah! My favorite spa in the city. They have the most amazing chocolate mint scrubs and . . . oh, sorry. I'm getting a bit off track here.) Anyway, I could do anything. Lounge around here or run over to Starbucks and read my new *City Girls* magazine.

(FYI: I'm *obsessed* with the horoscopes in *City Girls* magazine. It's crazy, but I feel like they really speak to me. And they're always right! Well, except for this week. Those stupid astrologers said I'm in a dry spell with love. Whatever. I'm totally fine. I'm just really busy. You know . . . a lot on my mind.)

God. What a fantastic day this is turning into. And I've almost forgotten about the whole Gwynn-being-engaged-thing, too!

See? I barely mentioned it.

I'm blow-drying my hair when the phone rings and I answer it without thinking.

"Victoria! *What* the hell are you doing?"

Oh my God. It's Karen.

Why am I so stupid? Why didn't I check caller ID? I bite my fist. Should . . . should I hang up?

"Hell-LO?" she barks.

Pause.

Pause.

She sighs loudly. "Look. I know you're there."

Aaack! How? I whip around, eyeing the corners of my bedroom suspiciously. Is Karen stalking me? I pull my fuzzy pink-and-white-striped bathrobe a little tighter around my chest.

"Victoria, this is ridiculous. You have five seconds to answer me. One . . . two . . ."

"Karen! Hi! Hello!" I spurt at last. "Did you hear that? My phone was acting up. So crazy! Anyway, what can I, um, do for you?" My cheeks are burning hot and I seriously think I might faint.

"Funny," she snorts. "Your phone isn't the only one *acting up* today."

Okay. Stay calm. Remember the plan. This is your day off, Vic. Your vacation. What's Karen's problem?

"I'm sorry? I . . . I don't understand?" I try to fake innocence, but my voice is shaky.

"I'm calling to see if you're blessing us with your presence today?" she asks sarcastically.

"On my day off?" I squeak, biting my lip and bracing myself.

Silence.

Fingers crossed. Did she buy it? Oh God. I'm dying here.

Suddenly there's a rustling sound and then an explosion of . . .

Of laughter?

I can't believe it. Karen is laughing? She's seriously laughing at me? No. She can't be. Perhaps she's laughing *with me*? Yes. Perhaps she's embarrassed for not remembering that today is my day off. And she's simply chuckling at herself for actually thinking otherwise and disturbing me at home.

Yes. Yes. I'm sure that's it. Ha-ha! I giggle along with her.

"Oh Victoria. Your work ethic is es—" Karen begins.

Ooh. Ooh. Is she going to compliment me? My work ethic is excellent? Exemplary? I knew it! Karen secretly likes me.

"Especially horrendous," Karen finishes off in exasperation.

"What?" I blink.

"Oh, you heard me. This is a joke, Victoria. I can't even get you to come into work on a regular basis."

"But . . . I took this day off. Don't you remember?" I ask, my voice wobbling.

"No, Victoria. I don't remember," she snorts. "And funny, it's not marked in my Outlook calendar either."

"But . . ."

"No buts. I've *had it* with your stunts, Victoria. You're fired. Do you hear that? Fired."

What?

My jaw drops. I can't believe this. *She can't fire me.* Can she? This is my vacation day! This is just a big misunderstanding, that's all. A scheduling error. It's not my fault!

"I . . . I don't know what to say. I thought you were pleased with the job I was doing," I sniff, lifting my chin a bit higher.

"At what?" she roars. "Skipping work? Instant Messaging your friends all day? And honestly, Victoria, do I even need to bring up the Starbucks incident?"

I knew it. *This is about the whole milk.*

"You have no respect," Karen continues. "I've never seen anything like it. You don't even try! Sales is hard. Sales is . . ."

Right then, my phone beeps. I have another call.

I shouldn't take it. Should I? Whatever. I'm already fired.

"Can you hold on a sec?" I ask.

"Oh no! Don't you *dare* put me on hold while I'm firing you. Don't even think . . ." Click.

"Hello?"

"Vic! Oh my God." Kimmie's voice explodes through the receiver. "I've been trying to get ahold of you! Wait. Why are you at home? Oh, whatever. Have you talked to Gwynn? Unbelievable. Seriously. Unfuckingbelievable! Engaged! Admit it. You think Bryan is cheating on her. Don't you? I'm telling you, Kaitlyn, baby. Something was going on."

"Listen. I can't talk. I think I'm going to get sick."

"I know. I know. Me, too!" Kimmie wails. "I mean, seriously. Gwynn? Engaged?"

I rub my temples. "No. That's not what I mean. Let me call you back. Okay?"

"Um . . . hello! Earth to Victoria. Our friend is EN-GAGED," Kimmie bellows. "We need to discuss this. What the hell is wrong with you?"

"I'm sorry," I say, my voice cracking. "I need to go."

"Hey, what's going on?" Kimmie's voice suddenly softens. "Are you okay?"

"I . . . I don't know. I think I just got fired."

I finally get Kimmie off the phone after swearing over and over again that, yes, I am fine. And, no, I don't want her to send Krabby Karen hate mail. Or hire a hit man. Or do anything else without consulting me first. But thanks for offering.

I flick on the TV, but Karen's voice keeps ripping through my brain. *"You're fired, Victoria! You're fired! You're fired! You're fired!"*

My cheeks flush with embarrassment. I can't believe this. What will I tell my parents? They'll be so disappointed. I can see Mom now—pursing her coral lips, patting her silver salon-curlered hair, and huffing, "Oh Victoria! How could you? Good people just don't go around getting fired."

What am I going to do?

Should I run into work with flowers and balloons? Storm into Krabby Karen's office and shamelessly beg for my job back? I'd swear to take my sales position more seriously. No more coming in late. No more e-mail. No more yakking on the phone with the girls all afternoon. I'd be the perfect employee. Completely transformed.

Oh God. Even if I did transform, though . . . let's face the facts. The sales job paid miserably. Mainly because I was so miserable at it. Ugh. I remember when I first interviewed, they said if I worked hard I could make over $100,000 the first year.

Yippee! I was *sold*.

Thinking back, I probably should have given a tad more thought to my career choice. Okay. Okay. I'll admit it, I didn't give it any thought at all. I had no idea what I was getting myself into. None. But at the time, I had dollar signs dancing in my head. I just wanted to get to Chicago ASAP and worry about the details later.

The $100,000 thing turned out to be a total joke (surprise, surprise). I think I barely cleared twenty-five that first year. And I *tried*. I really did. You know . . . *kind of.* I mean, it's boring stuff. Who honestly cares about processors, airports, firewalls, and blah, blah, blah? It's like reading some awful cryptic code:

Intel® Pentium® 4 Processor w/HT Technology 3.0GHz, 256MB DDR400 SDRAM, 1MB Cache, 800MHz FSB, 52X CD-RW, 80GB hard drive, 10/100/1000 LAN, Microsoft® Windows® XP Professional

Eww. Just the thought of it makes my brain go numb. Forget it. I can't go back. It was pure torture, sitting at that stupid desk all day. Pretending to care about computers. Pretending like I knew what I was talking about. No. I'm through.

Um . . . and who am I kidding? Krabby Karen would never take me back.

But I won't have a paycheck anymore. And it's not like I can go without a job for very long. I have a little money saved up, but not much.

So what do I do now?

Chapter 4

"**I** CAN'T BELIEVE IT. She *actually* fired you?" Kimmie yowls, her crazy red curls bouncing all around her head. "What a bitch."

Meet Kimmie. She's every Irish stereotype you've ever heard of, all wrapped up into one adorable ball of energy. Loud. Obnoxious. Wild hair. Freckles. Fair skin. (In fact, she won the whitest legs contest in college four years straight.) And since she's from a huge Southside Chicago family, where you learn to drink before you walk (not really, but close), Kimmie has the astonishing ability to drink obscene amounts of alcohol in one sitting. I adore her.

As soon as Kimmie heard the news, she immediately called Julia and Gwynn for an emergency girl's meeting that night at Gramercy—our favorite Lincoln Park bar. It's the best. Very chic. Very *in*. All white and stainless-steel décor. Funky white egg chairs. And a cascading waterfall behind the bar. It's definitely a "be seen" kind of place.

"I'm so sorry, Vic," Julia says softly, her forehead wrinkled with concern. "Are you okay?"

I nod miserably, letting my chin fall into my hands. We're sitting in one of the back booths tonight, so hopefully no one can see how truly terrible I look.

"We have to *do* something!" Kimmie bangs her fists on the shiny table. "We have to, well, we have to, like . . . sue."

"What?" Julia shakes her head, clearly amused. "We can't sue."

"Oh yeah? Well, why not Ms. Soon-to-Be-Fancy-Pants Law-yer?" Kimmie demands, jutting out her freckly chin defiantly.

"Because it doesn't work like that," Julia says. Did I mention she's in her second year of law school? "It's a little thing called at-will employment. Legally, they have the right to termi-nate Vic at any time for any reason, with or without cause or notice."

"Blah, blah, blah. Lawyer-speak!" Kimmie cries. "What the hell kind of contract is that?"

"It's pretty standard," Julia says matter-of-factly. I watch as Julia throws her long dark waves into a ponytail and pushes up her silver wire-frame glasses. It just kills me how much Julia re-sembles a fine porcelain doll. Smooth skin. Fluttery lashes. Rosy cheeks. She barely looks real. Let's just say, she drove all the guys wild when she was growing up in the city and going to all the best prep schools. Her parents never let her date, though. They stressed grades, no goofing around. So it's no surprise that Julia turned out so serious, so responsible, so calm. (Okay. Yes. She's basically the exact opposite of me.) She's not even drinking tonight because she has a big exam tomorrow.

Anyway, as the super-cute waiter with the blond floppy hair (whom we nicknamed Blondie months ago) takes our order and flirts it up with Kimmie, Julia is already mapping out my plan of action.

"I think this is a good thing. I really do," Julia says. "You hated sales. Now you can find a job you're really excited about."

"Like what?" I ask, wriggling my nose. "I'd rather die than take another stuffy desk job. I want something different. Some-thing exciting. Something . . ."

All of a sudden Julia's eyes light up and she snaps her fingers. "You know. I did hear about this new thing . . ." She stops midsentence, looking doubtful. "Oh, I don't know. It's silly."

"Come on. Spill it. Don't be a tease," Kimmie says.

"Okay. Fine." Julia bites her lip and pushes up her glasses. "This is ridiculous, but I was listening to *The Mix* radio station the other day, and Eric and Kathy were talking about this trendy new job. I guess it pays really well and whatever. It's called . . . a wingwoman."

A wing . . . what?

Kimmie bursts out laughing. "A wing . . . *who*?"

"I know. I know. It sounds absurd. It's called a wingwoman." Julia giggles. "I guess they're, like, really hot girls who men hire to help them pick up women. That's it. And they get a hundred dollars an hour or something."

$100 AN HOUR?! I nearly fall out of the booth.

Kimmie snorts. "Um. Last I heard that was called prostitution."

"I don't know," Julia says. "Supposedly it's the new It job, whatever that means. And, well, Vic does have a knack for setting people up."

My palms are suddenly sweaty. And my pulse is racing wildly. "That's right. I do!" I bubble, my eyes sparkling with excitement. "What a cool job. Can you imagine? Getting paid to go out all the time. Helping the rich and glamorous find true love . . . wow."

"Okay there, slow down," Kimmie says, pushing red curls out of her face. "You're starting to worry me. You wouldn't actually consider something like that . . . would you? It sounds like some creepy escort service."

I cough awkwardly, gazing down at my empty martini glass. "Oh no. No, I don't think so. You're right." But inside I can already see myself flitting around the city with my sack of lucky arrows, seeking out soul mates for the dating challenged. It'd be the greatest job in the world! And come on, how cool would it be to make $100 an hour? That's a lot of money. Let's see. An average night out:

8 P.M. to 1 A.M. = 5 hours

5 hours × \$100 = \$500

\$500 in one night?! That would be incredible. Just think. I wouldn't have to scrounge around for cash anymore. And with that kind of money, maybe I could even . . .

Shop at Barneys.

Oh my God. I've wanted to shop at Barneys my ENTIRE LIFE. Mom used to take me there when I was little to window-shop. We only went to browse for "ideas," though, so later when we shopped at the cheaper department stores we'd know which knockoffs to buy. For Mom, this was purely an educational trip. Her daughter needed to know how to shop smart.

But for me, it was something so much more. As soon as we pushed through the heavy glass doors and the sweet flowery perfumes tickled my nose, I was love struck. It was like a whole different world, where everything (and everyone) was beautiful. I loved gazing at the rows and rows of plump leather bags. Racks of gleaming belts. And the rainbow of vibrant lipsticks. I felt special just being around all the new and luxurious things. It was *almost* like having them.

Ah! I remember trotting through the store, hand in hand with Mom. She'd reach out and finger a delicate red scarf and gasp at its soft indulgence. But once she flipped the price tag over, her face would grow cold and hard. "Psshh," she'd puff. "We can get the same thing at Sears in Oakbrook for half the price. Just wait." But I always dreamed about buying that red scarf. Taking home that sweet delicious perfume. And happily strutting out of the store, swinging my very own black Barneys bag.

Sigh.

Stop. Stop it right now. I'm being ridiculous. I mean, come on . . . me? A wingwoman? I don't care how much it pays, it's a silly idea. *Crazy!* It's probably some weird escort service like Kimmie said.

But what if it isn't?

"Wait a minute. I KNOW!"

" Kimmie cries, her voice jerking me back into reality. "Maybe you could be a copywriter with me? We're hiring."

Hmm. A copywriter . . .

"Now that's a thought," I say, bobbing my head up and down. I *have* always been a teensy bit interested in advertising. Haven't I?

Okay. No. But . . . it could be cool.

Kimmie is a junior copywriter at Lambert Advertising—the best agency in the city (so she says, anyway). She loves it, and all her work stories always sound so fun. Crazy brainstorms. Wild photo shoots. Plush parties. I mean, I'm sure it's not *quite* as exciting as matchmaking, but I'm thinking it'll probably be easier to explain to Mom and Dad. And it's definitely a smarter career choice. Yes. Absolutely. A smarter career choice. And that's exactly what I need to be thinking about . . . not some dreamy matchmaking job.

I peer over at Kimmie, biting my thumbnail. "Do you think?"

"Totally!" Kimmie beams excitedly. "I'll try to get you an interview."

Good. Great. Now all I have to do is get that silly image of me playing merry matchmaker out of my head and everything will be just perfect.

Blondie finally drops off our new icy cold cocoatinis and Julia's Perrier. He flashes a killer grin and jets off. Kimmie licks her lips.

"That one's mine," she whistles, clinking glasses with Julia and me. "He gets cuter every time. What a hottie tottie."

And that's when I see Gwynn rushing into the bar. Her face is pink with happiness.

"Hi girrrls!" Gwynn coos as she swaggers over to our table. She has on a pair of Earl jeans, a crisp white tuxedo shirt, and a cute floppy turquoise driver's cap (à la Cameron Diaz). She flips her pin-straight blond hair off her shoulders and bends down to kiss each of us on the cheek.

Good ol' Gwynn. She looks as polished as ever. Fresh shimmery highlights. Glossy red lips and nails. Cute pudgy nose. And that cool modelesque mole right above her lip. It amazes me how Gwynn always looks like she could walk a runway on a second's notice.

"So sorry I'm late," Gwynn says, absently checking her watch. "Today has been *insane*. All the calls to make. So many people to tell about the engagement." She sighs. "You guys have no idea."

Oh, right. You should probably know a little more about Gwynn. She had time to make all those calls today because she doesn't *exactly* work. Gwynn got her degree in communications so she could help her famous fashion-designer father, Erik Ericsson, with his public relations. (Erik makes all this crazy haute couture stuff. Stars *love* him. But just between you and me? I think his things are sort of weird. I mean, frilly gowns made out of feathers?)

Anyway, Gwynn's idea of PR is shopping all day and going out all night, and telling everyone she knows how fab her father's dresses are. In Gwynn's defense, she does know E-V-E-R-Y-O-N-E. And, well, Erik doesn't seem to mind her "unconventional" PR methods.

Sigh. I really wish I didn't need to get a new job—I'd *kill* to go shopping all day. But it's hard to be jealous of Gwynn for long. She's super generous, always picking up a cute top or some dangly earrings for us girls. And she always lets us raid her closet for last-season stuff.

"Congratulations," I finally say, giving Gwynn a warm hug.

"You must be so excited!" Julia cries.

"Oh yes," Gwynn says breathlessly, scooting into the booth

next to Julia. I wonder what it feels like to be engaged? I bet it's weird. I bet you feel older. More mature.

Yeah. Totally. I mean, I remember Gwynn and me as college freshmen, giggling about the day we'd get engaged. We thought we'd be so smart. So sophisticated. Hmm. Come to think of it, I also remember Gwynn saying she wanted a really small, romantic reception. Nothing crazy or elaborate . . . no matter what her high-maintenance mother said. I wonder if Gwynn still wants something intimate? Oh, I'm sure she does. I mean, she mentioned the Lincoln Park Zoo. I could see that being cute and quaint. Can't you?

I inspect Gwynn carefully as she chats with Kimmie and Julia. Funny, she doesn't really look more mature. No transformation. No "whole new Gwynn." No *woman*. Nope. She just looks like the same ol' Gwynn I met in college. Maybe a little glowy in the cheeks. But that's about it. Kind of disappointing, to tell you the truth.

Suddenly Blondie appears again with four lemon drop shots. He slides the tray onto our table. "I hear you ladies have some celebrating to do tonight." He winks at Kimmie. "It's on the house."

"Oh my gosh! Thank you so much," Gwynn gushes.

"Can we get another round of cocoatinis when you get a chance?" I add.

"Sure thing," Blondie says.

"Ooh. Can I get a Perrier, too?" Gwynn lifts her perfectly red manicured finger in the air, calling after Blondie. (Is it just me? Or is she flicking her left hand around more than usual? Trying to show off her sparkly new ring?)

He writes down her order and disappears.

"So. What's going on?" Gwynn asks excitedly. She flips her hair off her shoulders with her left hand. (See! There's the wedding hand again.)

"What do you mean . . . *what's going on*?" Kimmie explodes, her green eyes wide with disbelief. "YOU'RE ENGAGED. Let's see the ring already!"

Gwynn takes a deep breath and very slowly places her left hand on the table.

Gwynn wasn't lying. It is BIG.

"Oh my God." Julia gasps, grabbing Gwynn's hand. "It's gorgeous!"

"Thanks." Gwynn smiles proudly. "Didn't Bryan do a great job?" She winks at me.

"I'll say. That thing is huge!" Kimmie lets out a loud whistle. "What a rock."

"Can I try it on?" Julia asks softly.

Reluctantly, Gwynn slides the ring off. She carefully hands it over to Julia, who slips it onto her delicate ring finger and holds it out to admire. "I wonder when Kevin will propose?" She sighs.

What?

Not Julia, too? I can feel chills prickling up my spine.

"Have . . . have you guys talked about that? You know. Um. Getting engaged?" I peep.

"Kevin thinks we're too busy." Julia frowns, pulling the ring back off. Kevin is Julia's boyfriend of almost two years. (I introduced them just after college. He was a friend of an old high school friend, and they hit it off immediately.) Kevin is an investment banker at J. L. McConnell in New York and he's always crazy busy. Julia says she doesn't mind the distance (they've always lived in different cities), but I'm really starting to wonder. She hasn't been visiting him in New York as much lately. And she was crying the other day when I picked her up for our mani-pedi appointment. She said they had a fight and it was no big deal. But I don't know. It sounded like there was more to it. MENTAL NOTE: NEED TO CALL JULIA

THIS WEEK AND ASK HOW THINGS ARE GOING WITH KEVIN.

My hands are shaking as I take the heavy platinum ring from Julia and hold it up to the light. I take in the three enormous round-cut diamonds. So this is what a $60,000 ring looks like.

Huh. It twinkles.

I slide the glittering circle onto my finger and stare, slowly rocking it back and forth so the light hits it at different angles.

Wow. All the sparkly colors. They glimmer like little rainbows. Look at them. Hundreds of tiny rainbows in there waving back at me. If I ever get married, I want something like this. (Um. But maybe a tad smaller? My hand feels incredibly heavy.)

That is, *if* I ever get married. And that's looking like a pretty big *if* these days. I haven't dated someone in . . . well, let's just say a very long time.

I give the ring back to Gwynn. "Shot, anyone?" I ask, reaching for a yummy lemon drop and scanning the bar for Blondie. We're going to need a few more of these shots ASAP.

I glance over at Gwynn as she blissfully replays the exact moment Bryan proposed—millisecond by millisecond.

Um. Make that *a lot* more shots.

Chapter 5

I THINK I'M GOING to die. Seriously. My head. It feels like it's about to explode. I really, really didn't need that last cocoatini last night. Or the lemon drop. Or the . . .

Ouch. What *did* I drink last night, anyway? I close my eyes tightly, wishing the needling pain in my head would stop. Ugh. Need more sleep.

The phone rings and I jump. Who'd be calling me this early—on a weekday? I swat at the bedside table, fishing for the phone.

"Hello?" I groan.

"Darling. I wasn't expecting you to answer. What are you doing at home? Why aren't you at work? Are you sick?"

Drats! It's Mom. Think fast. I can't tell her I got fired.

"I feel awful," I moan dramatically. "Let me call you back."

"Oh dear. Do you have orange juice? Drink orange juice. Have you been taking your vitamins? Should I call the family doctor?" Mom sounds worried, and I feel rotten for lying to her. I can practically see her wringing her hands out in Naperville, the suburb where I grew up. She's probably sitting at the kitchen table, the warm sun flooding through the bay windows, with those big fat curlers on her head as she applies a fresh coat of Avon all-day gloss. (She *loves* her coral lipstick.)

"No. No. Don't phone the doctor," I say quickly. "It's just a bit of a cold. But . . . um . . . can I call you later?"

"Of course, dear. Of course. Just one thing, though," she clucks. "Since I have you on the phone. I heard about your friend the Ericsson girl today at Club. Gwyneth? I always thought she had such a pretty name. Just like that actress, Gwyneth Paltrow. Gorgeous woman. Don't you think?"

I close my eyes, pressing my throbbing temples. "Gwynn, Mom. Her name is Gwynn." Fire. My head is on fire. Definitely going to explode. Clear some room.

"Ah, yes. That's right. Gwynn. Is that short for Gwyneth? Like the actress?"

"No, Mom." I sigh, throwing a pillow over my head. "It's just Gwynn."

"Oh right. Anyway," Mom chirps, "you girls must be thrilled!

This being your first friend getting engaged. Won't it be super someday when *you* get engaged?"

"That would require a boyfriend, though. Wouldn't it?"

"Yes. I suppose so," she trills. "But that'll happen soon enough. Did I tell you about . . ."

"Listen," I groan. "I really feel miserable. Let me call you later."

"Yes. Yes. Call me later. Don't want to pester you, dear. Ooh! I almost forgot. Rick and Claire's wedding is a week from Saturday. You *will* be there, won't you?"

Oh. Right. In high school, Rick was my boyfriend and Claire was my best friend. Long story short: they were sleeping together the entire time Rick and I dated. And unfortunately, we still run into one another because my mom and Claire's mom, Linda, are still best friends. They just pretend like it never happened. It amazes me.

"Arghh! I forgot about that." I grumble. "Do I really have to go?"

"Of course," she snips. "What would I tell Linda? And be honest now. Wouldn't you regret missing Claire walk down the aisle?"

"Nope. Can't say I would."

"You two used to be so close. I never understood what happened there."

I close my eyes. "She was sleeping with Rick."

"Oh now, you can't believe every rumor," she puffs.

"I walked in on them!"

Mom clears her throat. "Yes. That was a bad situation. It was ages ago, though."

"Five years is not ages ago," I correct her.

"Right. Well. It was very nice of Claire to invite you. She's making an effort. You need to also."

"Yeah. More like an effort to throw it in my face. To prove once and for all that Rick is officially hers."

"Oh Victoria . . ."

"Fine. I don't want to talk about this anymore. If it's that big of a deal, I'll go. Okay?"

"Good!" I can hear her clapping with delight. "Why don't you wear that pretty peach dress I got for you? The one that was on sale at Sears? Hmm? No black. Black does nothing for you. And . . ." Blah, blah, blah.

Once we get off the phone, I lie in bed for a few minutes and stare up at all the cracks in the ceiling. Sun is flooding through the windows, making me feel a tiny bit better. It's so warm and cozy.

Yep. I really do like my apartment. It's pretty typical for a one-bedroom starter in Lincoln Park. Super tiny (like six hundred square feet). Ancient appliances. Horrendously bad plumbing (as in, I have to pull a rusty chain to flush the toilet). And all for the outrageous sum of $1,200 a month.

I know. I know. It's way too much money, but when I saw the gorgeous stained-glass window in the living room and the cute paint-chipped fireplace (à la Pottery Barn), I had to have it. Okay. Fine. I'll admit it, I also like that it's on Armitage Street—only the BEST shopping spot in Chicago. Well . . . besides Oak Street with Kate Spade, Jil Sander, Hermès, and *Barneys,* but that's completely out of my league. So Armitage is just right for me. It's a cozy little patch in Lincoln Park. (Never mind that I have to share my neighborhood with a particular breed of Chicago girl—the gold-digging Lincoln Park Trixies, with their sparkly silver Jettas, no-foam lattes, and big bouncy ponytails. They all look identical and have the exact same goal in life: marry rich. *Very, very rich.*)

Despite the Trixies, I love Lincoln Park. The tree-lined streets are filled with the most adorable corner cafés and fantastic boutiques—like Sugar.

Oh, Sugar. It's the cutest shop ever, with the most amazing

designer stuff for ridiculously cheap. I stop by there at least every other day. You should really check it out. (Um. But can you be discreet about it? We don't want the whole world crowding in there and snatching up all the best deals, now do we?)

Anyway, Kimmie and Julia live over in Bucktown, a slightly edgier and more up-and-coming neighborhood with lots of funky lofts, quirky shops, and eccentric cafés. They're both jammed into apartments very similar to mine (old and tiny). But Gwynn? Oh, no. She lives down on the Gold Coast, on the corner of Michigan Avenue and Oak, in a glitzy high-rise condo (compliments of her handy-dandy trust fund). Gwynn's condo is completely loaded and completely brand-new. Living room, dining room, and bedroom all by Design Within Reach, Limn, and a bunch of obscure foreign artists (friends of her father's, of course). And her kitchen is fully stocked with every Williams-Sonoma gadget imaginable. (I know these details because it's all Gwynn could talk about for a month straight when the designers were creating "her look.")

So you'd think Gwynn would be super uppity since she's a trust-fund baby and all. Right? Well, she's not. Not really. In fact, I didn't even know her parents were wealthy until sophomore year, when she pulled up in a shiny red BMW convertible. She hid her money well as a freshman (said she didn't want to stand out), but by sophomore year she figured people already liked her or didn't, regardless of the size of her checkbook.

Her money never caused a problem . . . not until we moved to Chicago. And we're not talking about big issues. But it just highlighted the fact that, well, Gwynn is different from the rest of us. While Kimmie, Julia, and I scrounged around to make rent that first year, Gwynn spent her days at the spa. It's not like she didn't invite us. (She even offered to pay!) The thing is, Gwynn just never seemed to understand why Kimmie and I *had* to work, and Julia *had* to study. I love Gwynn. I really do. But sometimes it feels like we live in two separate worlds. Worlds that move farther apart all the time.

Okay. Okay. Enough about this. I can't stay in bed all morning. I throw back the fluffy white duvet cover and crawl out of bed, swaying a bit on my feet. I put on my bathrobe and shuffle into the closet-sized kitchen to make some coffee.

I'm instantly repulsed. There are piles of crusty plates and soggy cereal bowls scattered everywhere. There's an old Giordano's pizza box flipped open on the counter. (Eww! Is that mold?)

This place is disgusting. What happened to my neat and tidy life? I need to clean. I need to get organized. I need to make a list.

I rummage through my bag and pull out a silver pen and my small red leather planner. FYI: I totally L-O-V-E my jade Hogan bag. I got it in some sketchy back alley the last time I was in New York with Julia, when she was visiting Kevin. I'm pretty sure the thing was stolen, because it only cost me $65. But, hey, I'm not complaining. It's fab. I adore it.

I grab the pen and furrow my brow in concentration. On the top of the page, I write: Grocery List.

Now let's see . . .

1. *Coffee beans*

Hmm . . . what else?

My eyes slowly drift over to the blue paint–chipped kitchen table. Ooh! Is that the latest *City Girls* magazine? *I totally forgot about that.* How fun. I glance down at my grocery list and wrinkle my nose. Maybe I'll finish this later. You know . . . just as soon as I catch up on all the latest Chicago gossip.

As I pad into the bedroom, I catch a glimpse of myself in

the hall mirror and stop. I lean forward and smile big, checking the lines around my eyes.

Yep. Still there. What should I do about these annoying little suckers? Maybe I should see a dermatologist? Ooh. Or I could try some of that antiaging serum. (La Bella? Or whatever that expensive stuff is all the Hollywood stars obsess over.) I pull open my robe and check my stomach.

Gross. There it is! I pinch the newly found flesh right below my belly button and sigh. I really need to go on a diet. What's happening to me? I'm getting wrinkles. I'm getting fat. My apartment is trashed. All of a sudden my entire life needs a makeover.

My thoughts are interrupted by the phone. It's Gwynn.

"So glad I caught you!" she exclaims. "Are you free for lunch? I'm absolutely dying to ask you something. Does two o'clock work for you?"

"Um. Sure. What's going on?" I ask curiously.

"I'll tell you at lunch. 'Kay? Meet me at Spiaggia's. You're going to adore this place. Trust me."

I can't believe it. I'm finally going to Spiaggia! This is *sooo* exciting. Kimmie told me people at her ad agency have paid almost $300 just for lunch. And Hollywood stars dine there when they're in Chicago. Eee!

But wait . . . I wonder what's going on? Why does Gwynn want to have lunch on a random Tuesday?

Ah! I bet she's going to ask me to be a bridesmaid. Ooh. Ooh. Or her maid of honor. How cool would that be? Not that I think she should marry Bryan all of a sudden. But if it's going to happen, at least I'll be in a high-ranking position.

People pay a lot of attention to you when you're the maid of honor. You're, like, the second most important person in the wedding. Okay. The bride. The groom. Then you. Well, maybe the parents fit in there somewhere, too. But whatever, you're definitely in the top ten most important people at the wedding.

What should I say when she asks me? I mean, this isn't the kind of thing where you just squeal: *Oh my God. Yeah, totally!* No. This is something Gwynn will remember forever. She's probably been planning this moment her entire life. (Or at least since we met.) I can't screw this up. I need to put some real thought into this. I need to sound eloquent. Sophisticated. Honored. Yeah. Yeah. That's a good word. I'm truly honored . . . (Hmm. Honored about what, though?)

That she picked me? Yes. Truly honored that she picked me as her maid of honor. Or bridesmaid. Although I'd be pissed if she only asked me to be her bridesmaid. I *deserve* this position. I really do. In fact, I should get the chance to present my case on why I deserve to be Gwynn's maid of honor. Yes. In front of a panel of judges. Like *American Idol*. But better.

I can see it now. Me. Standing onstage in a bikini. Oh wait. Scratch that. No bikini competition. It would be much more tasteful than that.

Let's try this again. So there I am. In a shimmering evening gown. Preferably blue or lavender. And I'd be speaking very eloquently into a microphone about how dear our friendship has been over the years and why I should be her maid of honor. How I was her roommate and very first friend in the college dorms. How I listened to her cry every time some jerk broke her heart. And how I set her up with Bryan. (That alone is proof that I should be her maid of honor. Don't you think?)

Ooh . . . wait! I know. Maybe the competition could be like *Survivor*. All the maid of honor candidates would be put to the test. Head-to-head. We'd have to run obstacles. See which one of us could make better time down the aisle. (Oh yes. This is brilliant!) Maybe I should mention this to Gwynn? She'd be grateful to know I've put so much thought into the position.

Again, another reason why I should be chosen as her maid of honor.

Eee! I'm going to be Gwynn's maid of honor. Should I call Kimmie and Julia and tell them?

No. No. I don't want to brag. That would be rude and very un-maid-of-honor-like. Hey, wait a minute.

Do I get to register as a maid of honor? I *do* need some items for my ratty kitchen. MENTAL NOTE: MAKE SURE TO ASK GWYNN ABOUT *ME* REGISTERING.

Ooh. I better get going. I don't want to be late and make a bad impression right off the bat. I need to show Gwynn how dependable I can be. How punctual I can be. You know . . . when I really set my mind to it. After all, I don't want her changing her mind at the very last minute.

Chapter 6

I JUST NEED to make one quick stop at Bloomingdale's before I meet up with Gwynn. It'll only take a sec.

"So how's your antiaging serum?" I ask the makeup lady, who is peering down at the rows and rows of sparkling jars and canisters in her domain. I point to a green glass bottle with elegant type that reads La Bella. (Yeah. Yeah. I know. I'm currently unemployed and I should probably be buying Neutrogena and sticking to a budget of some kind. But come on, this is an emergency. I'M GETTING WRINKLES. This is no time to skimp.)

The older lady glances up to reveal frighteningly dark eye makeup and fake eyelashes.

"Ooh! Our wrinkle serum is *amazing*. One of our best

products. A real miracle worker!" she says, waving her arms in the air dramatically. "I'm Dorthea, La Bella specialist. Pleased to serve you. And you are?" she asks, smiling expectantly and extending her hand for me to shake.

"I . . . um . . . I'm Victoria," I say, shaking her hand awkwardly.

"Victoria, it's a real pleasure to meet you!" She beams. "What can I help you with today?"

"I guess I'm interested in the miracle worker," I say. "I think that's what you called it?"

"Ah, yes!" Dorthea smiles enthusiastically, pulling out a glass tester bottle. "This is a fabulous product, like I was saying before. It energizes and tones the skin. Youth in a bottle. An instant face-lift!"

"Really?" I say excitedly. "I'd like to buy a bottle then."

"Fantastic." She smiles. "What a splendid gift for your mother. She'll be very pleased. And may I say, La Bella guarantees 100 percent satisfaction, so if she's not pleased, she can . . ."

"Actually it's for me," I explain.

Dorthea laughs. "For you? Oh no, dear. This product is all wrong for you. Let me recommend something for your skin type." She leans over the counter, peering over her tortoiseshell glasses to examine my skin. She smells faintly like brown sugar. "Is your skin dry, oily? Or a little of both?"

"Mmm. Dry, but . . ."

"Right. So. This five-step cleansing system is ideal for you. See." She flips open a pamphlet and points to a diagram. "First you use the cleansing gel. Then this specially formulated . . ."

"That's nice, but I really want the wrinkle serum." I smile, pointing to the green glass tester bottle.

"Right. I understand. But that's only for skin types showing signs of aging. Yours isn't, so it's not appropriate. Mmmkay?"

"Ooh! But it is. See?" I smile as wide as I can and point to the wrinkles forming around my eyes.

She stares at me blankly and turns back to the pamphlet. "Right. So. After you apply the oil-absorbing tonic, you use . . ."

"I want the wrinkle serum," I say firmly.

She raises a heavily penciled-in eyebrow. "I'd appreciate it if you wouldn't interrupt me. Mmmkay? I don't like losing my place. Now. Did I mention that this legendary La Bella collection even comes with a roomy bag and . . ."

"Okay. Look. I'm really sorry, but I'm kind of short on time. So if you'd just sell me the . . ."

"Are you insinuating that my time isn't valuable?" she snaps. I notice that her bright-orange lipstick trails off her lips and sprays into the wrinkles around her mouth.

"No! Not at all. I just want to buy this serum," I say, holding up the tester bottle.

"Now lookie here," Dorthea says, narrowing her eyes. "I'm simply trying to help you find the *correct* solution for your skin type. Mmmkay? And now you've insulted me. So if you wouldn't mind, please step away from the counter."

What? I look around to see if there are any other makeup ladies to help me, but unfortunately, I'm stuck with Dorthea the skin-care Nazi.

"Ma'am. Please remove your hand from the counter and step away," she says.

"Okay. Okay. Okay. Listen. I didn't mean to offend you . . ."

"I apologize, but I can no longer serve you at this time," she says, sternly folding her arms behind her back like a soldier.

Now she's pissing me off. She can't *refuse* to serve me. What happened to the customer is always right? I mean, the employees at Neiman Marcus might be a bit rude and snippy, but at least they serve you! Now it's down to principle. *She has to sell this to me.*

I grab the tiny glass bottle and dangle it over the counter. "I. WANT. TO. BUY. THIS."

She stares through me like I'm not even there.

"Hello!" I shout. "Do you understand? *I* am the customer. *You* are the salesperson. You sell. I buy. Get it?"

No reaction.

"Look. I'm not leaving," I hiss. "Just sell it to me. Okay?"

Nothing.

Oh my God. This is ridiculous. I dig into my Hogan and grab a $20 bill and slap it on the counter. "Here. Think of this as an apology. Okay? Can I buy it now?"

She eyes the bill and then looks away. I can't believe I'm doing this. I'm bribing a makeup lady. I slap another $20 bill on the counter.

"There," I say.

She delicately takes the two bills and slips them into the pocket of her mint-green smock. Then with her chin slightly raised, she places a small glossy white box with a white ribbon onto the counter. She carefully unfolds a Bloomingdale's Brown Bag and drops the box inside.

"That'll be $285," she says, not even looking me in the eye.

WHAT? I didn't want to skimp . . . but $285?! I'm fuming as I hand over my credit card. Unbelievable. I just spent $325 (bribe included). This stuff better be freaking amazing.

"Thanks," I mutter, snatching the bag off the counter. I check my watch.

Shitty! I'm late for lunch with Gwynn. I sprint toward the door, dashing past the Kiehl's, NARS, and Acqua di Parma counters. Ooh. Is that a cellulite roller over there? I've always wondered if those things work? MENTAL NOTE: CHECK OUT THE ROLLER LATER.

•

I'M PANTING AS I FLING open the door to Spiaggia's. Woo. I need to catch my breath. Leaning over and resting my palms on

my knees, I take a few deep drags of air. I check the time and
frown.

"Can I help you?" asks a stiff-looking blonde with frosty
pink pursed lips.

"I have lunch reservations," I wheeze, feeling a drop of
sweat trickle down my cheek.

Classy, Vic. Classy.

"Party's name?" she snaps.

"Gwynn. Gwynn Ericsson."

"Right," she says, checking something off a list behind the
maître d' stand. "This way, please."

As we step into the elaborate dining room, my breath catches.
I see immediately why Hollywood stars dine here. It's amazing.
Light. Airy. Like a royal ballroom decorated for a wedding.
Enormous bundles of fragrant tiger lilies burst from every table.
And there are those cool white linen seat covers with the big
bows bustled in the back. (I love those!)

We weave our way in between the tables, and I notice I'm
terribly underdressed in jeans (Evisu, from Gwynn's closet, but
still). This place may serve stars, but it's not L.A. casual. All
the other ladies are immaculately pressed and starched. A very
proper parade of Prada, Escada, Gucci, Yves Saint Laurent,
and Dior. Full hair and jewelry. We're talking diamonds, pearls,
platinum, and plastic. Yep. It's definitely a nip and tuck kind of
place. (Oh my God. Freaking out. Is that Jude Law? I think it is!
I heard he was in town shooting that movie . . .)

"Vic—hi!" Gwynn stands up as I reach the table, giving me
a quick kiss on each cheek. "Sit down. Sit down. What would
you like to drink?"

A waiter suddenly appears at our table, a fresh white towel
hanging from his arm.

"Um?" I wriggle my nose. "Whatever you're having?"

The waiter eyes Gwynn's glass, scribbles down the order and
disappears.

As we sit down, I notice Gwynn is wearing a pleated Burberry skirt with a smart black top and matching cashmere sweater thrown around her shoulders. Oh God. Why did I wear jeans? *Why?*

Gwynn leans in a bit, her nostrils flaring excitedly. "Don't you just adore this place?"

I nod enthusiastically. "Very wedding-y." Um . . . I don't think that's officially a word, but whatever. It shows that I'm already in the wedding frame of mind. Again, why I am the *perfect* maid of honor choice.

"That's exactly what I was thinking!" Gwynn raves, beaming at me like I'm the smartest person alive.

Ha! I'm a total shoo-in. *Da-da-da-dum, here I come.*

"So," Gwynn says, after our minuscule pear salads arrive. "I'm sure you guessed why I asked you to lunch."

I smile and nod, trying my best to appear clueless.

"Bryan and I would like you to be part of our special day."

Obviously.

"We'd like you to be . . ."

Eee! I'm going to be Gwynn's maid of honor. I can feel myself getting choked up. Gosh. I didn't realize I'd get so emotional. I thought I was a shoo-in, but . . . okay . . . remember the speech. Think refined. Think eloquent. *I'm truly honored . . .*

"My personal . . ."

Here it comes . . .

"My personal . . . attendant," Gwynn finishes, her eyes gleaming.

Wait a minute. What?

Personal *who?*

I roll the two little words around in my head. Personal attendant. Personal attendant. What does that *mean* exactly? I feel like I've heard the term before. Is it some new politically correct name for maid of honor? It sounds important. I guess . . . *kind of?*

Maybe it's a step up from maid of honor? Yes. Yes. I'm sure it is. I'm sure I'll still be standing up with Gwynn in a gorgeous floor-length gown, holding her bouquet and straightening her train. (Um . . . that is, if she ever makes it down the aisle. I have to be honest, this whole Bryan/Kaitlyn thing still really, really bugs me. But innocent until proven guilty, I guess. No need to burst Gwynn's bubble. At least not right now.)

"Yes!" I hear myself gush. "I'd be honored to be your . . . um . . . I'm sorry, what did you call it? A personal . . . what?"

"My personal attendant." Gwynn smiles excitedly.

"Right," I say, scratching my head. "What is that, you know, exactly?"

"Oh my gosh." Gwynn suddenly puts on a business face. "A personal attendant is *incredibly* important. You'll help the wedding planners with everything. Run errands. Make lists. Coordinate stuff. You know. Make sure the wedding is, like, totally perfect."

That's not exactly what I had in mind. But . . .

"So you'll do it?" Gwynn asks, her eyes glittering with anticipation.

"Sure," I say. "Um . . . I mean, absolutely!"

"You will?" Gwynn squeals. "I'm so excited! This will be so much fun."

"I can't wait," I say weakly.

"Ah! I knew you'd say yes! I just knew it," Gwynn cries happily. "Here, I wanted to get you something." Gwynn scoots a thin ivory box with a silky white ribbon across the table toward me.

Ooh! I love Gwynn's presents. She always goes all out. For my twenty-first birthday, she flew us all down to Miami for the weekend and picked up the tab for everything. Luxury hotel suite. Room service. Limo. All of it. It was *sooo* nice of her.

I eye the pretty ivory package eagerly. I wonder what's inside? A Pucci scarf? (She knows I'm dying for one like hers.)

Or wait! We were checking out the cutest blue Kate Spade wallets the other day.

My heart flutters as I untie the ribbon and open the box. I can hardly wait to see . . .

"It's a wedding planner!" Gwynn bubbles. "Just like mine." She holds up a matching ivory binder. "So we can stay organized and in sync. All the wedding plans are bound to get crazy!"

"Oh right. Of course," I say, scratching my head. How odd. I thought Gwynn wanted a small wedding. How much planning could there possibly be? I finger the elegant binder.

"Okay. So. Let me give you the details." Gwynn claps her hands cheerfully. "Eva is my maid of honor—Mother said she had to be since she's my only sister and all. Angel and Dawn are my bridesmaids, and . . ."

Wait a minute. She already has a maid of honor? She already has bridesmaids? I don't get it. Where do I fit in?

Should I ask?

"Oh! And before I forget, Mother wanted me to give you this. It's from the wedding planners. She hired *three*! Can you believe that?" Gwynn places a glossy cream envelope between us.

Ooh. Maybe it's a list of stores where I need to register?

"You can read it later. I'm sure it's nothing major. After all, we do have *three* wedding planners. Oh! And just a warning. Mother tends to go overboard with this stuff." Gwynn laughs and takes a sip of her wine. "She means well, though. You'll see."

Now hold on a second.

"You still want a small, romantic ceremony, right?"

"Totally!" Gwynn gushes. "We're thinking six to seven hundred people. You know . . . eight hundred at the absolute tops."

Gulp.

EIGHT HUNDRED PEOPLE.

Oh dear God. I should have known. This is Gwynn we're talking about. Nothing is ever simple or small.

I plaster on a smile, but inside I'm wondering what the hell I just got myself into.

"Oh right. And Mother wants to throw Bryan and me an engagement party—next Friday!" Gwynn chatters. "I know. It's in ten days. Completely insane. We just got engaged. But with it being a six-month engagement, everything has to happen fast. Snap. Snap."

•

MY HEAD IS STILL REELING by the time I walk into my apartment. I throw the mail on the kitchen table and dump my bag on the floor. Armani comes bounding through the hallway, meowing happily. He flops down next to my feet and curls into a black furry bundle.

"Hi, buddy." I pat him on the head.

I shuffle into the living room, grabbing the dictionary off the bookshelf and flipping to the "P" section. Personal attendant. Personal attendant. Per-son-al . . .

Hmm. No entry.

Sigh.

I cautiously eye the glossy cream envelope peeking out of my Hogan. Do I even dare open it? I finger the smooth expensive paper.

Oh stop! I'm just being silly. How bad can it be?

Mrs. Lucinda Ericsson
900 North Michigan Avenue
Upper Penthouse Suite
Chicago, IL 60611

Dear Victoria,

We are extremely pleased that you will be assisting with the wedding details. It certainly goes without saying, but Gwynn's wedding is deeply important to our family. I'm sure you are aware that Gwynn's father, Erik, is a very important figure in the fashion industry. All eyes will be on his daughter's wedding. Celebrities, world-renowned designers, and perhaps royalty will attend. [Royalty? I didn't know that Gwynn knew royalty! She's been holding out on me! Oh my God. I wonder if she knows Prince William?] *Everything simply must be perfection. We are counting on you to assist Gwynn, myself, and the wedding planners—Polo, Pierre, and Philip—in any way you can.*

Contact Franco, my assistant, between 9 and 5 if you should need me.

Thank you,

Mrs. Ericsson

P.S. The wedding planners asked me to include this small list of requests for you to complete.

P.P.S. Please sign the enclosed Confidentiality Agreement and send it back to Franco immediately. We need to ensure that the wedding details are strictly hush-hush.

I gawk at the next page. Oh my God. Panic. Are they kidding? This must be a joke. They can't honestly expect me to do all these things in the next ten days. Can they?

Victoria, honey bun,

You're such a doll for helping us with the details. We owe you a million, ba-zillion kisses. Call if you run into trouble. Toodles.

XOXO,

Polo

1. *Confirm catering order at Marché restaurant. Tell them to arrive promptly at six o'clock for party setup. Très important!*

Make sure they provide linens, utensils, china, crystal, and at least five servers (hot and dressed formally, of course).

2. Pick up party favors at Coach (the flagship store on Michigan Avenue). Be sure to count the goodies—sixty Nantucket wrist purses and sixty Hamilton money clips. FYI: the store manager is ditzy, ditzy, ditzy. So make sure the gifts are wrapped in their signature "C" paper as requested.

3. Call City Girls magazine. Give them the heads-up that little Gwynnie-pooh is having her engagement party next Friday. Their photographers will be drooling! Mrs. Ericsson wants Gwynn to get as much press as possible. The bigger the event the better! Call the press room. Ask for Tia.

4. Pick up the handmade invitations at Crane's at Water Tower Place. Address them (see attached list) and hand-deliver them ASAP. Gwynn simply adores the idea of hand delivery. So different. So chic.

5. Confirm flower arrangements . . . exquisite . . . tight bundles . . . baby pink peonies . . . Orrefors crystal vases . . .

6. Call Coppola Winery . . . three cases Syrah . . .

7. Pianist's limo . . .

8. Harpist . . . French . . . truly the best . . .

9. . . . and on . . . and on . . .

OH. MY. GOD. These guys—Polo, Payton, Perry . . . um . . . whatever—have completely lost their minds. I flip to the next page and scan the list of addresses for hand delivery. Highland Park. Lake Bluff. Hinsdale. All these places are in the suburbs! It would take an *entire day* to deliver these—at least. Besides, who hand-delivers? Ugh.

My cell phone rings. I check caller ID. It's Kimmie.

"Where have you been?" Kimmie demands. "I've been trying to call you! I got you a job interview!"

"You did?" I squeal.

"Yep. You're officially interviewing for a junior copywriter position at Lambert! Thursday at nine o'clock."

"SHUT UP!" I shriek wildly. "Me? A soon-to-be copywriter at Lambert?!" This is great! I can picture it already. Me. Typing away furiously at a computer all day. A sharp number two pencil tucked behind my ear. Writing, well, whatever copywriters write. (I'll figure that out later. I mean, how hard can it be? They're just words.)

Ooh. I need to put my résumé together. I need to do research. I need to . . .

Wait. I'm interviewing on *Thursday*? That's only two days away! What am I going to wear?

E-M-E-R-G-E-N-C-Y.

CITY GIRLS

Leo

Breathe. Work may have you a tad stressed out. Try an extra workout session—in bed or out of bed—to mellow. Good news, little singletini. This is your lucky week with love. Sparks are about to fly. Keep your eyes peeled for a new love interest (or two!) in an unexpected place.

YOUR WEEK AT A GLANCE

STRENGTHS: LOVE
WEAKNESSES: Evil tight clothes
CONQUESTS: It's heating up . . .
TO DO: Trust your instincts. Don't be afraid to stretch your wings and watch your world take flight.

(New love interests? Eee! Bring on the boys!)

Wedding Bells to Ring for Chicago Socialite

By Jay Schmidt

Gwynn Ericsson of Chicago and Bryan Goldstone, formerly of New York, announced their engagement this week (see page 8). But sources say the lovebirds are already on the rocks. Ericsson furiously denies the claims. "We couldn't be more in love!" she states. "Just look at my Harry Winston. It's huge! If that doesn't say love, what does?" Looks like only time will tell if her diamonds keep their dazzle all the way down the aisle . . .

Chapter 7

I. AM. SO. EXCITED.

Only a few days ago I was just a lowly computer sales rep taking orders from Krabby Karen. But today? It's my big interview at Lambert. I just *know* this is my ticket into the exciting world of advertising. Martini lunches. TV commercials. Photo shoots for glossy ads. It's the world of glamour. The world of glitz. The world of . . . of . . .

Well, whatever. It's going to be great. Me, Victoria Hart, the bright emerging copywriting talent at Lambert. There's just one teensy-weensy problem.

I can't stop thinking about the wingwoman job.

I know. I know. What's wrong with me? It's absurd. I need to forget about the whole thing. (But can't you just see me flitting around Chicago like Cupid? It would be so much fun . . .)

Stop. Stop it right now. Being a copywriter is the smarter career choice. Yes. I'm absolutely convinced this is the job for me. Swear. No more thinking about the wingwoman job. I'm focused. See? Now all I have to do is go land the job. Easy breezy. I've got everything under control.

My thoughts slowly drift back to reality. Back to Starbucks, which is where Kimmie and I are waiting for our tall skim mochas with extra whip. Hmm. And now that I think about it, we've been waiting for quite some time. I check my watch.

"Ah! It's after nine o'clock." I grab Kimmie's arm in panic. "We're late! Should we go? I think we should go."

"Are you crazy? Our coffees will be up in a sec. Relax."

"Are . . . are you sure?" I squeak. "I think I might go. I mean, this is my soon-to-be career. My future. I don't want to blow it before I even get hired." Oh my God. I can't believe it. I'm late again! What's wrong with me?

"Five minutes is nothing." Kimmie flicks her hand. "Trust me. The art director you're meeting with won't even be in the office yet. I think the last time Lotty interviewed someone, they waited two hours, then rescheduled because Lotty ditched work that day."

"Really?" I gasp, barely able to contain my excitement. You can ditch work at Lambert? I'm *sooo* made for this job. They *have* to hire me.

I take a deep breath and peer around the café, dabbing on a bit of sheer pink lip gloss. It's really packed in here this morning. The windows are even steaming up. My eyes anxiously scan the puffy morning faces waiting in line. Ooh. I adore that tangerine trench coat. So cute. Is it from Banana Republic? My gaze shifts farther down the coffee line to . . .

To him.

Ah! Who is *he*? He's gorgeous—totally Orlando Bloom-ish. Yum. My eyes linger over his thick dark wavy hair, his sexy square jaw that's shaded with scruff, his dark sparkly eyes that . . .

Oh my God.

He's looking right at me.

I whip around. He totally caught me staring at him. Lusting over him. HOW. EMBARRASSING. I can feel my cheeks burning hot.

At that moment, our drinks are called. *Finally*. I snatch up my mocha and quickly peek over my shoulder to see if he's still looking. And to my horror he's now waving. Arghh! What do I do? I smile awkwardly.

That's when I hear Kimmie laugh. "What's up?" she calls over to the Orlando Bloom look-alike.

They both smile and wave.

"That's my creative director—my boss. Nice guy," Kimmie whispers, as she turns and starts making her way through the crowd.

As we reach the door, I glance over my shoulder to steal one last look.

He glances over and grins.

Ah! So cute!

•

AS WE WALK the last few blocks on Wacker Drive in the fresh, cool Chicago morning, I notice Kimmie's outfit for the first time. She's wearing tight white Theory pants, a punk black motorcycle jacket, and an arm full of clanky silver bracelets. Her red Irish curls are wrapped and twisted up into a wild knot. She looks very hip, very cool, very artiste.

Now me, on the other hand?

I'm feeling okay with my upper half. I have on a lemon-colored vintage Versace blazer (another hand-me-down from Gwynn) and a pink satin ribbon tied in a floppy bow around my waist. But my bottom half? *Terrible.* I'm squished into my new torturously tight Seven jeans. Long story short: Kimmie talked me into trying on the stupid things and . . . *the zipper got stuck.* (I know. I know. The luck!) And they made me buy them after the alterations department had to actually cut the jeans off me in the dressing room. So embarrassing. (But at least the tailor very nicely offered to stitch them back together.)

I've done hundreds of lunges to loosen them up, but they're still whorishly tight. I can hardly breathe in the suckers. And just between you and me? I'm absolutely positive my butt looks like a wide-load truck in them.

Kimmie swears the jeans are great. That Sevens are cut to

give you more butt. "Think J.Lo. Guys love it." But come on! Who seriously wants *more* butt? Hmm? WHO?

"Are you sure about these jeans?" I whisper frantically to Kimmie as we make our way through the white marble lobby of Lambert Advertising. "Maybe I should go back to my place and change? It wouldn't take too long if I grabbed a cab."

"Um. Are you nuts?" Kimmie blurts, rolling her eyes. "You look amazing in those jeans. *Amazing.* If I didn't know you better, I'd think you were fishing for compliments."

"I'm not fishing," I mutter. But in the back of my head, I can hear the *beep-beep-beeping* noises going wild: W-I-D-E L-O-A-D. Clear some room!

We're nearly to the elevators when suddenly a wave of ice-cold fear hits me and I feel faint. My head is light. My lips tingly. My palms sweaty.

Oh my God.

What am I doing?

I abruptly stop. People swoosh past me, bumping me with their briefcases and computer bags. But I don't care. I'm sick with panic. I . . . I don't even know what I'm doing. I'm not prepared. I clutch my Hogan with a death grip. Did I even bring my résumé? They're going to see right through me. See that I don't belong in advertising. I don't even know how to write an ad! (Or dress myself for that matter. Just look at these jeans!)

This is a mistake. I should leave. I should . . .

"HEL-LO. Are you coming?" Kimmie's voice interrupts my thoughts.

I shoot her a look of pure terror.

She tilts her head, giving me a funny look. But her face quickly softens, and I see the flicker of understanding in her eyes. She gets it. She knows what I'm feeling.

"Don't worry." She grins, wrinkling her freckled nose. "I felt the same way when I interviewed."

"You did?" My eyes grow wide.

Kimmie nods. "Yep. I puked twice."

Okay. I guess if Kimmie can do this, I can, too. I take a deep breath and hop onto the elevator. Here we go . . .

As we step onto the thirty-fourth floor, I instantly feel the energy. Everything is ultra chic, high design. Think Herman Miller. Silver accents. Light wood. Splashes of fun color. Loads of natural light. There are huge flat-screen TVs hanging from every lobby wall. Hip music blares from the intercom. There are young trendy people with artsy glasses talking in clusters all around. Their cheeks flushed. Their hands waving about. And the best part? No one seems to be working!

Can you say heaven? I'm going to fit in just great. Now all I have to do is get them to hire me. Fingers crossed!

Kimmie gives me a quick tour around the office. Kitchen. Bathroom. Vending machines. Executive row. People to impress. People to ignore. Who's hot. Who's not. Who's the office brain, the office suck-up, the office slut. Who's sleeping with who. You know . . . the basics.

My head is spinning by the time we navigate over to Kimmie's workstation. Kimmie peels off her leather jacket and hangs it neatly on a silver hook. Then she throws her Timbuktu bag onto a plush red beanbag chair, flips on her computer, and plops down on a turquoise swivel chair.

"So what do you think?" Kimmie grins excitedly.

"This place is so cool!" I squeak.

"Ready to throw up yet?"

I nod.

Kimmie laughs. "Consider yourself lucky. At least you know where the bathroom is."

"Wait. You didn't?"

"Nope. See that plant?" Kimmie points to a brown sickly tree withering in the corner. "It's never been the same."

We both giggle, then Kimmie decides she should probably tell HR I'm here for my interview.

"Stay here. I'll be right back," she says, disappearing down the hall.

I take a seat in Kimmie's chair and sip my coffee as I check out her workspace. Kimmie works primarily in fashion and cosmetics, and her walls are plastered with slick print ads and storyboard sketches. There are high-gloss lipstick ads for Revlon. Hot and steamy Calvin Klein spreads. And a big sexy $8\frac{1}{2}$ × 11-inch shot of Uma Thurman with silver Ray-Ban aviators slipping off her sun-kissed nose. A Post-it note sticking to the photo reads *Can we zoom in on the sunglasses? Make Ray-Ban logo 50 percent larger.*

So cool!

I lean over to read a handwritten note by her keyboard and . . . oh . . .

OH. NO.

A big splash of coffee lands on my new Seven jeans. Great. Just great. So typical. I'm about to go into the biggest interview of my life, and I spill on myself and look like a big slob. Way to make a good first impression.

I quickly snag a Kleenex and dab at the coffee, hoping it'll come out. No luck. It smears more. Now what?

Ooh. Maybe I can suck it out? (Mom's secret trick!) I know it sounds kind of weird and creepy. But it works. Swear.

I look around real quick to make sure no one is coming, then lean down, lift the jean fabric to my mouth and suck. I can taste the sweet chocolaty coffee on my tongue. Ah! It's working. I knew it. Mom's brilliant! I'll have to let her know she saved the day.

Suddenly I hear someone clear his throat. Uh-oh.

I slowly look up to see . . . *him*. Tall, scruffy, super-sexy *him*. My Orlando Bloom from Starbucks. Kimmie's boss! He's even cuter up close in his cashmere V-neck and suede loafers. My breath catches. And, well, I notice he's giving me a very odd look.

"Um . . . hi," I say, smiling awkwardly. I can feel my face blazing hot. He must think I'm a complete freak. *Oh, hi there. Don't mind me. Just licking my pants.* Very classy. Very ladylike. Well done, Vic. Well done.

"Coffee stain," I say, pointing to my jeans.

"Right." He nods, looking clearly amused. "Is Kimmie around?"

"She . . . um . . . she just . . ." Oh my God. Could I stutter anymore? "Kimmie will be right back."

"Cool," he says, pulling his funky black glasses off his head and slipping them onto his nose. "I'll drop by later then." He turns to leave, then stops. "I'm Patrick, by the way."

"Victoria." I extend a hand. "I'm interviewing with Lotty today."

"I see," he says, his dark eyes twinkling playfully. "Well, good luck."

"Thanks," I whisper, feeling a few goose bumps erupt as I watch this sexy, sexy man turn and walk down the hallway.

Wow.

MENTAL NOTE: MUST GET TO KNOW PATRICK.

Fingering the stained part of my jeans, I walk over to the enormous windows just outside Kimmie's workstation. What an amazing view. I can see the entire city from up here. Lake Michigan. Chicago River. Sears Tower. Hancock Building. Everything. What a gorgeous morning. Bright blue sky. Puffy white clouds. I see a lone sailboat raise its sail. Ah . . . I love spring in Chicago. Today is going to be a good day. I can feel it.

"Excuse me." I feel a tap on my shoulder. "Are you Victoria?" asks a smart-looking woman draped in all black, wearing horn-rims.

"Um. Yes. That's me," I say.

"Welcome to Lambert," the woman says, holding out her paper-thin hand. "I'm Bridget from HR. If you could just come with me, I'll take you to Lotty's office. She's the art direc-tor you'll be interviewing with today."

"Great!" I say brightly.

Bridget leads me down a long hallway, past row after row of offices. (Ooh. I wonder which one is Patrick's?) We eventually end up in front of a large, dimly lit corner office.

Bridget pokes her head inside, knocking lightly. "Lotty?"

No answer.

Bridget knocks again. "Hello? Lotty? It's Bridget from HR."

Still no answer.

Bridget turns and smiles at me nervously. And just as she's raising her hand to knock again . . . a tiny ball of color bursts out from under the desk.

"Holy mama!" I howl. Bridget and I both jump back.

I slowly take in this itty-bitty freckled woman standing before us. She looks all of age twelve. She's wearing a shiny magenta leotard and neon-green leg warmers. Think bad eighties Jazz-ercise video. She's barefoot. Her frizzy hair is sticking out in wild flames of gold, fuchsia, and crimson. And she's waving around a silver sequined fairy wand above her head. This is Lotty, I presume.

Gulp.

"I love your look today," Bridget says very seriously.

What the . . . ?

"Thanks. I'm a princess." The odd little creature curtsies and starts flitting around her office.

OH. MY. GOD. Total freak. This can't be who I'm inter-viewing with. *It just can't be.* I shoot Bridget a look of pure terror.

"Lotty is working on the Barbie account," Bridget whispers. "She likes to . . . um . . . *really* get into her work."

I nod as if this sort of thing is completely natural. No biggie.

"Right. So . . . Lotty," Bridget says, stepping carefully into the office, which is flooded with pink Barbie everything—pink dream house, pink Corvette, pink camper, and mounds of pink Barbie boxes. "This is Victoria Hart. She's interviewing for the junior copywriter position. Is this a good time?"

Lotty shrugs, plopping down onto the blue office carpeting. She grabs a Malibu Barbie doll and stuffs it into the pink Corvette.

"Great. So. Here's Victoria's résumé," Bridget says, placing a silver clipboard on Lotty's toy-cluttered desk. "You two have fun!"

And with that, Bridget leaves. I stand in the doorway for a few minutes, shifting awkwardly from one foot to the next and cursing Kimmie for not warning me about this loco Lotty character.

"So how long have you worked at Lambert?" I finally ask Lotty.

"Call me princess," Lotty says without looking up.

"Oh. Of course. Sorry!" Um. Are you kidding me? Is this lady for real?

Silence.

More silence.

Good. Great. This is going well . . .

Suddenly Lotty looks up at me, her eyes narrow. "Do you like Barbies?"

"Um . . . sure? I mean, yeah. Totally. I love Barbies!"

"RIGHT ON!" Lotty squeaks, jumping to her feet. "I need Barbie headlines. Hundreds of them. Think intelligent. Think sexy. We need to capture the tension between the two. Do you know what I'm saying?" Lotty asks, waving her arms dramatically above her head.

Oh God. Oh God. Is this some sort of weird test? I nod obediently, trying my best to look like I have a clue.

"Hmm." Lotty looks at me skeptically. "Close your eyes. Try picturing the dichotomy. Feel the tension between intelligent and sexy. Imagine nerdy versus sex kitten. Dorky versus hot. I need to know you're feeling it. Are you feeling it?"

Um. *W-H-A-T?* I close my eyes, desperately trying to picture something. *Anything . . .*

After a few moments, I peel open one eye. Lotty is staring at me intently. I quickly snap my eye shut again.

"Okay. Stop," Lotty huffs, her hands on her hips. "It's not meshing. I can't work with this! The energy is off. You need to go."

"I'm sorry?"

"Go. The interview is over," Lotty says, plucking a Barbie horse from her desk and twirling its golden mane.

"That's it? No questions? No nothing?" I can feel my cheeks burning hot. "Can't I at least . . . ?"

"No can do." Lotty sighs, clearly bored. "Wanna take home a Barbie?"

I shake my head. Is she joking? I stare at this tiny woman in disbelief.

"Suit yourself," Lotty mutters, flinging the Barbie at the wall. "I don't like these skinny things, either."

I can't believe this. What just happened? I wander back into the lobby in a daze. I quietly sign out with the receptionist, hand over my visitor's badge, and leave.

What a disaster.

•

AS I'M WALKING into my apartment, Kimmie calls my cell phone.

"I just heard!" Kimmie cries. "I'm so sorry. I forgot how wacko Lotty gets when she starts a new project."

"Don't worry about it," I say, dropping my Hogan on the floor. "I'll find something else."

Just then, my other line beeps in. It's Mom. Ugh. I don't want to talk to her. Come to think of it, I don't really want to talk to anyone.

"I need to go," I tell Kimmie. "I'll call you later. Okay?"

I switch the cell phone to silent. What a terrible week! I absently start flicking through the stack of mail. Let's see. Marshall Field's. AT&T. Comcast. Wow, I really miss my paycheck right now. And that's when I see it. The postcard.

Be a
WINGWOMAN
It's the hottest job in the city.
Party, pick up, and get paid for it!

Oh my God. I can't believe this! It's a sign. *FATE*. I was supposed to flub that interview today. It's all part of the grand Victoria Hart plan. I was born to be a wingwoman! I flip the postcard over.

Why Be a Wingwoman?

It's exciting! All you do is go out, introduce guys to hot chicks, and get paid $100 an hour.

Why Does It Work?

- A guy with a hottie on his arm is more likely to attract women. Period.
- Ladies are cutthroat. They always want what they can't have.
- Girls trust guys with other women. It's like a seal of approval.

Want In?

We're always looking for fabulous, fun, and fearless girls. Call Chicago Wingwoman and sign up for training today.

I mean, it really is a sign. Don't you think? God. I knew I should have called about this job from the beginning. I KNEW IT. What was I thinking with the whole Lambert thing?

I grab my cell phone and punch in the number. I'm so happy I could kiss the postcard. This is going to be so great. I'm going to be the city's latest and greatest matchmaking talent. I'll be famous for helping Chicago's most eligible bachelors find love. And, well, it's a smart career choice, too. You know . . . *kind of*. It's just a tad different, that's all.

Now I just need to figure out how to tell the girls . . . *and Mom and Dad*.

But the girls will never let me live this down. Kimmie thought it was an escort service! And my parents will totally freak. Especially Mom. This isn't exactly the kind of job she can brag to all her friends about at Club. (And she *loves* doing that. I remember when I landed that computer sales job. She was whipping out my business card to everyone. "Victoria is in sales these days! Very important job. See, here's her business card." It was *sooo* embarrassing.)

Hmm. On second thought, maybe no one needs to find out. Maybe it can be our little secret. You know . . . just for now.

Chapter 8

CHICAGO WINGWOMAN
EMPLOYEE HANDBOOK

Welcome to Chicago Wingwoman! Where you can party, pick up, and get paid. This handbook reviews the Top Ten Tips we share with all our employees. We hope this information makes your job easier and more fun.

1. Look like a million bucks.
Clients expect a hot wingwoman to go out with, so always be at your sexiest. Botox, eye lifts, brow lifts, lip injections, chemical peels, and other plastic surgery procedures are strongly encouraged. (Chicago Wingwoman offers 50 percent reimbursement.)

2. Arrive early.
Always show up to gigs ten minutes in advance. This'll

give you time to grab a drink, scope out the bar scene, and identify potential hotties to introduce to your client.

3. Be outgoing and ready to party.
Clients pay an arm and a leg for our services. You need to be the life of the party. The social butterfly. The star. So have a drink to loosen up. But don't get drunk. You're on the clock.

4. Know the basics about your client.
Is he shy or outgoing? Does he like blondes or brunettes? Is he looking for love or a hot hookup? And don't forget the easy ones! Name, age, occupation, hobbies, and where he grew up. These tidbits will be useful throughout the evening.

5. Work the room.
Strut your stuff. Smile. Laugh. Flirt. Introduce your client to as many women as possible. His happiness is your number one priority. So hustle. Collect phone numbers. Do whatever it takes to hook him up. Smiling client + hot babe = good wingwoman. So get after it.

6. Always compliment.
Girls love a little flattery. Tell her you love her shoes, hair, jewelry, lipstick, glasses, handbag, drink choice, or anything else you can think of. It's one of the easiest ways to break the ice and make the introduction. If you get denied, smile, laugh it off, and keep going.

7. Brag shamelessly.
Tell her your client is the CEO. He's a Little League coach.

He saved a child! The juicier the better. It's your job to make your client look as desirable as possible. So start bragging.

8. Stay positive.
Never react poorly (e.g., laugh, cry, hide, run away, or pretend to be someone else) if your client is not attractive. Get over it. Your job is to find him a woman. So think of it as a challenge and get creative.

9. Bar hop.
If you're not having any luck with the ladies, change your venue (the busier the better!). Maybe your client would be more comfortable at a sports bar. Or perhaps a funky lounge? Be ready to stay out all night if you have to.

10. Don't hook up.
It goes without saying, but Chicago Wingwoman strictly prohibits dating clients. This means no kissing or romantic relations of any kind (no matter how attractive he is). You are not a date. You are his wingwoman. Act like one.

SO WELCOME TO CHICAGO WINGWOMAN!
The only place where you can party, pick up, and get paid. Please let us know if you have any questions. We look forward to seeing you at training.

Sincerely,
Kate Darsy
Talent Trainer and Scheduling Manager

I report to wingwoman training Friday at eight o'clock sharp. (I'm so proud of myself. Not even five days after losing my job and I'm already on a new career track.) "Make sure you look gorgeous!" Kate told me on the phone. "We'll be taking your composite shots and the more you look like a model or actress, the better. Just pick someone and go with it. Think Gisele Bündchen. Think Angelina Jolie. Think . . . well . . . whatever. Inspire yourself."

Right. Okay. Absolutely.

The Chicago Wingwoman office is down on State Street. Its lobby is small, but immaculate. Completely minimalist. High breezy ceilings. All windows. No furniture. Just a few sunflower pillows scattered around on the gleaming hardwood floors . . . for decoration? To sit on? Who knows.

As soon as I arrive, they usher me into a small photo studio draped in sheer white sheets and snap about a million photos. I have to be honest. I tried for Kate Hudson, but it didn't work out so well. The crazy photographer with dragon tattoos kept screaming, "More chest. More chest. I need to see more chest!" And I kept howling back, "I'm flat. I'm flat. I'm really, really flat!" I don't think dragon boy had ever worked with someone under a C cup before. Let alone an AA. But whatever. The first day on the job is always a bit rocky. Right?

Eventually I'm led into a large sterile-white training room. There's a long dry-erase board at the front of the room and four rows of stadium seating with thick gray binders placed at each desk. I'm told to take a seat and start filling out the paperwork in the binder.

I nod and find myself in a room filled with the most stunning women I've ever seen. I'm instantly intimidated. They all look like they walked right off the page of a fashion magazine, with cool shimmery makeup, silver chandelier earrings, bright gauzy tank tops barely holding in their chests, and skintight James, Joe's, and Angel jeans.

Grrr. *Now* would have been the time to wear my Seven jeans.

I take a seat in the front row and start filling out paperwork. Name. Address. Telephone number. Social Security number. Blah, blah, blah. And then I get to a series of questions:

1. How much do you weigh?

Hmm. Now that's odd. I wonder why they need to know that? Maybe for insurance reasons? I bite my lip and scribble down my weight: 135. Eww. I quickly scratch out the numbers and write 120. (I know what you're thinking, but I'm not lying. Not technically. You see, I *do* plan on weighing 120 just as soon as I start that diet. Or buy that cellulite roller!)

2. What's your breast size? Please circle one and indicate if they are real: A, B, C, D, DD

WHAT? Why are they so obsessed with my breast size? How is it even relevant? Hmm? I peek up from my binder and see immediately that all the other girls are at least in the C and D camp. Okay. Fine. These girls just got lucky. My cheeks grow hot as I scratch down AA. Pathetic, Vic. Pathetic.

I quickly scan the rest of the questions:

3. Have you ever slept with or had romantic relations with a coworker and/or client?
4. Do you have any special talents we should know about, such as modeling, acting, dancing, stripping, massage therapy?
5. How often do you work out? Would you be interested in a personal trainer?
6. Which diet do you adhere to? South Beach, Atkins, Weight Watchers, the Zone?

7. Would you ever consider plastic surgery? Please circle which procedure: Botox, Breast Enlargement, Breast Lift, Brow Lift, Chemical Peel, Collagen Injections, Face-lift, Liposuction, Other
8. . . . and on . . . and on . . . and . . .

That's when a tall bony woman in a smart black suit and Manolo slingbacks clacks into the training room. Her slick blond highlights are pulled back into a chic bun. Not too tight, not too loose. Her high cheekbones and nose are slightly pointy, and her glossy peach lips are pursed. She gracefully folds her thin arms across her chest and carefully inspects every girl. Once she finishes, she lifts her pointy chin, taps on the desk with her silver pen, and says, "Good morning, ladies. I'm Kate Darsy and I'll be your wingwoman instructor this morning."

We all clap, but Kate promptly raises a slender hand to silence us. "We have a lot to cover, so please pay attention and take notes," Kate says, tucking a shiny blond strand into place. "I'd like to start by welcoming you to Chicago Wingwoman. You are now part of the most advanced dating service ever created. You are an elite matchmaker, a social butterfly . . . *you are a wingwoman!*" She pauses for emphasis. "The wingwoman approach is highly unique and effective. Men pay steep fees for our services, so we must deliver at all times. With that being said, please turn to page three in your binder; I'd like to reveal the three words all wingwomen live by."

We diligently flip to page three in our gray binders. It reads:

Fabulous
Fun
Fearless

Kate clears her throat, lifts her pointy nose, and starts *tap-tap-tapping* her silver pen in the palm of her hand. "As a wingwoman, you should embody these terms. Fabulous. Fun. Fearless. Chicago Wingwoman accepts nothing less. Say them out loud."

"Fabulous. Fun. Fearless," we all repeat.

"Good," Kate says, sliding onto the desktop and crossing her long elegant white legs. "Let's start with fabulous. As a wingwoman, you must always look and act fabulous. That means stepping up your wardrobe. After all, Chicago Wingwoman is the *best* wingwoman service. Our clientele is strictly upper-crust. They expect special treatment. That's why we pay you a higher hourly rate and give you an additional $1,000 each month to spend on expenses like drinks, cover charges, and appearance. A significant amount simply must be spent on clothing, hair, and makeup. We have an image to uphold, so we encourage you to wear only the highest-end clothing from Saks, Neiman's, Barneys, and other exclusive boutiques."

Oh my God. My heart flutters. I really *can* shop at Barneys!

"Keep in mind," Kate continues, "this isn't free money. You have to bring in ten gigs a month to keep it. And for every gig you come up short, we cut your check by a hundred dollars."

Arghh. Ten gigs? That sounds like a lot . . .

"And that's not all." Kate raises an eyebrow. "If you receive negative reviews from clients, we cut your check even more. $200 per complaint. And on the third complaint, we'll be forced to terminate you."

Gulp.

"Right. So. Let's move on to fun," Kate snaps, taking a sip of her bubbly Perrier. "Wingwomen must always be fun. You need to appear happy, upbeat, even when the evening is going poorly. Men hire us to have fun. So make sure their glass is always full and that they're having a fantastic time."

Kate slides off the desk and begins pacing from one side of the room to the other, her black Manolos clacking with every step. "Now lastly, ladies, you must be fearless. Dating is cut-throat. These women won't be any nicer to you than they are to men. So do whatever it takes to get a woman's attention. And I do mean . . . *whatever*."

The morning goes on and on and on. And we all scribble notes as fast as we can, desperately trying to keep up as Kate explains how there are generally two kinds of men who hire wingwomen: Shy Guys and Workaholic Guys. We should identify which type our client is before we proceed. Shy Guys need more encouragement. We should make sure they feel comfortable. Tell them they look nice. Make any last-minute adjustments to their hair or wardrobe. Do anything we can to build their confidence. We should look for quieter girls for them. Maybe not the star of the party.

Now for the Workaholic Guys, they tend to be good-looking. They typically have both confidence and money. Their main problem is they don't have time to date. That's where we come in. Move fast with these guys. Introduce them to as many girls as you can. Workaholic Guys tend to be easier clients to manage. So once you're experienced, you should be able to book two or three of these gigs a night. And Kate just keeps talking and talking, and *tap-tap-tapping* her silver pen . . .

My hand is aching a few hours later, but Kate is still rambling. Never accept tips. Never catch a ride with a client. Never go to a client's apartment or hotel room. We suddenly hear a light knocking on the training room door. In stroll two women. A gorgeous black woman in head-to-toe Gucci who looks remarkably like Tyra Banks, and a tall strawberry blonde with a thin aqua dress slipping off her shoulders, a mouthful of gum, and the biggest breasts ever.

Kate smiles. "Ah, yes! I'd like to introduce our most successful wingwomen to date—Lexi and Redd."

Lexi flashes her best glittery smile and waves like a beauty queen.

Redd blows a bubble, then tousles her big hair.

"These wingwomen are incredibly talented," Kate continues, pointing her pen to a row of gleaming gold plaques on the wall. "And as you can see, they were each Wingwoman of the Month on two occasions. This is an extremely prestigious award. We take it very seriously. To win it, a wingwoman must earn $10,000 in one month."

We all peer up at the plaques. And yep, sure enough, there's Lexi and Redd dominating the Wingwoman of the Month awards.

"Think of them as the masters today. Your mentors," Kate says, waving at them. "They'll take you through several exercises this afternoon. Show you the best wingwoman techniques. And tell you how to handle worst-case scenarios. You'll each shadow them on a real-life wingwoman gig sometime in the next week. So schedule a time with them before you leave."

We all nod enthusiastically.

"So I guess I'll leave it to the masters now," Kate says, lightly fingering her chic blond bun. "Good luck out there," she tells us. "And always remember: fabulous, fun, fearless. You are wingwomen now. Make us proud!" She turns and *clack-clacks* out of the training room.

The afternoon training session is drastically different. Lexi and Redd divide us into two groups and we all rotate. Lexi is *supposed* to explain why the wingwoman approach works and how we should play into it. But she spends most of the time shrieking wildly into her cell phone. *"Damn it. How many times do I have to tell you? Victoria's fucking Secret!'"*

She ends up propping us all on stools with pink hand mirrors and watching us apply our makeup as she barks away on her cell phone. Every once in a while she pulls the phone away from her ear, slaps a woman's hand, and hisses, "No. It's not perfect. Do it again!"

Then we rotate to Redd. She snaps her gum and explains

how we should do anything to get our clients phone numbers. "Make a fool of yourself. Brag shamelessly about the client. Be pushy. Lie. Anything. *But if they're rich and handsome, don't be stupid. Keep 'em for yourself.*" By the end, Redd has us running laps in the hallway in our heels. Her raspy voice barking after us, "Move, move, move! Chase down those girls. Your client is counting on you. Get that phone number. Go! Go! Go!"

When I get back to my apartment, my head is pounding and my feet are killing me. I have four messages on my answering machine—all from Polo, Pierre, and Philip about Gwynn's engagement party next Friday. (Ooh. I *really* need to get on those to-dos.) I'll deal with it tomorrow; I can't bear to think about it right now. Especially since I need to get ready for my training gig with Lexi and Redd! (By the time I got to the sign-up sheet, tonight was the only time left. Sigh.)

I patter into my bedroom and dump all my new wing-woman materials onto the bed. There are flyers and business cards. (Kate said we have to hand out a hundred flyers a week. I know. Are you kidding me? I guess there are tiny codes on the back, so they know how many new clients I'm bringing in.) Anyway, there are books on Chicago nightlife. (Kate said we're supposed to know all the hottest spots.) There are loads of discount cards for exclusive gyms, manicures and pedicures, Botox, you name it. And then there's the extremely confidential client roster! (Kate said we're dead if we show it to anyone.) I turn to the first page and skim the names, wondering if I'll recognize anyone?

No.

No.

I flip to the next page and that's when I see it . . . Bryan Goldstone.

Wait a second.

My jaw drops.

Bryan Goldstone? As in, Gwynn's fiancé? I can't believe it!
I knew Bryan was up to no good. I just knew it. First the ex-
girlfriend rumors and now this? Oh God. Should I tell Gwynn?

I bite my lip and close my eyes. Why did I have to set them
up? Why? To tell you the truth . . . it was an accident. I barely
even knew him. Another friend of a friend thing. I feel so responsible! And I'm a wingwoman now. *I should have known better.*

Arghh! I can't tell Gwynn yet. No. Not until I get to the
bottom of this.

Chapter 9

WHAT A NIGHTMARE. Today couldn't have started
off any worse. I woke up to find my ass plastered
on the cover of every *City Girls* magazine in the
city. *Sooo* humiliating. (Thank God you can't see my face!) I
tried calling that twerpy reporter about a million times, but his
ice-cold assistant kept informing me that Jay Schmidt was "out."

Yeah. Whatever.

But I have even worse things to worry about. My first solo
wingwoman gig is tonight—and I am so nervous. Yep. The
training is over. Last night I shadowed Lexi and Redd at Fulton
Lounge with the cowboys (and we all know how horribly that
went!), and tonight I'm on my own. It's just me and my client.
I have to get serious. I'm absolutely determined to make things
go a million times better. I'm simply going to relax and use my
natural matchmaking skills.

Ooh. But first things first.

I need to go shopping.

Like Kate said in training this week: *"As a wingwoman, you need to look and act fabulous at all times. That means stepping up your wardrobe."*

I head straight to the bank and cash my first $1,000 expense check from Chicago Wingwoman. I can't even begin to explain how exhilarating it is to hold ten crisp $100 bills in my hands and know that they're all mine. Not for rent. Not for the phone bill. Not for anything but clothes. Okay. Fine. Drinks and cover charges, too, but whatever. This is so exciting!

Next stop? I walk right into Barneys and buy the most *amazing* dress. A steamy-hot peach chiffon frock by Chloé. It has to be one of the happiest moments of my life. For the first time ever, I get to prance out of that store with my very own Barneys bag swinging from my fingertips. I'm so happy I could cry. It's almost enough to make me forget about the whole mortifying butt photo thing.

Well, until I see two girls parading down Michigan Avenue, gawking at the cover of a *City Girls* magazine and shrieking with laughter. Then I want to go hide in a dark hole again.

Damn last night!

Tonight is going to be different, though. I can feel it.

•

So HERE I AM at the Living Room waiting for my first official client to arrive. The Living Room is a hot hangout at the W Hotel in the Loop. It's *très* hip. Ultra-high vaulted ceilings. Long dramatic curtains swooping down to the floor. Lush leather couches. It's all super plush, super swanky. I was thrilled when I heard my client, Mr. Lewis, wanted to meet here.

My hands shake as I lift my sour appletini to my lips. What's my problem? Calm down. Breathe. I'm a trained professional, for Christ's sake. Get it together, Vic. Get it together. Mr. Lewis is going to be here any second. I have to appear cool, composed, sexy. Like this is no big deal.

Yeah. Exactly. No big deal. I shift uncomfortably on the trendy metal barstool, and my mind races all over the place.

What if I screw up again like last night?

What if all the girls think I'm a freak?

What if they yell at me? (Oh God.)

What if my client takes one look at me and says, "You're not hot!" and demands a refund? (That would *almost* be worse than my butt photo.)

What if . . .

Stop. Stop it right now. I'm being ridiculous. Everything is going to be fine. I think the key is to drink more. Get a little loose. Last night I only sipped on one martini all night and my nerves probably got to me. But not tonight. No sirree! I'll just put away a few more of these yummy appletinis and then I'll be good to go. (I know the Chicago Wingwoman Handbook says I'm only supposed to have one or two, but I'm also supposed to be fun. Right?) I slurp down the rest of my tangy drink and signal the bartender to bring me another one *pronto*.

I look down at my outfit and smile. At least I have the whole "fabulous" thing covered. Kate at Chicago Wingwoman would be proud. My Chloé is amazing! And my honey waves are twisted up in a delicate black ribbon, and I've got on the most adorable dangly silver heart earrings. I'm absolutely love, love, loving my look tonight. It's such a shame that I'm on the clock and *not* on a date.

Sigh.

Well, at least I'm making $100 an hour.

Speaking of the clock, I glance at my watch and see that it's after eight. *Mr. Lewis is late.* Oh God. What if he took one look at me and fled? What if he's on the phone this very minute complaining to Chicago Wingwoman?

Another appletini arrives. I immediately take a big gulp and scan the crowd. We're supposed to meet at the bar. (He has my picture, so he'll find me.) I feel myself relax as all the drinks I slurped down finally start doing their thing. I listen to the DJ spin funky beats from the overlooking balcony.

How many of these appletinis have I had, anyway? Ooh. I should probably be keeping track. But they disappeared so quickly. Maybe three? Four? Hmm.

Suddenly I feel a tap on my shoulder. I whip around to see . . .

Hey, wait a minute.

Don't I know . . . ?

Suddenly it dawns on me.

Oh my God. Patrick? The sexy, sexy guy from Lambert? My Orlando Bloom? KIMMIE'S BOSS?

It can't be.

But it is . . . it's *him*. The same dark sparkly eyes. The same sexy stubble. The funky black glasses are gone, but it's him. One hundred percent him.

My head spins. "What are you doing here?" I blurt, my heart thumping madly.

"Um. Hi." Patrick grins, raking a hand through his dark messy waves. "Weren't you in the office the other day? You're Kimmie's friend, right?"

I nod, biting my lip.

Ah! I can hardly breathe. He's even hotter than I remembered. I quickly take in his tall muscular frame. His wide shoulders. His strong arms. His sexy jaw.

Wow.

Patrick furrows his brow. He pulls a card out of his jeans pocket. "Are you Victoria Hart?"

"I am," I say slowly, my mind racing all over the place. Is he . . . ?

"I'm Patrick Lewis," he says. "Your client."

My jaw drops.

No!

He can't be?

This is Mr. Lewis? "Shut up!" I whoop. Oops. Did I just say that out loud?

Patrick cocks his head, giving me a very strange look.

Um. Apparently I did. "Right. So. We should, you know, shut up and get to work." I laugh nervously, clapping my hands together.

Patrick's cheeks are hot and flushed.

Eww. Awkward silence. Think of something to say. Quick!

Um . . . nothing is coming to me except really, really stupid things like: *You're hot, you're hot, I can't believe how hot you are.*

Not exactly appropriate.

"Would you like another drink?" Patrick finally asks, pulling uncomfortably at his camel cashmere turtleneck.

"Sure!" I say brightly. "Should I meet you over there?" I point to a cluster of leather couches that are overflowing with exotic purple sequin, silk, and beaded pillows.

Patrick nods and heads over to the bar.

Oh my God. What is going on here? I don't know whether to be insanely ecstatic to be spending time with the sexiest guy ever, or totally bummed out because my job is to hook him up with someone else.

Ooh. Quick. Is he a Shy Guy or a Workaholic Guy?

Drats! What if I can't tell?

Once Patrick has our drinks, we cozy up on a leather couch. And I have every intention of keeping things strictly business. *Swear.* I very professionally give him my business card and ask him all the basic questions like Chicago Wingwoman suggests:

Know the basics about your client.
Name, age, occupation, hobbies, and where he grew up.
Is he shy or outgoing? Does he like blondes or brunettes?
Is he looking for love or a hot hookup?

But before I know it, we're just chatting away. I end up telling him all about my hellishly bad interview with Lotty, which sends him roaring with laughter. We keep chuckling and joking, and he tells me all about how he loves to travel, cook, and play the guitar. And how he loves spending lazy afternoons out on his sailboat, cruising Lake Michigan. (Could he *be* any more romantic? And his voice! I didn't notice it before, but it's so deep and smooth and sexy.)

A tiny voice far, far in the back of my head tells me that I should really get to work. That I'm not here to flirt with the client. That I have a job to do. But I can't help myself. I'm having such a good time and . . .

"Well, I guess we should, you know, try this whole wingwoman thing?" Patrick finally says.

Pout. "Yeah. I guess we should," I say halfheartedly, setting down my empty appletini with a *clink*.

Come on. Snap out of it, Vic! You're here to work. Be professional.

"Right. So. Do you see any women you'd like to meet?" *Say no. Say no.*

He narrows his eyes, surveying the crowd. "I don't know," he says at last. "What about her?" He points to a leggy blonde leaning up against the bar in hot pink heels.

Hmph. Of course he has to pick the most amazing woman ever.

"Great," I say, forcing a smile. "I'll go work some magic."

Eww. Did I really just say "work some magic"? It sounded so cheap, so whorish.

As I wobble over in my silver strappy heels, all the alcohol rushes to my head. The room is suddenly blurry and tilting a bit with every step. Um . . . I think I'm a bit tipsy. In fact, I can't exactly feel my feet or legs. Not a good sign. I drank too fast. *Why do I always do that?*

Suddenly I realize I'm standing right in front of the leggy blonde with absolutely no clue what to say. None.

I smile up at her stupidly, my head swirling. Whoa! I think I need to sit down. Or drink some water. Or something.

Leggy squints at me in disgust, whipping around and whispering something to her girlfriend, who is equally blond and tall and gorgeous. I hate them both.

Okay. Stay calm. All I need to do is focus and then I won't be so drunk. I pinch myself, hoping this'll give my brain something to focus on besides the room spinning. I glance over at Patrick and give him a thumbs-up. He winks. Oh super. Why did I do that? Now he thinks I have this whole thing under control. I look up at Leggy, then back at Patrick. I can feel myself panicking.

Think, Vic. Think. How hard can this be? I just need to strike up a conversation, like they taught us in training, then motion for Patrick to come over. Easy breezy.

Geesh! What's my problem? Be fearless, like Kate said.

I take a deep breath and tap Leggy on the shoulder. I'll just compliment her.

She turns around and sighs dramatically. *"Yes?"*

"I love your . . . um . . ."

Quick. What am I complimenting her on?

I do a brief up-down, frantically looking for anything to latch onto. Anything unique or different. I immediately notice that she's perfect. Utterly and disgustingly perfect. Long silky blond hair. Long lean legs. Cute little Meg Ryan nose. She probably gets compliments right and left. I need to say something different. Something truly unique to get a good conversation going.

Leggy raises a sharp eyebrow, clearly annoyed.

"Um . . ."

Shitty! Come on. Spit something out, Vic! *Anything*.

"I love your . . . um . . . nostrils!" I finally blurt. HER

NOSTRILS? Oh dear God. Did I really just say that? My head feels so heavy and fuzzy, it's hard to tell.

Leggy looks horrified. "Freak!" she huffs, whacking me in the stomach with her green minibag.

I clutch my side. "I'm ss-sorry. I didn't mean . . ."

"Get away from me!" she cries, waving over the bartender. *Oh no.* I can't get kicked out of the bar.

I totter back over to Patrick in defeat.

"No magic?" Patrick grins, his dark eyes twinkling playfully.

"Very funny." I smirk. "She wass-sz . . . a bitch." Oh my God! Am I slurring now, too? Classy, Vic. Very classy.

Patrick shakes his head sympathetically, handing me a glass of water. Is it just my imagination or is he finding this entertaining?

Don't slur. Don't slur. "Do you see anyone else?" I ask very, very carefully, trying my best to sound professional. Grrr. I could just shoot myself for drinking so fast. I wanted to loosen up, not get wasted.

"What about that one?" Patrick asks. I squint, doing my best to follow his gaze over to a very blurry brunette in a skimpy-skimp outfit—shiny red camisole, frayed jean miniskirt, and gold stilettos.

"No problem. I'll be back," I say, taking a big gulp of water and handing the glass back to Patrick.

Okay. This has to go better than my last attempt. Right? *Anything would go better.* I stagger over to the brunette, much more focused this time. Much more prepared. Well, as prepared as I can be after four or five appletinis. Um . . . or six?

I can do this. I can . . .

"So," I say, casually sliding my elbow onto the bar next to her. "Do you hang out here a lot?"

The brunette's face lights up. Her lips are sticky red like candy. "Oh my God. No way! Are you hitting on me?"

I jump back a few steps, nearly toppling over. My cheeks are suddenly on fire. "What? Oh no. You don't understand."

"HOW CUTE!" the brunette hoots. "You're a lesbian."

"Oh no! I'm not . . ."

"Kristy! Quick, grab the camera." The brunette smacks her short pudgy blond friend in the back. "Hurry!"

I glance over my shoulder to see Patrick shaking his head in amusement. Fabulous.

"I . . . I have to go," I tell the brunette.

"Wait! Don't leave!" the girl yells. "Can I take a picture of you? We just moved here from Iowa. We've never seen a lesbian before."

•

AFTER ABOUT TEN MORE incredibly unsuccessful attempts to strike up conversations with random women, my head is throbbing and I officially feel like a big loser. I slink back over to Patrick in defeat.

Patrick pats the spot next to him on the couch. "How's it going? Any luck?"

I shake my head and sigh. "It's not you. It's me," I say miserably.

Then I see a cluster of pretty businesswomen in pin-striped suits sitting at the bar and that's when it hits me. *A plan*.

"Follow me," I say. "I have an idea."

As we weave our way through the trendy bar crowd toward the suits, I quickly finish formulating my strategy.

"What are we doing?" Patrick whispers with a conspiratorial grin.

"Okay," I say, turning toward Patrick. "See those businesswomen over there? I'll *accidentally* spill that brunette's martini. Then you swoop in and buy her a new one. You know . . . play the nice guy. She'll think you're a rock star and hopefully you'll hit it off." I stare at him breathlessly. "Got it?"

"Whatever you say," Patrick laughs. "You're the wing-woman."

We nudge our way up to the bar so we're standing right next to the suits. I wait until just the right moment and . . . *whoosh*. I slide by the brunette and knock the martini out of her hand.

CRAAA-AA-AAASH.

"I am *sooo* sorry!" I gasp. "I can't *believe* I just did that!" That's when Patrick rushes up beside me. He flashes an adorable grin.

The suits smile. And is it just me or are they checking him out? I mean, I'm sure they are. *He's so cute*. How could they not be?

Oh goody. I clap my hands in glee. My wingwoman powers are working! (I *knew* I was born to do this.)

Patrick quickly pays for a new martini, and they're all laughing and having a fantastic time.

"So you're a creative director. That's wonderful!" one suit says, peering over her thick black glasses. "Do you have experience in the beverage industry? I'm the Midwest VP of marketing for Evian. We're always looking for agencies to partner with."

"Actually," Patrick says with a smile, "Gatorade is a very big client of ours and . . ."

Hold on a sec. They're not supposed to be talking shop. What's going on here? Wait. They're exchanging business cards, too? No. No. No. I need to intervene. Steer this conversation in the right direction!

I wiggle myself into the center of the group. "Oh my God. Patrick is an amazing creative director!" I gush, putting a hand to my heart. "But he does so much more! And he's single. Did I mention that?"

Patrick raises an eyebrow.

"Oh yes!" I bubble on. "He's such a catch. And he loves giving back to the community."

"Really?" the suits bob their heads, looking impressed. "How so?"

"Oh . . . well . . . um . . ." I smile painfully, pulling at my dangly heart earring and stalling for time. "Patrick is really into . . . um . . . you know. Helping kids be . . . creative. After all, he's a creative director. Ha!" I let out an awful high-pitched laugh and slap the mahogany bar. "He's amazing with all that creating stuff."

The suits smile at me blankly.

"Right. Well. And then there's always . . . you know . . . the whales."

THE WHALES? Oh dear God. Where did that come from?

"I do love the whales," Patrick says, very, very seriously.

"Yep. Good ol' Patrick. He's such a goody-goody!" I squeal, slapping him on the back. "And single, too. Did I mention that?"

"My husband is a marine biologist. I should give you . . ."

Husband?!

My eyes dart down to their ring fingers.

Bling. Bling. Bling. Three diamonds right in a row. They're all married.

Drats!

Stupid, Vic. Stupid. MENTAL NOTE: ALWAYS CHECK THE RING FINGER.

Patrick and I quickly excuse ourselves and collapse onto the leather couches.

"Great plan," Patrick teases.

"I'm sorry." I sigh pathetically. "I was awful tonight!" In fact, I'm probably going to get fired. I suck.

"Sorry for what?" Patrick laughs. "I had a good time."

"How?" I ask incredulously. "You deserve a refund!"

"Maybe I'll look into that." Patrick winks. "Are you free sometime in the next few weeks?"

"Oh yeah. You can count on it," I say, mock saluting him. "Victoria Hart. Wingwoman extraordinaire. At your service."

For better or for way, way worse.

Chapter 10

FROM: gwynnie_pooh@girly.com
TO: victoria_hart@vongo.com
PRIORITY: *Standard*
SUBJECT: Reminder
Vic—hi!
Don't forget to send Mother your Confidentiality Agreement. She called me in a tizzy over the stupid thing today. I guess she fired her assistant, Franco, this week and she's losing her mind. Whatever. Just between you and me? I'm thrilled she finally gave Franco the boot. He was such a stiff! Anyway, gotta run. Send the form ASAP. 'Kay?
    Kisses,
    Gwynnie
    P.S. So glad you're my personal attendant. Isn't this a blast?
    P.P.S. You're planning on getting highlights before my party, right? They're looking a little shabby. Just want to make sure all the pictures turn out fab!

Sunday morning, I get a call from Chicago Wingwoman. I'm absolutely convinced I'm fired. After all, I drank excessively, flirted with the client, and failed to introduce him to a single woman. My overall performance for the night? A big fat disgusting F.

"Hello. This is Kate from Chicago Wingwoman," Kate says sharply. "We got a call from Mr. Lewis this morning . . ."

Yep. Here we go. I'm so out of a job. Twice in one week! That has to be a record. (Or at the very least, he complained and I'll get a $200 deduction from my next expense check.)

"Mr. Lewis was extremely pleased with your work last night. Said you were quite the pro."

What? "Hardly." I laugh.

"Excuse me?"

"Um . . . nothing."

Kate pauses. "Right. So. I have you booked for two more gigs this week. Tuesday and Thursday night. I'll have my assistant e-mail you all the information. Sound good?"

"Absolutely," I say, already doing the math in my head. Wow. I made $600 last night. I'll probably make the same Tuesday and Thursday night. That's almost $2,000—in one week!

I patter into the bedroom giddily. This is fantastic. Maybe I should go shopping again? After all, I do need to look fabulous! Just like Kate said: *fabulous, fun, and fearless*! I throw open my closet doors, yank out my new white denim skirt, a yellow-and-white-striped top, and a pair of red ballet flats. Very cheerful and springish, I decide. Maybe a tad chilly for April, but who cares? It's bright and sunny out and I'm in a fantastic mood. (Okay. Fine. And I've been dying to wear my new skirt. Can you blame me? It's adorable with the red stitching on the pocket!) I sweep on some lip gloss and grab my keys. And right as I'm about to slam the door, my eyes zoom in on the thick stack of pink Chicago Wingwoman flyers. Ooh. Right. I guess I should try to get rid of a few of these . . .

•

OKAY. SO. I try handing out flyers on Armitage Street. Honestly I do. But I feel stupid! What if I run into someone I know? *That would be awful.* So after a few minutes of flirting with the corner Starbucks manager, I talk him into displaying a stack by his register. I mean, Kate just said I had to get rid of them. She didn't say *how.*

Brilliant, Vic. Brilliant.

Now I can spend the rest of the afternoon shopping at Sugar. As soon as I swing open the red wooden door with its glittery nameplate in big cursive letters, I find myself relaxing. I love everything about it. How it's so small and cozy inside. How there are the sweetest vanilla candles flickering all around. And how the quirky owner, Cici, always has the most amazing new things. *"Victoria! Look at this new blue beaded top. Straight from Spain. Only forty dollars."*

Wow. $40?!

Cici knows how to get me every time.

There are hidden gems everywhere I look. Sparkly sapphire brooches. Darling silk sashes. Exquisite handmade sequined tank tops. A couple of chunky leather totes. Marc Jacobs blazers. (Oh my God. I adore that berry-colored one. It would look fabulous with those white jeans I bought last week. And come to think of it, it would look super cute with the denim skirt I have on. Don't you think? I'm so getting it!) Anyway, Sugar is also known for the most incredible vintage dresses— from black satin frocks to elegant lace sheaths. I'm dying for the opportunity to wear something formal, so I can splurge on one (or two) of them.

A few hours later, I stroll out of the boutique with happy bundles of bags stuffed under each arm. I'll be honest. I could really get used to this wingwoman job. I simply love having money to burn on clothes like this. I need to be careful, though. I've nearly spent the entire expense check already. Can you believe that? IN THREE DAYS. Looking good and going out all the time may be a bit more expensive than I anticipated.

•

LATER THAT WEEK, I meet my second client, Everett, at a comfy little place called Webster's Wine Bar. I'm wearing my new berry-colored blazer with a silver metallic tank top and jeans. (*Adorable.*) Everett is waiting for me at a tiny black-and-white-checked table near the front windows facing the street. He waves. I notice there are two wineglasses, a glowing tea candle, and a bottle of cabernet on the table waiting for me. Actually, it looks a bit romantic. A bit like . . .

Uh-oh. I stop midstep.

Everett knows I'm not a date. Right? He gets the whole wingwoman concept. RIGHT? Oh God. What if I have to explain how my job works? This could get awkward.

I approach the table, smiling nervously. Everett quickly stands and gives me a hug.

"Nice to meet you," he says warmly, his cheeks flushed.

"Same," I say, still a bit on edge.

I immediately like Everett, in a big brother kind of way. He's a roly-poly type with a pink nose and cheeks. He's slightly balding and a tad on the short side. But he's so sweet. And he has the most striking violet eyes. It turns out Everett is the *personal assistant* to the *celebrity assistant* of Jerry Springer. How cool is that? I guess it's a four-year plan. You do the time, then hope Jerry's celebrity assistant finally quits, or gets fired, or kidnapped, or something. Then you can maybe, *just maybe,* get promoted.

Anyway, Everett quickly confesses to me that he's a bit "dating challenged." I guess it was his sister's idea to call Chicago Wingwoman. Everett wasn't so sure. But he wants to find love, so here he is.

"I haven't been out with someone in over three years," Everett admits sadly.

"Why not?" I ask.

"I . . . I get so nervous around women. I start sweating and . . . I don't know. Women are scary. I guess I gave up." Everett lifts his cabernet to his lips.

"Maybe we can help you out," I say, surveying the crowded wine bar for potential girls to match with Everett. He's definitely a Shy Guy, so we need someone a little sweeter and quieter. "Have you seen anyone who catches your eye?"

Everett hunches over a bit and nods shyly, swirling the red wine around in his glass.

"Who?"

Everett discreetly tilts his head toward the bar. "I think she's amazing," he whispers, his violet eyes wide and honest.

I swivel around in my wooden chair. "The cowgirl?" I point to the smiley bartender with black pigtails and gold cowboy boots.

"DON'T LOOK!" Everett squeaks, his neck and cheeks all blotchy red.

I flinch. "Sorry. Sorry."

Everett's forehead is suddenly speckled in tiny beads of sweat, and his pudgy hands are shaking.

"Are you okay?" I ask.

He nods, wiping his forehead with a white linen napkin.

"Do you want me to go and say hi to her? See what she's like?" I ask, already pushing back my wooden chair.

"NO!" Everett wails, grabbing my arm feverishly and pulling me back into my seat. "She won't like me."

"That's crazy! How will you ever know if you don't talk to her?"

Everett sighs. "Look at me. *She'd never be interested.*"

"That's not true," I say.

Everett wrinkles his pink nose and shakes his head.

I give Everett a quick once-over. He has on a pair of out-dated Levi's, tennis shoes, and a stained white polo with dark chest hair peeking out the top. Pretty basic. Pretty blah. Sure, he could stand to lose some weight. And sure, he could use a good haircut. But there's still something about him. Something sweet. He has a nice honest smile and his violet eyes are just amazing! But he could be so much cuter . . .

That's when it hits me.

"Everett?" I ask cautiously. "How would you feel about getting a makeover?"

"I don't know . . ." I can already see the sweat starting to pour down the sides of his pink face.

•

THE FOLLOWING DAY I meet Everett at Maxine, an adorable three-story white brick salon and spa on the Gold Coast. (Yes. Yes. You remember. My favorite spa.)

"Wow. Your hair looks amazing!" I squeal with delight, bouncing up and down behind Everett's salon chair. Marco, my regular hairstylist, just gave Everett the most incredible cut. I kiss Marco on the cheek, then twirl back around to take another look at Everett.

It's unbelievable. It really is. I never realized a haircut could make such a difference. Everett's once lifeless and slightly re-ceding brown hair is now cropped about an inch off his scalp and tousled just slightly.

"And look," Marco raves, pushing up the sides of Everett's hair. "He can do a minihawk."

I giggle. "Just what Everett wants, I'm sure."

"Hmph." Marco sniffs, smoothing Everett's new hairdo back into place. "It's just another option. That's the sign of a good cut, you know." Marco stands back to admire his work, shifting from one tiny hip to the other and clucking his tongue.

I lean down to take an even closer look at Everett's cut. "Wait. Did you *lighten* his hair, too?" I ask incredulously.

Marco flicks his hand and purses his lips. "Perhaps a smidge."

"Brilliant." I clap my hands. "Absolutely brilliant!"

We twirl Everett's chair around, so he can see himself in the salon mirror for the first time.

"So," I ask Everett cautiously. "What do you think?" Marco and I both hold our breath, and I cross my fingers behind my back.

Everett leans forward on his elbows and stares at his reflection for a long moment. Oh no. He hates it. He totally hates it. And he's going to start oozing sweat like last night. But instead, he breaks out into a big grin.

"I like it." Everett reaches up and tugs at a piece of freshly highlighted hair. "I mean, it's definitely different."

"YES!" I whoop, jumping into the air and giving Marco a high five. This is so great. I should tell Kate at Chicago Wingwoman about this whole makeover idea. We could expand our services. Or maybe I could do it myself. Do people actually give makeovers for a living? Talk about a cool gig! Maybe I should look into it . . . you know . . . just for fun.

"Nice job." Everett smiles shyly.

"Yes. Yes. Thank you." Marco snips his scissors together and bows dramatically. "Thank you."

"Off to manis and pedis," I say cheerfully, grabbing Everett's arm and leading him up the salon stairs.

•

AND I MUST SAY, our big makeover day is going along just fabulously. We keep checking more and more things off our list:

Sports mani-pedi	Total success.
Sports facial	Ditto! Total success.
Chest hair waxing	Painful, but a success.
Back waxing	Very painful, but we swore to Everett it was worth it.
Eyebrow waxing	Ooh. I've never heard a grown man cry like that . . .

After we finally leave Maxine, we head straight over to the Banana Republic flagship store on Michigan Avenue. Banana Republic will be a great starter store for Everett. Nothing crazy. Nothing too expensive. Just some nice basic stuff. After flipping through a couple of *GQ, Esquire,* and *Details* magazines at the spa, we decide on Everett's new look. We're going for "Casual Cool, Yet Professional."

Everett spends the next few hours stuffed in the dressing room as I zip around the men's section, snatching up dozens of fun brightly striped dress shirts and polos. I hand him flat-front trousers and hip three-button blazers under the dressing room door. And Everett models everything so we can mix and match leather belts and loafers.

Ooh. The outfit he's modeling right now has to be my favorite by far. Everett sports a black pin-striped blazer with a funky green paisley shirt, dark-wash jeans, and black loafers. The jeans make him look a tad bit taller, and the shirt and blazer are cut really well and hide his slightly pudgy belly.

I LOVE IT.

I throw my hands on my hips and grin proudly. "You look great!" I squeal. "Really, really amazing."

Everett's entire face lights up. "Really?"

I nod happily, turning him around in front of the full-length mirrors so he can take a look. Then I basically give him a quick Fashion 101. Socks should always match your shoes. Shirts should always be ironed, preferably dry-cleaned. (Stains are not okay. Ever.) Concert T-shirts? No. Cell phone belts? No. Fanny packs? *Puh-lease*. And on, and on, and . . .

It's nearly three o'clock when we stumble out of the store, lugging bags and bags of clothes, belts, and shoes. We're both starving, so we head over to the RL café, right next to the Ralph Lauren store. It's a bright sunny afternoon and we sit under the quaint navy awning at one of the white linen-clothed tables. We both order RL burgers.

"So you really like my new cut?" Everett asks for about the millionth time. I swear he stopped at nearly every mirror in Banana Republic to inspect his new tousled hair.

"Absolutely. It looks great!" I bubble.

So Everett and I end up talking about everything as we munch on our burgers. All his fun new clothes and shoes. The Cubs' upcoming season. (We're both huge fans!) The new sports bar opening up in Wrigleyville. Everything.

"Do you really think this'll work?" Everett finally asks, his violet eyes wide. "My cowgirl will actually like me after all this?"

I smile warmly. "She will if I have anything to do with it. I mean, you have to do what you have to do to get the girl."

"Right. Right. Do what I have to do." Everett sighs. "You're so lucky. You must be great at dating . . . being a wingwoman and all that. I'm so jealous."

"Hardly." I cough, nearly squirting water out my nose. "I told you I was good at matching other people up . . . *not myself.*" I wipe my nose with a napkin. "I've dated a lot, but no one very seriously. I always seem to screw things up one way or another."

"Looks like we have that in common," Everett jokes. "At least you're not thirty and the only person you know not married."

"I'm working on it," I say, twisting my clear straw in a knot. "My first friend just got engaged."

"I see." Everett shakes his pudgy head knowingly. "That's a tough one."

We're both quiet for a few moments. Everett finishes his lunch. And I gaze across the street at the old Chicago Water Tower with its brick and ivy-clad walls. Everett's right. It is a tough one. I watch as tourists buzz all around snapping photos and pointing to their crumpled city maps.

Suddenly I feel so . . . lost.

Chapter 11

SO GLAD IT'S FRIDAY.

I'm E-X-H-A-U-S-T-E-D. But I officially made it through my first full week as a wingwoman. I'll admit it, it could have started off a tad smoother. But, hey, no one's perfect. Right? Besides, things got a million times better. Everett's makeover was a blast, and I totally think he has a shot with his cowgirl. We made plans to meet up in a few weeks to see if he's ready to talk to her. And last night, I had my first success! I set up a meaty *Chicago Tribune* sportswriter with a spunky redhead at ESPN Zone. And it only took me forty-five minutes.

I felt like Cupid. (Well, sort of a . . . new-millennium Cupid. You know?)

Anyway, tonight is Gwynn's engagement party. This entire week I've been running around like mad. Out all night on wingwoman gigs. Racing around all day taking care of last-minute engagement party tasks. Confirming this. Checking on that. I think I talked to Polo about a million times this week—talk about a high-strung guy. Whoa.

I mean, Polo nearly hyperventilated when the bride-and-groom ice sculptures were delivered late. Swear. He was in full crisis mode—ready to send me off on a private jet to Alaska for emergency replacements. (I know. *Crazy*. How in the world does Polo know skilled Inuit ice artists? I was afraid to ask.) All I can say is thank goodness the original sculptures arrived.

Meanwhile, I gave Tia at *City Girls* a heads-up about the party, I picked up the Coach favors, which all had to be re-wrapped because they weren't in the signature "C" paper (I thought the Coach store manager was going to murder me when I explained our little problem), and I *kind of* hand-delivered the invitations. That is, I had FedEx hand-deliver them.

Ha! Brilliant plan. And as long as none of the guests blow my cover, no one will ever know.

So with all that, the flowers, wine, catering, my new shimmering blond highlights, and everything else, I spent a whopping $6,500 this week on my Visa. (Gasp!) I know. I know. It's disgusting. I've never had a balance like that in my life! I'm surprised my card hasn't exploded from overuse. My wingwoman checks will cover some of it. But still. Luckily, Polo said he'd cut me a check from the wedding account tonight. Thank God.

My cell phone has been ringing like crazy all afternoon. Polo keeps calling, asking my opinion on one thing or another. Pleated table skirts versus smooth skirts? (I mean, honestly, does it matter?) Then Kate from Chicago Wingwoman called to confirm a last-minute gig at Zentra tonight. (It's not until eleven o'clock, so I'm praying Gwynn's party will be winding down and I can slip out. Fingers crossed.)

Right. So. I think I'll just relax a bit before I get ready for Gwynn's party. I shuffle into the kitchen to pour myself a glass of pinot grigio, but my eyes land on a bottle of SKYY. Hmm. Maybe I should mix myself up a Singletini instead? I can't even remember the last time I had one of those. (Maybe five, six months ago? At Kimmie's mini martini party?)

Let's see. I open the fridge. I don't exactly have all the ingredients, but whatever. I'll improvise. Yes. Yes. I mean, cranberry juice? Orange juice? What's the difference?

Just as I'm stretching out on the fluffy white couch with my fresh drink, my cell phone rings. Tell me it's not Polo *again*?! I check caller ID, but I don't recognize the number.

"Hello?" I answer cautiously.

"Hey there. It's Patrick. Your client."

I freeze.

Suddenly I can't remember how to speak.

"I hope you don't mind me calling," Patrick continues, "but I had your business card . . ."

Silence.

"Victoria? Are you there?"

"Um. Yeah. Yes. Hi. I'm here!" I stutter. "Can I, um, call you right back?"

"Sure," Patrick says slowly.

"Okay. Bye." Click.

"OH MY GOD!!!" I shriek. *Patrick just called me.* I race into the bedroom and leap onto my bed with excitement. Okay. Calm down. Think. I need to come up with something really witty to say. Like . . . um . . . I don't know? Ah! What if he's calling to ask me out? Is that against Chicago Wingwoman's policy? *I think it is.*

I jerk upright in bed, sitting cross-legged. Okay. Deep breath. I need to call him back. I quickly navigate into RECEIVED MESSAGES and dial Patrick's number.

"Hi!" I say brightly. "What's going on?" Breathe. Breathe. Think clever. Think witty. Think anything.

"So I was wondering if . . . ," Patrick begins in that deep, sexy voice of his.

Oh my God. He's totally asking me out.

"If you're free the Friday after next?"

"Totally!" I cry.

"That's great! Because I really need a good wingwoman."

Oh.

Right.

Of course.

He needs a wingwoman. What was I thinking? Like Patrick would ever call to ask me out! Dumb, Vic. Dumb.

"Cool," I say, trying to keep my voice as steady and professional as possible. "Just let me know where and what time."

"Awesome! I'll check with the guys and let you know. A big group of us are going out. Is that all right?"

"No problem," I say, penciling the appointment into my red leather planner. "I'll let Kate know. She usually handles the booking. She might need to call you and confirm."

"Great," Patrick says. "Well, I guess I'll talk to you later then."

I crawl back onto the couch and try not to be too disappointed. It could be worse. Right? He could have gotten me fired after last Saturday's disaster. Armani pads over and curls up next to me.

"Hey, chubs," I greet the big happy fur ball. Armani closes his eyes and starts purring as I scratch his tummy.

I sip my drink and watch the end of *Dirty Dancing* on TNT. My all-time favorite movie. Nothing beats the dance scene at the end. I LOVE IT.

Sigh.

Ooh. I check the time. It's six thirty! I better start getting ready for Gwynn's engagement party. Kimmie and Julia are picking me up at seven. I'm still singing the movie-credit music as I patter into my bedroom to pick out something to wear. I grab my cell phone off the bed and start singing into it as my microphone: "Now . . . I've . . . had . . . the . . . time . . . of . . . my . . . li–ii–ife. And I owe it all to yoo–oo–ooou!" I bite my lip and nod my head.

Just then, I hear something.

I freeze, looking fearfully around my bedroom. "Who's there?"

Hey, wait a minute.

Is someone saying my name?

Where is it? Is it coming from . . .

My cell phone?

I must have accidentally hit the redial button. Which means . . . *oh no.*

"Hello?" I ask cautiously, my cheeks blazing hot. Please let it be someone, anyone but Patrick. Puh-lease?

"Victoria?" I can hear Patrick's deep voice. He's laughing.

I close my eyes. *This is a nightmare.*

"Do you always serenade your clients?" he teases. "You're quite the singer."

"Thanks," I say miserably. "I didn't mean . . . you weren't supposed to . . ."

"No worries. It'll be our little secret. Just a perk to being your client."

Mortified. Totally mortified. I'm sure I could get fired for that. You know. Harassing clients. Torturing them with my horrifically bad voice. I quickly take a big gulp of my drink.

Okay. I need to calm down. Forget about it and focus. I have to figure out what to wear tonight. Kimmie and Julia will be knocking down my door in less than fifteen minutes and I have to look amazing. I mean, *City Girls* magazine will be snapping photos. I can't have *another* terrible picture showing up on the cover, now can I?

Just then, my doorbell rings, interrupting my thoughts.

Drats! The girls are early.

I hate it when they're early . . .

Chapter 12

I FEEL TERRIBLE. It's not like I meant to be late to Gwynn's engagement party. You know? It's just that things didn't work out the way I planned. For starters, I couldn't figure out what to wear. (And let's not even mention the whole serenade incident.) Then Julia burst into tears right as we were walking out the door. She said she and Kevin were still fighting over the whole long-distance stuff. Poor thing. She was such a mess. So we couldn't just leave! (Just between you and me, though, I don't think Julia is telling us everything. She seemed way too upset. And she was being all weird and cryptic about stuff. Saying things had changed and she wasn't feeling like herself. I don't know. Maybe it's my imagination?)

By the time our cab pulls up to Gwynn's Gold Coast highrise, it's a little after eight. *We're over an hour late.* Gwynn is going to kill me! We shove dollars at the cab driver and stumble into the chilly April night. We're all dressed like it's the middle of summer—no jackets and flashing legs and shoulders. Kimmie sports a funky orange Betsey Johnson dress that's dangerously short. Julia wears a shimmering silver slip dress that's absolutely to die for. And I'm strutting a killer black pleated skirt, a slinky charcoal camisole, and my new turquoise stilettos (from Sugar, of course).

As we approach Gwynn's ivy-covered entryway, we spot a cluster of photographers bundled up and waiting by the curb. I eye them carefully to see if my dear friend Jay Schmidt happens to be one of them. But nope. No Jay. (Thank God.)

"Strike your pose, ladies. Look hot," Kimmie belts, knocking me in the ribs.

"Are my eyes still puffy?" Julia sniffs.

I wipe a smudge of mascara from her cheek and smile. "Nope. You're good to go."

That's when the photographers swarm around us with a flood of flashes.

(Whoosh-whoosh.)

Oh my God. The lights. They're *blinding*.

(Whoosh.)

I try my best to smile sexily, but I can feel my eyes squinting painfully.

(Whoosh-whoosh.)

I desperately want to cover my eyes, but I force myself to stand there smiling in the bright lights.

(Whoosh-whoosh-whoosh.)

Besides, it's kind of fun. I could get used to this. I flip my freshly highlighted hair off my shoulder and pucker my lips a little. (If only I could see.)

"I feel like a movie star." I giggle.

(Whoosh-whoosh.)

"Turn to your side," Kimmie orders.

Ah! That's right. What am I doing? Side shots are *always* the best. They make you look much thinner. I quickly swivel around, but my right stiletto heel catches on something and oh, oh no . . .

I reach frantically for Julia's arm to balance myself, but I miss and grab the strap of her silver slip dress by mistake.

Snap.

"I. AM. SO. SORRY!" I gush to Julia as we ride the elevator up to Gwynn's condo on the twenty-third floor. "The photographers totally promised they wouldn't print the shots of your chest. I made them swear!"

"It's fine." Julia sighs, fiddling with the temporary knot we tied in her strap.

"You'll totally have to sue them if they do," I say helpfully.

Julia laughs. "I'm sure that won't be necessary."

"Right. Right. I'm sure, too," I say. But the truth is, I'm not so sure. Jay told me the same thing. Just the thought of my butt photo makes my cheeks flush feverishly. I still haven't told the girls about that. I haven't told anyone about that. (Well, except you. And I know you'll keep it to yourself. Right?)

As we step off the elevator and up to Gwynn's door, I can feel myself getting nervous. God. We're so late. I really do feel bad.

Right then, the door flings open.

We all jump back.

It's Gwynn. She's wearing a flowy mint-colored satin dress (looks like Prada's new Resort Collection) and sexy two-toned Stella McCartney pumps. Her red lips are carefully lined and glossed. Her blond hair is pulled back into a perfect chic bun, and she's dripping with diamonds. She looks a little upset, though. (Okay. Maybe more than a little.)

Oh dear God. She totally knows I FedExed those invitations. Dumb, Vic. Dumb.

She grabs me by the arm. "Where have you been?" she hisses.

"I . . . We . . . ," I stutter.

Gwynn looks like she might cry. Why do I always have to screw things up?

"You're late!" Gwynn fumes, glaring at me. "I can't believe you. You're my personal attendant. Could you please act like one?"

"I'm really sorry," I say quickly. "It's just that Julia and Kevin . . ."

"Whatever," Gwynn huffs, rolling her eyes. "I need to go mingle. Just shape up. 'Kay? And grab me some champagne and aspirin. This whole being-nice-to-everyone thing is totally giving me a migraine."

"Um. Sure," I say, watching Gwynn click off into the all-designer crowd. We follow her into the condo.

I thought she'd be a tad more understanding about Julia, given *her* recent issues with Bryan and his pushy mother. But no . . .

"Hey, did you see who's here?" Kimmie hisses, handing me a big bubbly flute of champagne and pointing toward the kitchen. "The mother-in-law with the standards Gwynn will never live up to . . . *Mrs. Goldstone.*"

Ah. No wonder Gwynn is in such a foul humor. Mrs. Goldstone *hates* Gwynn. And nothing would make her happier than to have Bryan move back to New York without her.

"You know . . . I heard Mrs. Goldstone hasn't spoken to her husband for over a month." Kimmie sucks in her cheeks and purses her lips. "She's still furious at him for opening that Chicago branch for Bryan to manage."

"I heard that, too," I say, taking a sip of crisp champagne.

I strain my neck so I can get a better look at the mother-in-law and her long pointy nose, dark piercing eyes, lavender Chanel suit with Ping-Pong-sized pearls, and perfectly Botoxed forehead. The ultimate New York socialite.

Gwynn fawns all around her, pouring more champagne, offering hors d'oeuvres. The poor girl looks like she's about to explode.

My eyes zip across the room. A typical Ericsson party. Oozing with money and more money. We're talking a pure Chicago celebrity crowd. I spot Michael Jordan in the corner chatting it up with Mayor Daley and Gwynn's father. Let's see, there's Jen

Schefft . . . the Bachelorette. Joan Cusack. (Don't you just love her? She's hilarious in *The Runaway Bride*.) And . . . OH MY GOD. Oprah is here, too! *I love Oprah.* I literally have to hold myself back from running over and hugging her. She looks amazing.

I sip my champagne and take in the rest of Gwynn's condo. It really is an amazing place. Utterly immaculate. All white, silver, and high design. Low-set sofas with tufted white cushions. Snow-white chaise lounges. And a super-trendy catwalk running down the middle of her condo and out onto the patio that overlooks the sparkling Chicago skyline.

I spot Gwynn's mom, Mrs. Ericsson, on the patio. She stands in a circle of lavishly dressed women—each wearing about ten pounds of jewels. She looks radiant under the moonlight, her platinum hair glimmering. She wears a fitted Calvin Klein cream dress that hits right below her knees with a chunky diamond bracelet hugging her left wrist. Her head is thrown back as she laughs like she just heard the funniest thing in the world.

Ooh. And there's Bryan. The fiancé. He looks terribly uncomfortable in his stiff black Prada suit, satiny mint shirt, and pointy black loafers. Gwynn dressed him, no doubt, to match her Prada vision. I lower my eyes and stare at Bryan suspiciously.

I'll admit it, normally I'd run over and say hi to Bryan right off the bat. I mean, I've always thought he was a nice guy. But . . . I don't know. This is the first time I've seen him since all the ex-girlfriend rumors. And, well, I just want to keep my distance. See if he's acting suspicious.

"How's the job hunt?" Julia asks, interrupting my thoughts. She pushes her dark hair off her shoulders and fidgets with her torn dress strap again.

"Oh . . . it's going," I say, shifting uncomfortably and avoiding all eye contact.

I know. I know. I should tell them about my wingwoman

job. And . . . okay . . . I should definitely tell Kimmie my first client was her boss (but I totally promised Patrick I wouldn't). Yikes. Why do I suddenly have so many secrets?

"I still feel awful about the whole Lotty thing!" Kimmie scrunches up her freckly face.

"Don't worry about it. I'll find something soon," I say, quickly trying to change the subject.

"Shit! The moo sisters," Kimmie hisses, smacking my arm madly. "Straight ahead. Quick! Don't make eye contact."

Oh super. There they are. Angel and Dawn—Gwynn's high school friends. The bridesmaids. They're the *worst*. Angel is the short mousy leader of the two, with a boring brown bob and pointy nose. And Dawn is a tall lanky blonde who's always hunched over and a bit sickly looking. Ugh. We've hated them ever since they visited Gwynn at U of I our freshman year. Angel and Dawn wore matching Chi Mu sorority gear the entire weekend (or as we called it, Chi Moooooo). Gag. And every chance they got, they turned our conversations into a big competition: *Who Knows Gwynn Better?* And nothing has changed. Absolutely nothing. They still wear the same geeky Chi Mu sweaters and sorority pins proudly fastened over their hearts. And they still try to compete with us every chance they get.

"Hi, giiirls," they coo in unison as they waddle over to us.

My skin crawls at the sound of their voices. So ooey-gooey sweet. So disgustingly fake. Just look at them. On the outside they appear nice enough. But their eyes tell the real story. Constantly looking away. Constantly inspecting. You know . . . they're the type of girls who are already moving their heads to say "uh-huh" before you even finish your sentence. They always agree. They always smile. And they always start whispering as soon as you turn your back.

It kills me that Gwynn picked *them* to be her bridesmaids

and not us. I'd be lying if I told you my feelings aren't hurt. (Don't get me wrong, I love being a personal attendant! But, you know . . .) I mean, Gwynn, Kimmie, Julia, and I used to have the best times. Gwynn was so wild and fun! She'd drive us all around campus in her red BMW convertible, our hair flying around madly. She'd run stop signs (knowing her looks would get her out of anything), catcall frat guys, and eventually pull onto the lawn of our apartment complex and park right under the droopy oak tree. "Looks like a parking spot to me!" she'd say, grinning like a tiger. God. I loved that Gwynn. Crazy. Carefree. Always up for anything.

But Gwynn isn't like that lately. Instead of dragging us to the latest VIP party or rushing off to the latest sample sale, suddenly she's all about wedding this, wedding that. I mean, she didn't even know Kate Spade was having a sale this week. How scary is that?

Just then, I feel a light tap on my shoulder. "Victoria—my sweet! At last we meet." I turn around to see the three cutest, most stylish men I've ever seen in my life. I instantly adore them.

"*Bonjour,* darling. I am Polo!" chirps the itty-bitty bald one with an enormous Crest White Strip smile. Polo blinks furiously, holding out his arms to hug me. I have to fight the urge to laugh. With his black trendy tuxedo and expensive leather flip-flops, Polo reminds me of one of those cuddly penguins at the Lincoln Park Zoo.

"Pierre, my dear. It is a great pleasure," rasps a very tall, serious gentlemen with a thin goatee. Pierre winks at me, takes a big sweeping bow, and showers my hand with kisses. I gather from the small tufts of silver hair sprouting at the sides of each temple that Pierre is the experienced one.

"Call me Philip," whispers the third man, Dior sunglasses propped on his head. He has that perfect blond spiky model hair and twinkly blue eyes.

"Um . . . hi!" I say brightly, my head spinning from all the champagne and their sudden introductions. I take a step back. So these guys are the wedding planners.

"Silly girl! I called your cell phone," Polo twitters, wagging his bony finger at me. "Are you ignoring me, *ma belle*? You are. Admit it."

"No . . . no really. I was going to call you back." I blush.

"Sure you were." Polo scowls playfully, stomping his little flip-flop. "And my date last night was supposed to call me today, too. *Mmmhmm*. Has he? *Non*."

"Oh stop." Philip whispers, patting Polo's shiny bald head. "Don't pay attention to Polo. He's feeling a bit snippy today."

I nod and give Polo a sympathetic look.

"*Moi?*" Polo gasps. "Psshh." He pretends to pout, but his lips instantly curl back into a smile.

"Enough nonsense," Pierre says, raising an eyebrow and pulling at his thin goatee. "Let's chat about FedEx. Yes?"

"*Oui.*" Polo beams. "Do explain."

Aaack!

Right then, the doorbell rings. Gwynn smiles grandly, then sweeps across the gleaming hardwood floors and swings open the front door. Her smile instantly fades.

In struts Kaitlyn Kingsley.

Gwynn's archrival.

Gwynn's nemesis.

THE ENEMY.

"Holy shit!" Kimmie howls, jabbing me in the ribs.

Julia shakes her head in disbelief.

I close my eyes. This is not good. Not good at all.

I hear the flurry of hisses and whispers taking over the room. Everyone knows the story about Kaitlyn. *Everyone*. She's rich, beautiful, and now one of the most powerful fashionistas in New York—having founded the wildly successful Red Envy clothing company. It's said that Kaitlyn's family has more money than the devil. (Whatever that means.) And they own a line of exclusive luxury hotels called K . . . and just about everything else in New York, so I hear.

FYI: Mrs. Goldstone L-O-V-E-S Kaitlyn. Adores her. Thinks she's absolutely 100 percent wonderful. Mostly because she lives in New York and comes from old money like the Goldstones.

Anyway, long story short: Kaitlyn is the ex-girlfriend I was telling you about. The one Kimmie and Julia spotted Bryan getting all cuddly with a few weeks ago. Those two dated all through college at some fancy East Coast place. But Bryan broke Kaitlyn's heart when he moved to Chicago after school and started dating Gwynn. (Well, after I kind of set them up. My family's friend Tyler worked with Bryan and, well . . . Gwynn just happened to go out with me one night and we bumped into them. So it was a total accident!) Kaitlyn has been on a mission to steal Bryan back ever since. And let's just say, nothing ever stands in Kaitlyn's way. *Nothing.* She's ruthless. And it looks like she's swooping back in town for the final rematch.

"Kaitlyn. What a surprise," Gwynn says icily.

"It's good to see you, too," Kaitlyn purrs, slipping out of her red tweed Marc Jacobs coat and black fur stole and dropping them in Gwynn's arms. "It's been forever. Hasn't it? I hope you didn't forget about me."

"Impossible." Gwynn flashes a frosty smile.

"Kaitlyn, dear." Mrs. Ericsson suddenly appears at Gwynn's side, nervously patting her platinum bob. "How on earth did you hear about our little soirée? Hmm?"

"Mrs. Goldstone extended the invite." Kaitlyn blinks innocently, swishing her long gorgeous blond hair away from her perfectly tanned face. "I hope that's not a problem?"

Gwynn's jaw flinches. "Not at all."

"Now . . . *where* is Bryan?" Kaitlyn's eyelashes flutter like mad. "I simply must say hello."

Bryan smiles tightly and looks incredibly uncomfortable as Kaitlyn flings her arms around him and drowns him in kiss after kiss after kiss.

My jaw drops. *The nerve.* Right here in front of Gwynn. I could strangle them both. I don't care if Bryan does look a tad uncomfortable. That's not enough. He could brush her off. He could . . . do *something.* Those rumors must be true!

Mrs. Goldstone stands to the side, smiling for the first time all evening. "Kaitlyn! I'm positively delighted you could make it."

Gwynn's nostrils flare angrily.

Uh-oh.

For the rest of the evening, Mrs. Ericsson keeps Kaitlyn as far away from her beloved Gwynnie-pooh as humanly possible. Kaitlyn is currently being held hostage on the catwalk, chatting it up with Mr. Ericsson and a few hot emerging designers. And Kimmie, Julia, and I are stuck in a circle of Old Marrieds listening to Gwynn talk about her wedding plans.

"Oh my gosh. And did I mention that Father talked Fred Sander into designing my dress? Can you believe it! Fred Sander!" Gwynn beams, brandishing a handful of wedding dress sketches from the ivory binder (the matching copy of mine) that she now carries everywhere. "Father said Fred is, like, the hottest new designer."

Blah, blah, blah. I'm so bored I can hardly stand it.

I love Gwynn. I really do. And all I want is for her to be happy and to have a wonderful wedding. But as personal attendant, I've already heard about these details. FOUR TIMES. From Polo, Pierre, Philip . . . and Gwynn.

"And it has the cutest little bustle," Gwynn gushes.

How much longer can this go on? I check my watch. Aaack!

It can't be. It's almost ten-thirty? I almost forgot about my wing-woman gig!

"That's wonderful," a woman in a lemon-colored strapless dress coos.

"Gorgeous," someone else remarks.

"Oh dear God. I really need to leave!" I blurt.

Oh no. Did I just say that out loud?

Heads turn.

Julia closes her eyes.

Oops. I did.

I look to Kimmie for help, but she just shakes her red curly head, her entire face looking like it's about to explode with laughter.

My cheeks are on fire. I didn't mean it like that! Swear. It's just that my gig starts at eleven and . . . and . . . oh thank God. No need to explain. It looks like Gwynn is too caught up in her wedding bubble to notice.

"And my hair," Gwynn babbles on. "It'll be swept up elegantly like Audrey Hepburn's. A little bun. A few wispy bangs. Very classic."

Mrs. Goldstone snorts.

"So when are you two thinking of having kids?" a woman in a smart black pantsuit asks, peering over her tortoiseshell glasses.

My ears perk up. At least five years, I'm sure. Maybe ten? I mean, thirty-four sounds like a good age to start. Right?

"Two years," she says, looking very serious and thoughtful. "Right about the time Bryan goes back to grad school at Northwestern. We're thinking we'll probably be ready to buy a house in Lake Forest by then."

What? My breath catches in the back of my throat. Kids? Grad school? SUBURBS? Gwynn *hates* the suburbs. What's going on? Where did all these plans come from? Gwynn never mentioned any of this stuff before. What happened to shopping, spas, and staying out late club-hopping? It's like Gwynn's morphing into an adult right before my very eyes. And it's happening so fast! (Who knew a ring could make someone change so much?)

Mrs. Goldstone looks equally upset by this new information. "I was under the impression that you two were moving to New York after the wedding," she challenges.

"How silly!" Gwynn laughs shrilly. "I don't know where you'd get an idea like that. We're staying in Chicago. We love it here."

Mrs. Goldstone frowns.

I look down at my watch again. I really need to get out of here. The trouble is, how am I going to slip out without anyone noticing?

Hmm.

I'll just have to be very, very stealth.

Chapter 13

UM. WELL.

My wingwoman gig starts in exactly fifteen minutes, and somehow Kimmie and Julia are tagging along. I know. I'm an idiot. All I had to do was slip out of the party and happily zip off into the night to meet my client at Zentra. But no. I had to slam my new turquoise stiletto in Gwynn's condo door and fall flat on my face. (Stupid shoes. I'm never wearing them again.) And instead of playing it cool, I had to open my big mouth and tell the girls I was jetting off to meet "old . . . um . . . high school friends" and how of course they should come along!

Now what?

This is going to blow my wingwoman cover for sure. Think, Vic. Think.

Our cab pulls up to Zentra, and I can already hear the techno music blaring onto Weed Street.

Un-cha.

Un-cha.

Un-cha.

My heart is thumping with the beat, and I seriously don't know what I'm going to do. I can't let Kimmie and Julia find out about my new job. Not yet! They'll never understand. They'll think I'm making another flighty work decision. But I'm not this time. This is different.

I think I actually like this job.

Okay. I need to stay calm. I can handle this. Kimmie and Julia will never suspect a thing. I have a plan: *I just need to get them drunk. Really, really drunk.*

We make our way up to the club—no line, no cover, no nothing, thanks to Kimmie and her scandalously short orange dress.

Sweet cigar smoke tickles my nose as we pull back the velvety plum-colored curtains. Fuchsia and lime lights swirl around our heads. White strobes blink sharply. It's all glam and glitz. Sequined bodies gyrating all around us. I make a beeline to the bar and immediately order us all a round of shots and cherrytinis. I scan the club nervously, my heart pounding. *Oh God. Please let my client be a no-show.*

But I see two guys (one tall, one stocky) huddled over a folded piece of paper and nodding. They point in my direction and start walking toward me.

Drats!

I quickly look away, slapping my hand on the bar and downing my drink. I've never wanted to disappear more in my life.

What am I going to do? Kimmie and Julia both stare at me like I'm totally losing it.

I smile weakly.

"Are you okay? You're acting really weird." Kimmie twirls a red curl around her fingertip.

"Absolutely," I peep. "I just haven't seen these guys for a really long time, that's all."

"Hey, hey, hey!" The two guys are now standing right in front of us. "Are you our lucky wing . . ."

"OH MY GOD. HI!!!!" I throw my arms around them. "It's great to see you. It's been forever! You have to meet my friends Kimmie and Julia."

"Hi there. I'm Aiden," the taller guy says. He's wearing a hip black blazer, funky red T-shirt, and frayed jeans. I can't help but notice that he's cute. Very Heath Ledger with beachy-blond waves, a sexy golden tan, and piercing blue eyes. He's going to be an easy one to set up.

"I'm Derek. Nice to meet you," says the stockier one. He's cute, but in a meathead kind of way. He looks like he spends every day at the gym pumping weights and sucking down protein shakes. His muscles are nearly exploding out of his skintight black T-shirt.

"I'm sorry. What's your name?" Derek asks me.

Shitty! We're supposed to be high school friends. Why is he being so difficult? He's blowing my cover! Quick. Stay calm. Think.

I roll my eyes playfully and slap Derek on the back. "Oh my God. You're *hilarious*. It's Victoria, silly!" I quickly turn to Kimmie and Julia and whisper, "He always was a bit slow."

The girls shoot me a strange look but start jabbering away with the two guys. No. No. No. This is not good. Not good at all. I need to break this party up fast before the girls find out I'm working tonight. I quickly order up another round of drinks and nervously tap my foot. I throw my Visa at the bartender, whip around, and shove the two cherrytinis at Kimmie and Julia.

"Here you go. Why don't you guys go dance? Hmm?" I softly nudge them toward the dance floor. "It'll give me some time to catch up with these guys. You know . . . it's been a while."

"Um. Okay." Kimmie and Julia give me more strange looks.

"I'm just going to grab some water first," Julia says. "Can't drink. I have a lot of studying to do tomorrow."

Great. Just great. Julia isn't drinking. How will I ever pull this off?

The girls finally move toward the dance floor, and I take a deep breath. Okay. I need to move fast. They'll be back before I know it. I glance over at Aiden and Derek and clap my hands. "Ready to meet some ladies?"

As we do a couple laps around the smoky, jam-packed club, I try to get as much information from my clients as possible. Turns out Derek is a personal trainer. (Surprise, surprise. That explains his gigantic muscles.) And Aiden helps manage his dad's properties. I guess his dad owns a couple of office buildings down on Wacker Drive. (From what it sounds like, Aiden isn't exactly hurting for cash.)

Anyway, Derek points out tons of glitzy women he thinks are hot—each super buff and wearing skimpier clothes than the last. I listen intently and then go off to do my thing. I have to say, I'm getting a million times better at being a wingwoman. The key is to act natural. Like I couldn't care less if these girls talk to me or not. I'm just making casual conversation. No biggie.

I sweep right up to a skinny Asian girl in shiny black plastic pants and a matching tube top. She has a crystal belly chain dangling around her ripped abs and baby blue feathers clipped onto her slick black hair.

"I love these!" I say, fingering a baby blue feather.

"Aren't they like the cutest?" Her dark eyes light up. I notice her makeup is amazing. There are huge glittery stars painted around her eyes and tiny red dots outlining her mouth. I've never seen anything like it.

"Wow . . . And your makeup! It's incredible. Did you do it yourself?"

"I got it done at Cocoa. Have you heard of that salon?"

I shake my head.

"WHAT? You totally have to try it. It's up in Boystown. Ask for Danny. He's like . . . oh my God . . . the best! He does my hair, too."

"Absolutely." I nod my head enthusiastically. "I'm Victoria, by the way."

"Mika," she says.

By the time Derek slides into the conversation, Mika and I are getting along brilliantly. It turns out she *loves* working out and is totally obsessed with the gym. Yep. And that's when I know I've officially made a match. I quietly back away, watching Derek and Mika chat it up.

Nice. I smile to myself. Well done, Vic. Well done. I'm getting even better at recognizing that moment between two people when it clicks or doesn't. There's just something about the way their eyes sparkle. The way their bodies start leaning closer together. It's the moment when I know it's okay to go. My work there is done. I've seen it with all the other couples I've matched up. Especially Kevin and Julia. But I'll be honest. I wasn't so sure about the spark I saw with Gwynn and Bryan. (Like I was telling you before, I didn't exactly mean to set them up.) Anyway, I have this awful feeling I screwed that one up. I think they're my first match gone wrong. It kills me! And I'm absolutely determined to get to the bottom of things. I just don't know how yet . . .

Ooh. What am I doing? I totally need to focus here. I nervously eye the dance floor. Kimmie and Julia seem to be having a great time. And it looks like Kimmie got the new cherrytini I sent her way. (If only Julia would have a drink. Her suspicious glances are making me nervous!) I just need to keep them out of the way for a tiny bit longer. I still need to set up Aiden.

That's when a hand slides around my waist. "Boo," a deep voice breathes into my ear.

I jump around to see Aiden grinning wide. He pushes his hair out of his eyes and hands me a cherrytini.

"Thanks," I say, looking up at him. Wow. He really is hot. But whatever. He's my client. And besides, he's definitely the kind of guy who knows he's good-looking.

"It's your turn," I say, waving my arm at the bar. "Take your pick. Should we do a lap to see who catches your eye?"

Aiden shrugs, keeping his blue eyes on me. "Sure, doll. Anywhere with you."

We start cruising the club and I point out beautiful woman after beautiful woman. Aiden nods but doesn't seem interested. He keeps his hand on my waist, which is a bit odd, but we are in a club. We have to stay together. Right?

"You're a picky client," I laugh, once we finally stop circling. We lean up against a tall circular glass table and sip our drinks.

"Not really." Aiden flashes a sexy grin and nuzzles my neck. "Let's go back to my place," he whispers.

I quickly pull away, placing a hand on Aiden's chest. "I'm sorry. But I'm working tonight. You're my client. I . . ."

And that's when I see Kimmie and Julia from the corner of my eye.

Oh no.

Julia narrows her eyes. How much did she hear?

"We're . . . (hiccup) . . . going home," Kimmie slurs, waving a finger at the door. She fiddles with the strap of her silver heel, nearly falling over.

"What are you doing?" I laugh, grabbing Kimmie's arm to steady her.

"They hurt." Kimmie pouts, flipping red curls out of her face. "I'm taking them off."

"Oh, no you don't!" Julia hisses. "Not here."

I avoid Julia's eyes as I give them each a hug good-bye. She gives me a hard look but doesn't say a word. She just turns and leads Kimmie away.

"Everything okay?" Aiden says, putting an arm around my shoulder and handing me another drink.

I nod, watching Kimmie and Julia stagger out of the club.

I can't believe I got away with that.

Um . . . I think I did. Right?

L e o

You are a beacon of sex. Sizzling hot. Sexy hunks seem to be at your disposal. When it rains, it pours. So take full advantage of the flood, little singletini. Be sure to keep your eyes wide open, though. While a tryst may feel like pure bliss, your heart might not be able to keep up.

YOUR WEEK AT A GLANCE

STRENGTHS: Über-stealth moves

WEAKNESSES: Dieting

CONQUESTS: Yum

TO DO: Share your talents. Don't be afraid to take someone under your wing and show him the way.

(*Ahem. Smug.*)

Bride-to-Be Goes Berserk

By Jay Schmidt

It was a star-studded night at Gwynn Ericsson and Bryan Goldstone's engagement party. Sources say things heated up toward the end of the night when ex-flame Kaitlyn Kingsley sat on Bryan's lap. Ericsson reportedly threw Cristal on the ex and called her a fat cow, a fashion whore, and other interesting profanities. "Gwynn was out of control," says Bachelorette Jen Schefft. "But wow . . . her Harry Winston is huge! So much bigger than the two I have." Unfortunately, Ericsson's rep couldn't be reached for comment.

Chapter 14

*R*ING-RIIING.

Ring-riii-iiing.

The next morning, I wake to the sound of my cell phone. So annoying.

My entire body is wrapped and twisted around in crisp sheets, and there's a cool breeze drifting across my face and arms.

Mmm. So snug and cozy—if only my stupid cell phone would stop ringing! Obviously I don't want to talk, because I'm not picking up. So stop calling.

Ring-riiiiiiiiiing.

OH FINE. I snap open an eye and . . .

Ah—light! Pain jets through my head. MENTAL NOTE: MUST DRINK SLOWER.

I press my temples for a second, then fish around on the floor for my bag, sifting through its contents until I find the source of the evil, evil sound. Stupid freaking cell phone.

I check caller ID. It's Kimmie. *This better be good.*

"Where the hell are you?" Kimmie shouts.

What? I'm at home. Aren't I? I hold the cell phone back from my ear a few inches, squinting in pain as I slowly skim the unfamiliar bedroom.

"I . . . I'm not exactly sure," I stammer, a rush of fear jetting through my veins.

I've never seen this room before! Everything is white. *Really white.* White walls. White carpet. White puffy chair. Airy white curtains floating high above my head. There are narrow windows running the entire length of the wall, which is at least twenty feet above my head.

"Are you at Aiden's?" Kimmie demands.

"What are you talking about? Aiden who?" I ask, scratching my head. I don't know anyone by that name. Do I?

"Hello! Your friend from high school? Did you sleep with him? You did, didn't you?" she squeals.

High school?

High school?

What is she . . . ?

Suddenly I yank the sheets up around my chest and freeze.

Oh my God. *My client?* Nooooo!

My head spins as images from the night before start rushing back to me. Engagement party. Slamming my stiletto in the door (ugh). Kimmie and Julia tagging along on my gig (double ugh). And . . .

Aiden.

Shitty! I was making out with my client Aiden.

I slowly peer over my shoulder. And yep, there he is, my client. He's propped up on an elbow, his sexy, tan torso sticking out from the sheets. He flashes a grin and points to himself, mouthing the words: *I'm Aiden.*

Arghh. I whip around, my heart thumping like mad. What did I do?

Quick. Think. I squeeze my eyes shut, desperately trying to remember. If only my head would just cooperate and stop throbbing for one sec, maybe I could think clearly.

"HEL-LO!" Kimmie cries. "We need to talk. Julia said you called Aiden your client? And that you were *working.* What the hell is going on? You're not a . . . a hooker, are you?"

Aaack! She's practically screaming. Did Aiden hear her?

"ARE YOU KIDDING?" I cup my hand over the phone. *"I. am. not. a. hooker,"* I hiss wildly. *"Are you completely insane?"*

I peer over my shoulder at Aiden and let out a nervous little laugh. I point to the phone and mouth: *She's cuckoo.*

Aiden laughs.

"Are you sure?" Kimmie snaps. "I know it sounds crazy, but you were acting really weird and . . . Julia said . . ."

"I'm hanging up now. Good-bye," I tell her.

"Oh no. Wait! What happened? Are you there? I'm sorry. I know you're not a hooker. Did you sleep with him? You can't just hang up on . . ." Click.

I flop back onto the bed and close my eyes for a few moments, trying to clear my head. Nice going, Vic. Well done. Way to be professional. Just hop in bed with a client. What was I thinking? I just don't *do* one-night stands. And I could get fired for pulling a stunt like this.

Geesh! I might as well be a hooker.

"Hi there," Aiden says, softly biting my neck and snapping me into the present.

Mmm. My entire body tingles.

But this *can't* happen.

"I need to go," I whisper, as his lips work their way from my neck to my stomach.

"Sure. Whatever you say," he murmurs, pulling himself on top of me. "I have a meeting. It won't take too long."

Well . . .

It already happened once. Might as well make the most of it. Right? Maybe I'll go in just a bit . . .

•

SO AS MUCH AS I WANT to have a tell-all session with Kimmie and Julia about Aiden, I've got bigger things to worry about as the clock inches toward noon. Like, my ex-boyfriend's wedding.

I still can't *believe* Mom talked me into going to this thing.

It's going to be so awkward and, well, humiliating. I don't want to see all my ex's relatives and his friends. And I certainly don't want to see him. I can hear the whispering now: *Isn't that Rick's ex-girlfriend? I can't believe she came to the wedding. Do you think she still wants him? She must.*

I'd rather do anything than go, but I promised Mom I would. So I'm doing what any other girl would do at a vulnerable moment like this—going shopping. Hey, if I'm going to wish them well, at least I have to look decent. Right?

I check my watch. It's a little past noon now. I'm meeting Mom and Dad at the church in Naperville at five o'clock sharp. I need about two hours to get ready. So that leaves me approximately two hours to find a drop-dead gorgeous dress. Where to?

Barneys.

I feel bad about not dropping by Sugar first. I mean, Cici does stock the most incredible vintage dresses. But it's just so much more thrilling to shop at Barneys . . . *now that I can*. I'll drop by Sugar later this week.

I dig my cell phone out of my bag as I wait for the "L" at the Armitage station. A receipt falls to the ground. My cell reads TWO MISSED CALLS. Kimmie again?

I bend down and pick up the receipt as I wait for voice mail to pick up. Zentra: $350?! *What was I thinking?* This wing-woman stuff is really adding up. Ooh. And come to think of it, Polo never cut me that check from the wedding account last night. Surely my credit card will max out any day now.

"WE HAVE TO TALK." Gwynn's voice rips through my cell phone. "THIS IS AN EMERGENCY. KAITLYN—THE FAT COW— MUST BE STOPPED. CALL ME!"

Oh dear God. I can't deal with that right now. I press delete and play the second message.

"Oh!" Gwynn huffs. "And get this. Angel got engaged!! ENGAGED?! AT MY ENGAGEMENT PARTY. Can you believe that? Right after you guys left. Unbelievable. I can't believe she'd do this to me. So rude. So tacky! SO UNFOR-GIVABLE. And on the night Kaitlyn shows up again? Ah! CALL ME!"

I stare at my cell phone in horror. Someone else is engaged now, too? What's going on?

•

WHEN I FINALLY STEP into Barneys, I'm immediately drawn to the cosmetic counter. I don't know what it is, but there's just something about all the soft sugary scents. The shiny tester bottles. The miniature lipsticks. The new sparkly spring shadows. The smooth, velvety crèmes. It's like I'm a little girl again and they're all just waiting there, calling after me: Try me! Try me! Try me!

And I . . . I can't stop myself.

I. MUST. TRY. THEM.

It'll only take a sec. Swear. And then I'll go find a fabulous dress.

I happily trot over to the Kiehl's counter and lather some of their facial moisturizer onto my hands. Wow. It's so silky. So luxurious. How much is this stuff? I turn the four-ounce plastic bottle around to check the price. $28. Hmm. Not bad.

After testing a few other lotions, I bend down over one of the makeup mirrors and inspect the faint lines around my eyes. I've been applying that La Bella serum every day like the directions indicated. But . . . I don't know . . . I pull the skin back around my eyes. Yuck. Those pesky lines are still there. They make me look *so old*. For $325, I expected better results. But the gross lines still look the same.

Sigh.

What is going on with my body?

Oh! And don't even get me started on my ever-expanding butt and tummy. It's . . . aaack . . . I can't even talk about it. Let's just say, it's totally out of hand at this point. In fact, it's almost time for a full-out emergency. We're talking starvation! Um . . . but I couldn't live without cheese fries. Chicago-style pizza. And, well, I have to have a few hot dogs from Wiener Circle every now and then. Um . . . and then there's chocolate. And . . . okay. Never mind.

Maybe I should (gasp!) join a gym?

I know. I know. I absolutely despise sweating and working out in general, but it might be my only option.

Eww. Suddenly an image flashes into my head. Me on one of those evil treadmills, red-faced, lungs about to explode, hanging on for dear life.

I think I might cry.

There has to be another way. Doesn't there?

Sighing softly, I step away from the mirror and let my eyes linger on all the shimmering perfume bottles. Vera Wang, Alexander McQueen, Marc Jacobs, Sensi . . .

Hey, wait a minute. An odd-shaped contraption catches my eye. Is that a cellulite roller? I walk over and inspect the silver gadget, flipping it around in my hands. It is! It's like the one I saw at Bloomingdale's the other day. Hmm. Maybe I don't need to hit the gym after all. *City Girls* magazine says these things are *unbelievable.* All the stars use them.

"How's my favorite wingwoman?" A deep voice interrupts my thoughts.

I jump, nearly dropping the roller on the floor. "What the . . . ?"

I whip around to see none other than Patrick.

Arghh!

I look up at Patrick, then down at the cellulite roller in my hand, then back up at Patrick's smiling face.

Why can't I be looking at something smart? Like a . . . a . . . I don't know . . . an Hermès scarf, a Fendi purse, or something—*anything* but a cellulite roller.

Oh dear God.

I instinctively hide the roller behind my back. "Um . . . hi," I say helplessly, feeling my neck and cheeks go flaming red. Suddenly the outrageously embarrassing image of me singing to Patrick on the phone last night comes flooding back. *Please don't say anything about the call. Please?* Ugh. Could this get any worse?

"What's that?" Patrick asks curiously, pointing behind my back.

It's getting worse. It's getting much, much worse.

"What do you mean?" I say defensively, putting my free hand on the cool glass counter and trying desperately to look casual.

"In your hand? What is it?"

Why is he being so nosy? I stare up at him blankly, my jaw flinching, praying he'll suddenly just change the subject or miraculously disappear in front of my eyes. *Poof.* Gone. Bye-bye.

Unfortunately, he's still staring down at me intently.

"What? This little thing?" I shrug, letting out an awful high-pitched laugh, flashing the cellulite roller in front of my face, then slapping it on the counter. "It's just a . . . um . . ." Oh God. Oh God. Think, Vic. Think. "It's just a . . . a massager." A WHAT?! A massager? I practically called it a vibrator!

"Wow," Patrick says, lifting up the cellulite roller and inspecting it carefully. "It's quite a complicated-looking gadget. Don't you think?" he asks, rolling the device back and forth on his arm and looking skeptical. "I guess it feels okay." He starts moving the cellulite roller back and forth across my arm.

I want to die. Right this very moment.

"What do you think?" he asks.

Well, I want to shrivel up and disappear, but other than that? "It feels awesome!" I exclaim, a little too excitedly.

"Huh," he says, raising an eyebrow and nodding. "Well, maybe I should get one then. I'd hate to be missing out."

"No!" I practically shout, snatching the roller away from him. "It's the only one. I . . . I was going to buy it."

"Oh right. Of course," Patrick says, looking slightly amused. "I forgot how competitive shopping at Barneys can be."

"I didn't mean . . . I'm sure they have another in back. Or you can take this . . ."

Patrick pushes a dark wavy strand out of his eye. "Oh no. You take it. I insist."

"Thanks," I say quietly, taking in his dark eyes, his scruffy jawline, his sexy . . .

Aaack! What am I doing? He's my client. And hello, I just slept with Aiden last night. *Another client.* Am I turning into a big slut? Good God, Vic.

Anyway, he just thinks I'm a good wingwoman.

"Ma'am. Can I help you?" asks a Nicole Kidman look-alike behind the cosmetics counter.

My eyes dart from Patrick to the cellulite roller, then back again. What do I do? I can't afford any extra credit card charges.

Before I know what's happening, I hear myself squeak, "I'd like to buy this."

I hold my breath as Nicole swooshes my credit card through the cash register. I am barely listening to her explain how this particular item costs $245 and is completely nonreturnable. *Please let it clear. Please let it clear.* I cross my fingers behind my back.

"Great," I say sharply. "Perfect."

Is it just me or is it taking longer than usual? MENTAL NOTE: POLO NEEDS TO WRITE ME THAT CHECK *TODAY.*

"I guess I should let you keep shopping then," Patrick says at last.

"Right. Okay. See you later!" I wave.

Right as I'm turning around, I hear Patrick say something . . .

"What's that?" I ask.

He looks flustered. "I was just, you know, wondering what you're doing tonight?"

"Well, in about four hours I'll be at my ex-boyfriend's wedding—alone. Pretty exciting stuff, let me tell you." *Alone?* Why did I say that? Now I look like a loser.

"I could be your wingman." Patrick grins playfully. "Only if there's singing involved. Of course."

Oh great. He thinks I'm so desperate I need a sympathy date.

"Oh God, no! I mean . . . no. I don't need a date. I actually . . . you know . . . *like* going to these things alone." Super. Now he thinks I'm a total dork.

"Right." He nods, his face suddenly serious.

"My parents will be there." Even better, Vic. Even better. *Stop talking. DO NOT SPEAK.*

Patrick cocks his head, smiling awkwardly. "Okay. Well, have fun at your ex-boyfriend's wedding."

"Thanks. I will!" I chirp. And with that, I turn on my heel and take the stairs two at a time up to the women's clothing section.

Okay. Focus. I need to focus. I steal a peek at my watch. Arghh! It's almost one o'clock already? I can't believe it. This is not good. Not good at all. I only have an hour left to find a super-amazing outfit. How could I let myself get so distracted like that?

My fingers sweep through rack after rack of designer dresses—ranging from truly hideous prints to unbelievably divine fabrics—but my head keeps spinning back to Patrick's sparkly eyes, his dark messy hair, the way his lips curled into a smile . . .

Oh my God. I have to get a grip. He's a client. And he's Kimmie's boss. He's off-limits.

I grab a handful of dresses and race toward the dressing room.

While I'm in the fitting room, my cell phone rings. I don't recognize the number.

"Hello?"

"Victoria! Hi! It's Everett. I hope it's okay that I'm calling you."

"Hey. What's going on?" I say, whipping around to inspect my butt in a clingy silver Laundry dress. Gross. I look like an elephant in this thing.

"It's an emergency," he whispers. "I'm at the gym and a girl just asked me out. What do I do?"

I laugh. "Well, do you like her? Is she cute?" I can practically see Everett standing in the corner of the gym, his stubby fingers clutching his cell phone with a death grip as sweat trickles down his pink face.

"Yeah. I think so."

"Then say yes, you goofball!" Wow. Everett really *is* bad at dating.

"Right. Got it. Bye."

After trying on about a dozen more frilly designer dresses, I finally find *the one.* It's by Miu Miu and it's absolutely to die for with a literally to-die-for price. I don't even want to think about it. I'm just going to close my eyes, hand over the card, and pray like hell it clears again. (After all, my ex-boyfriend's wedding is no time to skimp, now is it?)

I'm flying down the stairs to the main level, when suddenly I spot . . .

Aiden?

I stop dead in my tracks. What is *he* doing here? I thought he had some big meeting at one of his dad's Wacker Drive properties? I watch as Aiden hovers over a makeup counter, talking to some trashy tanning-bed chick with bleached-blond hair. (Definitely not the Nicole Kidman look-alike waiting on me before.) She's wearing a tight white smock unbuttoned to reveal enormous breasts. Her head is thrown back and she's laughing hysterically.

"You are just *too cute!*" Boob Chick purrs, leaning toward Aiden and squeezing her chest together under his nose.

My heart thumps wildly. What is he . . . ? Who is she . . . ?

I slither down the remaining steps, watching as Aiden leans in closer, resting his elbows on the glass counter. He looks down longingly at her chest, tickling her cheek with a makeup brush and letting it sweep down her neck.

Boob Chick, of course, is loving it.

My heart feels like it's about to pound right out of my ears. I can't believe this. Just what does he think he's doing? How could he? Aiden was in bed with me just a few hours ago! (Never mind the fact that I was just fantasizing about another client. Obviously that is *completely* different.)

He whispers something in Boob Chick's ear, then turns to leave.

Oh no.

I'm standing in plain sight. He'll . . . he'll know I was spying on him. I duck behind a rack of designer belts, totally frantic.

No use. He'll easily spot me behind this dinky thing.

What do I do? I look right, then left.

Oh dear God. He's coming this way. I have to do something! Quick. Hide!

I dive behind one of the silk scarf counters, but my foot catches on the edge of a display. There's a huge crash as the entire Ralph Lauren glass table smashes onto the tiles. Glass flies everywhere. And a rainbow of silk scarves floats down all around me.

This can't be happening. It just can't. I grab one of the shimmery gold scarves and pull it down over my head, closing my eyes. Don't let Aiden lean over. Don't let him check to see if everyone is all right. Just keep walking, Aiden. Keep walking.

I hear someone clear their throat above me.

No.

Let me disappear. Pretty please?

"Are you okay, ma'am?" I hear a soft voice above me ask.

I peek out from under the gold scarf. It's Nicole. Thank God.

"I . . . I'm really sorry," I stammer. "I think I fell. Or I don't know what happened. I can clean?"

"That's okay," she says. "I'll call maintenance."

I poke my head out into the aisle, watching as Aiden pushes through the store doors and struts into the dreary Saturday afternoon. Wow. That was close.

My cell phone rings. It's Everett again.

"I HAVE A DATE!" he yells.

"Everett—that's fantastic!" I whoop. "Congratulations."

At least one of us is having a good afternoon . . .

Chapter 15

KIMMIE CALLS as I'm driving my silver VW Bug up to the church.

"Guess what?" she screeches. "I have the most fabulous, sensational, wonderful news! Sit down. Are you sitting down?"

"I'm driving; what do you think?"

"Ooh. Testy, testy." She clicks her tongue. "Has your sex high worn off from last night?"

"You could say that." I consider telling her about catching Aiden with that trashy Boob Chick this afternoon, but I really don't want to rehash last night and the whole hooker idea she concocted. *(And obviously I'm not telling her about my crazy little crush on her boss!)*

"You know . . . I didn't like that Aiden guy," Kimmie grumbles. "I got a bad vibe from him."

"Okay. Whatever." I sigh. "Listen. You better not be calling to say you're engaged. Because that's all people are phoning me about these days. Angel got engaged at Gwynn's party last night."

Kimmie lets out a loud whistle. "Gwynnie-pooh must be thrilled. But no. I'm not calling about an engagement. I, for one, still remember our pact. Long live the singletinis, baby!"

Thank God. At least *someone* remembers.

"I do have a date, though," Kimmie blurts.

"You do!" I shriek. "With who?"

"DJ," she says excitedly. "Remember Blondie from Gramercy?"

My mind drifts back. Back to the night I got fired and we all met out for drinks. Oh yeah! Blondie—our waiter? "Shut up!" I scream. "He's hot. Steamy hot. Ouch! When did he call? How'd he get your number?"

"I have my ways," she lowers her voice mysteriously.

"I'm impressed." I whistle. "I want to hear all about it, but I gotta run. I'm in the church parking lot."

"That's right. The *wedding* is tonight. I still can't believe you're going. You're a hell of a lot nicer than I am."

•

As I WALK UP to the ivy-covered church, the same quaint Naperville church I went to when I was growing up, my stomach knots up. I just can't believe Rick and Claire are getting married today. It was all sort of a bad joke until now. (You know. *Ha-ha. My evil ex best friend is marrying my ex-boyfriend. Feel sorry for me.*) But tonight, it's really going to happen. They're really getting married.

It's not like I still have feelings for Rick anymore. Seriously.

That was, like, what? Five years ago? Six? But it still feels weird. Back in high school, I thought he was *the one*. And I know this is so, so incredibly awful of me, but every time I'm around Rick and Claire (unfortunately it's every once in a while with that whole my-mom-and-Claire's-mom-are-still-best-friends thing), I have this uncontrollable urge to blurt, "I've slept with him! Ha! I've had sex with your fiancé. S-E-X. And it was really, *ree-eally* good."

I know. Who thinks like that? I could probably go to hell for having such wicked thoughts so close to a holy site. I peer up at the overcast sky. Maybe I should take cover from sudden bolts of angry lightning?

The church looks beautiful inside. As much as I want to say it's horrid and oozing with pink and tacky taffeta, it's not. It's actually very simple and elegant. There are bundles of white peonies at each pew, tall white candles flickering all around, and sheer white fabric draped artfully around the altar. It's pretty.

I take my place in line, waiting for an usher to seat me. I guess one good thing about this evening is that I simply adore my dress. It's jet black with these itsy-bitsy spaghetti straps that crisscross all the way down its low neckline. And it playfully swishes around my knees all Spanish-dancer-like with a satin bow that ties snugly around my stomach. The dress was made for me, accentuating all the right places (shoulders, collarbone, and legs) and hiding all my "problem areas" (butt and tummy).

As I get closer to the front of the usher's line, I scan the pews for Mom and Dad. I immediately spot Mom's silver bubble of hair off to the right. She's wearing her favorite mint-green suit, complete with matching pumps, bag, and eye shadow. (How many times do I have to tell her . . . *too much matching*.) She waves excitedly with a lacy white handkerchief.

I take an usher's arm and point in the direction of my parents. I notice how strong the usher's arm feels. I glance up at him and notice that this usher is hot. *Very hot.* Solid football build. A total Tom Brady kind of guy. (Gotta know your football to chat with clients.) Maybe coming to this wedding wasn't such a bad idea after all?

Mom gasps as I scoot down the pew toward her. She grabs my arm and yanks me down next to her.

"You're wearing *black*," she hisses.

"So." I shrug, smoothing out the front of my dress.

"You look nice." Dad leans over and smiles.

"Thank you. So do you." I wink at him, admiring his smart navy suit, starched white button-down, and silk red tie. His full head of silver hair is neatly combed to the side and his sky blue eyes are gleaming.

Mom frowns, wringing her hands nervously. "You're not supposed to wear *black* at weddings."

I roll my eyes, absently flipping through the program. "Says who?"

"I don't know *who*," Mom huffs. "But you're not supposed to. Everyone knows that. It makes a bad statement."

"Oh Mom. It's fine. I'm not trying to make a statement."

"Well, you are," she sniffs. "And it's not good."

"Judy, leave it alone." Dad puts an arm around Mom's padded shoulders and gives her a squeeze. "Victoria looks nice."

Mom inhales sharply and looks away, but I can hear her mind ticking: *Good people don't wear black to weddings. Everyone knows that. Everyone!*

Grrr.

"See." I elbow Mom a few minutes later. "She's wearing black, too!" I point triumphantly to a waify girl dressed in head-to-toe black—black dress, black shoes, black bag, and a black pashmina thrown dramatically around her shoulders.

"She looks like a tramp," Mom says, pursing her coral lips tightly.

Whatever. I give up. We sit shoulder to shoulder in silence as I scan row after row, checking out all the cute, annoyingly rail-thin girls. Am I the only one with some extra pounds to hide? Wait. Is that . . .

Aaack! Don't look. It's one of my clients. That meaty *Chicago Tribune* sportswriter and the cute redhead I set him up with at ESPN Zone. (Hmm. That's a little soon to ask someone to a wedding. Isn't it?) I frantically grab a Bible from the pew and hold it up to my face as if I'm studying the verses very, very carefully.

Oh God. Please don't let them see me. *Please.* I'm with my parents! I can't even imagine explaining the whole wingwoman concept to Mom. It would be disastrous. Once my client is seated at the other side of the church, I put the Bible back down. Whew. That was close.

And that's when the organ music begins.

I swivel around in the pew and watch as the bridesmaids begin their proud march down the long skinny aisle, one by one. I recognize most of them from high school.

Step together.

Pause.

Step together.

Pause.

Each of the bridesmaids wears the typical I-am-an-important-person-in-this-wedding-and-you're-not smile plastered on her face. And as they make their way down the aisle, I sit on the edge of my seat, just waiting to nitpick anything tacky or obnoxious. But the dresses are actually quite cute. Ivory. Silk. Tea-length. With the tiniest ribbons at the waists.

"Gorgeous," Mom whispers as the girls pass our aisle.

At that moment, there's silence. The wooden door behind the minister's podium cracks open and Rick squeezes out in a black tuxedo with tails. It looks like he's sweating slightly and . . .

Oh my God. When did he get so, well, well-built?

I can't believe this. *Rick is hot?* What's going on? Isn't it some unspoken rule that ex-boyfriends are supposed to look fat and repulsive without you? They're *definitely* not supposed to look better than they did when you dated them!

The bridal march starts and the doors in the back of the sanctuary fling open. There are *oohs, ahs,* and a few gasps as the congregation stands.

"Oh my. Doesn't Claire look stunning?" Mom dabs her eyes.

I force myself to look. I haven't seen Claire in nearly a year. And as my eyes focus in on her, I'm surprised at how different she looks. She's thinner than I remembered. And much more . . . sophisticated. (Is it the way her hair is swept back?) Claire's dress is very simple. Silk. Strapless. Classic. Her cheeks are rosy. Her eyes are twinkling. And she's absolutely glowing with happiness. So is Rick. They laugh nervously when their eyes meet for the first time. Is she crying? Is *he* crying? Wait. Why is everything so fuzzy?

Oh my God.

I'm crying.

WHAT AM I DOING? I can't *cry* at my ex-boyfriend's wedding. I . . . I'm supposed to be mad, angry, bitter, cruel, flippant . . . anything but crying.

Sniff.

But I'm not mad or angry or any of that. I don't know what I am. As they say their vows, though, I feel this awful flood of fear wash all over me. I feel so old. I'm almost twenty-five years old and I'm not even close to this stage in my life. Nowhere near it. And here's the funny thing. I never thought I wanted to be for a while . . . but maybe I do? It looks so sweet. So . . . I don't know. It's just so scary. I'm not ready for all this.

"They look so in love," Mom snuffles, reaching for Dad's hand.

Sniff. Sniff.

And the rest of the wedding is a bit of a haze.

·

Wow. I DON'T KNOW what came over me at the wedding! It was crazy. I'm fine now. Swear. Totally back to normal. You can't tell anyone I cried, though. Okay? I mean, honestly, who cries at an ex-boyfriend's wedding except psychos storming down the aisle trying to call the whole thing off? And I am certainly not that girl. No sirree. I just came to wish them well. And . . . okay . . . fine. Because Mom guilted me into it. But whatever. I'm here. Right?

When we make it over to the country club, I'm shocked to discover that the reception is dry. As in, no alcohol. Nada. Zip. Zilch.

I know. I know. Unbelievable.

How is this even possible? How am I supposed to get through this night without a single drink? Hmm? I want a refund. No wedding gift for them. That Mikasa gravy boat? It's heading straight back to the store!

"Isn't that smart, dear?" Mom clucks. "What a great way to save money. We should consider a dry reception for you if you ever get married one day."

"Yeah," I grumble, rubbing my temples. "Great idea. Just super."

Ugh. What I wouldn't do for a cherrytini . . .

"How's work, dear?" Mom chirps as we sit down. "Have you landed any big sales?"

My stomach tightens. "Good. Great. It's going really well." Okay. Definitely need to change the subject ASAP.

"My daughter is in sales!" Mom announces to our entire table. "If you ever need a computer, be sure to call. She's the best!"

Claire's great aunt and uncle from Milwaukee smile and nod politely.

"Victoria, where's your business card?" Mom whispers. "This is a great networking opportunity."

Oh dear God. Here we go again with the business cards.

"I didn't bring any," I say sharply, praying she'll get the hint and drop the subject.

But oh no. Not Mom. She starts rooting around in her handy mint-green bag (with all the slots and pouches she raves about) . . . and sure enough . . . plucks out two fresh business cards and scoots them across the table at the older couple. "Here you go," she clucks. "Anything computers. Call our Victoria anytime!"

I smile weakly, my cheeks hot with embarrassment.

If only Mom knew the kind of sales I was in . . .

By the time Rick and Claire take the dance floor for their first dance—to "The Way You Look Tonight"—I'm bored to tears. I absently finger one of the white peonies on our table.

I need a drink.

I *sooo* need a drink.

I'm not an alcoholic. Swear. *You* try going to an ex-boyfriend's wedding. Without a date. *With* your parents. SOBER.

At this point I'd take a cheap wine cooler. Maybe someone has a six-pack of beer in his car?

Sigh. It looks like I'll have to settle for fresh air.

"I'm going to take a walk," I say. Mom and Dad nod.

I wander around the hallway for a bit and eventually make my way into the kitchen. It has to have some alcohol. Doesn't it? A bottle of sherry? Some vermouth? Anything? I push open the swinging kitchen doors and stick my head inside.

I slowly scan right, then left. The kitchen is dimly lit. Not a soul in sight. Whew—the coast is clear.

I step inside, quickly pulling the doors shut.

"Hi there," a deep voice suddenly says.

Aaack! I jump back, my heart dropping into my stomach with a thud. I whip around to see who's there . . .

It's my usher friend.

Relief washes over me. "You scared me!" I cry, clutching my stomach.

"Sorry about that," he says, flashing me a sexy grin. "Are we looking for the same thing?"

"Maybe," I say, biting my lip.

He pulls a bottle of chardonnay from behind his back and dangles it between us. "Something like this?"

I smile devilishly. "How'd you guess?"

He unclips his tuxedo bow tie and hands me the bottle. We sit on top of the kitchen counter, our feet swinging back and forth as we take turns swigging chardonnay from the bottle.

A little while later, I step back into the wedding reception on the arm of my new friend. As we make our way onto the dance floor, Mom gives me a thumbs-up. "That's the spirit!" I hear her whisper to Dad.

The usher and I dance and dance. And I have to admit, I actually have a pretty good time. He's a funny guy. Turns out he has the hots for a girl he works with at Deloitte & Touche. And, well, being the helpful wingwoman I am, I give him a few tips. You know . . . don't act too interested or needy. Just be friendly. Ask her loads of questions. Show that you're a good listener. And on, and on, and on.

At the end of night, he can't thank me enough. I give him my business card and he says he'll be in touch to set up a gig. (Looks like I have a new client! Way to work, Vic. Seriously. *Very* industrious.) Wow. This wedding turned out so much better than I anticipated! I even chatted with Rick and Claire on the dance floor for a few minutes. (Can you believe that?)

Yep. I have to admit, I'm in a pretty good mood as I *clack-clack* down the hall toward my car.

Now, if I could just forget about Aiden and that trashy Boob Chick . . .

Chapter 16

EWW.

The next morning as I'm shuffling into the bathroom, I catch a glimpse of myself in the vanity mirror. My face is so puffy. (I knew I shouldn't have chowed that second piece of wedding cake!) I look down at my thighs. Gross. I'm blowing up like a big blobby whale. If I don't pull it together, I'm going to have to join a gym. And you know how much I don't want to do that. I turn on the sink faucet and splash water on my face.

Maybe I should go back to bed? At least I can't eat while I'm sleeping. I throw myself into bed, sending pink wingwoman flyers scattering everywhere as I pull the covers over my head.

Ugh. I can't believe I have a wingwoman gig tonight. I'm exhausted. This is going to be pure torture. I just need a night off!

The phone rings, but I don't move. I don't care who it is. I'm not interested. I'm busy sleeping. I'm in a coma. I'm dead.

Hi. You've reached Victoria. Leave a message.

"Hey, babe. It's Aiden."

I freeze, my heart suddenly racing. What do I do? What do I do?

"Just calling to see if you wanna hang out tonight."

I jerk upright in bed, hugging my legs tightly. Should . . .

should I pick up? No. No way. I'm mad at him! He was all over Boob Chick.

Well—maybe I'm overreacting a teensy-weensy bit? It's highly possible. In fact, the more I think about it, *she* was the one all over *him*. Yeah. Totally. He probably doesn't even like her. Or maybe she's only a friend?

"Call if you . . ."

"Hello?" I gasp, grabbing the phone. Geesh! Breathe. Don't sound so desperate. "It's . . . um . . . Victoria."

"I know, doll. I called you. Remember?"

"Oh right." I laugh nervously. "So . . . um . . . what's going on?"

"You tell me," he says. "Wanna hang out tonight?"

"I'm working, but maybe afterward?" I say, trying not to sound too eager.

"Cool. Give me a call when it's over."

Well. Maybe I don't need to *completely* forget about Aiden. I just won't be his wingwoman anymore . . .

Right. Absolutely.

•

AHEM. I WAKE UP Monday morning absolutely glowing. Last night was amazing. And, well, let's leave it at that. It kind of bothers me that Aiden left in the middle of the night—he mumbled something about needing to get up super early today for another big meeting—but whatever. I'm not going to let that ruin my high.

My wingwoman gig went fabulously, too! It was at Wrigley Field for a night game. My beer-bellied client, Marty, was a total Cubs fanatic—decked out in a blue-and-white Mark Prior jersey, Cubs beer helmet, and a huge CUBS ARE #1 poster (he really wanted to get on TV). We sat in the bleachers, drank

Old Style beer, waved at the center fielder, and chatted with every female sitting in our section.

I finally hit a home run at the Cubby Bear bar when I spotted a curly haired brunette with rosy cheeks and her very own Mark Prior jersey. (Boys' size, very flattering. Maybe I should get one?) They hit it off immediately. *Score.* I was literally skipping on the way home to meet Aiden.

And I'm still smiling as I roll out of bed, throw on a cute red tracksuit, and bounce down to the corner Starbucks. Kimmie called in sick and Julia doesn't have class until later, so we're meeting for coffee. (We used to do this all the time. But, well, we're all so busy these days.)

"Morning." I smile blissfully, sliding into a wooden chair across from Kimmie and taking a sip of my tall skim mocha with extra whip.

"Look at this," Kimmie snickers, smacking a pink piece of paper on the table and pushing a few red curls out of her face. "It's that weird escort service Julia was talking about. Who knew prostitution was making such a comeback?"

Arghh! It's my wingwoman flyer. My eyes dart over to the cash register and the stack of flyers. Okay. Stay calm. She has no idea it's mine.

"Yep," I say nonchalantly. "Funny what people do for love."

Kimmie eyes me suspiciously but doesn't say a word.

"Hi, guys," Julia says brightly, pulling up a chair and setting down her caramel macchiato and flaky croissant.

"How are things with you and Kevin?" I ask, desperate to change the subject.

Julia's face falls. She takes a long sip of her macchiato. "I'm going to New York this weekend. I don't know . . ."

"I'm sorry," I say, giving her a quick hug. "I'm sure everything will work out. You two are the perfect match."

Julia nods, but her eyes are red. She pushes her long dark

hair off her shoulders and sniffs. And for a second, I think I see a flicker of fear or . . . I don't know. Is she hiding something?

Oh no. No. How crazy! Why do I keep thinking that? I'm sure it's just my wild imagination. This is Julia we're talking about. She has nothing to hide. She's so calm. So put together. Finishing up year two at Loyola law school. Top of her class. A job lined up at Peterson & McNally. I'm being ridiculous. Right?

On my stroll home from Starbucks, my cell phone rings.

"Hello. Victoria? This is Kate from Chicago Wingwoman. Is this a good time?"

"Um . . . sure," I say slowly. Oh no. She knows. She totally knows I'm sleeping with a client. I'm *sooo* fired.

"Great. Chicago Wingwoman is hosting a fashion show this Friday at Bloomingdale's to launch the new Rico label. This is a huge press event for us. I need you there all day. This shouldn't disrupt any of your work, since your gigs are at night."

Whew. "Sounds exciting!" I say brightly. "Am I helping set up? What time should I be there? Anything you need."

"Actually." Kate clears her throat. "I need you to be a model."

I burst out laughing. "Me? A model?"

"I'm sorry, but this is mandatory for all wingwomen," Kate says crisply. "Report to Bloomingdale's Thursday morning at nine o'clock sharp for rehearsal. And Victoria . . . this clothing line is extremely confidential. Keep it hush-hush. Okay?" Click.

I think I'm going to get sick.

I stop in the middle of the sidewalk, my entire body shaking in fear. This has to be a mistake. I mean, me? A real-life model walking down a real-life runway? What a nightmare. Especially in my blobby state. I stare at my cell phone in horror. I . . . I have to call Kate back. Tell her no! I quickly dial up the Chicago Wingwoman office, but all the lines are busy. Shitty! What am I going to do?

Oh dear God. What if I trip? What if I fall flat on my face like Carrie Bradshaw in *Sex and the City*? I'd die. Or even worse . . . what if everyone starts whispering about how fat I am? I swivel around and ruefully examine my butt and thighs.

Hopeless.

This calls for drastic measures. I definitely need to join a gym. No doubt about that. And, well, I think I need to call Mom. You'll see . . .

"Nonsense, darling!" Mom trills a few minutes later. "You were a skinny minnie at Claire's wedding. You shouldn't lose an ounce."

"But it's an emergency!" I wail.

"Hmm." She clicks her tongue. "Are you doing this for a boy?" She sounds hopeful. "Anyone your father and I can meet?"

"MOM!!"

After about twenty minutes of begging and pleading—*tell me, tell me, pleeeease?!*—she finally coughs it up.

The Hart Family Diet Secret.

I know. I know. Why haven't I asked before? Well, it always sounded so drastic and severe. So desperate. But this is an emergency. I have to model. *In four days.*

She's breathless as she whispers the instructions. "Since you have less than a week, we'll put you on the most extreme level. Listen very carefully . . ."

"Thank you! Thank you! Thank you!" I squeal, surprised by how simple the diet sounds.

"Don't tell a soul," Mom hisses. "This diet has passed down through generations of Hart women. You're now in the know. Be very, very careful. It's potent."

Geesh! See what I mean? So dramatic. It's a diet, not an atomic bomb.

Chapter 17

OKAY. HERE'S THE THING with Gwynn. I love her. I really do. But she's suddenly got this insane notion that the entire world revolves around her. And I do mean the *entire* world.

Gwynn totally freaked on me for not calling her back Saturday morning. She whined on and on about how I was *her* personal attendant and she really needed me. I mean, Angel got engaged at *her* engagement party! And Kaitlyn Kingsley is back in town—indefinitely! Her perfect little engagement is falling apart! How could I possibly be doing something more important? Did I not care about her at all?

I tried to explain to Gwynn that Angel is a cow and will probably end up divorced within a year. But for some reason, this comment didn't go over so well. Gwynn completely twisted my words all around, and even accused me of insinuating that she and Bryan would end up divorced! Like I'd actually say something like that?

Ugh. And then I got to hear all about evil, evil Kaitlyn. "THE NERVE. Scouting out new talent for her trendy Red Envy fashion company? Ha! She's here to break up my engagement—*I know it*. But we're going to stop her. You just wait. I'm devising a plan."

Oh no. I hate it when Gwynn devises plans.

I managed to get Gwynn to stop crying and plotting against Kaitlyn by changing the subject to the wedding itself. She cheered up immediately and happily chatted on and on about how she was going to a private wedding-cake tasting at the Chicago Culinary Institute this week. Some über-famous chef wants to create the divine mocha truffle cake of her dreams.

I'm sure that's helping her diet along just brilliantly. Oh wait, that reminds me! I forgot to tell you about that e-mail Gwynn sent me the other day. I guess Polo, Pierre, and Philip put her on this super-strict, super-hush-hush bridal regime. It went something like this:

- 1,000-calorie-a-day diet.
- Daily massages at the Four Seasons.
- Private bride-to-be yoga sessions in her condo. *[I guess it's all the rage. Makes you look refreshed and absolutely radiant on your wedding day. Better than sex, she wrote.]*
- Floral reviews at her parents' penthouse.
- Wedding therapy twice a week with her mother. *[Purely for preventive mother-daughter stress.]*
- Posh menu reviews at mk, NoMI, Charlie Trotter's, and so on.

Isn't that completely out of hand? Just like this conversation. I finally get Gwynn off the phone after swearing I'll go to lunch with her sometime this week and after listening to her remind me a ba-zillion times (and I'm barely exaggerating) to check my e-mail. More wedding to-do lists.

Swell. Can't wait.

I reluctantly switch on my computer, bracing myself for all the wedding crap. I quickly skim my inbox. Let's see. Two messages from Mom. One from Kimmie. One from Gwynn. And this really bizarre one . . .

```
FROM: cory@webtalk.com
TO: victoria_hart@vongo.com
PRIORITY: Standard
```

SUBJECT: Seeking wingwoman

I got your business card from a friend. I'm a big partyer and I'm looking for a hot, fun, very open-minded bisexual wingwoman to help hook me up with bi girls. I have a big thing for them. Are you game?

Cory

OH. MY. GOD. Where do these people come from? I've been getting all kinds of these messages lately. One guy actually asked if I'd be interested in a threesome with him and his girl-friend. Eww. And this other guy offered to pay me $5,000 to find his true love in a week. Here's the catch. He's married and wants to know if that's a problem.

Are you kidding me? Maybe I'll stop handing out business cards. I'm getting enough gigs, anyway.

Next message . . .

FROM: kimmie_ohaggan@lambertagency.com
TO: victoria_hart@vongo.com
PRIORITY: *Urgent*
SUBJECT: !!??!!
GUESS WHAT?
DJ sent me flowers! Peach tulips. I LOVE TULIPS.
Should I call and thank him now? Or wait until tomorrow? I'm thinking tomorrow. I don't want to seem too eager . . .
Call me when you get a sec.
Kimmie

Ooh. Things must be heating up with Kimmie and her new guy. She said their date Saturday night was *amazing*. Picnic on the beach. Champagne. Something about a quiche? Anyway, I'll reply later. Next message . . .

FROM: gwynnie_pooh@girly.com
TO: victoria_hart@vongo.com
ATTACHMENT: shower_priorities.doc
PRIORITY: *Very Urgent*
SUBJECT: Need your opinion—ASAP!

Okay. So. I'm thinking about getting all the brides-maids gym memberships. Would that make it totally obvious that I want them to drop some serious poundage? Be honest.

I just don't know what to do. Angel is totally chunking out these days. Did you see her at my engagement party? Gross. Talk about oink-oink. I mean, I love her (never mind that we're in a huge fight over the whole her-getting-engaged-at-my-engagement-party thing), but come on! Get it together. What am I supposed to do?

How awful would it be if I was surrounded by fat people during my wedding ceremony? Hey, come to think of it, it would make me look super thin. Tough one. What do you think?

Oh yeah. And I was thinking about throwing in a scale, a couple of *Fitness* magazines, and some workout videos. Sort of go with a theme. What do you think? Good idea? Bad idea? Let me know ASAP.

Kisses,

Gwynnie

P.S. There's a tiny to-do list from Polo, Pierre, and Philip attached. I think it's about the shower. Can you believe it's coming up so soon? Beyond, beyond excited! I don't care what Mother says—Birdie is not throwing it!

SHOWER_PRIORITIES.DOC
Bonjour, honey bunny.

You're simply smashing for helping us out. Thanks a billion! Toodles.

XOXO,

Polo

1. Create a picture timeline of Gwynn and Bryan's relationship—from when they met in college until now. IMPORTANT: Make sure Gwynn looks thin and glowing in all photos! Preferably shots focusing on her right side to show her sexy, sexy Cindy Crawford mole. She despises her left profile. Bryan just needs to be in the shot *somewhere*.

2. Write a cutesy short speech. You know. Mention what an amazing and incredibly beautiful friend Gwynn is, and how you could only hope to be half the person she is. Gwynn is a goddess. La-di-da. You get the idea.

3. Send an e-mail out to all the girls attending the party and request that they wear black to the shower. Gwynnie will be wearing white and she must be the radiant angel of the day. Do you think there's any way you could convince the other girls not to wear makeup? Hmm. Probably not. Just a thought . . .

4. Give Tia at *City Girls* magazine a jingle about the shower. Tell her we want some pre- and post-party shots. See if we can get Gwynnie's best gifts on a spread with some celebrity wedding gifts. (A-list celebrities only, though!)

Oh dear God. Are you kidding me? I stare at the list in disgust.

•

THAT EVENING I have a happy hour gig at John Barley-corn—a popular neighborhood pub in the heart of Lincoln Park. The redbrick bar is known for its vibrant stained-glass windows, original tin ceiling, and old model ships. (I guess the gangster John Dillinger used to be a frequent patron there, too. But now it's mostly packed with Big Ten graduates fresh out of school.) Anyway, my client's name is Oscar O'Flaherty and he's turning out to be a W-I-L-D one.

With his carrottop hair, crazy freckles, and short five-foot-eight stature, Oscar looks about sixteen and barely old enough to drive. He talks about a million miles a minute and . . . my God . . . he has so much energy. He's constantly hopping up and down, up and down from his barstool. Pointing to this girl. Jabbing me in the ribs about another girl. I can barely keep up. No wonder he can't get a woman. He's like a toddler with a mad case of ADD.

About ten minutes into the gig, Oscar's clear blue eyes suddenly light up. "Shit. I forgot!" he blabs, ripping out a résumé and slapping it on the slick mahogany bar. "Quick. Memorize it. I gotta look smart. Professional. A real ace. Make sure to tell the ladies I'm a vice president. They love that stuff. I'll give you a hundred dollars every time you mention it. Eh? How's that sound?" Oscar buzzes, taking a quick sip of his Amstel Light and smacking his lips.

"Um. I really shouldn't accept tips," I say, running a hand through my hair and motioning to the bartender to bring us another beer. In fact, I specifically remember Kate saying tips are against Chicago Wingwoman's policy.

"Sure you should." Oscar winks, scratching his carrottop head. "I gotta get myself some love. So you get to skimming and leave the tips to me. Eh?"

I take a deep breath. What a wacky guy. I quickly eye Oscar's résumé. And it really is quite impressive . . . or at least it sounds impressive.

Vice President, O'Flaherty & Sons Securities, 2002–present

- Traded $15 billion matched book in T-bills and bonds
- Increased gross trading profits by 16 percent annually
- Generated $8 million gross profit in 2003
- . . . and on . . . and on . . .

Looks like he went to Indiana University. Majored in finance. And now works for his dad's trading company. Hmm. Not bad. I start scoping out the packed bar, filled with all the fresh college grads, looking for potential matches. Oscar doesn't exactly seem like he's on the hunt for true love. So I'm thinking a nice hot hookup will do the trick. As my eyes float across face after face, I start to feel a bit old. I barely even recognize any of these faces.

Gwynn, Kimmie, Julia, and I used to hang out at John Barleycorn all the time. Gwynn would pick us up in the Loop in her red BMW convertible, and we'd fly up Lincoln Avenue, throw the keys to the valet, and skip inside. Come to think of it, I even introduced Julia and Kevin here. That's right! God. Those were the days. But, well, Gwynn sold her BMW a few months ago and bought a big boring black Range Rover. (I couldn't help but laugh. What does Gwynn need with a monster SUV? Is she planning to go off-roading on Michigan Avenue?)

"Hey. Hey. What about her?" Oscar suddenly jumps up from his stool and gawks at a tall leggy blonde. He yanks me by the hand toward the back of the bar.

"She went in there. Go! Go! Go!" Oscar squeals like a child.

"THE BATHROOM?" I ask incredulously. "Are you joking? We should wait until she comes out. You know . . . play it cool. Besides, I didn't even get a good look at . . ."

"No way!" Oscar pouts. "I'm paying you big money. Get in there." Oscar shoves me toward the women's bathroom. "Tell her I'm a vice president. Eh? Tell her I'm good in bed. Tell her anything! She's such a hottie. I waa-aant her!"

WHAT. A. BRAT.

The next thing I know, I'm standing over the sink and washing my hands, waiting for the blond girl to emerge from the stall. I inspect my new lavender beaded top in the mirror. Very cute. I bought it at Sugar this afternoon. Cici was so happy to see me! I felt really guilty for all my recent Barneys purchases, so I bought this top and a pair of jeans and the most adorable lime slip dress. I mean, I'm out nearly every night. It takes *loads* of clothes. Thank God I'm getting my next expense check soon.

That's when I suddenly realize I'm *still* washing my hands.

What the . . . ? Did the blonde leave without me noticing? I grab a paper towel and wipe my hands. How odd. I bend down and peer under the three stalls. And I'm relieved to see two pointy hot pink shoes with rhinestone bows staring right back out at me. Whew! She's still in . . . oh . . . oh no . . . they're walking . . .

Thwack! The stall door slams right into my forehead.

"Oh my gosh. I'm so sorry!" A high-pitched voice shrieks. A girl bends down next to me, her cold fingertips resting on my shoulder. "I didn't see you . . . wait. Victoria?"

I can already feel the needles prickling down my spine. *"Kaitlyn?"* I squeak.

SHITTY.

It turns out Kaitlyn is grabbing a few drinks with Bryan and some friends. She's just sure Gwynn was invited. "Why wouldn't she be?" she says innocently. But as I hobble out of the bathroom, I see Bryan standing over at the bar, grinning wide and slapping down his Visa for another round of drinks. He looks as tall and thin as ever in his black tailored Hugo Boss suit. But no Gwynn. Hmph. They're up to something. I just know it.

I quickly duck out of the way. I can't let Bryan see me or I'll have to run over and say hi. That would not be good. Not good at all. Can't let anyone find out about this wingwoman thing. (And somehow I don't think Kaitlyn will tell Bryan about our little meeting.)

"She was horrible!" I huff to Oscar a few minutes later, rubbing the purple knot on my forehead. "She swore she only dated presidents, CEOs, and pro basketball players. Sorry, VP."

Oscar shakes his carrottop head. "I can't believe she punched you! Wow. You really are a good wingwoman. Thanks for going after her like that."

"No problem," I mumble, my cheeks flushing feverishly. (Oh my God. I had to tell Oscar *something*.)

Forty-five minutes later, Oscar has his arm slung around a cute brunette with a pudgy nose. He was amazed at how fast I worked the room. Little does Oscar know, the pretty brunette was a girl I knew from U of I. It was a breeze chatting with her and just pure luck that they hit it off. (That's our little secret, though. Okay?)

As I wave good-bye to the new pair, Oscar slyly hands me a $100 bill and pats me on the back. "What a rock star!" he whispers. "You can be my wingwoman anytime."

Eww. Oscar is *sooo* cheesy! I bet he was dying to use that *Top Gun* line all night.

Chapter 18

FROM: cory@webtalk.com
TO: victoria_hart@vongo.com
PRIORITY: Standard
SUBJECT: RE: Seeking a wingwoman

Hi there,

Thanks for getting back to me so quickly. I'm sorry
to hear you're not bi. I have to ask . . . are you sure?
A lot of girls just don't realize they are. Think
about it and get back to me.

Cory

P.S. Are you at least hot?

I'm chomping on my breakfast as I quickly scroll through
more strange e-mail. I've officially started the diet. Did I tell
you? It's an all-broccoli regime. (Raw broccoli, not cooked.
Supposedly cooking deactivates a special enzyme or something
like that?) I'm supposed to drink tons of water and sprinkle all
my food with this super-secret ingredient. We'll see. Mom
insists broccoli is the perfect food. Packed with calcium, fiber,
potassium, and vitamins A and C. The fiber fills you up and it's
low carb. "Low carb is very in!" she clucked. She swears the
results are amazing.

Yeah. Okay. All I know is the grocery cashier thought I was
a total wacko last night when I rang up seven pounds of broccoli and ten gallons of water, then dared to ask if they had a
few more heads of broccoli in back. (Hey—I'm supposed to
eat two pounds a day! Seven just isn't going to cut it.)

And, well, brace yourself. I'm joining a gym.

The super-exclusive Muse Gym on North and Clark. I
know. I know. I hate working out. Detest it! But this is a total
do-or-die situation. I simply must lose my pooch and blobby
butt by Friday. How hard can it be? I'll lift a couple weights.
Do some push-ups. Run on the treadmill for twenty minutes
or so. (Definitely need to focus on cardio.) Done. The end. I
can go home. Eat more broccoli. Brew some coffee. And have a
nice, relaxing and healthy morning. Easy breezy. I zip up my
new furry orange fleece and smile to myself.

Hmm. I'm feeling better about this workout thing already. Yes. I can see it now. I'll be a pillar of good health. A fitness queen. People will look at me and say, "Wow. How does she do it? She's so healthy. So put together." Hmm. I'm actually feeling a bit giddy. I can't wait.

As I step inside the club, clutching my shiny black discount card (compliments of Chicago Wingwoman), I'm speechless. The place is, well, amazing.

Bright lights bounce all around, glaring down on the freshly painted walls and gleaming hardwood floors. The air is cool and light, unlike most muggy gyms. Everything is so sterile, so new. I can actually smell the lemon from the cleaners they use.

There are people everywhere, zipping from one machine to the next. They're checking out their cute matchy-match outfits in the wall-to-wall mirrors. Flipping magazines. Adjusting their iPods. And trendy ultra-fit trainer ladies dressed in all-black Nike workout gear and full makeup walk around with important-looking headsets, supervising the whole scene.

I turn around in a daze. Where should I start? Everything looks so complicated. There are lines and lines of awkward-looking contraptions with strange belts and moving arms. Water bottles and towels are neatly folded at each machine. And . . . ooh . . . there's a yoga studio! I've always wanted to try yoga. Everyone who does yoga is so thin and muscular. I mean, hello! Madonna? Gwyneth Paltrow? Hey, is that a kick-boxing studio, too? How cool would that be?! Yes. MENTAL NOTE: DEFINITELY WANT TO TRY KICKBOXING. I can see it now. I'll learn all kinds of secret self-defense moves. I'll be strong. Buff. Confident. It'll be the best. Now all I need to do is join. Hmm. Now where would membership be? Is it . . .

"Can I help you?" A blond, bouncy Nike Lady interrupts my thoughts. She's wearing one of those black uniforms, but hers is skintight with the hoodie unzipped and revealing an ungodly amount of cleavage.

Whoa. I nearly gasp. Don't look, Vic.

"Sure. I'd like to . . . um . . . join the club." Those can't be real. *They can't be.* They're like the size of my head.

"Great," she says, chomping her gum. "Come with me. We'll do a tour first."

Nike Lady yanks me all around the club, pointing out various studios—three spinning studios, two Pilates studios, two yoga studios, one step studio, one kickboxing studio, one dance studio, and every other kind of studio you can think of. Indoor beach volleyball courts, basketball courts, tennis courts, squash courts, swimming pools. She recites award after award the club has already won. (Hmm. Didn't this gym just open? Is that even possible?) She walks me by the ultra-exclusive spa with "oh my God, the best masseuses in the world!" and the club's very own specialty plastic surgeon.

What the . . . ? Did I hear that right? I smile like this is the most normal thing in the world.

Our last stop is the locker room. It's so cozy. It smells like crisp, linen sheets and looks like a page straight out of Pottery Barn. There are warm towels lining the perfectly paint-chipped shelves, and bundles of orchids clustered in every corner and nook. Staff members are dressed in all-white uniforms, standing by the locker room door ready to replenish water and towels at a second's notice. Wow. I never knew working out could be so, well, so luxurious.

"I'm sold," I squeak, handing her my wingwoman discount card.

"Sorry?" Nike Lady asks.

"I'd like to join." I grin, barely able to contain my excitement. "Right now!"

"Good decision." She nods, eyeing the shiny black card.

"You're a lucky girl. We have a six-month waiting list. But since you're a wingwoman, you can join immediately."

FABULOUS.

I follow her over to a tall circular glass table with a pair of funky silver stools.

"I'm going to grab the paperwork," Nike Lady says. As she disappears into the spandex and fleece crowd, I admire all the rock-hard bodies lifting the weights around me. Up down. Up down. It looks so easy . . .

"Victoria—hey! How's your head?"

I whip around to see short, freckly Oscar from John Barley-corn. He's all smiles and peering up at my forehead. "Knot went down. That's good. Man. I gotta thank you for last night. That girl was great! A real lion in bed . . ."

I quickly raise a hand and laugh. "I don't need details. Trust me."

Oscar winks. "Right. Cool. So . . . there's this girl here at Muse Gym that I've had my eye on for a while. Think you can help me out?"

"Ooh." I scrunch up my face. "I can't right now."

Oscar looks hurt.

"Thursday night?"

"Great!" Oscar's clear blue eyes light up. "Oh and hey—here's a couple business cards. Hand 'em out to hot chicks. Make sure to mention I'm a vice president, too!"

"Absolutely," I say, fighting back a laugh. *Because ladies love that stuff.*

Nike Lady eventually comes back with a stack of papers the size of a full ream. She's also carrying a small purple shopping bag with MUSE GYM spelled out in tiny white letters on the sides.

Ooh. Goodies.

She takes a seat, flips open a glossy yellow folder, and says, "So tell me. What kind of body are you looking for?"

"Um . . . I don't know. Don't I kind of have to keep mine?" I laugh.

Nike Lady gives me a blank stare.

"Seriously," she says. "We sculpt bodies here. If I don't know the look you're after, I can't do my job."

I can feel my neck and cheeks turning red. All of a sudden I feel like I'm taking a quiz that everyone else knows the answers to but me.

"Well, I guess I'm looking for fit and healthy. You know . . . thin. Normal looking?" I hold my breath, praying this is an adequate answer.

Nike Lady stares at me as if to say . . . *that's it? That's all you have to say about your body shape?* She pauses to give me more time to rethink my pathetic answer.

"Look at the pictures." Nike Lady points to the yellow folder. The photos range from Gaunt Anorexic to Rambo Chick. I stare in horror. Is this a joke?

"Um. Okay. Just give me a second." I stare at the pictures painfully.

Focus, Vic. Focus.

"I bet no one picks Rambo Chick," I finally blurt. "Talk about stuck in the eighties." I look up at Nike Lady's ripped arms and orange leathery tan. I instantly realize I should close my mouth, and never speak again. Yep. Total Rambo Chick wannabe. Dead ringer.

"Not that there's anything wrong with that look or anything. I mean . . ."

Oh dear God. I close my eyes. Maybe I should just leave.

"How about this look?" Nike Lady points to Gaunt Anorexic.

"She's a bit thin. Don't you think?"

"Hardly." Nike Lady huffs. "This model is the *ideal* weight. The ideal smooth physique with the effortless, I–don't–work-out-or-even-have-to-try look."

"I guess so," I say, ogling the model's bony frame and sunken-in abs. I mean, I want to drop a few pounds . . . but I don't need to look like a starved teenager!

Nike Lady checks something off on her clipboard and abruptly gets up from her stool.

"Okay. Stand up. I need to see the material I'm working with."

Material? I cautiously get up from my stool.

"Turn around slowly." She taps my right shoulder. "That's right. Turn. Turn. Turn. Now stop."

I stand still, holding my breath. I can feel Nike Lady's eyes burning into the back of my thighs and butt.

"Ah-ha! Here's a problem area." I feel something sharp poke into the back of my right thigh.

SHUT. UP. Is she circling my fat like one of those bad sorority movies? I look over my shoulder and thankfully it's just the end of her pencil.

"Hmm. Here's another problem area," she says. I feel another poke, slightly lower this time. I hear more scribbling on her clipboard.

"Okay. Turn toward me," Nike Lady orders. She leans closer, her eyes narrow, inspecting every inch of me. After several moments of excruciating silence, she clicks her tongue, tosses the clipboard on the table, and launches into her fitness synopsis. "So. The good news is, you're fairly thin. A little poochy. But we can work with that. The bad news is, you're soft. Your thighs are flabby and your butt . . . let's just say . . . it needs a lot of work."

Ah! I think I'm going to cry. She called me poochy. I mean, I know I am—*a little*—but did she really have to say it? Out loud? I quickly scan my immediate space. Did anyone hear? There are two beefy guys flirting with each other by the front desk, but they seem oblivious. Whew.

"When's the last time you did lunges? Or lifted weights?" Nike Lady demands.

"Um . . . I don't know. Not for a while, but . . ."

She rolls her eyes and lifts a hand to silence me. "We have a ton of work to do with you. Have you ever thought of liposuction?"

My jaw drops. "I . . . I'm only looking for *natural* solutions," I manage to say.

"I see. That's too bad," Nike Lady says, shaking her head. "Our surgeons work wonders. We're going to have to put you on a strict fitness plan if surgery isn't an option."

Um. Is this lady insane? What kind of gym pushes plastic surgery?

I think Nike Lady can sense my disapproval.

"Look," Nike Lady snips. "Just to be clear. We take working out very seriously. If you aren't committed, then maybe this isn't the club for you."

"No. No. I'm committed. Swear," I assure her. I mean, I'm on an all-broccoli diet, aren't I?

"Good. Because we don't let just anyone into our club. This is the best gym in the city," she says proudly. "Everyone wants to be here. We give women the bodies they've always dreamed of. We avoid slackers. We avoid casual workout girls. You know the kind. They sign up. Buy the new workout gear and you never see them again." She pauses, then leans in secretively. "To be honest, most people sign up for gyms and never even go to them."

"No!" I gush, praying she won't look down and see my new glowing-white Nike Shox tennis shoes.

"That kind of behavior is simply unacceptable at Muse Gym," she snips.

"Absolutely. I understand."

"I knew you would," she says, staring at me intently.

Oh God. All I want to do is lose my butt and tummy. Ten pounds max! This woman is nuts.

Nike Lady hands me a heavy black pen.

"Now if you would just sign here . . ."

Chapter 19

FROM: gwynnie_pooh@girly.com
TO: victoria_hart@vongo.com
PRIORITY: Beyond Urgent
SUBJECT: Kaitlyn alert!

CALL ME AS SOON AS YOU GET THIS E-MAIL. I don't know what to do. After you told me you saw Bryan and Kaitlyn at John Barleycorn, I snooped around in Bryan's work e-mail.

I found dozens of messages from Kaitlyn. They've been e-mailing for weeks now—and Bryan hasn't said a word! I can't believe it. I think Bryan is cheating on me.

They're going to Tsunami for sushi at noon tomorrow. You have to follow them! I can't lose Bryan to Kaitlyn.

HELP!

Gwynnie

P.S. Oh! And I just read my *City Girls* horoscope and it's the worst. It says to brace myself for bad energy. What the hell does that mean? God. This is all Kaitlyn's fault. She must be eliminated!

P.P.S. Have you started on that picture timeline for my shower? It was Polo's idea. LOVE IT. Try to include that shot of Bryan and me in Cabo. I look so cute in that white Moschino bikini. Don't you think?

P.P.P.S. Did you hear Dawn is engaged now, too?! Do you think she's copying me? Be honest.

So. Here I am. It's a bright, chilly Wednesday afternoon and I'm officially on my first stakeout. I'm dressed in head-to-toe black with an orange Pucci head scarf and gigantic black Fendi sunglasses on. Just because I'm on a secret mission doesn't mean I can't look fab. Right? *And I couldn't resist.* The Fendis are total knockoffs from a Michigan Avenue street vendor, but the Pucci scarf is the real thing. I've been dying for one ever since I saw Gwynn's. It's just too cute. (Another Barneys splurge. I know. I know. I need to stop. I'm blowing through cash like crazy on clothes and going out . . . and don't even get me started with Gwynn's wedding stuff. Even with my wing-woman checks and the two wedding checks Polo cut me, it's all adding up again!)

"What are they doing? Talk to me," Gwynn demands. I have my cell phone on walkie-talkie mode per Gwynn's request.

"They just left Tsunami. They're walking west on Chestnut."

Beep. "Oh my God. Bryan is taking Kaitlyn to his apartment!" Gwynn wails. "Tell me what's going on! Are they walking close? Holding hands? Snuggling?"

"Are you kidding? Get a grip, Gwynn. They're not snuggling!" I hiss. "Don't you think I'd mention a detail like that?"

Gwynn doesn't respond. Good. Looks like I've shut her up for a moment. Now I can focus. Really scope out the scene. I feel like James Bond, my eagle eyes taking in all the details. I can feel my brain memorizing their every move, piecing together this mysterious Bryan/Kaitlyn puzzle in my head.

Honestly. I think I missed my true calling in life. I mean, I'm good at matchmaking. But what if I should have been a spy? A secret agent? Or . . . in the CIA? I should really look into something like that. Don't you think?

I carefully keep my distance from my subjects, trailing a full block behind. I glance down at my *City Girls* magazine every now and then and post up wingwoman flyers on light poles so I don't look suspicious. (Nothing like multitasking!) Most of the time, though, my eyes are fixed on Bryan and Kaitlyn. They stroll happily down the sidewalk side by side— Bryan with his short cropped hair and sharp navy suit, and Kaitlyn with her silver beaded slippers and gorgeous wavy blond hair flowing all around her black Burberry trench coat.

At that moment, Bryan whispers something in Kaitlyn's ear and she throws her head back, laughing hysterically. Hmm . . . they look pretty cozy together. *Very suspicious.*

Then Kaitlyn loops her arm through Bryan's.

Uh-oh. Is this considered snuggling? I look down at my cell phone in a slight panic. Should I tell Gwynn?

Mmm . . .

No. I don't think so. It's innocent enough. Right? Just a friendly linking of the arms. No big deal. No need to freak Gwynn out . . . *yet.*

Beep. "What's going on now?" Gwynn barks.

"Nothing," I say quickly. "Still walking."

Kaitlyn and Bryan stop abruptly and peer over their shoulders.

Aaack! Can they hear the walkie-talkie?

I frantically hold up my *City Girls* magazine in front of my face. My hands are shaking and my heart is about to leap out of my chest. *Don't see me. Don't see me.* (Ooh. What page is this? I *love* Reese Witherspoon's sea-green dress.)

Good God. Focus, Vic. Focus.

After a few seconds, I cautiously poke my head above the magazine and see their backs safely turned away. Whew. That was a close one.

They slip inside a cozy brownstone—Bryan's brownstone, to be exact.

"They just entered Bryan's apartment," I say, bracing myself for Gwynn's fury.

Beep. "I KNEW IT!" Gwynn shrieks. "Get in that apartment! You have to spy on them. NOW."

Oh dear God.

Cautiously . . . very, very cautiously I tiptoe my way to the front of Bryan's brownstone and stare up at the big bay windows glowing with light. How? How on earth am I supposed to sneak into Bryan's apartment? Hmm? Just barge right in and say hello?

Um. Yeah. *Swell idea.*

I eye the front door with its massive bronze lock. I wonder . . . is there a back entrance? I tiptoe to the far right edge of the brownstone, then all the way over to the left side. Both chain fences have sturdy locks dangling from their handles.

Should I climb the fence?

I glance down at my Kenneth Cole boots.

There has to be another way . . .

I gaze up at the glowing bay windows again. I guess I could peek inside one of the windows? And before I know what I'm doing, I'm wedging my way between the prickly line of shrubs and the building. My heart is racing wildly. I seriously can't believe I'm doing this.

Beep. "What's going on?" Gwynn cries.

"Chill out. I'm working on it!" I growl.

Beep. "Let me know as soon as you see something. Anything! And if that bitch puts one finger on Bryan, I want you to kill her! Rip her pretty little head off."

Yeah. Okay. Will do. *When did Gwynn turn psycho?*

I take a deep breath, reaching up as far as I can, grabbing the window ledge and carefully pulling myself up. And if I strain my neck . . . just enough . . . I can peer into Bryan's living room. Ooh. It's nice. Really nice, actually. It looks like a page ripped right out of Crate & Barrel. Smooth beige couches. Bearskin throw blankets. Cozy chic. Who knew Bryan had such great taste?

I lift myself up a bit higher on the ledge so I can see Bryan and Kaitlyn standing in the doorway. And, well, they both have their clothes on, so that's good. Right? I let out a huge sigh of relief. Kaitlyn is saying something. Bryan nods. Kaitlyn hands Bryan a glossy blue folder.

Ooh. Ooh. There's an exchange!

I squint hard, but I can't quite make out the words on the blue folder before Bryan stuffs it into his Tumi bag.

Beep. "I'M DYING HERE. WHAT THE HELL?" Gwynn howls.

Shitty! *That was loud.* Kaitlyn and Bryan whip around, eyeing the bay window suspiciously. I let go of the ledge, sending myself flailing into the shrubs and white gravel.

Ooof.

I yank the cell phone to my mouth. "SHH!" I hiss. "You're blowing my cover!"

Beep. "Sorry!"

What if they saw me?

I scramble to my feet, quickly dusting off my black pants and jacket and straightening my orange head scarf. I need to go. I need to get out of here. Fast! Stuffing my cell phone into my leather jacket pocket and stepping onto the sidewalk, I run smack into . . .

"Kaitlyn!" I squeak, breathing in her distinct Chanel No. 5 perfume. Oh God. Oh God. I'm so busted. I can feel my face getting all splotchy red. My signature guilty look. (Good thing Kaitlyn doesn't know me very well.)

"Fancy seeing you here," Kaitlyn says, giving me a sugary smile. "Seems like we keep bumping into each other."

Grrr. She is so . . . ooh . . . .wait a minute. Wow. *I love her lipstick.* It's the most amazing color. Like a wild glistening sunset. Vibrant reds and oranges. Pale blues. Delicate pinks. I'd kill to know where she got it. Maybe I could just . . .

No! Absolutely not. I can't ask. *She's the enemy.* And Gwynn would murder me. Act like a spy, Vic! Interrogate and infiltrate. Get information.

"We certainly do keep running into each other," I say, pointedly rubbing the small purple bump from our unfortunate bathroom incident. "What brings you to this neighborhood?"

"Just visiting a friend," Kaitlyn says, raising an eyebrow as if to challenge me. "What about you?"

HA! A friend? Why doesn't she just say Bryan? *Because she's trying to hide something, that's why!* Hmph. I have her all figured out.

"I live in the neighborhood," I answer crisply, which isn't a complete lie. Armitage Street? Chestnut Street? Same thing . . . *kind of*. Whatever. It's all on the North Side.

Bryan suddenly steps out of his apartment building. He waves at the two of us as if everything is completely normal, then checks his mailbox.

"Hey, Vic." Bryan tilts his head and smiles. "Are you meeting Gwynn over here?"

I nod nervously. (Please don't look at my splotchy face. Please!)

"Would you give her a message for me?" Bryan asks, dropping a bundle of shiny magazines and envelopes into his Tumi. "Tell her to give my mother a ring. She's coming into town in a few weeks and wants to talk about florists."

"No problem." I smile.

Kaitlyn sighs dreamily, fingering a shiny blond strand as Bryan walks down the sidewalk. "What a shame," she murmurs.

"What's that?" I narrow my eyes.

"Oh nothing."

My eyes dart from Kaitlyn to Bryan, then back again. I don't know what these two are up to, but it's not good. Not good at all. I'm absolutely certain of it after today. Now . . . if I can just figure out what?

Beep. "UM. HEL-LO? THIS ISN'T FUNNY. WHERE ARE YOU? WHAT THE FUCK IS GOING ON?" Gwynn's voice explodes through my leather jacket.

Kaitlyn narrows her eyes and tilts her beautiful blond head. "Hey . . ."

"Gotta run!" I say brightly, already bolting down the sidewalk.

Wow. I didn't realize this personal attendant stuff was going to be so dangerous.

•

"I CAN'T BELIEVE BRYAN!" Gwynn screams into my cell phone a few hours later. "How could he?"

"You're not listening to me," I say impatiently. "Nothing happened. Kaitlyn gave him a blue folder. That's it."

I inspect my crow's-feet in the hall mirror. The gross little wrinkles aren't getting any better. What the hell? I'm turning into an old ugly singletini! Should I call La Bella and complain? I'm *not* witnessing a miracle. Not even close. Hmph.

"I don't believe you," Gwynn cries. "Something happened and you just won't tell me. Admit it. You saw them having sex!"

Breathe, Vic. Breathe.

Stop dreaming about strangling Gwynn. It's not healthy. Seriously. And I love her. She's just stressed out. And I would be, too. Bryan is acting really shady.

"You're being ridiculous." I sigh, padding into the kitchen for some more water. "Look. You have to act normal. Okay? We'll never find out the truth if you automatically jump down Bryan's throat. You'll be forced to admit you snooped through his e-mail and that you sent *me* spying on him. You don't want to do that. Do you?"

Gwynn thinks about this for a long moment. Then she barrels right back. "BUT I HATE HER. Can't you do something?"

"Right. Like call my hit man?" I say sarcastically. "I did the best I could! Did you check his bag for that blue folder?"

"Nothing!" Gwynn huffs. "I found nothing! Just a bunch of stupid mail and some brochures for our honeymoon, which was supposed to be a big surprise, and now I know he's taking me to Bali. What do you think of Bali? I feel like it's overdone."

I don't get it. I saw him put that blue folder in his bag. "Are you sure? Did you check his Tumi?"

"I'm perfectly capable of looking through a bag! Thank you very much," Gwynn snips.

Ooh. "Was the Bali brochure blue?" I ask. That might be it. I mean, folder? Brochure? Same thing. It's not like I had the best view while hanging off the window ledge. You know? Give a girl a break.

"Mmm . . . *not exactly.*" Gwynn sighs. "It was more teal . . . or indigo. Actually, it's the exact color of the Marc Jacobs new racer sling bag. Have you seen it? So cute! Special edition. I think they call the color native navy. But whatever, it's completely *not* navy. And . . ."

Oh dear God. Never mind; I should know better than to ask Gwynn a simple question like that. Blue is never . . . *just blue.*

I check the clock on the kitchen wall. Oh no.

"Listen. I've gotta run," I say. I have a wingwoman gig tonight at the Living Room (that hip bar where I first met Patrick), and I can't be late.

Owww.

And suddenly my stomach isn't feeling so well . . .

"Why?" Gwynn whines. "Come over. I'm depressed."

"I can't. I really have to go," I say, sitting down on the couch and doubling over. Ugh. My stomach is so gurgly and weird! It must be all the broccoli I've been gnawing on.

"Where are you going?" Gwynn whines.

"Out."

"With who?"

"Um. Hi. Are you my mom?" I laugh, then immediately regret it as my stomach does flip-flops. Laughing hurts. God. I can't wait until Friday. I've never hated broccoli more in my life. It's like munching on weeds! And that secret ingredient isn't much better. It's like dirt and salt. Gross.

"Do you have a secret date?" Gwynn teases.

"Yeah. I wish. I'm hanging up now."

Gwynn giggles. "Hope he's a cutie."

"Good-bye!" *Click.*

•

ABOUT A HALF HOUR later, I'm jumping out of a cab and bursting through the doors of the Living Room. I glance at my watch. Whew. Five minutes to spare. I make my way over to the bar, checking out all the men crowded about and wondering if one of them is Ben, my client for the night. Hmm . . .

Hot.

Hot.

Cute.

Adorable.

Sooo adorable.

Mmm. Just okay.

Eww. (Please don't let it be him.)

"Can I get a cocoatini?" I tell the bartender. God. My stomach isn't feeling any better. Maybe I should order a ginger ale. That's supposed to be soothing. Right?

"Victoria Hart?" asks a nice-looking guy with dark floppy hair and big brown puppy eyes.

"That's me." I smile. "You must be Ben."

After a few questions, we're ready to go. I have all the information I need about Benny boy. Financial consultant. Originally from Cincinnati. Big family. Likes dabbling in the kitchen. Enjoys kayaking. Loves baseball. And coaches Little League at Oz Park on Saturdays. Overall? Nice guy.

"Ready?"

We circle the dimly lit bar, weaving in between clusters of leather couches and velvety stools, and I try my best to ignore my grumbling stomach.

"Do you like her?" I ask, tilting my chin toward a brunette in a skimpy chocolate-colored dress.

Ben shakes his head. "Too slutty."

I shrug and point to a perky, cheerleader-type girl with a blond pixie cut. "What about her?"

"She's okay." Ben scratches his head, continuing to skim the crowd. He gestures toward a gaggle of girls all decked out in silky tops, Marc Jacobs jeans, and expensive wedge heels. "How about her?"

"The Jessica Simpson wannabe?" I ask.

Ben nods excitedly.

"Let me go check her out. Stay here."

I saunter over to our prospect, then . . . *no way*! She has a bag just like mine—but white.

"Wow. Is that a Hogan?" I point to the trendy carryall bag slung over her shoulder.

The girl grins excitedly and nods, obviously thrilled to have her bag noticed.

"I love it! I have the jade one!" I say, quickly surveying her girlfriends for Ben, just in case she doesn't work out.

"Isn't it the best?" she gushes.

"Totally," I say. We smile at each other for a long awkward moment. Quick. Think of something else to say.

"We were just talking about the DJ," the girl bubbles. "Do you know what time he goes on? We love to dance!"

Ooh. Dancing. *Now there's an in.* "Hmm . . . I'm not sure," I say, already piecing together the story about how Ben is my roommate's brother, who (gosh!) loves to dance! I motion for Ben to come over.

At that moment, the DJ appears on the overlooking balcony. Music rips from the speakers, and all the girls start squealing and bouncing up and down. *Fantastic timing.*

This is looking good. Hopefully I can hook this girl up with Benny fast and jet. I'm exhausted after the stalking business this afternoon . . . and something is really, *ree-eally* wrong with my stomach.

"I'm Victoria, by the way," I say, extending a hand.

"Madison," the girl says.

Ben arrives at my side looking wide-eyed and hopeful. "Hi!" He grins stupidly.

Oh no. *Keep your tongue in your mouth, Ben.* Grrr. Why does he have to look so eager and desperate? Not good. Not good at all. This might be harder than I originally thought.

And yeah . . . it takes about 2.2 seconds for Madison to give us the official brush-off. Ben and I watch her and her friends race wildly toward the dance floor. Away from us.

"Don't worry about it," I tell Ben, patting him on the shoulder. "Let's find another one. Look at all the girls you have to choose from." I gesture toward the flock of females at the bar. "Pick one."

And after about two hours of tirelessly approaching nearly every woman at the Living Room, we finally stumble across a girl who's sitting at the bar with two of her friends. She's very natural. Very pretty. She has straight brown hair and the cutest twinkly eyes, like she laughs all the time.

"What about her?" I ask.

"How did we *miss* her?" Ben asks, already looking enamored.

Turns out the girl's name is Kara. And about two minutes after the introduction, our friend Kara looks pretty much enamored with Ben as well. They're smiling and laughing. Their heads leaning toward each other. I see sparks.

Sigh.

Looks like my job here is done.

"Have fun!" I tell them.

As I walk toward the door to leave, I have to admit, I'm feeling pretty good. It looks like Ben and Kara really have a connection. They look so happy, so cute together. It must be nice . . .

I feel a sharp pang in my chest. It's been a long time since I felt a real connection with someone. I mean, Aiden is great and everything, but it's only been a few days. A few days that pretty much consisted of him drunk-dialing me. (Um. Okay. And one late-night hookup.) It'd be nice to have a tiny bit more. But maybe Aiden feels the same way?

All of a sudden, I feel a hand squeeze the right side of my waist.

"Hey, hey, hey!" I whip around, smacking at the hand. "What the hell do you think . . . ?"

I lift my head to see . . . "Patrick?"

What is *he* doing here?

"Sorry!" Patrick says, holding his palms up in surrender. "Didn't mean to scare you."

My heart flutters. Ah! So cute. I breathe in his sweet, sexy cologne and feel my head getting light. "No . . . no problem," I say, closing my eyes and trying to shake it off.

"Are you on your way out?" he asks, gesturing toward the door.

I nod, suddenly wishing I wasn't.

"Me, too," he says. "You wanna walk part of the way?"

Are you kidding me? *Yes!*

"Absolutely," I say, looking down at my four-inch gold satin pumps and praying they'll play nice. Not exactly my best walking shoes. But whatever.

Patrick slips his navy corduroy blazer around my shoulders and offers me his arm, and we're off. I love the feel of his coat around me. So warm. So safe. So perfect.

We talk and laugh as we leisurely stroll through the breezy night air. Patrick chats about work. About some big deadline on Friday for a new super-hush-hush account. And I tell him about my ridiculous walkie-talkie stakeout today, which sends him howling in laughs.

"Victoria Hart." Patrick squeezes my arm. "You're something else. Do you know that?"

"Um. Thanks . . . *I think?*"

As we cross the Chicago River and slowly make our way up Michigan Avenue, I find myself awestruck by how gorgeous the night is. All the glittering lights above our heads. It's so magnificent. So alive. Almost as if the city has its own pulse. Its own heartbeat.

We're both quiet for a while. Maybe it's because we're tired. Maybe it's because we don't want to break the magical silence. Or maybe it's because of . . . something else? Whatever it is, the silence feels good. It feels right. By the time we reach State and Rush Street, I'm starting to shiver.

"We should get you a cab," Patrick says quietly, rubbing my arms to warm me up.

"I guess so," I say, not moving an inch. There's just something about this walk: I don't want it to end.

We smile awkwardly at each other.

"Well, thanks for walking . . . me . . ." And before I know what's happening, Patrick pulls me toward him, his hands cupping my face gently as he very, very slowly kisses me over and over again.

Once we finally say good-bye, Patrick puts me in a cab and I zip off into the night. My head falls back against the cab seat and I close my eyes tightly. Wow . . .

Double wow.
Who cares about Aiden?

Chapter 20

I HATE THIS. I hate this. I hate this.

All I want to do is crawl back into bed and continue daydreaming about Patrick. Instead I'm forced to torture myself at Muse Gym. *I have to.* The fashion show is tomorrow and I haven't dropped a single pound. In fact, I think I've gained some! Arghh! And my stomach is K-I-L-L-I-N-G me. It's all weird and twisted up inside. This can't be normal? Maybe I should call Mom . . .

What a disaster.

So here I am . . . dripping with sweat. Calves burning. Face on fire. And my lungs are about to explode as I desperately try to keep pace with this evil, evil treadmill.

I hate working out.

I hate this treadmill.

Treadmill = devil.

To the left of me, I've got Biff. The next poster child for protein shakes. To the right, I've got itty-bitty Barbie Workout Queen. She's fully equipped with matching sneakers and accessories. They're both gliding effortlessly on their treadmills. Taking long beautiful strides. Barely breaking a sweat. I despise them both.

I check the time. Nine minutes. (What! *That's it?*) I can't believe this. I'm never going to make it thirty minutes. Ever. Oh dear God. I'm having trouble breathing. Am I having a heart attack?

I sneak a peek at Barbie's time: one hour, twenty minutes.

Shut the hell up. Are you kidding me? I wasn't even planning to stay at the gym that long! Should I stop the machine? Just give up?

No. No. I can't. What if someone sees me? They'd think I'm a poser. An out-of-shape chick who can't even make it ten minutes on a treadmill. This is so embarrassing! I thought working out was supposed to make you feel good about yourself. Exhilarated. All I feel is terrible and, well, tired.

Ooh. I know. I'll simply pause the machine. You know . . . pretend I'm taking a teensy-weensy break. Just getting a quick sip of water at the fountain by the bathroom. No one will ever notice if I don't return. Right? That's respectable.

I cautiously press the PAUSE WORKOUT button and step off the treadmill.

"Just getting some water," I announce loudly to Biff and Barbie. "I'll be right back. One second."

They both shoot me strange looks and continue with their smooth workouts.

I bolt straight for the door and out into the dark cool morning toward home. BED, HERE I COME!

·

MY CELL PHONE rings right as I'm entering Bloomingdale's a few hours later. It's Mom.

"I can't believe you didn't tell me, darling!" Mom chirps. "I always said you were a born model. Didn't I say that?"

My heart thumps wildly.

"What are you talking about?" I gulp.

"Don't be silly! The fashion show, dear. I got the Bloomingdale's invite in the mail today. I'm in their Premier Insider program. Lots of savings!" she says proudly. "You didn't think you'd keep this a secret. Did you?

AAACK! "What did the invite say?" I ask frantically, biting a thumbnail.

"Well, let's see. I need my reading glasses." I hear papers crumpling in the background. "It says . . . join us for the new Rico label launch. See the latest Summer Collection from this sizzling New York designer. Hosted by Chicago Wing-something-or-other . . . and then there's a list of models with you at the very top! And to think, I almost threw out this month's newsletter."

That would have been *tragic*. I close my eyes. Thank God she missed the wingwoman thing!

"And it was so odd," Mom chirps away. "I called Kimmie so she could save your dad and me a seat, and she didn't know about the show, either. I'm sure it just slipped your mind! But don't you worry. I told her everything. And we'll all be there!"

"YOU'RE KIDDING? Right?" My voice is shaking and I'm close to tears. "You told Kimmie?"

"Why yes, darling! I hope that's okay?" Mom twitters away. "I assumed you'd want us there. Now . . . tell me. This is why you wanted my secret diet, isn't it? I knew it wasn't about a boy. You always were a terrible liar. Never could keep a secret."

"I have to go," I say, feeling faint.

"Oh yes. Yes, of course. But real quick. Tell me. What are you wearing? The ladies at Club are dying to know. I told them all about it! I hope this new designer works in pastels or flowery prints. Request something in pink. It really is your best color. Nothing black. Black does nothing for you."

"I'll see what I can do," I say dizzily. "See you tomorrow."

"Wonderful, dear. We'll be there! Don't you worry about your father and me!"

I can't believe this. My wingwoman cover is blown. Everyone is totally going to find out now. I think I'm going to cry. Ugh. *And what is going on with my stomach?* I should have said something to Mom. This crazy gurgling and churning can't be normal . . .

Oh no. What am I doing? I'M SUPPOSED TO BE AT REHEARSAL.

I check my watch. I'm fifteen minutes late. Drats!

I cautiously poke my head into storage room B, no clue what to expect. The entire room is draped in black curtains. Mirrors are leaning up against every free spot. People are dressed in head-to-toe black, arms stuffed full of colorful clothes, shoes, scarves, you name it.

Half-naked wingwomen stand incredibly still like manne-quins as people fuss all around them. I see there are two tables in the back of the room. One labeled STAFF, one labeled WING-WOMEN. The table for staff has a lavish assortment of flaky pas-tries, croissants, and buttery muffins. There are heated pans of hash browns, bacon, and eggs.

I'm drooling.

The table for wingwomen has a slightly different array of food. There are tiny boxes of nonfat Special K cereal, nonfat Silk soymilk, strawberries, bananas, yogurt, carrots, celery, broccoli (ugh!), fat-free ranch dip, hummus, and blah, blah, blah.

My body is instinctively drawn toward the staff table. I don't know what it is, but this uncontrollable urge suddenly comes over me. And I . . . I can't stop myself. *I'm starving.* All I've had is broccoli for the past three days. Maybe this is what my stom-ach needs. *Real food.* Meat! I reach out and pluck up a tiny piece of bacon and . . .

Just as I'm about to bite down on the warm, crispy, delicious little sliver, a ghost-white woman with black razored hair rushes my way. Her face is flushed and she's panting, her clipboard jammed under her arm.

"What are you doing?" she demands, yanking the piece of bacon out of my hand and throwing it on the floor. "You can't eat this stuff. Can't you read? The wingwoman table is over there!"

"I . . . I'm sorry." My hands are shaking. "It's only one piece?"

"Whatever. Don't let it happen again," she snips. "I'm Elle, the stylist for this show, so do whatever I say and we won't have any problems. Got it?" She clicks her tongue. "Now get over to hair, makeup, and wardrobe—pronto! Our artists need to check your coloring and hair texture and note any problem areas." She gives me a quick once-over. "I'm thinking there may be a few."

What's up with everyone wanting to identify my problem areas? Do people enjoy making me feel like a big blobby cow? My eyes wander over to the hash browns. So hungry . . .

"Snap. Snap." Elle raises an eyebrow.

I shuffle over to an empty hair station. But my mood lifts instantly when I see Marco, my hairstylist from Maxine, bounce up behind my chair.

"Victoria!" Marco shrieks, throwing his arms around me and kissing each cheek. "*You're* in the show? How fab! I got hired to do hair."

Marco and I chat away happily . . . until he starts taking sections of my hair and teasing them straight up into the air.

I raise an eyebrow. "Marco. What are you doing?"

"Don't worry!" he says cheerfully, twirling my chair around to face him. "I have something *special* in mind for you."

Hmm. I don't know if I like the sound of that . . .

About an hour later, Marco declares me finished. He steps back to admire his work, narrowing his eyes and shifting from one tiny hip to the other.

"Perfection," he whispers.

I'll admit it, I'm curious. *Really curious.* Because my head feels about ten pounds heavier. Marco spins me around to face the mirror and squeals, "Ta-da!"

Gulp.

"Marco!" I gasp. "What did you do?" I reach up to touch the

two massive wings jutting out from my head. "I look like . . . a bird!"

"You don't like it?" Marco pouts, folding his arms across his chest. "But it's perfect for the wingwoman theme! *Perfect.*"

"Can't we tame . . ."

Suddenly a tall Italian man with long slicked-back hair and a hip linen blazer appears before us. "Foo-king fabulous. A foo-king piece of art. You are God. Er . . . God of de hair."

Marco's eyes twinkle with delight. "Thank you! Thank you!"

"I am Federico." The Italian man with the thick accent offers Marco and me his hand. "I am de designer. I have . . . er . . . how do you say? De vision?"

I shake his hand. "It's nice to meet you. I'm Victoria."

Elle dashes over to my side. "Enough chitchat," she hisses. "You need to get dressed." She yanks me out of the hair station chair and thrusts me into wardrobe.

"Um . . . okay. Bye!" I wave to Marco.

Elle explains to the junior stylists that Federico's vision for me is sex. I need to look like I just got fucked. (I know. I know. Are you kidding me? How am I ever going to explain this to Mom? This isn't exactly the baby pink floral thing she suggested.)

It's nearly five o'clock when I finally get home and get all the makeup off my face and hair spray out of my hair. People have been poking and pulling at me all day. I'm so exhausted and my stomach is about to explode. And I can't believe I'm meeting Oscar at Muse Gym in two hours! I was already there once today . . . and I *hate* that place. All I want to do is curl up in a ball and die. I never thought I'd say this, but maybe a desk job doesn't sound so bad. This wingwoman job is starting to take over my life.

Lifting my head up from the couch, I notice there's a message blinking on my answering machine. I check caller ID. It's Gwynn. Ugh. Do I dare listen? I cautiously hit PLAY and brace myself.

"*You have to help me.* Kaitlyn must be stopped! She called Bryan last night—AT MY PLACE. Bryan got all weird and whispery, and took the call in my bedroom. I . . . I can't handle this, Vic. You have to do something! You have to break into his apartment! *I need that blue folder.* And it's not the Bali brochure. I don't care what you say. It's not blue! I'll get you the key. No one will ever know. Call me!"

Ugh. Erase message.

•

THIS. IS. SO. EMBARRASSING. I'm meeting Oscar at Muse Gym any minute and, well, I can't believe I'm telling you this, but . . .

Oh my God.

I have the worst gas ever.

It's like death. I don't know what's going on. My stomach is a raging monster. I swear to God, I think my apartment windows were even fogging up. Armani wouldn't get near me. He just hissed, growled, and batted a furry black paw at me every time my stomach roared. I called Mom and she was all hoots.

"This isn't funny!" I hiss into my cell phone, eyeing the gym doors for Oscar. "It's ghastly! What should I do?"

"Oh darling!" Mom tee-hee-hees. "I told you it was potent. Don't worry. This happens to your Gramms, too."

I close my eyes, practically in tears. "I don't care if this happens to Gramms! Make it stop!" I wail. "I hate this stupid diet. It doesn't even work. I'm *gaining* weight!"

"Nonsense. It's working fine. It's only water weight. You'll see . . ."

Yeah. Whatever.

Remind me never to listen to Mom again. Ever.

That's when I see Oscar bursting through the glass gym

doors. He looks like his regular ball of freckled energy, decked out in a gray Adidas half-zip windbreaker and matching pants.

"Victoria!" He gives me a quick hug. "How's my wing-woman? Eh? Sorry I'm running late. Crazy at work. Just crazy! So are you ready? Hmm? I've had my eye on this babe for a while." He rubs his hands together. "I can't wait for you to work your magic."

"Me, too!" I smile weakly.

I follow Oscar's carrottop head through the steamy cardio section. Suddenly he stops and wrinkles his face up. "Jesus. *What's that smell?*"

Oh dear God. I can feel my face turning fire red. This is so embarrassing. *Stupid diet.* "I . . . I'm not sure. Should we keep walking?"

"Ugh. It's disgusting!" Oscar gasps, pulling his half-zip over his nose.

I should just go home. This is humiliating. Other people are scrunching up their faces and fanning their noses. Do they suspect it's me? I just need to play it cool. I can't believe this. I hate this diet. I HATE BROCCOLI. I'm never eating another disgusting green stalk again.

I keep my head down as I follow Oscar through the gym. He weaves his way in between silver bench presses and groups of people chatting and comparing biceps.

"There!" Oscar points. "There she is. God. Isn't she gorgeous?"

I gaze out over the field of treadmills and there, striding away, is a tall black-haired beauty with a long ponytail who's ripped in every way. We're talking killer abs, chiseled biceps, and sculpted legs. Geesh! I want to know what diet she's on.

"Let's go!" Oscar hisses. "There are two open treadmills next to her."

Oh no. *Not the treadmill again.*

Reluctantly I mount the evil machine next to Chiseled Girl as Oscar hops on the treadmill next to me. Oscar is already trotting away and flicking through the latest *GQ* by the time I press the FAT BURN option. The treadmill zips into motion. I listen to my Nike Shox *pound-pound-pounding* against the moving belt and . . . ooh . . . hey now. It's going a bit too fast. How do I make this thing go slower? Make that *a lot* slower.

Hmm. I was on a slightly different machine this morning. And this control panel is so . . . so complicated. So many knobs and buttons. I punch a green arrow . . . and oh . . . oh no! This is *waaaaaa-aaay* too fast. I grab onto the handrails in panic, my legs desperately trying to keep up with the whirring black belt.

Chiseled Girl pulls a white iPod headphone out of one ear and smiles, her long black ponytail whipping back and forth. "Need help?"

I slam my palm onto the red PAUSE button. "Oh no. Got it! Everything's under control." I grin, wiping my forehead.

"Cool," Chiseled Girl says. "Just checking. These new machines with the TVs are a bit tricky." She pops her headphone back in and continues her long beautiful strides.

Ten minutes later, I'm gasping for air and Oscar is flipping out on me. "Do something. Talk to her! Do you think I'm running for my health?"

"Right. Okay," I gasp. (God. I just want to stop. My stomach really, really hurts! But what can I do? I'm on the clock.) I turn to Chiseled Girl and tap her rock-hard shoulder.

She pulls out a white headphone and smiles.

"I'm sorry. Do you work out here a lot?" I gasp, gripping the handrails so tight my knuckles are white. *Terrible question, Vic. Terrible.*

"Yep," Chiseled Girl says, barely breaking a sweat as she glides effortlessly on her treadmill. "Do you?"

"Totally," I wheeze, wiping sweat off my forehead. "All the time. Me and my good friend *love* the gym." I point to Oscar.

Oscar's head jerks up, his blue eyes wide and hopeful.

"Working out is the best," I ramble on, very aware that my face is red and blotchy, and sweat is pouring off my body. "I'm totally not one of those girls who signs up and never shows up again." I give her a knowing look. "You know the kind."

"I do." Chiseled Girl laughs and puts her headphones back in. Oscar moans.

I tap her on the shoulder again and flash a glittery smile. "It's me again." I pant.

Chiseled Girl smiles tightly and pulls out her headphones. "Yes?"

"Can I borrow your magazine?" I ask, pointing to the glossy mag with a frosty blue mountain on the cover. (Aaack! I'm dying here. I need to get off this machine ASAP.)

She hands me the magazine and . . . oh . . . oh no! She's putting in those stupid headphones again. Quick. Think of something.

"I just love . . . um . . ." I eye the outdoorsy magazine frantically. "Climbing! Don't you?" Eww. *Climbing?* Isn't that super strenuous? And like, really, really dangerous? "And my friend Oscar loves it, too!" I hear myself blabber.

Oscar scratches his red head and shrugs helplessly.

"Really?" Chiseled Girl says. "Where do you two normally go?"

Arghh! I should have seen that question coming.

"Um. You know . . . the usual," I say, my eyes scanning the pages frantically. "That place in . . . Indiana."

Chiseled Girl wrinkles her nose. "That's kind of flat. Isn't it?"

"Um . . . did I say Indiana? I meant, India . . . you know . . . the Alps." My voice wavers. I think my lungs are on fire. Is that possible? I eye the red extinguisher on the wall.

Chiseled Girl squints. "That's in Europe. Do you mean the Himalayas?"

"Oh right. Totally!" I laugh. "What was I thinking?"

Okay. That's it. I can't take this machine anymore. I leap off the treadmill and throw my hands on my knees. "I'm just going to . . . [gasp] . . . grab some water. Do you guys need anything?"

Chiseled Girl shakes her head.

Oscar shoots me a panicked look and hops off his treadmill. *"I don't climb,"* he hisses.

"Sorry about that. I got confused. Honest mistake. Don't worry, though. I've got everything under control."

And I do. Or . . . I thought I did. I don't know what happened, though. I followed Chiseled Girl all over the gym, doing pull-ups, sit-ups, lunges, you name it. And now she won't stop doing push-ups. *She's a maniac.* I've never seen anything like it. Up down. Up down. I can barely get a word in. And oh my God . . . my arms are so puny. I can't handle many more. Up down. Up down. What am I going to do? I'm at my wit's end. And I've tried E-V-E-R-Y-T-H-I-N-G.

> *"Your abs are amazing. Can you show me some moves?"*
> *"Um. Sure. Try three hundred of these and . . ."*
> *"Those red spandexy shorts are so cute. Are they comfy?"*
> *"No."*
> *"Right. So. You never said. Do you climb a lot?"*
> *"Actually I went pro last year."*
> *"Can you show me how to use this heavy silver thing?"*
> *"Um. That's a trash can."*

Oscar tugs at my arm like a frantic child as Chiseled Girl heads toward the door to leave. "Do something!" he pleads.

I race over to her side. "Hi. Me again!" I wave. "Thanks for all your help with the treadmill and abs. And sorry about that silly trash can thing. I was totally joking. Swear."

"No problem," she says, swinging a green bag over her shoulder. "Well, have a good one!"

"WAIT!" I blurt. "Can we . . . um . . . buy you a smoothie at the gym juice bar? To say thanks."

She gives Oscar and me a funny look, but finally nods her head. "I guess so."

As we stand in line, Chiseled Girl puts on a green Nike hat and dabs on some clear lip gloss. Oscar gawks at her like a toy he simply must have.

"Oh. I'm sorry! You met Oscar, right?" I ask, handing her a fresh raspberry smoothie. "He's the greatest workout friend," I gush. "He keeps me motivated!"

"That's so sweet," Chiseled Girl says, taking a sip of her smoothie. "So what do you do, Oscar?"

He whips out a business card. "Vice president. O'Flaherty & Sons Securities. Maybe you've heard of it?"

"Why no. No, I haven't." Chiseled Girl bats her eyelashes, taking Oscar's arm. "But tell me all about it." Oscar winks at me as they push open the heavy gym doors and step out into the cool evening air.

F-I-N-A-L-L-Y.

Chapter 21

MY PHONE RINGS in the middle of the night. What the . . . ? Who the . . . ?

I rub my eyes, checking the fuzzy green numbers on the alarm clock. One fifteen?! I throw a pillow over my head, but the phone just keeps ringing and ringing.

Oh fine. I swat at the bedside table, grabbing for the phone. I check caller ID. It's Aiden. Hmm. Yesterday I would have jumped, but yesterday Patrick hadn't kissed me yet. Do I really want Aiden to come over? No. No. I'll just tell him no.

"Hello?"

Music blasts into my ear. "H–E–L–L–O?" Aiden shouts above all the thump, thump, thumping. "IT'S ME. ARE YOU UP?"

"Where are you?"

"I'M AT JOE'S!" he slurs. "CAN I COME AND SEEE-EEE YOU?"

"Aiden, it's late."

"WHAT? CAN I COME OVER?"

Sigh. "Look, Aiden, I don't know . . ."

"GREAT. I'LL BE OVER IN A FEW." And he hangs up before I can say anything else.

What? How did that just happen? I bolt upright in bed and flick on the light. Joe's is only a few blocks away. He'll be here in a few minutes! I look down at my ratty T-shirt and boxers.

Oh no. This definitely won't work. Can't let anyone see me in these. I scramble over to my closet, stubbing my toe on the edge of the bed.

"Oo-uch!" I wail, flopping onto the floor and pinching my toe in pain. I finally manage to throw on some kicky sweatpants and a tank top. Thank God my stomach is starting to feel better.

The doorbell rings. I run into the hallway and hit the intercom.

"Victoria? It's meee-eee! Let me in," Aiden slurs.

I hit the entry button.

What am I going to do? I fling open the door. Aiden falls into the entryway, nearly whacking his head on the small wooden bookcase under the hall mirror. I catch a whiff of an icky mix of smoke, booze, and his Escada cologne. Good. He's clearly too drunk to do anything but sleep.

I frown. "Let's put you to bed." I swing his left arm over my shoulders and lug him toward the bedroom.

I wake up a few hours later with my head hanging off the side of the bed. Aiden's baseball hat is on the floor next to a couple of pillows, but there's no sign of Aiden. No shoes. No boxers. No nothing. I pad into the living room.

"Hello?" I call out.

No answer.

"Aiden?"

What a jerk. He wakes me up in the middle of the night and then leaves without saying good-bye?

I check the time on the microwave. It's five o'clock. And my eyes feel swollen from no sleep. I'm dead. The fashion show is today. The makeup girls are going to *kill* me.

I crawl back into bed and angrily pull the covers up around my chin. I can't believe Aiden. And to think I actually liked him. (Or I thought I did. Didn't I?) Armani prances across the duvet, settling into a black ball on my stomach. I sigh, scratching him behind the ears. He twists his cute furry head around and purrs up at me.

"You're one of the only good men left." I peer down at the little guy. He looks so happy. So content. What a good life. Sleeps, eats, and bats around a pink jingly ball. Is it possible to be jealous of a cat?

I switch off the bedside lamp and I must nod off for a bit, because I start having the most bizarre dream. Elle is screaming, "Fucked! You need to look like you just got fucked!" I try to explain to Elle that I don't exactly remember what getting fucked looks like. Could she please elaborate? Then I realize Elle is my mom. "You know, darling. Grunt. Get some color in your face." That's when Aiden offers to help put me in the mood and we start making out on the runway as Mom cheers us on. Only to realize that I'm actually making out with Patrick.

I wake up in a cold sweat. Whoa.

What the hell was that?

•

LATER IN THE MORNING, I desperately try to keep my eyes open as Marco yanks my head back and forth, teasing my hair higher and higher. He's much more serious than normal.

"I want your wings *huge* today," Marco mumbles. He narrows his eyes, deep in concentration as he jerk, jerk, teases, and sprays. Jerk, jerk, teases, and sprrraaayyys some more.

There's a cloud of hair spray all around me. The more I cough, the more he sprays. I let my eyes flutter shut for a moment, replaying last night in my head. The more I think about it, the angrier I am. Angry that Aiden called so late. Angry that he disappeared without saying good-bye. I deserve better. Don't I?

Ugh. I feel nauseous. Partly because I'm starving. But . . . wow. I feel so thin. My stomach is sunken in. My butt is tighter. It's, well, it's amazing! The Hart Family Diet Secret is a miracle. I can't wait to tell Mom.

Marco finally finishes and kisses me on both cheeks, and Elle pushes me toward wardrobe. "Let's go. Let's go. You're already behind schedule." She presses a button on her headset and barks into the mouthpiece. "We're en route. Prepare now."

As soon as we reach the wardrobe station, a stylist with olive-green glasses grabs the bottom of my T-shirt, and with one yank and snap of the bra, I'm completely topless.

What the . . . ? I jerk my arms up around my chest, attempting to cover as much skin as possible. I might be flat-chested, but come on! I'm still modest.

"Stylists. Remember. De vision is sex," Federico yells from across the room.

Elle nods. "Do you hear that, people? Like yesterday. We're going for that just-got-fucked look!"

Oh dear God. I really wish she'd stop saying that—*just got fucked*. My cheeks flush feverishly as I suddenly remember last night's dream. God. That was so messed up.

"Nice breasts," mumbles the stylist. She clips a bracelet around my wrist. "Very perky."

"Um . . . thanks," I say, rubbing my neck uncomfortably. "Most people just call them small."

The stylist giggles.

"Tarin! Where the fuck is her bra? Hmm?" Elle growls. "Tell me. Did it just walk off the table last night?"

"I'm not sure," says Tarin, the girl with the olive-green glasses.

"Well, find out!" Elle orders. "Jesus. Do I have to do everything around here?"

They finally locate the black leather bra and my outfit is complete. I'm officially Federico's just-got-fucked vision. I look in the mirror and . . . oh . . .

Oh no. This is not good. Not good at all. Mom is going to freak. My outfit consists of a microscopic leather bra, ripped fishnets, a shredded lace skirt, and no shoes. And my hair? Let's not even talk about the massive bird wings jutting out by my ears. (What was Marco thinking?)

Right then, I spot Kimmie squeezing through the backstage crowd. (Whew! Thank goodness I have *some* clothes on!) Okay. Stay calm. She'll never put two and two together. I mean, she seemed to buy the I-want-to-be-a-model story I told her. And, well, Chicago Wingwoman is just hosting the show. No one knows they're supplying the models, too. Fingers crossed. If everything goes my way, my secret will stay safe and sound.

Uh-oh. Who is Kimmie with? Is that . . .

PATRICK?

Panic. What is *he* doing here?

"Hiii!" Kimmie squeals, slipping her arms around my waist and giving me a hug. "I can't believe you've wanted to be a model all this time! Why didn't you ever say anything?" She suddenly stops, looking me up and down. "Good God. Have you lost weight? You look like you haven't eaten all week!"

"You have no idea," I say, my eyes fixed on Patrick.

"What are you doing here?" Patrick and I say at the same time.

Kimmie looks confused. "Do you two know each other?"

"No," I blurt.

"Yes," he says.

I smile nervously, avoiding his gaze. "Kind of. We met . . . um . . . you know . . ."

"At work," he finishes off.

Ha! That's right. Brilliant answer. "We met the day I interviewed at Lambert," I say breathlessly.

Kimmie slowly looks from Patrick to me, then back again. "Uh-huh. Right."

Oh no! She's not buying the story. Quick. Change the subject.

"Did you save two seats for my parents?" I ask Kimmie.

"Yep. Julia and I are sitting with them." Kimmie looks at her watch. "And I should probably get back. I just wanted to say hi."

"I'm glad you're here," I say, pulling Kimmie in for a hug. And I am. In fact, I almost want to sit her down and tell her the whole story. No more lies. But there isn't time right now. And would she really understand?

"Wouldn't miss it!" Kimmie bubbles, giving me a squeeze. "You look *amazing*. I can't believe my best friend is a real-life model!"

"Hardly." I roll my eyes. "Now go. You're making me nervous."

Patrick stays behind with me. He carefully eyes my outfit. "You look great."

"Thanks," I say, wrapping my arms around my stomach, suddenly very aware of all the skin I'm showing. "So what are you doing here?"

"You're wearing my new client." Patrick grins. "I'm helping launch the Rico label today."

"Wait a minute. Your big hush-hush client is Federico?" I ask incredulously.

Patrick laughs. "Actually my client is Ms. Kingsley. She owns the Rico label."

"MS. KINGSLEY?" I squeak. "As in Kaitlyn Kingsley?"

"Yeah. She's with Red Envy. Do you know her?"

"Oh . . . you could say that."

Suddenly there's a big commotion by the storage room doors. And speak of the devil—in struts Kaitlyn with a fully decked-out entourage of Naomi Campbell and Kate Moss wannabes. Kaitlyn slides off her platinum Gucci sunglasses and tosses her thick blond waves over her shoulders like a scene straight out of *Charlie's Angels*.

"Oh God," I groan, rolling my eyes.

"I can see you're a big fan," Patrick says.

"Huge."

Kaitlyn sweeps through the room, air-kissing cheek after cheek and waving like a queen.

She swoops up to Patrick, kissing his left cheek. "Amazing work on the Rico label, sweetheart. Love it!"

"It's a pleasure. As always," Patrick says.

Kaitlyn's gaze shifts to me. Her jaw flinches. "Victoria. I didn't realize *you* were in the show. What a small world."

"Isn't it?" I say sharply.

"I'm surprised they selected *you*." She clicks her tongue. "You're not exactly the Rico vision."

WHAT. A. BITCH. Maybe I could help Gwynn strangle her? I smile tightly. "I guess someone thought differently."

"Guess so," Kaitlyn says icily, turning on her high Prada heels.

"So about the other night," Patrick says quietly, stuffing his hands in his pockets.

Oh no. His tone sounds weird. He's totally going to tell me it was a mistake. It was a silly slip and it'll never happen again.

My cell phone starts ringing.

"Can you hold on a sec?" I lean down, rooting around in my Hogan. By the time I find my cell phone, the ringing stops.

"I'm sorry. What were you saying?" I brace myself for the inevitable brush-off.

My cell phone starts ringing again. Grrr.

Patrick leans in and gives me a quick hug. "Nothing important. You're busy. We can talk later."

My breath catches as I take in his sweet, delicious cologne. And suddenly I have an urge to pull Patrick toward me by his belt loops and wrap his strong arms around me . . .

I close my eyes, trying to shake the thought.

"Are you okay?" he asks.

"Oh yeah. Fine. Just hungry," I say quickly.

My cell phone is still ringing.

His eyes search mine. "Okay. Well, good luck."

I smile and wave good-bye as I click on my cell phone. "Hello?"

"Vic! Hi! It's Gwynn. Did you get my message?"

Oh no. She sounds frantic. I should have let the call go straight to voice mail.

"No. No, I didn't." I lie. Suddenly the storage room grows dark and someone lets out a loud *"Shh."*

"I made a copy of Bryan's key. Can you break into his place tonight?"

"Are you crazy?" I howl. "I'm not breaking into your fiancé's apartment!"

A few heads snap around to eavesdrop.

"Pretty please?" Gwynn pleads. "I have to know what's going on. We need to find that blue folder!"

"I don't know," I whisper. "I really think the blue folder is the Bali brochure."

Just then, Elle comes running up in a complete panic, motioning for me to cut the conversation—*now*.

"Um. Listen. Let me call you later," I squeak.

"We're lining up!" Elle hisses.

I hold up my index finger, letting Elle know I only need a second.

"What's going on?" Gwynn huffs. "This is important. I need your help. Kaitlyn is ruining my life!"

Elle narrows her eyes into two devilish slits. Clearly waiting is not an option. "Do not fuck with me!" Elle growls, ripping the cell phone out of my hand and slamming it shut.

Oh God. Gwynn is going to flip. I'll have to call and beg forgiveness later.

"When I say it's time to line up, you line up," Elle rages, shoving me in line.

Music blares from the speakers. Wingwomen start making their way down the runway. My entire body starts to shake. I wave over at Lexi and Redd, who are farther up in line. Lexi is busy text messaging on her cell phone and barely looks up. And Redd gives me a quick nod as a stylist tries to squeeze her enormous breasts into a lime green bustier.

"It's freezing," I whisper to the Gothed-out Asian girl in front of me. Her eyelids are smeared black and her orange hair is slicked up into a bristly mohawk.

She whips around and glares at me. "*Do you mind?* I'm trying to focus," the girl snaps. "This could be my big break."

Wow. Okay. I take a few steps back, so she can focus . . . or whatever.

I hear *oohs* and *ahs* from the audience. My stomach suddenly feels queasy. And my palms are sweating. There are only a few wingwomen left in front of me. Goth Girl fingers the edge of her mohawk as a stylist adjusts the leopard-print scarf cinched around her waist. She takes her place by the curtain. She's on next.

Marco suddenly appears behind me. He looks frazzled as he pulls at my wings. He jerks them higher and higher, then spraaays.

Elle runs up, panting. "Quick. Turn around."

"Is everything okay?" I ask, my heart racing.

Elle rips off my shredded lace skirt and holds up a pair of pale pink sequined underwear with baby white wings sewn to the rear. "Put these on."

"What?" I blink.

"You're next," Tarin whispers.

"Victoria. I don't have time for this shit! Ms. Kingsley made a last-minute request. She wants you to wear these, so put them on. *Now!*" Elle hisses. "And it'll be a great promotional shot with the pink wingwoman banners."

I stare at the hideous pink garment in horror.

Oh no. No way. This must be a joke!

Goth Girl whisks through the curtains, finishing her walk. Aaack! *It's my turn.*

"You're going to ruin the entire show. Is that what you want?" Elle growls, thrusting the underwear into my hands. "Put them on, you little bitch!"

My jaw drops. "I . . . I . . . okay . . ." I bend down and slip on the sequined pink underwear with the baby white wings. I swivel around and stare down at my butt, which is barely covered by anything.

This can't be happening.

"Go! Go! Go!" Tarin squeaks in panic. "We need her onstage."

"I . . . I can't do this." I grab the curtains with a death grip, my eyes filling up with tears. *I'm going to kill Kaitlyn.*

"YOU HAVE TO GO!" Tarin shouts hysterically, pushing me onto the stage.

"But my butt . . ." I whip around, looking for someone, anyone to help. But the curtain already swooshed shut and I'm all alone . . . onstage. I turn toward the audience, shaking. Someone shoves me into the light and I stumble a bit, then stop. The audience is silent. The lights are glaring and my chest is about to explode.

This is it. I'm dying. I just know it. This is what it feels like to have a heart attack. Did I tell Mom I loved her? Did I . . . ?

"Woo, Victoria!" I hear Kimmie hoot.

Oh thank God. Something familiar. I'm not dead . . . *yet.*

I take a deep breath and before I know what's happening, I'm walking. I'm actually walking down the runway.

Oh my God. I can't believe I'm doing this!

Breathe.

I can feel my hips swaying in little figure eights just like we rehearsed. And suddenly it's like I'm standing outside my body, just watching myself go. Who is this person swishing all sexy-like? I hardly recognize myself.

And it's kind of fun.

I pivot at the end of the runway and make my way back toward the black velvety curtain. There's a buzz in the audience. Cameras start flashing like mad.

Not fun anymore.

Everyone's staring at my butt. At my practically naked butt. I want to die.

What if everyone is cringing in disgust? What if these stage lights accentuate all my icky cellulite? I *knew* I should have used that new cellulite roller more. And I swear . . . if Jay Schmidt is out there, I'm ripping his camera to shreds.

I have a sudden urge to plop down in the middle of the stage, scooting myself back toward the curtains. Laughing. Waving. Like this is exactly what I planned to do. But to my surprise, I keep swaying figure eights, figure eights all the way to the curtains.

I did it. *I actually did it.*

•

A BIT LATER, I stand on tiptoe in the jam-packed reception room trying to find familiar faces. Ooh. Is that Jay Schmidt? *It is!* He races for the door as soon as we make eye contact. (What a twerp.) And then I spot Kimmie and Julia waving excitedly. "Vic, over here!"

I smile and wave back.

As I get closer, I see Patrick standing next to my dad. They're both chuckling about something. Mom's face lights up when she spots me. I can already see her bright mint eye shadow and coral lips. (I *really* need to talk to her about her makeup again.) She elbows Dad in the ribs and pats her silver curls. "She's coming. She's coming. Quick. Get the camera, honey."

"You were awesome!" Kimmie says. "And nice wings." She lowers her eyes mischievously.

I bite my lip. Did she figure it out? *I'm sure she did.* How much more obvious could it get?

"You were fantastic!" Julia says, checking her watch and scrunching up her pretty porcelain face. "I hate to run. But my flight leaves for New York soon." She gives me a quick hug and disappears into the crowd.

Mom pulls me to the side, her hands clasped tightly, her eyes wide. "What did I tell you. Hmm? The diet works like a charm. Doesn't it?"

I nod happily. My stomach may never be the same, but it worked!

Kimmie hands me an icy glass. "Mangotini, just for you."

"Oh, thank you! You're the best," I say, clinking glasses with the group.

That's when I see Aiden. My stomach tightens.

Drats! Did I tell him about the show last night? I don't even remember.

"Hey, doll," Aiden says, sauntering up and squeezing my waist. "Killer outfit up there. Maybe I can get a closer look later on?"

Patrick glances at Aiden's hand on my waist, then shoots me a funny look.

"It *was* killer, wasn't it?" Mom says excitedly, snapping a picture of me on her new digital camera. "Look!" she points to the LCD screen. "What a nice picture. Want to see the shots of you onstage?"

"She only took about a hundred," Dad teases.

I laugh. "I'd rather not see my monster butt just yet."

"Oh darling, it was only showing a smidge," Mom trills. "And it was very thin . . . and sexy. Right, Kimmie?"

"Mom!" I cringe.

"I'll say," Aiden says, narrowing his eyes and sliding a finger down my side and nuzzling my neck.

Eww. I jump back, shooting him an evil look. Not in front of my parents! Not in front of . . . Patrick! *What is he thinking?*

"What?" Aiden says innocently.

Patrick furrows his brow. "I better be going," he says quickly, not meeting my eyes. "I have to get back to the office."

"Don't leave!" I blurt. "Um . . . I mean, are you sure you have to go?"

"Positive." Patrick shakes hands with my dad, then walks off into the crowd.

"Yeah. I gotta run, too. I'm checking out a new building for my dad." Aiden grins. "I'll call you later, babe. Okay?" He leans down and kisses me on the cheek. The tiny hairs on the back of my neck stand up.

I smile at Dad nervously.

He frowns.

Leo

The stars are busy stirring up trouble for you, little singletini. And there are loads of steamy secrets brewing (not just yours!). Proceed with caution. You may feel uneasy about what the future holds. Trust your intuition. When the dust settles, you'll be standing tall. Keep your chin up. Your reward is worth the wait.

YOUR WEEK AT A GLANCE

STRENGTHS: YOU. ARE. JAMES. BOND.
WEAKNESSES: Big fat mouth
CONQUESTS: Things could get interesting . . .
TO DO: Be patient and keep an open mind. Big surprises await.

(Hmph. I do not have a big fat mouth!)

CITY GIRLS

THE MUST-READ MAG FOR THE CHICAGO SINGLETINI

Was Goldstone Caught Red-Handed?

By Jay Schmidt

Gwynn Ericsson's golden boy was spotted with a swarm of wingwomen at the recent Bloomingdale's fashion show. Sources say, "He was flirting like crazy. You'd never guess he was engaged!" It's rumored that Goldstone was there to support ex-flame Kaitlyn Kingsley, who owns the Rico label. But Goldstone furiously refutes, "This is ridiculous. I was shopping . . . *for my soon-to-be wife.* Don't you people have anything better to do?" Um. To answer his question: no, we don't.

Chapter 22

FROM: gwynnie_pooh@girly.com
TO: victoria_hart@vongo.com
ATTACHMENT: more_shower_stuff.doc
PRIORITY: *Very, Very Urgent*
SUBJECT: Help!

OH MY GOD. I'm totally freaking out! My shower is tomorrow. It's supposed to be this big magical day, but everything is turning into a huge mess. I'm in the worst mood ever. I mean, I nearly fired Polo yesterday for stepping on my toe! (Whatever. It really hurt!) Anyway, no time to chat. I'm late for my mani-pedi. See the attached.

   Kisses,

   Gwynnie

P.S. Sorry about leaving those nasty messages on your voice mail. I didn't realize your cell phone died and you were trying to call me back. I thought you hung up on me!

MORE_SHOWER_STUFF.DOC
Hello, sweet pea!

   It's your favorite little Frenchie. I must admit, my sweet, I'm losing my mind. With the shower suddenly being held at Birdie's house, things are getting crazy, crazy, crazy! (What a loony lady!) Call if you run into trouble. Kiss. Kiss. Toodles.

XOXO,

Polo

1. Run by Blackbird and convince the head chef, Franz, that it *is* possible to create a mini Eiffel Tower out of pink cake. I mean, the famous French chef Jean-Claude Moreau made the Statue of Liberty out of tiny white marshmallows. You see. How hard can it be? *Non?* I tried explaining this to Franz . . . but he hung up on me. Psshh! Anyway, we simply must have this cake. Gwynnie's heart is set on it. It's *très romantique.* So bat your pretty eyelashes, honey bunny. Flirt. Flirt. Flirt.

2. Bring the following items to the shower: pink pencils, pink 4 x 5-inch note cards, disposable cameras, 100 rolls of toilet paper (I'll explain later), makeup remover (in case girls look too cute—remember Gwynnie must be the radiant angel of the day!), birdseed, Kleenex, and lots and lots of those Claritin pills.

3. Bake five dozen pink chocolate chip cookies (heart shaped, of course!). Use four drops of red Esco food coloring to achieve the exact shade of pink we're going for. Don't use a heart-shaped cookie cutter, though. Shape them by hand. The cookies will be much more organic and artistic that way. And Gwynnie just adores the idea of "food as art."

4. Don't mention Birdie in front of Gwynnie. She's trying this new experimental "pretend" method, where she doesn't acknowledge things she doesn't like. Her therapist thought it might reduce her stress. (Can I just say? You Americans are very odd.)

•

"I'M SO CONFUSED," I confess to Everett on Saturday. It's a warm, sunny May afternoon. Vibrant blue sky. White pillowy clouds. Red azaleas and sweet cherry blossoms blooming all around. We're sitting on the bridge at Lincoln Park Zoo, jeans rolled up and our feet dangling in the cool water as we lick ice-cream cones and watch paddleboats spin around.

"This Aiden guy sounds like a jerk," Everett says, wrinkling his pink nose and wiping his mouth with a napkin. After running all of Gwynn's errands and ordering cookies from Sweet Thang bakery over on North Avenue (you didn't think I'd actually bake those, did you?), I met up with Everett. We went shopping all day in Bucktown (I snagged the jazziest little Marc Jacobs top at Jolie Joli). Then we eventually wound our way through Lincoln Park and up to the zoo.

"I think you're right." I sigh, slumping my shoulders and taking a bite of my sugar cone. "What's wrong with me? I can set everyone up but myself. And, well, I can't even do that these days."

"Stop! What are you talking about?" Everett says, nudging me. "I thought you set Oscar up *twice.*"

"Yeah. On one-night stands. How hard is that?" I mutter sarcastically. "All of my real couples are breaking up. Gwynn and Bryan are going down in flames. Even Julia and Kevin are on the rocks. I'm starting to think this wingwoman job is a mistake. I mean, it's all I do these days! Post flyers. Stay out late. Sleep until noon. Get up and do it again. At least with a desk job, it was always nine to five and I wasn't lying to everyone I care about."

"Tell them the truth. Who cares?" Everett cries. "So you're a wingwoman! They'll get over it. You can't quit, though. Look at what you've done for me. I'm almost ready for my cowgirl! Only a few more pounds." Everett smiles, tapping his shrinking belly.

It's true. Everett does look good. He's wearing a hip gray fitted T-shirt, dark-wash Diesel jeans, and Ray-Ban aviators. (A far cry from the rumpled jeans and stained polo he had on the first time we met.) It even looks like he went back to Maxine to have his hair trimmed and his eyebrows shaped. And I swear he's at least ten pounds thinner.

"Don't be so hard on yourself," Everett says, pushing up his aviators. His violet eyes are so warm and friendly. "Are you just upset about Aiden?"

"Maybe." I bite my lip.

"I'm sorry." Everett shakes his head. "But he really does sound like a jerk. You'll find someone else. Someone much better."

"Will I?" I peer out over Swan Pond and up at the Chicago skyline nestled between the budding trees. "I . . . I think I'm scared," I say at last. "I'm having all these weird feelings and I'm so confused. I don't know what I want. But I know I don't want to be left behind."

"It's okay to be scared," Everett says, swinging an arm around me and squeezing my shoulders. "And it's okay to be in a different place than your friends. Look at me. All my friends are not only married, but they have a van full of kids. And I don't even have the nerve to ask out the girl of my dreams. It doesn't mean I'm left behind. It just means I'm not ready to leap. I haven't found the one."

My eyes fill up with tears. "What if I can't find the one, either?" I watch the two plump white trumpeter swans flutter about. They splash and frolic, dipping their orange beaks in the pond and flicking water. The beautiful white birds eventually settle down and let their long graceful necks curl toward each other. Are they flirting? Are they fighting? Are they soul mates? How does anyone know for sure?

"You will." Everett smiles. "Just like I will." He leans back on his hands and swishes his feet around in the pond water. "You're a wingwoman! It's your job to find love."

"How scary is that?" I sigh.

Everett rolls his eyes. "So tell me more about Patrick. I have a feeling about this one."

And we sit there in the lazy afternoon sun for hours, just swinging our legs in the cool water, and laughing and talking. I tell Everett everything I know about Patrick. How we met. How we kissed. All of it.

And then we plot our plan for Everett and the cowgirl . . .

Chapter 23

SUNDAY IS GWYNN'S shower . . . in the suburbs. Lake Forest to be exact. It's a bright, beautiful day and I'd rather be doing anything but attending it. *Julia is so lucky to be in New York.* Don't get me wrong, I love Gwynn. But I saw the agenda (Yes, there is an agenda. Does that surprise you?), and this shower sounds, well, interesting. Goofy games. Something about bridal hats? I guess Gwynn's crazy old grandmother, aka Birdie, demanded she throw the shower. Let's just say, Gwynn is less than thrilled. "You don't understand. The woman is senile. Cuckoo! She'll forget she's even throwing the thing!"

Kimmie and I drive up the long windy cobblestone drive-way, which is tangled with weeds and yellow wildflowers. And I have to admit, Birdie's place is not what I expected. I pictured the typical Lake Forest property. A traditional redbrick and white-pillared home. Immaculately groomed lawn. Smartly trimmed hedges. Maybe a marble fountain or two? Instead we pull up to a rather funny-looking cottage. Slightly lopsided, to tell you the truth. Think Hansel and Gretel. There's a swooping thatchlike roof with shingles splashing across the front like waves. It has the tiniest windows. And a big droopy Swiss-chalet balcony hanging over the arched ivy-covered entryway. Very whimsical. Very fairy tale.

Kimmie and I unpack the car and make our way to the front door. Kimmie carries a small ornately wrapped gift in one hand and a bouquet of yellow tulips in the other. I have an over-stuffed Barneys bag jammed with pencils, note cards, and photos of Gwynn and Bryan (for the timeline), and a blue Tiffany box (with a $200 sterling silver Audubon spoon inside).

I know. I know. How ridiculous is my gift? A single spoon. Whatever. It was $200! What do you even *do* with a $200 spoon? And why on earth would you put it on your registry? Do you honestly use it? Or do you just set it out and admire the shiny thing? At least I finally talked Mom into splitting it with me. You should have heard her huff and puff, though. "Tiffany? Psshh. What a new bride needs is practical things from Sears. Like towels. You can never have enough towels."

Dear God.

I'm thinking it's a good thing she couldn't make it today. (It's her Club's annual bake sale at Naperville Public Library. Their biggest event of the year!) I don't think she would have enjoyed herself among all the uppity ladies.

Just then, the door swings open and there stands Polo. "Hello, honey bunnies!" he sings, rubbing his shiny bald head. He gives us both a peck on the cheek and takes our bags, gifts, and flowers in one big sweeping motion. "Come in! Come in! Isn't this exciting?"

I smile. Polo isn't wearing the trendy tuxedo today, but there's still something about the way he waddles about that reminds me of a penguin.

"I can't believe it! *Can you?*" Polo trills. "Our little lovebirds will be walking down the aisle before we know it." He wipes his eyes dramatically. "My job is such a joy!"

"Polo, it's just us." I laugh. "We know Mrs. Ericsson is driving you mad."

"Oh thank God." Polo's entire body goes limp. He draws a hand to his forehead. "I can't wait until this dreadful thing is over. And this Birdie character is causing all sorts of trouble. Look! It's ruining my clear complexion," Polo huffs, pointing furiously at his shiny head. "And, it's making me go bald."

"You didn't have hair to begin with." I giggle. "Remember?"

"True." Polo pouts. "You get the point, though."

The doorbell suddenly *brr-rings.* Polo jerks upright and starts shooing us away. "Go! Go! Grab some champagne." He scoots us toward one of the tuxedo-clad waiters and flutters back to his position by the door. I can already hear him reciting the same speech to the arriving guests . . . *"My job is such a joy."*

"Please select a hat, mademoiselles." Pierre suddenly appears and bows. He motions to a long cherry table piled with fancy hats. All in different shades of pink.

Kimmie and I exchange looks. "Do we have to?" we whisper.

Pierre rubs his dark thin goatee. "I'm afraid so. Mrs. Ericsson's orders. It's supposed to be fun."

Right. Of course. Fun.

Kimmie picks a gigantic hot pink hat with a white satin bow, and I grab a small felt one with pale pink flowers and tulle around the crown. We gingerly put them on and giggle. We look ridiculous.

As we make our way into the living room, I have to laugh. Birdie definitely didn't forget she was throwing a shower. The entire room is exploding with pink streamers, bows, and balloons. We're talking pink cookies. (I had them delivered first thing this morning. I know. I know. Brilliant plan.) Pink candles.

Pink champagne. There is pink absolutely everywhere. I feel like I've just entered some awful secret side room in Willy Wonka's Chocolate Factory—a sickeningly sweet pink cotton candy room. The lyrics "Oompa Loompa doom-pa-dee-do . . ." start playing in my head.

And there are the Old Marrieds—the same ladies who were at Gwynn's engagement party. They all stand there stiffly, chatting away in small clusters around the living room, draped in their very proper pink hats. (How on earth did they manage to dig normal-looking hats out of that pile?) The Old Marrieds are absolutely identical. All tall. All elegant. And all carefully sipping their pink champagne and laughing lightly. They're immaculately dressed, each wearing pounds of jewelry and makeup with their noses pointed slightly down.

I spot our little Gwynnie-pooh in an elaborate pink poufy hat with pink and white ribbons looped all around. She's standing in the middle of the room with her mother. Her cheeks are glowing with joy and she's laughing at something a short grandma type just said. It's crazy watching her. Was she born to be an Old Married?

I shake my head, hoping this image will disappear. But it doesn't. She's still standing there. Perfectly poised in her perfect white piqué dress and pearls. Just perfect, perfect, perfect. Soon it'll be all over. She'll officially be one of them and she won't want anything to do with us. She'll leave all the singletinis in the dust . . .

"No way! Is that a bird?" Kimmie knocks me in the ribs. "Look!"

And there, clicking around on the terra-cotta tile floor, is a fluffy red bird with a green and purple chest and a stubby orange beak. It stands about two feet tall.

Kimmie walks right up to the red feathery thing and bends down next to it. The bird twists its red head and clucks up at her. "Should I pet it?"

"Sure you should!" a crackly voice bellows.

We both whip around to see Birdie. *Gwynn's grandmother.* I've heard so many crazy stories about Gwynn's grandmother and all her exotic birds, but Gwynn's never let us meet her. And, well, I have to say, it's clear that she's a bit . . . um . . . different. Birdie's an itty-bitty old lady with a shiny red cane. White frizzy hair. Loads of white powdery makeup. And giant black horn-rims with sparkly crystals on each tip. Her face is round and her wrinkles are deep. And when she smiles, her eyes get squinty and her red lips and white teeth take up her entire face.

"That's Mac. He's a macaw. You better watch him!" Birdie snaps. "He bites!"

Kimmie jumps back and Birdie cackles, thumping her red cane on the tiles. "I'm just joshing ya! He's the sweetest thing." She hobbles over and bops the furry red bird on the head. The bird swoops into the air and flutters back down on Birdie's shoulder.

Polo stomps over to Birdie's side, his brows deeply furrowed. He throws his hands on his hips. "Madame, please. Remember Gwynnie explicitly said Mac was not allowed at the party. *Under any circumstances.*"

"Oh pooh," Birdie huffs, pushing the fluffy red bird off her shoulder. "We were just having a bit of fun. Weren't we, girls?" Birdie winks at Kimmie and me. "No need to get in a tizzy." Mac flutters down to the floor. And is it just me, or is the bird giving Polo the evil eye?

Kimmie pushes a red curl out of her freckled face and grins at me. "Should we grab some champagne?"

I nod. As we're pouring pink champagne we see Mrs. Gold-stone and Kaitlyn arrive. They're both wearing head-to-toe black. (Mom would faint.) Pierre is trying desperately to get them to put on a pink hat. But he's failing miserably.

"Madame, please!" he begs Mrs. Goldstone. "Just a small one. *Non?*"

"Looks like someone's here to stir up trouble," Kimmie whispers.

I raise an eyebrow. "Which one?"

I glance over at Gwynn. Her smile disappears. And I can practically see her blood pressure skyrocketing from across the room. Before I can blink she is immediately at my side.

"Can I see you for a second?"

Uh-oh. Here we go. Shooting Kimmie a helpless look, I follow Gwynn down a long tiled hallway and into a small library with blue stained-glass windows and massive chocolaty leather couches. Gwynn plops down on a couch, clicks open her silver compact, and applies a fresh coat of red DiorKiss lip gloss. She fingers the mole just above her lip. "Didn't I tell you Birdie was nuts. Hmm? She's out there telling people she's a pirate. DID YOU HEAR HER?"

I burst out laughing, then immediately regret it when I see Gwynn's hurt face. She clicks her compact shut and throws her head back on the couch.

"It's not funny! Birdie thought Angel was *me*. She followed her into the bathroom and tried giving her condoms for the wedding night. Can you imagine? WHY DOES SHE EVEN HAVE CONDOMS?" Gwynn shrieks, her cheeks bright red. "She's eighty-one!"

"I'm really sorry," I say, patting her knee. "Is there anything I can do?"

"Make her keel over?" Gwynn sighs, puffing a pink hat ribbon out of her face. "Anyway, that's not why I brought you in here. Look at this!" She thrusts a crinkled piece of paper into my hands.

```
FROM: goldstone@thegoldstonegroup.com
TO: bryan_goldstone@thegoldstonegroup.com
PRIORITY: Critical
SUBJECT: We must talk
```

Dearest Bryan,

I've been trying to phone you all week. We need to talk immediately! As we've recently discussed, I'm deeply concerned about your future with the Ericsson girl.

I've always let you make your own decisions—where to go to college, what to study, whom to date. Even when you decided to move to Chicago, I stayed quiet—hoping it would be temporary. But I refuse to stand by and watch you make the biggest mistake of your life.

You could have your pick from the finest families in New York—a Whitney, a Vanderbilt, a Landon, a *Kingsley*. You deserve a girl with class, a girl with drive, a girl like Kaitlyn. You two were meant for each other. I can't stand to see you walk away from that.

I know you'll do the right thing. Break it off and come back to New York. It's where you belong.

Best,

Mother

After I finish reading, I gaze up at Gwynn. Her eyes are red and watery, and her small delicate hands are balled up into two angry fists.

"I found this, too!" she wails, shoving another piece of paper my way. It looks like a string of Instant Messages . . .

KAITLYN: Hi! Like what I showed you yesterday?
BRYAN: Loved it.
KAITLYN: Nice. That's what I like to hear.
BRYAN: Gwynn won't be happy, though.
KAITLYN: What? Too hot?
BRYAN: Much too hot. I need to see more.
KAITLYN: Are you sure?

```
BRYAN: I think so. We can do better.
KAITLYN: When can we meet?
BRYAN: How about lunch on Friday. My place. Gwynn has a
    dress fitting. She'll never suspect a thing.
```

Uh-oh. I put a hand over my mouth. This is bad. *Really bad.*

"You have to help me!" Gwynn cries. "I have to know what's going on!"

"What can I do?" I say weakly.

"Break into Bryan's apartment," she says, handing me a small silver key. "I'm counting on you."

Aaaack!

My mind is racing as we return to the party. Mrs. Ericsson snaps her fingers at Gwynn to socialize, and I drift over to a chair.

This is completely nuts. I can't believe I just agreed to snoop around Bryan's apartment Saturday. Apparently Gwynn put the Bali brochure back in Bryan's Tumi. (Yeah. I know.) So now I need to find it again to prove that's all it is . . . or dig up something else blue and suspicious. I down my entire flute of pink champagne, then immediately regret it.

Bad, Vic. Bad.

Drink slow. Gwynn will kill me if I get drunk at this thing. She has enough to worry about with Kaitlyn and Mrs. Goldstone stirring up trouble . . . and Birdie on the loose.

Right then, Birdie whistles and thumps her red cane. "It's game time! Take your seats." Her voice crackles. Fluffy red Mac is perched on her shoulder again. Polo is already batting at the feathery thing, but the big red bird keeps clucking down at him angrily. Poor Polo.

"Okay," Birdie quacks. "We'll start with one of my favorites . . . oh dear . . . what's it called again?" Birdie scrunches up her powdery white face.

"The purse scavenger hunt," Philip says cheerfully, already sweeping around the room with his pink lacy basket, handing out pencils and game cards. Mrs. Ericsson sits primly on the edge of a pink upholstered ottoman, patting Gwynn on the knee.

Hmm. On second thought, I think I'll have one more flute of champagne. I mean, I need to loosen up a bit. Get in the festive spirit. Right?

That's it, though. *Just one.*

But one drink turns into two and then . . . well? I don't know what happened. I mean, I may have grabbed a few more flutes from one of those handy little silver trays floating around the room. But only a *few.*

Okay. Maybe four. (Hiccup). Or five? But on a positive note, this silly shower is turning out 100 percent better than I expected. I'm having the best time ever! We played purse scavenger hunt (I won!), bridal bingo, and this weird game with toilet paper?

I love showers.

Who would have thought? Ooh! And I've gotten to tell all these hilarious tales about little Gwynnie-pooh . . .

"And there was this one time when Gwynn *thought* she walked in on Bryan cheating on her with some trampy girl. But it turned out to be his roommate's naked girlfriend confused about which bed to crawl into. Ha! Or so Bryan says."

The Old Marrieds are roaring with laughter. Hmm . . . or I think they are? It's kind of hard to tell at this point. Everything is a tad blurry.

"God. Gwynn's face was classic!" I howl, letting out a loud snort.

That's when Angel and Dawn join our conversation. And is it just me? Or is there a sigh of relief coming from the Old Marrieds? I grab another flute of champagne and sip away happily as Angel and Dawn show off their glittery engagement rings and bask in all the *oohs* and *ahs* over their wedding details.

"So when are *you* getting married?" Angel asks, fluffing her brown bob and directing the attention to me. She raises an eyebrow and smirks meanly.

"What?" I nearly choke on my champagne.

"Yes. Yes. What about you?" Birdie clicks up with her red cane, Mac fluttering close behind. "I'm sure you have a Mr. Right about to pop the question. Hmm?"

I take a big swig of champagne and close my eyes, frantically trying to think of my last *acceptable* date.

Hmm. Nothing is coming to me. Call me crazy, but I don't think a random hookup with a hottie counts. (Well . . . there is Patrick. And wow, that kiss was amazing! But no. Forget about it. He's my client. It was an accident. Nothing more.) What a sad, sad thought. I haven't had a proper date in, well, I don't know how long.

I can feel the panic starting to gurgle in my stomach. What am I supposed to say? A dozen faces stare back at me intently, waiting for my answer. I smile and laugh nervously. What's wrong with me? Surely I have a guy just waiting to get down on bended knee . . .

Right?

What kind of girl *doesn't*?

Hmm . . .

"I'm a lesbian," I hear myself blurt.

OH. NO. Did I just say that?

"Yep. No guys for me. I'm girls all the way!" I try my best to grin casually, but my head feels so fuzzy.

Oh dear God. What the hell am I talking about? *Girls all the way?* HAVE I GONE MAD? I down the rest of my champagne and look around desperately for one of the cute waiters. Nowhere to be found. Drats!

Angel glares at me, her face on fire. And Dawn purses her lips, looking like she might burst out laughing (or into tears?) at any moment. I might be a teensy bit tipsy, but I'm not so far gone to think that Gwynn wouldn't murder me if she overheard this conversation.

"I've always wondered about . . . lesbians." Birdie clucks her tongue. "What's that like? Do tell."

"What's *what* like?" I gulp. *Please don't ask about sex.*

A couple of the ladies clear their throats, anxiously looking around the pink living room for any possible reason to excuse themselves.

"Oh dear, not the sex!" Birdie cackles. "I meant, you know, to be a lesbian. Out of the closet. Is it difficult?"

"Not at all!" I chirp. "It's great."

Stop it, Vic. Just stop. You're being completely ridiculous.

"In fact, it's kind of like being a vegetarian," I hear myself say. Oh. Dear. God.

"Really?" Birdie scratches her wild white hair. "Is that so?"

"Totally!" I beam.

At that moment, Gwynn walks up. She's not smiling. In fact, she looks like she might strangle me.

"Take vegetarians." I clear my throat. Yes. Yes. This is good. I eat broccoli. "You know . . . they might crave a steak from time to time. But they don't order one. Because, well, that's not on their menu . . ."

I stop talking and smile painfully at Gwynn.

No one says a word.

The Old Marrieds look horrified.

Birdie thumps her red cane impatiently. "And . . . ?"

I'm dead. *I have no idea what I'm talking about.*

But I have to say something. I close my eyes.

"It's . . . um . . . really about choice. And . . . um . . . what kind of menu you need." I nod, suddenly realizing my head is spinning wildly. Maybe no one even noticed my story. I mean, honestly, who listens to polite conversations at these things, anyway?

Wow. How did I get so drunk? Did they put something in these drinks? I should really talk to Polo about the stiff drinks they're serving. It's a tad inappropriate at a shower. Don't you think?

Gwynn pinches my side hard. "Can I speak with you?" she asks, smiling tightly.

"Now?" I turn to her. "I'm in the middle of a story."

"Now," she growls.

"Okay. I'll be right back!" I wave to the circle of ladies. "Don't worry. It'll just be a second."

Gwynn pushes me into the guest bathroom and slams the door.

"What are you doing out there?" she hisses.

"I'm sorry," I say.

"You're sorry. SORRY?" Gwynn howls, narrowing her eyes. "Do you even know what I'm going through today? I have a future mother-in-law dissecting my every move. Kaitlyn whispering rumors that Bryan and I are on the rocks. And a crazy grandmother passing out condoms! I don't need you making things worse!"

"I'm sorry," I say again. "How can I help?"

"How can you help?" Gwynn lets out a loud snort. "I'll let you in on a secret. You're my personal attendant! Your JOB is to help me. You should be at my side at all times. Making sure that *I* have a drink at all times. That *I* am having a good time at all times. Your world should be revolving around me, me, me!" she huffs, flipping her blond hair off her shoulders. "God. What part of being a personal attendant do you not understand?"

I stare at her in disbelief. Why is she speaking to me like this? *Hi, Gwynn, remember me? I held your hair back while you puked in college. I picked you up at the emergency room on Christmas Eve when your parents were in Cannes. I drove you to St. Louis at two in the morning when you were dating that Cardinals player. And I stalked your fiancé last week and I'm about to break into his apartment. AND THIS IS WHAT I GET FOR IT?*

She's so mean. When did Gwynn become so . . . so evil?

(Hiccup.)

Oh no. Now I'm getting worked up from all the champagne, from getting yelled at, from everything. All I can manage to say is "Mean. Just mean."

(Hiccup.)

Gwynn shakes her head. "Yes. The way you've been acting is mean. I'm glad you realize this." She crosses her arms, pouting. "So are you going to shape up?"

I nod, because I don't know what else to say or do.

"Good." She sighs. "Now let's get back to my shower. Oh—and slip a couple Ambien in Kaitlyn's drink. I'm sick of hearing her whiny voice. It'll put her right to sleep."

I nod again helplessly.

As we walk back into the party, I hear Birdie thumping her cane again and announcing that it's time to start opening gifts. I take my position as gift logger next to Mrs. Ericsson, and do my best to construct a bouquet out of bows and a pink paper plate. (I don't get why this tradition is necessary—is it for another hat? Gwynn has plenty of hats!)

When the shower is over, I help lug gift after gift out to Gwynn's Range Rover.

No *"Thank you for the beautiful $200 spoon."*

No *"Thank you for helping with my shower today."*

No *"Thank you for breaking into my fiancé's apartment."*

No nothing.

(Hiccup.)

Chapter 24

THAT NEXT FRIDAY, I meet Patrick and his friends at Gramercy and I'm really nervous. Patrick and I haven't had a chance to talk about the kiss. And . . . I don't know? He was acting so weird when he left the fashion show last week.

Ugh. My stomach feels queasy. (Thank God I stopped eating broccoli or it'd be so much worse!) I need to calm down.

I flash my ID at the bouncer and enter the ultra-trendy club. I immediately spot Patrick and a group of guys standing at the back bar. They're laughing, slapping one another's backs, and looking like they're having a grand ol' time.

Okay. Deep breath. Act cool. Like everything is completely normal. I mean, that kiss was nothing. No big deal.

My eyes meet Patrick's. I see a flicker of . . . something. A smile? A laugh? His face quickly hardens, though.

"Hi," Patrick says sharply, handing me an appletini and avoiding all eye contact.

"Um . . . thanks," I say, feeling my breath catch as Patrick's fingers brush against mine. I look up at his face and see his jaw flinching. *Is he mad at me?*

"Guys, this is Victoria—our wingwoman extraordinaire for the night." Patrick breezes through introductions. "And Victoria, these are the guys—Blake, Damon, and Frankie."

Blake seems a bit on the intellectual side—stiffly pressed polo and tasseled loafers. He looks like he belongs standing in front of a college classroom and lecturing all day. Damon seems, well, goofy. Laughing eyes. A bit of a jokester. And

Frankie? He's clearly the wild one of the bunch, with his black messy hair, tight white club shirt, and enormous grin.

"Sweet," Frankie says, shooting me a big flirty grin. "So you're a wingwoman, huh? Are you, um, seeing anyone?"

"Dude. You're not supposed to hit on *her*." Damon smacks Frankie on the back of the head, smiling apologetically to me.

"Ooof!" Frankie scratches his black messy hair. "What? Are wingwomen like . . . off-limits or something?"

"Please excuse Frankie." Blake rolls his eyes, sipping his scotch. "We don't take him out a lot."

I instantly like Patrick's friends. They remind me of Ross, Chandler, and Joey, straight off the *Friends* cast.

"No problem." I laugh, taking a sip of my appletini.

"Damn. Check out that hottie!" Frankie whistles at a Lindsay Lohan wannabe in a flowy pink dress, a chunky white belt, and a fresh Mystic Tan.

All four of their heads whip around to steal a glance.

Patrick nods at me. "You heard the man. Go work your magic."

I smile, hoping to catch Patrick's eye. But he's staring off into space, his hands jammed into the pockets of his tailored black pants. Maybe I can pull him to the side later on? Ask him what's wrong?

"I'll be back," I say, racing to catch up with the girl.

Hmm. The closer I get to the girl, the more she actually looks like Lindsay Lohan. It's remarkable!

"Excuse me," I say, tapping the girl on the shoulder. "I bet you get this a lot, but . . ."

"Back off," the girl snarls.

Whoa. I take a few steps back. "I'm sorry?"

"Back off," the girl huffs. "I'm not giving autographs tonight. Go away."

Are you kidding me? What the . . . ? That's when I see a

monstrous bodyguard in a black suit. The same bodyguard I recently saw in *City Girls* magazine. Pictured with Lindsay Lohan.

Oh my God. *No . . . it can't be?*

I take a closer look at the Mystic-tanned girl and realize that . . .

"You're Lindsay Lohan!" I shout.

"Cody, take care of this. *Now.*" Lindsay flicks her hand in my direction.

The beefy bodyguard takes a step forward.

"No need." I shrink back. "Just a . . . um . . . a misunderstanding. I'm leaving. Going away. Gone." I smile stupidly and wave.

OH. MY. GOD. I can't believe I saw Lindsay Lohan. And she just told me to back off!

I zip back over to Patrick and the boys. Frankie's eyes are wide with anticipation.

"And?" he asks eagerly, rubbing his hands together.

I shake my head. "Not going to happen. Ms. Lohan wasn't feelin' the love tonight."

"Wait. Are you saying that she . . . ?" Frankie's jaw drops.

I nod.

Frankie snatches his beer bottle and jets off toward Lindsay and her entourage. Damon and Blake race right after him.

Patrick and I laugh. But as soon as Patrick catches my eye, he stops and frowns.

"Are you okay?" I ask quietly.

Patrick ignores my question, quickly surveying the bar.

I touch his arm lightly. "Listen. Can we talk?"

Patrick jerks his hand back, his face like a sheet of ice. "I don't think we need to. You made things pretty clear a few days ago."

"What's that supposed to mean?"

"Nothing," Patrick grumbles. "Look. You're here to do a job. Can you just do it?"

"Sure," I say quietly, folding my arms across my chest and looking down at my feet. This has to be about Aiden. *It just has to be.* Everything was fine before that.

Frankie runs over, smacking Patrick on the back. "Dude. This is the best night of my fucking life. We're hanging out with Lindsay Lohan! *The girl can party.* Get the hell over here."

He dashes back without waiting for an answer.

"In a second," Patrick calls after him, stuffing his hands farther into his pant pockets.

"Patrick, is this about . . . ?"

"Her," Patrick interrupts, motioning toward a hot Latina in a gauzy white dress and gold ballet slippers. "Think you can hook me up with her?"

I look up at Patrick, searching his dark eyes. His stare is hard and angry.

"Fine," I say. If that's how it's going to be. "Fine."

And about three exhausting hours later, I've officially set up all four of my clients. Frankie is currently in heaven, making out with two Czechoslovakian models in a leather cushy booth. Every time he comes up for air he tells me either (a) he loves me or (b) I'm the best wingwoman in the entire fucking world.

Damon already went home with a hot hippie musician. Blake is sipping scotch and engaged in a heated conversation with a smart-looking Andie MacDowell type. And Patrick is still flirting it up with the gauzy white dress girl. She's been spastically throwing her head back in laughter for the past three hours. I'm seriously starting to worry about her neck. Whiplash?

Whatever. Good. Great. Looks like my job here is done. I throw my Hogan over my shoulder and strut over to Patrick.

"I'm leaving," I say. "Bye."

"Okay." Patrick's face falls briefly. "Well, thanks."

"No problem." I eye the gauzy white dress girl up and down. Her long dark silky hair is spilling over her bare back.

She really is a gorgeous girl, but she's drunk beyond belief! "It looks like you're all set."

"Guess so," he says. The girl suddenly starts pawing at Patrick's chest and making weird kissy noises.

I raise an eyebrow and smirk. "Have fun."

As I'm waiting in line for a cab home, my arms crossed tightly around my stomach, I realize tears are rolling down my cheeks and my shoulders are starting to shake. Oh God. This is so embarrassing. I angrily wipe a few tears away with my hand and try desperately to control my breath.

Why am I so upset? Patrick isn't worth crying over. I'm his wingwoman for Christ's sake. I did my job tonight. I should be happy.

But I'm not. I'm miserable.

If only I had a chance to explain. That I don't even like Aiden. That I . . . I like Patrick. Arghh!

My shoulders begin to shake uncontrollably now and the tears are in full flood mode.

And that's when I see Patrick. He's walking out of Gramercy, *alone*. I wish I could hide. My face is wet with tears. My eyes are so puffy. My nose is running and I don't have a Kleenex, so I'm sniffing loudly. Come on, line. Move! I just want to grab a cab and go home.

I put my head down, praying Patrick will walk right by. But he doesn't. When I look up, he's standing right in front of me.

Oh dear God. Could I look any more pathetic? I might as well paste a huge sign on my forehead that reads: HEY—I LIKE YOU. I'M CRAZY ABOUT YOU.

This is sooo humiliating.

"Why didn't you tell me you were seeing someone?" Patrick finally asks.

"I'm not," I snuffle. "We've gone out a couple times. That's it."

"It looked like more than that to me," Patrick says skeptically.

"Well, it's not, Mr. Nosy."

Patrick cracks a smile for the first time all night. "I *am* being nosy, aren't I?"

"So where's your girl?" I sniff.

Patrick shakes his head. "She's not exactly what I'm looking for."

Oh! I get it. Patrick only came out here because he still needs my help. *Because he still needs a wingwoman.*

"Fine," I say, wiping my eyes roughly, brushing past him and heading toward the bar entrance. "Let's go find you another girl."

Patrick grabs my arm. "That's not what I mean. I don't want another girl," he says firmly.

"What *do* you want?" I bark, feeling the anger bubbling in my chest. "Because you're really starting to confuse me."

Patrick rubs his scruffy jaw. "I'm not sure."

"You know what? I'm done. Okay? You need to call on Monday and get yourself another wingwoman, because this isn't working out. I can't . . ."

Suddenly Patrick pulls me toward him and starts kissing me furiously, his hands tangled in my hair. My entire body tingles as I let go into the kiss, into Patrick. "I want you," he murmurs between kisses. "You're what I want . . ."

"Hey—get a room!" Frankie howls, staggering out the door with a lanky model tucked under each arm.

And I don't know how long Patrick and I stand there, just kissing and laughing, but I have never felt happier in my entire life.

•

THE NEXT DAY, I sip an icy Frappuccino as I trot over to Bryan's brownstone apartment. It's warm outside, and the air smells like fresh-cut grass and barbecue. I can't stop thinking about last night. Patrick and I grabbed late-night Chinese and a bottle of chardonnay and took a cab over to Belmont Harbor. We went out on his sailboat and lazily cruised Lake Michigan, sipping wine as we cuddled, and gazed at the stars and the glittering city lights. It was incredibly romantic.

We laughed and flirted and shared stories until sunrise. He admitted how he was crazy about me ever since we first met (when I was licking my jeans before my interview—so embarrassing!). And how he was jealous when he saw me with Aiden at the fashion show. He told me all about his parents and sister in New York. How his dad owns a small ad agency called Nine Communications. And how he's pressuring Patrick to move back and take over when he retires. (What's up with everyone pressuring people to move to New York? Geesh!) Patrick feels torn. After all, he loves his job. He loves Chicago. And, well, he just met someone pretty special . . .

Me! Me! Me!

I told him all about my parents in the suburbs. How Kimmie, Julia, and I met in college. How Gwynn is driving me nuts with all her wedding lists and stalking stuff. How I decided to become a wingwoman. *Everything.* (Okay. I didn't tell him I lied about the cellulite roller. But you know . . . *almost everything.*)

Sigh. What a night.

I stare at my cell phone, debating if I should call the girls. Normally I'd want to spill something like this ASAP, but for some reason, I feel like keeping it to myself. I just don't want to spoil things. Besides, Julia is still in New York, and I don't want to disturb her and Kevin. And oh dear God . . . Kimmie would F-R-E-A-K.

Yeah. I should really wait. I mean, I don't even know what Patrick and I are yet. If we're anything at all? Maybe it was just a one-night thing for him.

What if it was more, though?

I hope so!

Suddenly I realize I'm standing in front of Bryan's brownstone. (God. I can't believe Gwynn talked me into breaking into her fiancé's apartment. This is crazy. INSANE.) I stuff my cell phone back into my Hogan and fumble around for the silver key Gwynn had made for me.

I carefully let myself inside, scanning the hallway—looking right, then left. Whew. Coast is clear. My heart thumps wildly as I hold my breath and slowly turn the key. I hear the door click as it unlocks.

I can't believe I'm doing this.

I poke my head inside Bryan's apartment, checking for any signs of life. It's silent, except for a soft wind whistling through the cracked kitchen window.

Okay. Good. It looks like Gwynn got Bryan out of the way as planned. Who knows how long I've got, though. I need to move *fast*. I tiptoe into Bryan's bedroom, quickly locating his black Tumi bag that's propped up against an oak desk. Ah-ha! I unzip the bag and quickly sift through its contents—thick manila folders, stacks of office papers, business cards, calculator, a folded-up *Chicago Tribune,* blah, blah, blah. Nothing good.

That's when my eyes land on a spread of colorful brochures sticking out from under Bryan's bed. I tiptoe over and pluck them up. Hmm. I briskly fan through the brochures. They're all honeymoon related—Tahiti, Saint-Tropez, Mykonos—but no Bali. And nothing blue! Hmm. I stuff the brochures into my Hogan so I can inspect them later. (I'll have Gwynn put them back ASAP. He'll never even notice they're missing.)

Just then, I hear a loud creaking noise.

AAACK! My heart pounds. Is someone there? I nervously scan Bryan's bedroom, checking for hiding places—under the bed? Under the desk?

I listen intently for any other creaking noises. When I don't hear a peep, I continue snooping around. I check Bryan's Black-Berry (without a password, I don't get far, though), then I move onto his mail pile, dresser drawers, dirty laundry (I know. I know. Eww!), and I find nothing. Nada. Zip. Gwynn is going to be livid. She's expecting answers. Hard evidence. *Something*.

Come on, Vic. Think. I flick on Bryan's computer, having no clue what I'm looking for.

That's when an Instant Message pops up onscreen.

```
KAITLYN: Sorry . I had to step away from the computer for
    a sec. I'll call you as soon as I get in town. Sound
    good?
```

The cursor is still blinking, just waiting for Bryan to respond. I quickly scroll down and read the full string of Instant Messages.

```
BRYAN: We need to finish this.
KAITLYN: What's the rush?
BRYAN: I think she knows.
KAITLYN: Bummer. Sorry. We should figure things out soon.
    I'm in New York for a couple weeks. After that?
BRYAN: Okay. The sooner the better. I'm starting to lose
    sleep over this. Call me.
BRYAN: Hello?
```

Uh-oh. I cringe. This is not good. Not good at all. I quickly press print. Come on, printer. Come on.

That's when I hear another creaking sound. It's even louder than before. *Is someone coming?*

Then I hear a key in the front door.

The door screeches open.

Shitty!

Ice-cold fear jets to my heart. I frantically clutch my chest. I'm dying. It's *for real* this time. Honest to God. I'm having a heart attack. I . . . I can't believe it. I'm going to keel over as an intruder. A burglar! Mom will be so disappointed.

"BRYAN!" I hear Gwynn shout. "WE SHOULD GO GRAB DELI SANDWICHES."

"Jesus, Gwynn. Why are you yelling?"

"I'M NOT YELLING."

I snatch the printout off the printer, stuff it in my pocket, and quickly scan the room.

Panic. Panicky. Panicking.

Should I hide? I eye the closet. Then what? Stay in there all night? Forget it. I have to get out of here! My eyes race around Bryan's bedroom. Think. Think. Think.

Ooh. The window?

I tiptoe over to the navy curtains and pull them back. Right as I'm unlocking the window, I hear the bedroom doorknob rattle.

Aaack! I desperately start jerking on the pane with all my might and oh . . .

Oh no. It's stuck!

I tug again.

Nothing.

"BRYAN. WHAT ARE YOU DOING?" Gwynn shrieks.

I hear something smack against the bedroom door. Her hand? Bryan's back?

I give the window one last yank and . . .

GOT IT.

"Jesus, Gwynn. Why the hell are you acting so weird?" Bryan grumbles, throwing open the door, just as I'm diving through the window.

Oof.

I do a nosedive right into the grass. Great. Just great. I'm starting to make a habit of this. I quickly scramble to my feet and start walking down the sidewalk as if everything is completely normal. As if I'm always flying out of windows. *Isn't everyone?*

Hugging my Hogan tightly, I pick up my pace. I need to get home to analyze these brochures and the hot little Instant Message string I discovered.

Gwynn is not going to be happy. Not happy at all.

Chapter 25

"TALK TO ME," Kimmie puffs as she jabs at a gray boxing bag. "Are you okay? I feel like you're keeping secrets."

We're about twenty minutes into a cardio kickboxing class at Muse Gym and my body has never felt this kind of intense pain in my life. I'm dying here. My arms are on fire. And I can barely lift my legs. Seriously. I don't know about this whole kickboxing thing . . .

I'll admit it, I was pretty jazzed about trying kickboxing at first. I mean, *hello.* I'm a single girl in the city. I need to know how to protect myself. And, well, let's be honest. People who kickbox have fantastically buff bodies. Especially arms. And it looks so cool. Don't you think? Jabbing at a boxing bag. Kicking out all your frustrations. It's so rough and tough. So empowering. So *Crouching Tiger, Hidden Dragon.*

It's been really hard, though. What the hell? And what's with all the strange grunting? It's kind of freaking me out. Can't these girls punch their boxing bags with their puffy red Everlast gloves without howling and growling? They sound like animals. Eww!

"Think we'll take a break soon?" I grumble through clenched teeth as I punch, punch, punch my bag. Sweat pours down my back. Geesh! Could this kickboxing studio be any hotter? It feels like a steam room. I think I need some water. I think I'm going to pass out.

"No talking. *Concentrate*." The kickboxing instructor gives Kimmie and me a death look. "You are a warrior. You are a fighting machine. Attack!"

Kimmie is a regular in this class, so she's been easily punching and kicking and practicing all kinds of advanced jabs, hooks, and uppercuts. (Oh my God. Who knew Kimmie was the next Rocky?!) I, on the other hand, am a first timer (I don't need to remind you that I'm a complete workout wuss), and my body isn't cooperating with these fight tactics . . . *at all*. In fact, my body is screaming hateful vulgarities at me this very second. Perhaps I should have opted for yoga? I'm more of a lover than a fighter.

"High energy, girls!" the kickboxing instructor shrieks over the pounding dance music. "Punch those enemies. Kick those bad guys. Punch. Punch. Kick. Kick."

OH. MY. GOD. I'm never going to make it through this class. Ever.

"I'm serious," Kimmie huffs, her freckled face red from all the kicking. "What's going on with you? Is there something you want to tell me?"

"No. Everything's . . . fine," I gasp, resting my boxing gloves on my knees. "Good God. Is my entire body supposed to feel like it's on fire? And my legs . . . they're practically numb!"

Kimmie flashes me a look of sympathy. "It gets better. Do you need water? Grab my bottle of Evian. Try taking deeper breaths and working through the pain."

I furrow my brow, taking a halfhearted jab and missing the boxing bag entirely. "I don't want to work through the pain. I want to take a nap," I grumble, wiping sweat off my forehead.

Kimmie giggles.

A total warrior chick with black face paint under her eyes, silky yellow boxing shorts, and a red bandanna glares at us. "Slackers," she growls.

Ah! How rude.

As we continue to punch, punch, kick, kick, my legs start to feel weak. *Really weak.* In fact, my legs are starting to shake wildly. What the hell? (Maybe I should sit down? How embarrassing, though! We're only twenty minutes into the class.) Oh screw it. I can't feel my legs. I'm dying here. I need a break. I plunk down on the floor.

Kimmie looks down at me and starts giggling. "Get up! What are you doing?" She grabs my arm with her boxing glove and yanks me up, but my legs are like jelly and I fall to my knees again.

"Girls," the boxing instructor snaps. "We're here to fight. Not relax."

"Sorry," I say, struggling to my feet. "I'm a fighter."

The boxing instructor narrows her eyes, clearly skeptical.

"No, really. Swear," I assure her, punching my boxing gloves together and running in place.

The instructor sighs, but turns away. "Fists up, everyone. Close your eyes. Imagine your biggest enemy. Picture all the things that pissed you off today. Now destroy them! Punch, punch, punch."

Thank goodness she's giving the kicking a rest. Whew.

"I just think it's weird," Kimmie yelps over the music. "You haven't been going out with us girls lately. You're never home. And, well, you're not doing anything weird or illegal, are you?"

I cough loudly, avoiding Kimmie's eyes. "You're kidding. Right?" My heart stops. I need to get Kimmie off this subject quick . . . before she gets me to spill the beans. That I'm a wingwoman. And that I've been (gasp) seeing her boss.

"Well, no," she pants, taking a swing at her bag. "I'm not kidding. I mean, at the fashion show, they were advertising wing—"

"Focus on your inner fight. Kill the demons! No chattering!" the kickboxing instructor shouts at Kimmie and me.

"Are you working on any new accounts at work?" I ask, desperately trying to distract Kimmie.

Kimmie narrows her eyes. "Why are you changing the subject? You're hiding something. Aren't you?"

"I don't know what you're talking about," I say, mentally crossing my fingers.

"Oh, you do, too!" Kimmie huffs, whacking her boxing bag. "Now tell me what's going on. I'm worried about you."

Those last words hit me right in the stomach. I don't want Kimmie to be worried. I mean, I'm fine. Great, actually. (Now that I have the Patrick thing figured out!) I wish I would have told the girls about my wingwoman job earlier.

"Look. I'm a . . ." Oh dear God. I close my eyes. I can't believe I'm about to tell her. She's going to die laughing. She's never going to let me live this down.

"I'm a wingwoman," I hiss.

"I KNEW IT!" Kimmie shrieks.

Warrior chick huffs angrily.

"Girls, please!" The kickboxing instructor stomps over to us, her fists on her hips. "If you can't focus like a fighter, you'll have to leave."

"And I'm dating your boss," I hear myself spill out, before I can stop myself.

I can't believe it. It's all out in the open! I scrunch up my face and put my boxing glove over my mouth, just waiting for the shit to hit the fan.

Kimmie's jaw drops. Her eyes are bugging out. "SHUT THE FUCK UP."

The kickboxing instructor stamps her foot furiously and points to the door. "Out. We only want fighters in this class. Not fakers!"

Warrior chick smiles smugly and continues to annihilate her punching bag.

"*I knew it.* I knew something was up with you two! You guys were acting so weird at the fashion show." Kimmie whoops, as we both pull off our puffy boxing gloves and race out of the studio. "I can't believe you're a wingwoman! *And I can't believe you're dating my boss.* The girls are going to D-I-E when they hear the news."

"Actually. Do you think we can keep this quiet?" I pull at my ear awkwardly. "You know . . . just between you and me? Patrick and I still need to talk about . . ."

"In your dreams," Kimmie roars, throwing a white towel around her neck. She clicks on her cell phone and taps in some numbers. "Julia! You're never going to believe this!"

Fabulous. Just fabulous. Leave it to Kimmie to keep a secret . . .

Chapter 26

FROM: gwynnie_pooh@girly.com
TO: victoria_hart@vongo.com
PRIORITY: *Incredibly Urgent*
SUBJECT: I did it!

I couldn't stand it any longer. I confronted Bryan about Kaitlyn last night. I told him I know all about the two of them!

Oh my God, Vic! We had a *huge* fight. He got so

pissed off. He told me to quit talking badly about
Kaitlyn and to stop being such a snoop. He said I was
ruining *everything*!

What should I do? I'm going crazy. And Mother is
driving me mad with wedding stuff. FYI: Polo is draft-
ing another list for you. I'll send it over soon.

Vic! I'm freaking out over here! What if I have to
cancel the wedding?

Help!

Gwynnie

P.S. I got a strange call from Kimmie the other day.
You're a wingwoman? Should I be worried? Let me know.

On Wednesday afternoon I meet Patrick for lunch at Le
Colonial, a trendy French-Vietnamese restaurant on Rush
Street. It's cool and dark inside. We sit upstairs in their private
enclosed patio on cushy wicker chairs, nestled between palm
trees and lush ivy.

The fan whooshes above our heads as we flirt and chat. After
our plates are taken away, Patrick clears his throat. "About Friday night."

Uh-oh. His tone sounds weird.

He's totally giving me the brush-off. I know it.

"I think we should . . ."

I can't take this. It's going to be humiliating. I . . . I have to
do something. "Absolutely," I cut him off.

He looks confused. "You think?"

"Yeah. No. Um . . . I don't know." I laugh nervously, bracing myself for the inevitable. He's going to tell me it was fun,
but it has to end. He's my client. My best friend's boss. Years
older than me! (Seven, actually.) It'll never work.

"I thought maybe we could, well . . ." He rakes his fingers
through his dark wavy hair, looking shy. "I'd like to spend
more time with you."

Ah! I'm so excited I want to scream . . . or laugh . . . or something.

Patrick looks worried. "What do you think?"

Okay. Act cool. For once.

"I'd love to," I say, managing to stay semicalm.

His face softens, and he takes my hand across the table. "That's very good news." He pulls his wicker chair around closer to mine and we kiss for a long wonderful moment. God. He's such a good kisser.

"Should we stop by my place?" I ask mischievously. "Before you go back to work?"

"Absolutely." Patrick grins, tucking a loose strand of hair behind my ear. "We might have to stay for a long while, though. If that's okay with you, of course?"

I nod happily, grabbing his hand to go.

Eeeee!

•

LATER THAT EVENING, I have a gig with Everett at Webster's Wine Bar, the same cozy place we met at a few months ago. He's sitting at one of their black-and-white-checked sidewalk tables, swirling around a glass of pinot grigio.

"Hi, Everett!" I wave as I make my way up the sidewalk.

He stands to greet me.

"Oh my God. Everett! You look *amazing,*" I squeal. "When did you get a tan?"

I carefully scan him up and down. I mean, I saw Everett a few weeks ago when we went shopping and ended up at the zoo, but he's dropped even more weight. And look! Everett even has a bit of a minihawk going on. (Marco would be so proud.) I love his outfit, too. A hip pink Ben Sherman oxford, Paper Denim & Cloth jeans, and leather sandals.

"You've been shopping, too!" I shriek.

Everett nods proudly. "And I've been on three dates since the last time I saw you. THREE."

I can't believe it. *I made Everett hot.* I'm so proud.

Everett taps his stomach. "Twenty pounds lighter and counting."

"Wow," I say, shaking my head in astonishment. "You look like an entirely different person!"

"Thanks." Everett smiles gleefully. "And you!" He gives me a quick hug. "I'm so happy. I told you I had a feeling about Patrick."

He hands me a wine list and motions for me to take a seat.

After I order a chardonnay, we scope out the scene and I notice Everett is suddenly nervous.

"So have you spotted your cowgirl?" I ask.

Everett nods a bit shyly, tilting his head toward the back bar. "Don't look."

I swivel around in my seat and take a peek.

"I SAID, DON'T LOOK!" Everett cries, hiding his flushed face behind the wine list. "Why do you always look?" he grumbles. Even his fresh tan can't hide his pink cheeks and nose.

"Sorry, sorry, sorry!" I say.

He lowers the wine list, his eyes squeezed shut. There's already a thin layer of sweat beads on his forehead. "Tell me. Is she looking?"

I slowly peer over my shoulder and eye the back bar. "No," I whisper. "You're fine."

Everett lets out a huge sigh of relief and takes a sip of his pinot grigio.

"What's wrong? I thought you were ready to ask her out." I say. "You look great. You know you do."

Everett wrinkles his stubby nose. "I thought I was, but . . . look at her. She's so pretty." He gazes back at his cowgirl. Tonight her shiny black hair is pulled back into a long ponytail. She has on a frayed white cowboy hat and sparkly red boots.

Everett wrings his hands, sweat trickling down his cheeks. "I can't ask her out. There's no way! Not yet."

"Do you want me to?" I ask.

"NO!" Everett shouts.

"Okay. Okay," I say, patting his arm lightly. "That's okay. Another time."

"Soon." Everett nods. "I promise. I thought I was ready. But I'm not . . ."

"No rush." I smile. "Like I keep telling you, you have to do what you have to do. We should at least have another drink, though," I say, shifting in my chair to look for our waiter. And just as I'm shifting my gaze back to Everett, I see . . .

Wait. Is that Bryan?

Ah! It is! And he's huddled in a dark booth with Kaitlyn and . . . *Mrs. Goldstone.*

No way. They must be up to something. I have to tell Gwynn!

"Everett. Do you mind if I make a quick call?"

As suspected, Gwynn freaks. "WHAT? I dropped Mrs. Goldstone off at the hotel after our florist appointment. And Bryan said he was working late tonight. WHAT LIARS!" Gwynn shrieks.

Everett raises an eyebrow, giving me a funny look. She's really loud.

I smile awkwardly.

"What are they doing? TELL ME EVERYTHING!" Gwynn demands.

I lean way back in my chair to get a better view, nearly toppling over. (Arghh!) And if I strain my neck . . . just enough . . . I can see Kaitlyn leaning close to Bryan, batting her eyelashes flirtatiously. Mrs. Goldstone is saying something, but I can't quite make it out?

"Hold on," I whisper to Gwynn.

Bryan looks furious. He's shaking his head. "Forget it, Mother. This discussion is over." He shoves his chair back, grabs his Tumi bag, and marches toward the door. I duck behind a wine menu and thankfully he doesn't see me. Or I don't think he does, anyway . . .

"*Bryan!*" Mrs. Goldstone calls after him. "Try to understand. I'm thinking of your future."

Kaitlyn scampers after him, her blond waves flowing behind her back. "You should listen to her," she purrs, putting a hand on his forearm.

Bryan shakes her hand away and rushes outside.

Kaitlyn puts her fists on her hips and huffs. And for one awful moment, her fiery eyes meet mine.

I scratch my neck awkwardly. "Hey."

"Oh, whatever!" Kaitlyn grumbles, stomping over to Mrs. Goldstone.

"WAS THAT HER?" Gwynn yells. "Tell her I hate her. Tell her to get her grubby hands off my fiancé!"

"It appears Mrs. Goldstone was showing her concern for Bryan's future again," I say. "By throwing Kaitlyn on top of him."

"WHAT?" Gwynn howls. "I hate that woman. I really do. How mad do you think Bryan would be—on a scale of one to ten—if I hired someone to smack the hell out of his mother? *Hmm?*"

I laugh. "I don't know. He looked pretty pissed off. He might think you're an angel."

Chapter 27

WEEKS FLY BY, and Patrick and I can't get enough of each other. We do everything together—eat, sleep, shop, you name it. We've strolled down Navy Pier to watch the fireworks. Sat in the blazing hot bleachers at Cubs games (I even saw my beer-bellied client Marty and his rosy-cheeked brunette—they both had their Mark Prior jerseys on! And they looked as happy as ever. *Yes!*). And Patrick has taken me to some of the hottest restaurants in Chicago: Japonais, L8, Rockit, mk, Carnivale. I've never eaten so well.

And not that you want to know this, but with all the amazing sex, I've actually been losing weight, instead of gaining. (Yay! Yay! Yay!) Maybe the broccoli jump-started it all, but *this* diet trick is much less painful. My thighs are finally shrinking back to normal and my dreaded pooch has almost vanished. Can you say pure bliss?

Everything is going so well. Too well, almost. Patrick is wonderful. My wingwoman gigs have been wildly successful. (Well, except for this odd gig at a bar mitzvah. Whoa. Who tries to pick up at a coming-of-age party?!) I finally set up my usher friend with his coworker at a happy hour for Chicago-area businesspeople. They were so cute together! Well, you know . . . from what I could tell. They kept throwing around weird acronyms and business jargon. (It was kind of hard to keep up, to tell you the truth.) Even Gwynn isn't driving me too insane with all her wedding stuff and outrageous stalking requests, despite the fact that it's already the end of July and

Gwynn will be walking down the aisle in almost six weeks. (Isn't that CRAZY?)

But here's something even crazier. I'll let you in on a secret, but you can't tell anyone. Okay? I think everything is so utterly fabulous, because . . .

I'm serious. You can't tell anyone.

I think I'm in love.

There. I said it. I think I love Patrick. Not that I'd tell him. Yet. But, well, I'm crazy about him. And I think he's crazy about me too. Eee!

I check my e-mail when I finally drag myself out of bed one morning. And there's a message from Gwynn . . .

FROM: gwynnie_pooh@girly.com
TO: victoria_hart@vongo.com
ATTACHMENT: dress_fitting.doc
PRIORITY: *Super-Super Urgent*
SUBJECT: Help!
Vic—hi!

I need your help. Mother is driving me crazy! She actually wants me to finally decide on a florist this week. What a nightmare. I mean, I can't make that kind of decision in one week. The pressure!

You have to help me. I need time to focus. And Polo, Pierre, and Philip are completely useless. (I don't know why we ever hired them. I swear they do nothing!) Something about nailing down a new wedding theme this week, so they need complete seclusion. I guess it's, like, really intense or something. Whatever. See the attached list. It's nothing major.

Kisses,

Gwynnie

P.S. I haven't brought up the whole Kaitlyn thing

lately. Bryan got so furious with me last time. Should I?

P.P.S. Oh yeah. I'm going ahead with the "get-fit" theme for the bridesmaids' baskets. I see your point about it coming across a bit insensitive, but I'm desperate. Angel's weight is totally out of hand! She's, like, at least 150 pounds. Can you imagine? Gross.

DRESS_FITTING.DOC

1. Call the bridesmaids about the dress fitting this Saturday. Remind them to wear a strapless bra and nylons for the proper fitting. Tell them not to eat the night before. They need to be at their absolute skinniest. Oh! And Mother thinks we should alter the dresses a couple sizes smaller, so the girls are forced to lose weight. What do you think? Good idea? Bad idea? Tell Eva she has to dye her hair back to normal, too. No hot pink! I'll murder her.

2. Order a crepe brunch at Socca's. Make sure to get me the Tuscany. It's to die for! Ooh—and remind Javier that I simply adore his lingonberry tart. See if he'll whip one up. Tell him you'll pick everything up at seven o'clock sharp. Make sure he includes silver and linens, too.

3. Set the food up at Fred Sander's studio. Maybe pick up some decorations to make it look cute and festive? His studio is on Grand and Wabash. Fifth floor. FYI: Fred is incredibly cool. One of the hottest fashion designers right now. So don't say anything stupid. Maybe try not to say anything at all.

4. Grab Starbucks for all the bridesmaids. I want a

> tall, extra hot, extra foam, double shot, half
> caf, soy, caramel macchiato with just a dab of
> whipped cream.
>
> 5. Pick up the bridesmaids and meet Mother and me
>   at Fred's studio. We'll have the bridesmaid bas-
>   kets with us. Mother is having them wrapped at
>   *Neiman's*.
>
> 6. Ooh. And bring the following items: digital cam-
>   era and video camera (make sure to get footage
>   of absolutely everything!), extra strapless bras
>   and nylons (in case the girls forget), Kleenexes
>   (I'll be a sobbing mess for sure!), aspirin,
>   hair ties . . . I feel like I'm forgetting some-
>   thing. I'll call if I think of anything else.
>   Thanks!

Has Gwynn completely lost her mind? Seriously. How am I supposed to explain this to her bridesmaids? "Um. Yeah. Gwynn thinks you're total fat asses. So don't eat. Okay? Ha-ha. Ho-ho. And she's having all your dresses altered two sizes too small to force you guys to lose weight. I know. I know. Isn't Gwynn the greatest?"

This should be fun.

I flip open my address book and dial Eva's number first, praying she's not home. Gwynn's sister might be three years younger than we are, but she's intimidating as hell. Maybe it's the hot pink hair, the body piercings . . . the drugs? Why can't Gwynn call her own relatives? Geesh!

Someone picks up. Music blares in the background.

"Hello?" someone screams over the thumping.

"Is this . . . um . . . is this Eva?" I ask, my voice shaking. She sounds pissed already. Maybe I should hang up. Pretend I never called.

"What the fuck do you want?"

Good. Great. It's Eva all right. FYI: her favorite word is *fuck*.

"Hi. This is Victoria Hart. Gwynn's friend?"

"I hate my sister's friends."

Right. So. This is going well. "I'm calling to remind you about the dress fitting Saturday."

Silence.

"Hello?" I wince, afraid of what she might bark next.

"I'm not going to a fucking dress fitting," Eva shouts. "I told Mother already. What the hell is her problem?"

"I'm sorry. Gwynn just told me to confirm . . ."

"Confirm this!" Eva shouts. The line goes dead.

Okay. So. Maybe I should talk to Eva about her pink hair some other time . . .

•

SATURDAY COMES FAST. *Too fast.* My eyes flutter open and I slowly focus on the alarm clock.

AAACK!

It's almost eight A.M.?

I'm dead. I was supposed to pick up brunch at seven o'clock sharp. I jump out of bed and throw on my orange fleece jumpsuit. I stuff my feet into my Nike Shox and stumble back across the room to give Patrick a kiss. He rolls over and mumbles something, looking so adorable. I wish I could crawl back into bed with him and . . .

No. No way. Focus, Vic. Focus.

"Bye!" I call as I run out the door.

I'm fuming as I storm down the sidewalk toward my silver VW Bug. God. What's my problem? Why am I ALWAYS running late? Maybe I really am severely time challenged or something. I wonder if it's a rare disorder that no one has discovered.

I could make millions on a cure. Right? Of course, I'd need to figure out a cure first . . .

•

I SLAM TO A STOP at a red light. Come on. Come on. I tap my fingers impatiently on the steering wheel. Gwynn is going to K-I-L-L me. I check my watch. It's almost eight-thirty. I was supposed to be at Socca's at seven!

I grab my cell phone. And after lots of fast talking (and promising Javier a big fat tip), Socca's agrees to meet me at Fred's studio on Grand and Wabash. Whew! Okay. Now I just need to stop at Starbucks.

Come on traffic. *Move.*

My cell phone rings while I'm standing in line to order everyone's coffee. It's Angel. I hit SILENCE and shove the cell phone back into my Hogan. I am so dead. Gwynn is going to be furious.

I finally make it to the register. "I'd like a . . . let's see." I root around in my bag for the coffee list, but . . .

Drats! Where is it?

I dump the contents of my bag onto the counter and rummage through all the crumpled receipts, loose change, Kleenex, notepads, red leather planner, sheer pink lip gloss, Stila compact.

It's not here.

The Starbucks barista clears her throat, looking anxiously at the long line forming behind me.

Screw it. "I'll take five tall skim mochas with extra whip." Everyone will just have to drink what I give them and like it.

I pick up Angel first on the Gold Coast. She looks pure PTA mom—head to toe. We're talking sharply pressed chinos, a cream cashmere sweater tied neatly around her heavily starched white button-down, and shiny dark hair pulled back into an antique-looking clip.

I roll my eyes as she opens the car door and sits down, properly placing her manicured fingertips on her knees.

"You're late," she says once we pull into traffic.

"Am I?" I act surprised, making my way over to Dawn's Gold Coast condo. Eva is meeting us there.

Gwynn is raging mad by the time we make it to Fred's studio. I hand her a mocha.

"Where have you been?" Gwynn demands.

"Traffic was terrible," I say, praying Angel and Dawn will keep their mouths shut.

"I wanted decorations! Where are they?" Gwynn huffs. "Why did Javier deliver the food? You were supposed to get it."

"Um. I'm not sure," I say, not meeting her eyes.

Polo, Pierre, and Philip shoot me sympathetic looks.

"Oh my God!" I hear shrieks from the front of the studio.

It's Angel, Dawn, and Eva. They're standing in front of their bridesmaid baskets with looks of sheer horror.

I quickly glance down at my feet. Don't laugh. Don't laugh.

"What do you think?" Gwynn's face lights up. "I thought we could all get fit together before my wedding! Work out together. Motivate each other. Maybe even do weekly weigh-ins together. Isn't it great?"

Angel and Dawn bite their lips. Eva looks like she's about to explode.

I *sooo* want to laugh.

"You're such a fucking bitch!" Eva finally blurts, throwing her basket on the floor. "I'm surprised you didn't get us a gift certificate for plastic surgery, too. You're sick. Do you know that? How are we even related?"

Gwynn gasps.

"Eva!" Mrs. Ericsson huffs. "Your mouth."

I briefly consider telling Eva that Muse Gym does happen to offer many plastic surgery options, but I decide to keep quiet.

"They're just gifts," Mrs. Ericsson says, turning to Angel and Dawn. "You girls can do what you like with them. Okay? So. Why don't we try the dresses on? Get to the exciting part. Shall we?"

As the girls slip into their dresses, I snap picture after picture. "Oh look!" Gwynn cries dramatically. "Look how pretty Dawn is in the dress. It's fantastic."

I nod. "Fantastic."

The truth is, the lavender dresses are horrific. I guess the wedding theme Polo, Pierre, and Philip finally landed on is Cinderella. So Fred designed the bridesmaid dresses to look like peasant dresses. They're ripped, frayed, stained, and just plain dirty-looking.

"I went for the whole evil stepsister look," Fred says, taking a swig from his highball glass. He looks terribly bored. "I picture messy hair, bare feet . . ."

"Wonderful," Mrs. Ericsson gushes. "Amazing work."

"Yeah. So. If you ladies don't mind, I need to fly. I've got a jet to Milan waiting. Big show next week."

"Absolutely," Mrs. Ericsson coos. "And thank you so much! Your work is . . ."

"Mother, get in the picture!" Gwynn yells. "Vic, don't miss this shot." I continue to snap away.

After a dozen more pictures, Gwynn spins around to face me. "Your turn."

"I'm sorry?"

"Your dress. You need to try it on," she says, handing me a long purple flowy number on a hanger.

I have a bad feeling about this.

As I slip the yards and yards of fabric over my head, I catch my first glimpse in the mirror.

Oh no.

"As personal attendant, your dress is incredibly special," Mrs. Ericsson explains. "You need to be comfortable. You need room to breathe. You need lots of pockets to stash bobby pins, Kleenexes, and lip gloss. And a hood to hide your earpiece, naturally."

"Earpiece?"

"Absolutely. You need to be in communication with Polo, Pierre, and Philip at all times," Mrs. Ericsson says.

I turn around to see my full reflection in the mirror.

Oh dear God. What am I wearing? A cape?

"Fred said this look was inspired by Cinderella's fairy godmother!" Mrs. Ericsson explains.

Right.

Gwynn pulls the hood over my head and ties the pink ribbon under my chin into an obnoxiously large bow. "There. Perfect."

"*Oui! Oui!* You look so cute," Polo, Pierre, and Philip cheer wildly.

I shoot them an evil stare. They pipe down immediately.

"What do you think?" Gwynn beams excitedly.

Arghh. If I tell her the truth—that I hate it—I'll forever be the bad guy. The girl that popped Gwynn's bridal bubble of bliss, well, even more than Eva did.

I glance over at Angel and Dawn. They grin evilly, clearly loving every minute of this.

"It's really . . . *something,*" I say at last, swooping the yards of purple material around my ankles. I swear, I have at least ten pounds of fabric hanging from my body.

"I knew you'd love it!" Gwynn squeals, clapping her hands excitedly.

This is a nightmare. I could pass for a Buddhist monk.

•

THAT EVENING, Kimmie and I go to the Funky Buddha Lounge—an über-trendy Moroccan bar in the West Loop—to meet my new client, Joe Maloney. Kimmie wouldn't stop begging to come along and watch me in full wingwoman action, so I finally gave in.

"Please, please, puh-lease," she pleaded, flopping onto her knees and tugging at my shirttail. "I'll be good. Promise! Just let me tag along."

"Fine," I finally grumbled. "I surrender. But you can only stay for a bit. And you can't say a word!" I told her firmly.

So here we are, five minutes early, perched on leopard-print benches and already sipping deliciously sweet mangotinis.

"This is so great!" Kimmie hoots. "So . . . tell me. Do you use cheesy pickup lines? Like . . . is it hot in here, or is it just *you?*"

I roll my eyes. "No! *I'm* not the one who's trying to take the girl home. Remember?"

"Yeah. Yeah. Yeah. How about . . . I'm new in town, could you give me directions to your apartment?"

"KIMMIE!" I wail.

"Ever played leapfrog naked?"

"Oh my God. What's wrong with you?" I giggle. "You're disgusting!"

"I know." Kimmie grins happily, slurping her frosty mangotini.

We sit in silence for a few minutes, just checking out the Funky Buddha Lounge's cool jazzy vibe and grooving to the wild African beats. There are gold-tasseled Moroccan rugs hanging from the walls, antique chandeliers dangling above, and this weird black netting sweeping dramatically down around the bar and the swanky corner booths.

"Eww. What if that's Joe?" Kimmie suddenly points to a Fabio-ish guy with flowing straw-yellow hair, hulky muscles, and orange leathery skin. He's squeezed into zebra-print pants and a shiny red muscle shirt.

I snicker, watching as Fabio carefully maneuvers toward the bar . . . toward us.

Uh-oh. He's scanning the crowd, obviously looking for someone. He catches my eye, tilts his head, and mouths—Vic-to-ria?

Gulp.

"It's Joe," I say through clenched teeth.

Kimmie jabs me in the ribs. "*Shut up.* What should we do? Should we run?"

That's when I remember the handbook:

Stay positive.

Never react poorly (e.g., laugh, cry, hide, run away, or pretend to be someone else) if your client is not attractive. Get over it. Your job is to find him a woman. So think of it as a challenge and get creative.

"Order us another drink—now!" I hiss.

Joe pushes his straw hair off his shoulders and waves. "Hi there!" he says. "Great to meet you!"

Oh my God . . . does he have *eyeliner* on? This is going to be a long, long night.

"Same," I say, nodding painfully. "This is my friend Kimmie."

"Awesome," Joe says, giving us a geeky thumbs-up. "Two wingwomen for the price of one. I love a bargain!"

Kimmie and I stare at each other, then burst out laughing. "Anything for our clients," I say.

After brief introductions, we find out that Joe is a professional bodybuilder, an aspiring actor (he was *almost* the butt double for Jack Black!), and currently a Hanes underwear model.

"Do you recognize me?" Joe asks, turning his head to the right, looking extremely serious.

Kimmie and I shake our heads.

Joe looks hurt, but quickly recovers. "Wanna see pictures?"

"Um . . . sure?" I shrug, shooting Kimmie a helpless look.

Joe pulls out his black Kenneth Cole wallet and starts flipping through pictures:

Joe—dripping wet, draped in nothing but a towel. (Ewwwww!)

Joe—pouting, unzipping his Levi's.

Joe—wearing cheesy overalls, no shirt, a hand raking through his locks.

Joe—lounging on a bearskin rug, nothing on but a black leather thong and a tool belt. (*OH. MY. GOD.* Is Joe secretly a porn star?)

"You ladies are going to have an easy job tonight." Joe winks. "I'm a chick magnet."

Kimmie snorts.

I shake my head in awe. This guy is unbelievable.

Two hours later, the three of us are, well, smashed. Kimmie is howling bad pickup lines to every woman in our immediate vicinity. And Joe and I are too drunk to even stop her anymore.

"Hey you!" Kimmie shouts at a preppy brunette in a lime plaid dress with a white sweater draped around her shoulders. "Can he be your lo-o-ove slave tonight? Hmm?"

The preppy girl narrows her eyes and stamps off.

Joe and I are screaming with laughter.

"Excuse me?" Kimmie pokes a gorgeous black woman in the arm. "I love your skirt! But . . . it'd look a hell of a lot better on his floor."

The woman laughs and turns back to her cluster of friends.

A little while later, Joe actually passes out at the bar. The bartender politely asks us to leave. And when we "not so politely" ignore his request, the bouncers basically throw us out of the Funky Buddha Lounge by the napes of our necks.

Oopsie.

I wonder if Chicago Wingwoman could find out about something like this? I'm sure getting a client kicked out of a bar isn't exactly good form. I should probably call Joe tomorrow and apologize for getting a bit sidetracked. I got him a couple phone numbers from some hotties earlier in the evening, but still . . .

Kimmie and I end up stuffing Joe into a cab, linking arms, and stumbling down the block.

"Pretty cool job." Kimmie lets out a huge yawn. "Think you'll keep it?"

Good question. I don't know. The job pays well, that's for sure. "I'll probably keep it until something better comes along," I say at last.

"Like a call girl? A madame? Or how about . . . a hooker?" She winks.

"KIMMIE." I thwack her on the shoulder.

She shrinks back, laughing. "Kidding! But seriously . . . don't you think you should find something more serious? You *are* turning twenty-five next week."

"Don't remind me," I grumble.

Chapter 28

FROM: gwynnie_pooh@girly.com
TO: victoria_hart@vongo.com
ATTACHMENT: bachelorette_party.doc
PRIORITY: *Super-Ultra Urgent*

SUBJECT: My last night as a free woman!

Vic—hi!

Real quick. Polo, Pierre, and Philip came up with the most brilliant ideas for my bachelorette party. I know it's still a few weeks off, but I guess there's no such thing as planning too early. Right? Can you believe I'm getting married in a month? So exciting! See the attached.

Kisses,

Gwynnie

P.S. How do you think my "get-fit" baskets went over? Good? Bad? Eva was completely rude—of course! God. She's a brat. I really regret asking her to be my maid of honor. I never should have listened to Mother.

P.P.S. Kaitlyn is back in New York for the next few weeks, so she won't be at my bachelorette party. SO HAPPY. Ding-dong, the witch is gone.

—

BACHELORETTE_PARTY.DOC

Hello, little honey bunny!

Hope things are well with you. Here are a few ideas for Gwynnie's bachelorette party. Let us know if you have questions. We'll be in and out for the next few weeks—shopping in Paris for *très* unique wedding décor. *Merci, merci!* Toodles.

XOXO,

Polo

1. We're picturing lavender since this is Gwynnie's wedding color. So do make sure all your fabulous decorations—flowers, balloons, banners, linens, china, candles, cups, twinkly lights, whatever else you think of—are lavender (not purple, plum, lilac, or grape!). It must match the exact

shade of lavender we're using as her wedding
color. No substitutes, honey bunny. I can send a
color chip if you'd like.

2. We're thinking your apartment is the most suit-
able place for the prebachelorette party festiv-
ities. It's in the most convenient location for
all guests. And, well, let's be honest, it'll go
best with lavender. We don't want to clash, now
do we?

3. Take down all pictures of yourself before the
party. Gwynn really wants the focus to be on her
that night. I'll send over some framed shots of
Bryan and Gwynn, and maybe you could hang those
on your walls instead? There's the cutest poster-
size shot of them hugging at the top of the Mat-
terhorn. I'll send over a bunch and you can pick.

4. Don't forget party favors! Give something
simple, but truly exquisite. After all, Bachelorette Jen Schefft and Swedish princess Victoria might be there. (Eee! Can you imagine?
Royalty!) I saw some crystal bracelets at Barneys the other day. They're made by that hot
Chicago artist, Kelsa Keller. You *must* check
them out. They're, like, the It item in Hollywood this summer.

5. Kaitlyn will not be attending the bachelorette
party. Please ask all guests to refrain from
mentioning her name, Red Envy, or New York in
general. Gwynn reacts very poorly to any associ-
ation to Kaitlyn Kingsley. In fact, if you could
ensure no K words are used at the party that
would be great. (She's still using her therapist's "pretend" method to reduce stress. But
yes, I agree with you . . . it's not working.)

6. Maybe you could whip up some elegant appetizers
   before you girls have dinner at Charlie Trotter's? FYI: I made a reservation for sixty-five
   guests. Charlie is shutting down his restaurant
   especially for you girls that night. Clap. Clap.
   Very exciting!

How depressing. I'm turning twenty-five today. No matter how many appletinis I slurp down, I simply can't shake the fact that I'm actually turning twenty-five! It's the year adulthood *supposedly* begins—and the fun ends. Gone are the days of immaturity. *Poof.* Gone are the days of borrowing money from Mom and Dad. *Poof-poof.* Gone are the days of getting wasted on a work night and calling in sick the next day (assuming I get a desk job again someday). *POOF.*

Nope. Being twenty-five means acting smart. Acting mature. Acting like I have it all together. Being on time for once in my life. (I know! Me? Mature? On time? What a joke.) I can't believe it. When I was younger, being twenty-five sounded so old, so far away. I remember thinking, I'll never be *that old*. People that old actually get up in the morning and eat toast and bagels in their smart white robes. They leisurely sip coffee, flip through the *Wall Street Journal,* and watch the *Today Show* before zipping off to their meaningful jobs. I mean, these people have mortgages, families, real careers.

But I am that old. And I don't have any of these things. I can barely pay my credit card minimum thanks to this new wingwoman job and Gwynn's wedding! I can hardly drag myself out of bed in the morning. And puh-lease, I'm about as close to having a family as I am to morphing into a man-eating alien.

Suddenly a wave of emptiness hits me. Is something wrong with me? Why am I so behind? Maybe Kimmie's right. Maybe

I should find a job that's a bit more serious . . . now that I'm *twenty-five*.

"Cheer up," Patrick says, tugging lightly on my ponytail. "Being twenty-five isn't so bad."

"Sure. Easy for you to say, Mr. I'm Thirty-Two!" I pout. "You've had seven years to get used to it."

"Woo." Kimmie lets out a low whistle. "Thirty-two. Huh? Looks like you only have a few good years left."

"True." Patrick laughs, holding up his beer in defeat. "I'm an old goat. I can take it. But being old has its benefits, too. We old fogies know what to do when we're feeling down and out. We drink."

"Oh yeah?" I challenge. "Well, we twenty-five-year-olds know how to put 'em down, too."

Patrick raises an eyebrow playfully. "Is that a dare?"

"Hey, you heard the birthday girl!" Kimmie cries. "What are you waiting for, boss? Grab us some drinks. Or wait, do you need me to grab your cane?"

Patrick laughs as he slides out of the booth at John Barleycorn and makes his way to the bar.

I glance around the table and smile. It's so great having everyone out together. (Well, almost everyone. Gwynn and Bryan couldn't make it. They auditioned musicians all day for their wedding orchestra and claim to be way too exhausted.) Kimmie and DJ look so in love. Although I hardly know DJ, he clearly adores Kimmie (and that gets my vote). And Julia appears absolutely elated to have Kevin in town. Tonight they seem completely in sync. Kevin keeps leaning over to kiss Julia on the cheek, and Julia is, well, glowing.

Hey, wait a minute.

Glowing is highly suspicious.

My eyes shoot down to her ring finger. That's the last thing I need. Another person engaged.

And to my delight . . . it's bare. Whew.

Bring on the drinks!

And after a few appletinis, I've almost forgotten about the whole depressing turning twenty-five thing and getting old. Yep. My birthday night is turning out just brilliantly.

Until . . .

"We have an announcement to make." Julia's face lights up. Kevin takes her hand.

I knew it. They're engaged!

"NO!" I suddenly blurt. Oops. Did I just say that out loud?

Kimmie crinkles her forehead and shoots me a worried glance.

Julia takes one look at the two of us and bursts out laughing. "Don't look so scared! It's a good thing!"

Oh thank God. I let out a huge sigh of relief.

"I'm moving to New York," Julia says at last.

"What?" Kimmie bellows.

"Why?" I cry. "What about law school? You can't quit!"

"I got my transfer approved today. I'll attend Columbia in the fall. That way Kevin and I can live together."

"And you guys can visit anytime!" Kevin adds. I watch as he leans over and kisses Julia's forehead. They look so in love. I mean, honestly, how can you not be happy for them?

"Why can't Kevin move to Chicago?" I blurt. Oops. I didn't mean for that to come out. Swear. I meant to say something more like . . . um . . . congratulations.

"I'm sure it's not that easy with Kevin's job," Patrick says quickly.

"I know. I understand. It's great," I peep. "Really." I rest my chin in my palms and try my best to look happy.

But my mind is racing. Is it possible to go through a midlife crisis in your twenties? (Hmm. Now that I think about it, it is possible. Very possible! Oprah was talking about it the other day. She called it the quarter-life crisis.) But surely I'm not . . .

Well, I have been feeling a tad lost lately.

I mean, first people started getting engaged. Now they're moving away? I hate getting old. I hate New York. The single-tinis are totally falling apart . . .

Geesh! Maybe I *am* going through a quarter-life crisis?

"Congratulations," DJ says, adjusting his blue-and-white Cubs baseball cap. "Should I go grab us another round to celebrate?"

"Sure," Kimmie says halfheartedly.

Patrick wraps his arm around me and squeezes my shoulders. "Yes. Congratulations you two," he says. "New York is an amazing city. My dad has been trying to get me to move back for years."

But Chicago is a great city, too! I feel like it's suddenly New York against Chicago these days. And Chicago is taking a total beating.

"We're going to miss you!" Kimmie sniffs, leaning over and giving Julia a big hug.

Kevin clears his throat. "We have one more announcement." Kevin smiles proudly.

Oh no . . . what's going on?

Julia takes a deep breath.

Her dark eyes are sparkling.

Her rosy cheeks are beaming.

"I'm pregnant," she whispers.

OH. MY. GOD.

L e o

Beware: your budget is on the verge of bursting. Curb your urge to splurge, big spender, or you'll be in the red fast. Think you're head over heels in love, little singletini? Watch out and use your head. Rocky roads ahead.

YOUR WEEK AT A GLANCE

STRENGTHS: Illegal parking
WEAKNESSES: Wedding dresses
CONQUESTS: Uh-oh . . .
TO DO: Breathe. Life is moving fast—whether you want it to or not. Enjoy the ride. And remember, not all change is bad.

(Ooh! That's right. I forgot to tell Polo to write me another check!)

Did Fashionista Bride Hire a Spy?

By Jay Schmidt

Bryan Goldstone filed a police report this week. Apparently several confidential brochures and a spare key were stolen from his apartment on Chestnut Street. It's rumored fiancée Gwynn Ericsson may be the culprit. Sources say she's wildly jealous of Kaitlyn Kingsley, so she hired a top-secret detective to investigate. "Lies. It's all lies!" Ericsson refutes. "I trust my fiancé completely. I'd never spy on him. What kind of person does that sort of thing?"

Chapter 29

RIGHT. SO. I'd be lying if I told you I handled the baby news brilliantly. But I think I did okay. I mean, I only flipped out a teensy-weensy bit. Hardly at all. In fact, the more I think about, I'm just positive no one even noticed. I mean, crying hysterically is completely natural. Right? They were just tears of joy. Oh my God. And like I meant to faint. It can happen to anyone! It's not my fault it happened . . . *twice*.

Oh, whatever. I called Julia a million times to apologize, and I promised to take her shopping at Baby Gap just as soon as all of Gwynnie's wedding stuff wraps up. Picking out baby clothes should be fun. Don't you think?

Mmm. Who am I kidding? I'm not ready for this sort of news. I'm just now getting used to Gwynn being engaged. And, well, I'm sure this means Julia and Kevin will be walking down the aisle soon, too.

Oh God. We really are growing up. I have a friend who's pregnant? Crazy! (Ooh. Wait a sec. I wonder if I'll get to be godmother. Now that's exciting! Godmother is a very, *veee-erry* high-ranking position.)

Okay. Stop. This is a child we're talking about.

Aaack! Can you believe I just said that? I know someone with a C-H-I-L-D. A baby. A . . . a . . . I think I'm going to get sick. (Is it possible to experience morning sickness *for* your pregnant friend?)

BEFORE I KNOW IT, it's the day of Gwynn's bachelorette party. I know. I know. I can't believe how fast this summer is flying! Gwynn will be walking down the aisle in less than a month—and my suspicions about Bryan are stronger than ever. Get this . . . I saw him strutting out of the Chicago Wing-woman office the other day. (I know. HE IS SO BUSTED.) I drilled Kate about it, but she wouldn't peep. She kept feeding me a bunch of client confidentiality junk. And . . .

Oh God. What am I doing? Focus, Vic. Focus. Gwynn will be at my apartment tonight at six o'clock on the dot and I seriously need to get snapping. I haven't done a thing for her bachelorette party. I still need to figure out which appetizers I'm making, what decorations I'm putting up, basically every-thing.

I'm so dead.

My cell phone rings. It's Polo.

"Hello?"

"Victoria! Hi! How's my little sweet pea?"

"Good. Great. Um . . . just finishing up some last-minute things for Gwynn's party," I lie.

Aaack! Polo knows. He totally knows that I'm not prepared for the party tonight. God. He's good. *Really good.* Does he have ESP?

"Fabulous, honey. Fabulous. When should I drop by?" he clucks.

Stop by?

Panic. Panicky. "No!" I shout. "I mean, no. No you really don't need to stop by. I have it all under control."

"Don't be silly. I'll help arrange the flowers, balloons, hang pictures. You *did* get the boxes I sent you, *non*? I shipped them FedEx—I know it's your favorite. Right, honey bunny?"

I eye the mound of FedEx boxes flooding my hallway, won-dering how the hell I'll ever find enough wall space to actually hang everything. "Oh yes. I got them all right."

"Wonderful! We'll drop by at five to make sure everything is perfection. Sound good? Great. Toodles!" Click.

"But . . . I . . ."

Drats! I check my watch. It's almost noon. I only have six hours to pull this party together. (Should I call Mom? Maybe she could help? No. No. I can handle this. Right?) I grab a notepad from the kitchen counter and start furiously scribbling down my plan of action. Time to get going.

First on the list:

1. *Buy crystal bracelets at Barneys.*

I throw my car into park right in front the Barneys entrance, ignoring the NO PARKING ANYTIME sign. No big deal. This'll only take a sec.

I shove my way through the glass doors and march straight to the jewelry section. The jewelry counter lady turns around and it's none other than the Nicole Kidman look-alike lady. Good. I like her. She recognizes me immediately and smiles.

Quick. All business. I have to move fast. "Do you have bracelets by Kelsa Keller?"

"We do," Nicole says, reaching into the display case and pulling out a black velvet tray of bracelets. She slides the tray onto the glass counter between us. "Very popular pieces."

My eyes scan over all the glittery crystals. Hmm. Now which bracelet can I honestly see a real-life princess wearing? (I still can't believe Gwynn actually knows a Swedish princess. You have to admit, it's beyond insane. *How do you even meet royalty?* MENTAL NOTE: ASK GWYNN HOW SHE MET PRINCESS VICTORIA.)

"Ooh. This one is cute!" I finger a crystal bracelet with tiny lavender hearts dangling from a sterling silver clasp. The right color. Perfect.

"It's my favorite, too," Nicole says.

"I don't suppose you have sixty-five of them?"

Nicole pulls a face. "I'll have to check."

As Nicole searches the back room, I tap my nails nervously on the glass counter, glancing at my car parked just outside. If Nicole doesn't hurry it up, I swear I'm going to get stuck with a stupid ticket.

Nicole returns from the back room. "We have sixty. Will that do?"

I scratch my head, glancing back at my car again. "I guess so. Sure. Can you gift wrap them, too? Quickly?"

"Absolutely," she says ringing up the bracelets. "Your total is $3,500. Will that be cash or credit?"

Whaaat? I feel myself breaking a sweat.

"I'm sorry. How much did you say?"

"$3,500," Nicole says, smiling politely.

Gasp.

I quickly do the math in my head. I guess that means they're about $50 a piece. That's reasonable for a bracelet. Right? I mean, a real princess *is* going to be wearing one. I take a deep breath and hand over my Visa.

I really need to tell Polo to write me another check. I keep forgetting . . . and I've been picking up all this crazy expensive stuff for Gwynn. Italian hand-beaded veil: $3,200. Swarovski and pearl tiara: $850. Bryan's custom platinum wedding band: $5,000. (Yikes! Come to think of it, I still need to give that to Gwynn.) My balance must be close to $10,000 or more at this point.

Nicole looks up from the register, her face crinkled. "I'm sorry, ma'am. Your card got denied."

My cheeks flush madly. *How embarrassing.* I knew it would happen sometime.

"Can you try again?" I whisper.

"I did. Twice." Nicole looks worried. "Can I try a different card?"

I don't *have* another card.

Aaack! What am I going to do? Think, Vic. Think. *I have to have these bracelets.* Oh dear God. How am I going to buy decorations? And pay for dinner at Charlie Trotter's? Should I call Polo? Have him cut me a check this instant? No. No. He'd murder me. I already told him I had everything under control. I can't admit that I don't. Can I?

"Isn't there something we can do?" I hear myself ask. Oh great. I sound like I'm prostituting myself out for sixty bracelets. This is a real low point for me. Even worse than the time I bribed the makeup lady.

"You could sign up for a Barneys card," Nicole says helpfully.

Yes! A Barneys card. Brilliant idea. Fucking brilliant! I'm so elated I could hop across the glass counter and hug my dear, dear friend Nicole.

"That would be great!" I squeak.

Nicole pulls out a credit card application from under the cash register and hands me a slick black Mont Blanc pen. "If you'd just fill this out."

Suddenly I remember my car. I whip around to see two parking attendants leaning down over the back wheel, holding something big and yellow.

What are they doing? What is that yellow . . . ? Oh no. Not the BOOT! I drop the pen on the floor.

"No, wait!" I shout, breaking into a full sprint. "Don't give me the boot! I'm right here." I fly through the doors and practically leap onto my silver VW Bug.

The two attendants stare at me like I'm completely mad.

"Is this your car, ma'am?" asks the gray-haired attendant with a beer belly, coughing and adjusting himself in his blue-uniform pants. The younger one is still crouched down around the back wheel.

"Yes! Yes, it is," I pant.

He points to the NO PARKING ANYTIME sign. "You can't park here, ma'am."

"I . . . I had no idea," I say. "I'll move it. I'll drive it away right now."

"Sorry, young lady. We have to follow procedure. Joe, attach the boot."

"No, wait. Please don't give me the boot! Shouldn't I just get a ticket or something? I don't understand!" I grab the younger attendant's arm frantically and . . . hey . . . wait a minute! It's Joe. Joe Maloney! My Fabio-ish client. The professional bodybuilder, aspiring actor, Hanes underwear model, almost-a-butt-double for Jack Black, and self-proclaimed "chick magnet." And he's a parking attendant, too? Wow. This guy gets around.

"JOE!" I shriek. "It's me, Victoria. Your wing—"

"Hi!" he cuts me off, his cheeks flushed, obviously not wanting his coworker to know about our gig.

"Can't you do something?" I beg Joe.

He shakes his head. "Sorry, I . . ."

"Look, lady," the older attendant says, peering over thick reading glasses. "You've got over $450 in outstanding parking tickets. Did you know that? That's a serious crime here in Chicago. Be happy we're not towing you and consider this a favor."

This can't be happening. I look helplessly from one parking attendant to the other. "I . . . I don't know what to do. I really need my car today."

"Well, we really need you to pay your parking tickets," the older attendant snorts.

"Can't we do her a favor?" Joe asks his beer-bellied coworker.

"Forget it," the older attendant says, shoving his glasses on top of his sweaty bald head. "We need $150 to take this here boot off your wheel. I don't give out favors. Only fines, sweetheart."

Joe looks worried. "Do you have that kinda cash on you?"

"No," I say. Ooh . . . but wait. "Can you guys hold on a sec? I'll get you the money."

"Look, lady, you've got five minutes," the older attendant barks. "Then we're outta here."

I sprint back into Barneys and up to the jewelry counter. "I'm ready to fill out the application."

Nicole eyes me questioningly but hands me a pen.

"So do these cards have cash advances?" I ask, not looking her in the eye.

"They do," she says hesitantly. "How much would you like?"

I hold my breath and do the math for today's purchases in my head. Let's see: $150 for the parking ticket, $200 on decorations, $100 on flowers, $100 for appetizer groceries, $300 on wine and champagne, and I'll talk to Polo about him charging the Charlie Trotter's dinner. (There's no way I can cover that!)

Gulp.

"$1,000 should do it," I say.

•

A FEW HOURS LATER, I'm standing in line at Party Co. on Halsted with lavender everything in my cart. Here's the problem. A lot of it doesn't *exactly* match. Okay. Fine. None of it matches.

I really tried, though. Swear. But no matter how hard I looked I couldn't find anything to match Gwynn's stupid lavender color chip. The candles are closer to plum than lavender. The balloons are dark grape. (In fact, they kind of look black in the bag.) The string of lights are hot pinkish purple. And the plastic cups and plates are light pink. I don't know what else to do? My only smidgen of hope is that Gwynn gets so drunk she doesn't notice.

I check the time. It's three o'clock! Polo is coming over at five. I still have to pick up flowers, make the appetizers, put up decorations, hang pictures, *everything* . . .

I finally make it home and it's nearly four. I'm doomed! I dump all the bags in the middle of the living room and begin tearing off wrappers and price tags.

Right then, my phone rings. It's Patrick.

"Hello?" I say, tucking the phone between my ear and shoulder. I grab a bunch of groceries and head for the kitchen.

"Hi there. How's the preparty? Are you girls getting crazy over there?"

"Very funny. I can't talk. I'm totally running late."

"Imagine that," Patrick teases. "I'll let you go. But real quick. Did I leave my wallet over there?"

"Yeah. I think I saw it this morning. I'll check and call you back. Okay?"

"Sounds good. Have fun tonight. Go crazy."

"Oh yeah. You know me. The wild girl." I giggle.

"That's what I like about you."

I click the phone off and start stuffing groceries into the fridge. I don't have time to make the goat cheese tarts, or the crisp apricot Brie, or the spicy Thai rolls, or the . . .

What am I going to do?

Why didn't I plan this better? My God. I'm twenty-five. I'm an *adult*. I should at least be able to plan a party. Polo is going to kill me. No wait, Gwynn is going to kill me!

All right. So. I don't have time to make food. I need to order something *now*. I flip open the phone book and scan entry after entry. Who's elegant? Um . . . and cheap?

I . . . I don't know. I've never ordered food for sixty-five people in my life. I quickly settle on Romo. Their prices aren't listed, but how bad can it be?

So the food is taken care of, now on to decorations. I still need to get ready, though. Okay. Shower first, then decorations.

Forty minutes later, all the candles are lit, the balloons are inflated, and I'm carefully balancing one foot on the back of the couch and the other on the radiator, trying my best to string up hot pink lights.

I jump down and view my work. In less than an hour, I've transformed my living room into a rainbow of purple. There are splashes of lavender, lilac, plum, pink, fuchsia, and grape everywhere. It looks good . . . *kind of.*

Okay. Fine. It's pretty bad. But maybe if I dim the lights no one will notice?

Now all I need to do is set out the wine and champagne, pay for the takeout when it arrives, and get dressed. Polo, Pierre, and Philip can fuss with hanging all the photos.

Right then, the doorbell rings. I press the intercom. "Hello?"

"It's us, honey bun!" Polo trills. "Let us in."

I fling open the door and wait for them to climb the stairs to my apartment.

"Sweetheart, you look dreadful!" Polo gasps, flicking his hand over his chest. "Are you sick?"

"It's good to see you, too," I snap. "I just need to get ready."

Pierre and Philip file in behind Polo. Pierre stops and checks his reflection in the hall mirror, smoothing back his silver tufts of hair. Philip pushes up his Dior sunglasses and flutters into the living room.

"Oh dear God!" Philip shrieks, cupping his hands around his cheeks. "What did you do? *Non, non, non!*"

My stomach knots up. I close my eyes. I guess it's worse than I thought . . .

•

GWYNN BUZZES MY APARTMENT at precisely six o'clock. Gwynn is always punctual. It's one thing I truly dislike about her. I scan my apartment one last time before I open the door.

It's flawless. Sheer perfection. I don't know how Polo, Pierre, and Philip did it. But my place looks amazing. They worked pure magic in the last hour. I'm in awe.

Basically they took down everything I put up—the hideous hot-pink lights, the unfortunate black balloons, the streamers, the banners, all of it. They left the dark plum candles, but arranged them in elegant clusters around the room.

They artfully hung black-and-white photos all over my walls: Gwynn and Bryan hugging; Gwynn and Bryan kissing; Gwynn and Bryan skiing; Gwynn and Bryan skydiving; Gwynn and Bryan doing every godforsaken thing you can imagine. And of course, they're both smiling flawlessly in every shot, their hair blowing all sexy and model-like.

Okay. I think my place is ready. I look in the hall mirror, fluff my hair, pucker my sheer pink lips, and then swing open the door.

"Hiii!" I say, giving Gwynn a quick hug. "You look *amazing*. Wow. I love your satin shoes. Are those Valentino?"

"Of course," Gwynn says.

"Princess!" Polo scampers over to Gwynn. He blows kisses all around her. "You're breathtaking. I can't even touch you, *ma belle.*"

"Oui, oui." Pierre and Philip bow and curtsy playfully.

"Don't stop!" Gwynn shrieks with laughter. "I just adore these three, don't you?" Gwynn gushes, her eyes already busily scanning my apartment.

I watch as she takes it all in. The candles. The photos. The immaculately wrapped gifts from Barneys. The sparkling wine and champagne glasses (Polo had them emergency shipped over from Georg Jensen). The freshly starched linen tablecloths and napkins just waiting for the steaming hot appetizers to arrive. She pauses. She looks confused.

"Where are the hors d'oeuvres?"

"They're coming," I say, smiling assuredly. *Arghh!*

"I hope they arrive soon." Gwynn's brow wrinkles. "Guests will be arriving any minute."

"Don't fret, honey bunny. Worrying gives you wrinkles. And we don't want that, now do we, princess?" Polo takes Gwynn's hand and escorts her over to the couch. "Let's sit down now. Philip? Will you pour Gwynnie-pooh some champagne? Hmm?"

Philip zips over with a bottle of champagne as Pierre parades into the living room with a giant pink penis sculpture. Pierre gently places the penis in the middle of the living room and smoothes back his tufts of hair. "The finishing touch. *Non?*"

I eye Gwynn worriedly. She isn't exactly a penis-statue kind of girl, but to my surprise she shrieks with delight. "That's fantastic! How perfect."

"I thought so." Pierre nods, wiping his delicate hands with a white handkerchief. "I commissioned a sculpturist from Italy. It just arrived today. Polo and Philip thought it was a bad idea, but I said . . . *non, non, non!* What's a bachelorette party without a big penis?"

"We had these made, too." Philip smiles bashfully, his blue eyes sparkling. He pulls out a pair of dangly platinum penis earrings. "Designed by Kelsa Keller. Just for you! *The only pair.*" He cups his hands over his mouth and squeals. "Aren't they fabulous?"

"I LOVE THEM!" Gwynn cries, snapping them out of Philip's fingers.

That's when the doorbell rings and my stomach leaps. Please let it be the food. Pretty-pretty please? They promised they'd deliver at six. It's ten minutes after. I grab my wallet and swing open the door.

YES. It's the delivery guy.

He's holding two huge blue plastic bins of food. "Where do you want these?"

"In the kitchen," I say, stepping out of his way.

He carefully sets down the bins, reaching into his back pocket and pulling out a receipt. "Here," he says, handing me the receipt. "I'll be right back. There's more downstairs."

"Okay," I say, looking down at the enormous blue bins. "Thanks."

Good God. This is a lot of food. But then again, it's appetizers for sixty-five people. I look down at the receipt and . . .

Holy mama! $750?!

How? I nervously scan the itemized list:

6 orders of Crisp Artichokes: $140
4 orders of Foie Gras: $95
6 orders of East Coast Champagne Oysters: $135
2 orders of Chilled Maine Lobster: $95
    Extra English Mustard Cream: $10
8 orders of Ahi Tuna Tartare: $140
    No anchovies in the caper vinaigrette
3 orders of Belgian Endive Salad: $50
    Extra Roquefort cheese and toasted pecans
1 order of Baked Goat Cheese: $25

Right. So. This is not good. Not good at all. I take a deep breath and open my wallet.

Oh no. I only have 1–2–3–$400 left! What am I going to do? Should I tell Polo I can't cover it? No. The three of them already had to fix my decorating today. They'll think I'm completely irresponsible. But my card is totally maxed.

Suddenly I remember Patrick's wallet. He called about it earlier. He left it on my dresser this morning.

No! *I can't.*

The delivery guy carries two more blue bins into the kitchen and then looks up at me expectantly.

"Just a minute," I tell him. "I need to . . . um . . . get my credit card."

I walk into the bedroom and sure enough. There's Patrick's wallet. This is so wrong.

I hold my breath as I hand over Patrick's platinum Master-Card. The delivery guy swipes the card.

Patrick will understand. It's not like I won't pay him back. Right? This is no big deal. Couples do this sort of thing all the time. Patrick and I are a couple. This is totally normal. What's my problem? God.

Lighten up, Vic.

Chapter 30

HONESTLY. The fire wasn't anyone's fault. Mmm. Okay. That's not entirely true. It was *my* dumb idea to close the curtains and move some of the candles onto the radiator. But . . . it's not like it was a major fire. And, well, I only sprayed the extinguisher for a second. It only ruined two outfits (Polo promised to pay their dry cleaning bill), and only a few people fled from the scene.

I'm thinking it's probably a good thing that the Swedish princess and the Bachelorette were no-shows. I bet I could get locked up and put away for starting a fire with a real princess or celebrity in the room. You know?

Anyway, everyone is slowly calming down. Polo, Pierre, and Philip are bobbing around the room, pouring guests more wine and champagne. And I'm busily throwing open windows to let out all the smoke.

"Just a teensy delay, honey bunnies," Polo says, wiping his bald head. "And penis hats on, ladies! We didn't have them custom-made by Japanese origami experts for nothing. Hmm?" (Geesh! What's up with wedding events and hats?)

Gwynn stomps up to my side, her platinum penis earrings swinging angrily. "Can I talk to you?"

Aaack! Here we go . . .

We step into the bedroom and Gwynn slams the door.

"How could you let this happen?" Her jaw flexes angrily.

"Look. It was just an accident," I say helplessly.

"An accident? You call ruining *my night* an accident?"

"Aren't you being a wee bit dramatic?" I say, wagging my finger at her. "Everyone's having a good time. Relax."

"Don't tell me to relax," Gwynn shrieks. "This is *my night*. I'll relax when I want to relax."

I scoot back a few steps—genuinely afraid she might pounce on me.

Gwynn leans forward, her eyes lowered into two angry slits. "You need to fix this. You need to turn this party around," she growls, pointing a red fingertip at me. "I don't care what you do. This is supposed to be one of the best nights of my life. *So get on it.*"

I stare at Gwynn in utter disbelief. What happened to my friend? Seriously. I don't even recognize her. She's morphed into some raging red-faced monster. Has she forgotten all the favors I've done for her lately? That I'm her personal stalker? Her very own 007 bridal agent?

"Didn't you hear me?" she barks. "I said fix it. *Now.*" With that, Gwynn spins around, checks her reflection in the full-length mirror, adjusts her crystal BACHELORETTE tiara, and stamps out of the bedroom.

Wow. I take a deep breath, following her into the hallway. Kimmie and Julia are waiting just outside the door.

"What the hell is *her* problem?" Kimmie mutters, wrinkling her freckled nose.

"Should we drop a Valium in her drink?" Julia blinks innocently, taking a sip of her bottled water.

"Try a tranquilizer gun." I shake my head. "Geesh! You'd

think she'd be in a good mood tonight. No Kaitlyn or Mrs. Goldstone breathing down her neck. But no . . . we have a royal pain on our hands!"

"Speaking of royalty. Where's the Swedish princess?" Julia whispers.

"No-show."

"That explains Gwynn's foul humor." Kimmie rolls her eyes.

"Well, the fire might have more to do with it." I grin.

"Ah yes, that." Julia winks.

I take a deep breath. "I guess I should probably get back in there . . ."

"Be strong," Julia says. "If all else fails, tell everyone you're a lesbian again. I hear that seems to work for you."

"Very funny," I snap, catching myself eyeing her stomach. (Is she showing yet? I still can't believe Julia is pregnant!)

I step back into the living room, my eyes gazing over my newly charred white couch and curtains. *My poor apartment.* I hope Polo is planning to pay for all this fire damage, too . . .

"Come on, girls. Penis hats on!" Polo waddles around the room, plucking origami hats off the floor and plopping them on girls' heads.

Kimmie suddenly appears, handing me another flute of champagne, which I down immediately.

"Let's open gifts. *Non?*" Pierre pulls at his dark goatee thoughtfully.

"*Oui. Oui.* Gifts!" Philip snaps his fingers excitedly.

I *knew* I forgot something.

My eyes dart over to the mountain of brightly wrapped gifts, glossy envelopes, and glittery bows. Should I steal one? Rip the card off and pretend it's from me? No. No. I may be a lot of things (stalker, snoop, what have you), but I am not a thief. (Okay. Okay. I know what you're thinking. I took

Patrick's credit card. But, well, that was just *borrowing*. I'm paying him back ASAP, so it doesn't count.)

I grab another flute of champagne. I'll get Gwynn something later. She'll never notice.

A little while later, I clap wildly from the back of the room as Gwynn opens gift, after gift, after gift. Lacy Calvin Klein lingerie. Black Versace corset. Leather whips. Furry handcuffs. Feathery boas. Silky robes. And everything monogrammed with GG.

"Too cute!" I howl as Gwynn unwraps a tiny white G-string with ostrich feather pompoms dangling from the back. I push my way over to Gwynn's side, yanking the lacy numbers out of her fingertips and holding them in front of her waist.

I let out a loud screeching whistle. "Bryan is going to love these little kitties. *Meeeow.*"

I stare into the crowd of blank faces. My head is spinning. Way too much champagne—way too fast! (How many times do I have to tell myself? DRINK SLOW.)

Polo comes toddling over to me. "Let's sit you down, sweet pea," he says brightly, twirling me out of the way and over to a glass of water.

"That was the last gift," Angel announces, checking something off Gwynn's gift spreadsheet. (I'm supposed to be in charge of that! But apparently after the fire, Gwynn didn't trust me.) "Oh wait. We're missing one," Angel snaps. "Vic's."

I KNEW IT. I should have stolen a gift.

"So?" Angel raises an eyebrow. "Where's your gift, Vic?"

"That's funny." I laugh nervously. "It was here a minute ago. Is it hiding behind some wrapping paper?"

"No," Angel says sharply. "I'm certain it's not."

My cheeks and neck are burning hot. "Um . . . maybe it's in my bedroom," I say. "Or maybe it slipped . . ." I let my sentence trail off as I stagger into my bedroom and close the door.

I can't believe this. She just opened over sixty gifts tonight. Like she *needs* my gift. Her parents are, like, ba-zillionaires. Gwynn knows royalty! And Angel is hunting me down for a gift?

Yanking open the top dresser drawer, I see it. The silk ivory negligee I bought to surprise Patrick with. It's brand-new. The tags are still on it. I have no choice.

I walk back into the living room and hand Gwynn a rumpled pink striped Victoria's Secret bag—no tissue paper, no card, just the bag. "Look what I found," I say as cheerfully as possible. "I accidentally left it on my bed."

Some snooty girls dressed in full black Dolce gear shoot me disapproving looks.

Gwynn pulls out my negligee and smiles. "How nice. Thank you." She stuffs it back in the bag. "Should we go now?"

·

AFTER CHARLIE TROTTER'S, we dashed over to Zentra. I rented the velvet leopard-print back bar, so we could drink and dance privately. The girls swarm around Gwynn all night, jumping up and down and squealing under the steamy hot lights. Polo and I take turns videotaping and flashing picture after picture, doing our best to capture every godforsaken moment.

Around two o'clock, the party starts winding down. Bouncers begin carrying girls out in bundles and stuffing them into cabs. Everyone wants to go home. Everyone that is, but Gwynn.

Suddenly Gwynn is a madwoman, dripping in penis paraphernalia and swinging from the pole onstage like a born-again stripper. She keeps shaking her hips, flinging her legs around the pole, and doing her best to slide down it sexily.

I give her a thumbs-up and she squeals back happily, waving her pink penis sippy cup and pointing to the video camera to make sure it's still taping. I give her another thumbs-up to say, yes, I am indeed taping.

Suddenly the bar lights flip on and the music stops. They're closing. Thank God! We can go home now. *This was the longest day ever.*

I hop up onstage with Gwynn. She's standing there all alone, her hair damp and sticking to her face. Her eyes are bloodshot and she looks confused.

"Where . . . (hiccup) . . . is everyone?"

"It's late. They all went home," I say.

"Did everyone have *f-f-fun* tonight?" She leans into me, her head wobbling.

"Oh yes," I say, leading her off the stage. "And you have hours of footage to prove it."

Right. So. This is when Gwynn bends over and pukes. Not the swift ladylike kind of puking, either. Oh no. This was the head-flinging, I-want-to-die kind of puking.

I softly rub her back, looking around desperately for Polo, Pierre, and Philip. Nowhere in sight. Gwynn lifts her head up, mascara running down her cheeks, lips trembling. She looks like she wants to keel over, but instead she curls up in my lap.

"It's okay," I say, wiping a sticky blond strand off her face. "We'll get you home."

"I found another message," she splutters, fumbling in her Louis Vuitton and pulling out a wrinkled piece of paper. "Look."

Uh-oh. I slowly unfold the paper, squinting in the hazy bar light.

```
KAITLYN: I know you're still mad about that night at Web-
    ster's Wine Bar.
BRYAN: It's not right. I trusted you. Let's just finish
    this. Okay?
```

KAITLYN: I know. I know. I have it all worked out now.
    Let's meet.
BRYAN: When?
KAITLYN: Next Saturday. You'll be in New York. Right?
BRYAN: Forget it. You know it's my bachelor party.
KAITLYN: Don't worry. It won't take long. This way, we
    won't have to worry about Gwynn in Chicago.

So *this* explains Gwynn's foul humor.

"I . . . (hiccup) . . . think he loves her," she mumbles, taking a big gulp from her penis sippy cup.

"Shh. You're just tired. Bryan adores you." *I think?*

There's a long pause. Her shoulders shake and I can hear her sniffling.

"I'm scared," her voice cracks. "I can't lose him. You have to . . . (hiccup) . . . go to his bachelor party. You just have to!"

It's in New York. *Is she crazy?*

"We'll talk about it later," I say. "Okay?" The truth is, I couldn't go even if I wanted to. I have a wingwoman gig that night. It's super hush-hush. And Kate is being all weird about it. Says it's for one of our top clients.

"I love him," Gwynn sniffs. "Even if the sex is . . . (hiccup) . . . bad."

Oh dear God. She must be more drunk than I thought.

Don't laugh. Don't laugh.

"*Sooooo* bad!" She wipes her nose. "I . . . I just want to be happy."

"You will be. Everything will be fine," I say, patting her back.

"Promise?" she asks. (Hiccup.)

"Um . . . sure? I guess so."

"Vic?" Gwynn looks up, her dark eyes watery and her BACHELORETTE tiara slipping off her blond head.

"Yeah?"

"I think I'm going to get sick again."

Oh goody.

Chapter 31

I AM A COMPLETE IDIOT. I can't *believe* I borrowed Patrick's credit card. How will I ever explain this? Not only did I charge Romo on his card, but I also charged Charlie Trotter's. (I had the card out to buy a few drinks, but the waiter put the whole bill on my tab!)

Grand total? $8,200.

I know. I know. I'm doomed.

I think I'm going to throw up.

Polo cut me the check today for $18,000 (to cover my credit card, too), which is great and everything. But I still have to confess to Patrick. I flick through the crisp stack of $100 bills, deep in thought. What should I do? What am I going to say?

The buzzer interrupts my thoughts.

Aaack! It's Patrick. My stomach knots up. Maybe I should send him away. Tell him I suddenly came down with a terrible case of . . . of well, whatever. *Anything.* Just go. Leave.

No. Forget it, Vic. YOU HAVE TO TELL HIM TO-NIGHT. He'll get his credit card statement soon or he'll check his online account. You'll get caught eventually. You have to come clean. He'll understand. Right? He has to . . .

"Hi there, pretty girl," Patrick says, handing me a DVD and kissing me on the cheek.

"Hi," I mumble, staring at my feet.

"Why so sad?" he asks, lifting my chin and looking into my eyes.

"We have to talk," I say at last.

Patrick steps back. "What is it? Are you okay?"

"Oh yes. I'm fine. Nothing like that. But I have to tell you something . . ."

Pause.

Pause.

"Ok-aay," Patrick says, raising an eyebrow. "Tell me."

"I screwed up," I blurt. There. I said it.

"Are you dating another client? Did you get fired?" Patrick teases.

I shake my head no. "I . . . um . . ." I wrinkle my nose. "I kind of . . ." Arghh! I can't do this.

"It's okay, Vic. Just tell me."

"I charged $8,200 on your credit card," I spurt, closing my eyes, waiting for the attack.

Silence.

I open an eyelid. He's staring at me in disbelief.

This isn't good.

"Say something. Please?" I say, biting my thumbnail.

"Are you joking?" he asks incredulously.

"I wish I was."

Patrick scratches his head. "I don't understand. How did you even have my . . . card? Oh! That's right. I left it here . . ."

"You see, my credit card was maxed and . . ."

"What? You're in debt?"

"Oh! It's not all because of *me*," I add quickly. "Honestly. It's all Gwynn's wedding stuff. And . . . and I've had so many wing-woman gigs lately! And going out all the time takes a lot of . . ." My voice trails off. This sounds like such a lie.

Patrick shakes his head. "I can't believe this."

"I'm really sorry. Polo wrote me a check today. Here's your money." I hand him the stack of bills.

He looks at the money and then at me. "I never thought

you'd do something like this, Vic. Maybe we've been moving too fast. Maybe I don't even know you."

What? No!

"Patrick, I'm so sorry. I didn't know what else to do. It was a stupid mistake. You *know* me. You *have* to believe me!"

"Why didn't you just ask?" Patrick sighs. "You could have called me. I would have let you."

"I know. You're so right. I . . . ."

Patrick reaches for the doorknob. "I should leave."

"No. Don't go! *Please?*" I cry, reaching for his arm.

He shrugs me away. "Vic, don't. I need time to think."

Oh no.

Chapter 32

I AM A BAD, bad person. I mean it. Beware. Don't trust me.

I lie.

I steal.

And my boyfriend hates me.

I feel terrible. I ruined everything. What if Patrick never forgives me? I mean, he was really, *ree-eally* mad. And he said he needed time "to think." Arghh!

I've been trying to . . . you know . . . give him time "to think." But how was I supposed to know that meant no contact whatsoever? I mean, I figured what's the harm in giving him a quick call . . . or two . . . (cough) . . . or five. And, well, I thought he'd be delighted if I dropped by his loft. I just wanted to say hi. *I was in the neighborhood.* And come on, who doesn't like being surprised with bacon, eggs, and toast in bed? It's only the best way to wake up. Right?

Whatever. Patrick didn't seem to think so. I have to be honest. I don't think I like this whole "thinking" thing. I mean, how long does Patrick need? I estimated a day? Two days tops? But it's been almost a week. ONE WHOLE WEEK. I'm dying here!

Ooh. Come to think of it, maybe I should call him again and ask how much longer this'll take. It's just a quick question. I'm sure he won't mind.

I punch Patrick's number into my cell phone.

Hi. This is Patrick. Leave a message.

Drats! (I wonder if he's screening calls?)

I stuff my cell phone into my Hogan and take another sip of my cherrytini. Thank God this night is almost over. It's been one of the wildest nights yet! Remember that huge wingwoman gig I was telling you about? The one Kate was so hush-hush about? Well, get this . . .

It was for a bachelor party.

In New York.

FOR BRYAN GOLDSTONE.

I know. How insane is that?! Bryan nearly had a heart attack when I hopped on the United flight with Lexi and Redd. He was convinced Gwynn put me up to the whole thing. But once we landed at JFK and checked into the W Hotel on Times Square, he was loads better. (I think all the vodka shots in our limo ride into Manhattan helped, but whatever.) And by the time we made it to Cielo, a super-chic club in the meatpacking district, Bryan was treating me like his new best friend. He tossed me his credit card and said to keep the drinks and the ladies flowing.

So Redd, Lexi, and I worked the crowd. Hot orange lights swirled above our heads as we squeezed our way through the sunken dance floor and picked out New York glam girls for our bachelor party boys. Let's be honest. It wasn't exactly diffi-cult. As soon as we flashed Bryan's platinum credit card and promised free drinks, girls were more than game. And I was on the lookout for Kaitlyn the entire time, too, but nothing. I guess that text message Gwynn intercepted was bogus! I don't know . . .

Oh, and get this. After Bryan's seventh or eighth beer, I even got him to confess why he's one of Chicago Wingwoman's top clients. (I know. I know. Way to sniff out the information! Well done, Vic. Well done.) Turns out it's because of all the crazy bachelor parties he's been throwing lately. All his buddies keep getting engaged!

Anyway, around midnight, we finally ended up at a seedy strip club over on Twenty-third Street with wall-to-wall mirrors and blue neon lights flashing everywhere. There's a small stage in the middle with a silver pole, currently occupied by a tiny red-head wearing a navy NYPD hat and brown leather chaps.

As I hunch over the sticky bar and jab my straw at a mara-schino cherry bobbing in my drink, I watch buff naked girls prance around. Most of the bachelor party boys had already straggled back to the W with a New York glam girl on each arm. Lexi and Redd had headed back a few minutes ago, too, but I said I'd stick around to make sure all the guys are happily hooked up. But I really just wanted to keep my eye on Bryan . . .

Every few minutes, I glance up to see more of the same. Bryan doing another shot. Bryan getting a lap dance by a school-girl with triple D breasts. Bryan getting a lap dance by a furry white sex kitten with triple D breasts. Bryan doing another shot. Bryan stuffing twenties into a tiger-print thong. Blah, blah, blah. Typical bachelor party stuff. Gwynn wouldn't be thrilled, but it's fairly harmless. I call home again to see if Patrick called yet (only my tenth call tonight). No luck. Each time I hear the dreaded: YOU HAVE NO NEW MESSAGES.

Grrr.

But that's when I see Kaitlyn! I bolt upright and rub my eyes. Is that really Kaitlyn . . . *in a strip club*? AT MIDNIGHT? I know they said they wanted to avoid Gwynn . . . but, wow, this must be really top-secret stuff.

Kaitlyn saunters over to Bryan, all sexy in a low-cut red sheath, and pecks him on the cheek. She tugs him over to a dark back booth and pulls a stack of documents out of her bag. Oh no. Here we go . . .

They hunch over the table talking. Kaitlyn flips though papers, pointing to a few things here and there. Bryan nods. God. I wonder what they're looking at? What are they saying? The suspense is killing me. *I need to find out.* I slide off the bar stool and consider my options:

a. Walk by casually? See if I can steal a glance?
b. Grab a seat at a booth nearby? Eavesdrop?
c. Stay here? Safe and sound?

Screw it. I'm doing a walk-by. Grabbing my Hogan, I make my way toward their booth. Bryan is probably so drunk at this point, he won't even notice. As I get closer to the table, I see Kaitlyn slide an arm around Bryan's waist. She hugs him, then . . .

Oh no. She's not . . .

Tell me she's not . . .

I cover my eyes, barely able to force myself to peek through the open space between my fingers as Kaitlyn puts a hand around Bryan's neck and kisses him.

And kisses him . . .

And kisses him . . .

Oh dear God. I stop midstep, heart thumping wildly. I didn't want to see that. I DID NOT WANT TO SEE THAT.

I look down at the floor, then back up at Bryan and Kaitlyn. Bryan is shaking his head and lightly pushing her away.

Good Bryan. Good boy. You could have pushed her away a tiny bit earlier, but, hey, you're drunk. It's your bachelor party. It's better than nothing.

Kaitlyn throws her hands on her hips, her chest heaving up and down. She smacks the stack of documents off the table, sending papers flying everywhere.

"Fine. Just wait!" she shrieks as she storms past me, blond hair streaming behind her. "Your mother will be furious."

Whoa! What the hell is going on? Did Mrs. Goldstone send Kaitlyn to seduce Bryan? A cheap last-ditch effort? Get her precious son drunk, then send in the ex-girlfriend? That's low. *Really low.*

Should I tell Gwynn about this?

I don't know. I mean, Bryan pushed Kaitlyn away. That should count for something. Right? What if Gwynn breaks off the engagement because of this? Because of what *I* saw? And what if Gwynn is miserable for the rest of her life now? I'd be partially responsible.

I . . . I can't take the pressure.

Right then, my cell phone rings. It's Gwynn.

Arghh! Perfect timing, as always. Should I answer? Oh dear God. She'll want to know what happened. And I can't tell her. I just can't. She'd never understand that Kaitlyn kissed Bryan, not the other way around. That Bryan pushed Kaitlyn away. Never.

Forget it. I'm keeping my mouth shut. It's for her own good. It is . . . seriously.

•

IN THE LIMO back to the W Hotel, I call home to check my messages again. Maybe Patrick called this time? I cross my fingers as I punch in my pass code.

"YOU HAVE NO NEW MESSAGES." *And stop calling, you pathetic loser.*

Ah! *What?* I stare at my cell phone in shock. Did I really just hear that?

No. I couldn't have. God. I must be exhausted. What a long night.

Leaning my head against the cool glass window, I watch glittery New York City whiz by. I gaze into the sea of headlights and yellow cabs. It's so alive and bustling, even at this hour. There are dazzling neon lights everywhere I look, flashing animated signs, massive video screens, and running stock market tickers. I can even see the brilliant Empire State Building twinkling like a big gorgeous star in the sky. And as much as I want to say I hate this city, I can't. It's too easy to love. No wonder Julia wants to move here.

As I climb out of the limo under the gigantic glowing red W, I look down at my cell phone again. I don't get it. Why hasn't Patrick called? Maybe I should call him real quick. Just tell him I'm thinking about him. That I miss him. That I'm a fool and . . . and . . .

No. Stop it, Vic. Patrick said he needed time to think.

But it's taking him so looooong.

And if the truth be told, I don't want him to think! What if he thinks himself right into not liking me anymore?

This is pure torture. I *have* to talk to him. I quickly dial his number, then immediately hang up.

Good God. VIC?!?!

What the hell is my problem?

Chapter 33

PATRICK STILL HASN'T CALLED.

Nine days and counting. I'm so depressed.

And to make matters worse, I accidentally gained back all the weight I lost for the fashion show. (Grrr.) And I got in a H-U-G-E fight with Kate. She booked me for a wedding gig September 8. *Gwynn's wedding.* (Yeah. I know. Are you kidding me?) Long story short: a guy from the bachelor party loved my work in New York and hired me for the wedding. And, no, I absolutely can't get out of the gig. End of discussion. Kate promised the client. (He's paying double.) If I back out, I'm fired.

Fabulous. Just fabulous. How am I supposed to play wingwoman and personal attendant on the same night? Hmm?

Ugh. And I can't believe I agreed to meet Kimmie for lunch today. This has bad idea written all over it. I'm crazy emotional, and what if I run into Patrick? I'll start crying on the spot for sure.

But Kimmie left a frantic message insisting that we grab a quick bite at noon. She said she was dying to tell me something face-to-face. So here I am . . .

I sign in with the Lambert receptionist, grab a visitor's badge, and head toward Kimmie's workstation. Just as I'm turning down the hallway, I run smack into the loco art director, Lotty. She's dressed in a nun's costume today.

"YOU." Lotty jumps back. "Bad energy!"

"Yep. That's me. Just a bundle of bad energy," I mumble. "Great to see you, too."

Lotty glares at me, then shuffles down the hallway reciting, "Jesus loves me! This I know, for the Bible tells me so . . ."

F-R-E-A-K.

I stick my head into Kimmie's workstation and can see immediately that she's bursting with energy, freckled cheeks glowing, green eyes shining brightly.

Something's up. Something is definitely up. I can't quite put my finger on it, but . . .

"Hiii!" she squeals. "Where have you been? Oh my God. I've been trying to call you!"

I nod, my stomach tight. There's just something about her perky tone. It sounds so unlike Kimmie, yet so eerily familiar?

"Yeah. I had a gig in New York and . . ."

"Whatever. Whatever." Kimmie flicks her hands around excitedly. "*Guess what?* You're never going to believe this. Never, ever, ever!"

It suddenly dawns on me. I take a few steps back. Oh . . . no.

"I'm . . ."

Oh my God. She's not? She can't be . . .

My eyes dart to her ring finger. Please, no! But yes. There it is. The glittering diamond, waving over at me.

My stomach drops to my feet.

I can't believe this.

"I'M ENGAGED!" Kimmie shrieks, jumping up and down and holding out her ring finger under my nose.

NOOOOO.

Not Kimmie. This is so much worse than Gwynn getting engaged. I thought Kimmie and I were in this together. Long live the singletinis. Now she's abandoning me, too?

I can't possibly be the lone singletini?

How awful.

How pathetic.

No. I refuse to accept this. Kimmie can't be engaged. This

simply must be a joke. That's the only logical answer. After all, she's only been dating DJ for . . . a few months. She can't just go off and get engaged like that. She hardly knows him!

Kimmie scrunches up her face. "Are you okay?"

Suddenly an uncontrollable urge to laugh washes over me. This . . . this is just hilarious. Ha! In fact, it's the funniest thing I've ever heard. Ha-ha. Ho-ho.

"Whoa." I sigh, wiping my eyes. "Good one, Kimmie. You almost had me there."

"What do you mean?" she asks, pushing a red curl out of her freckly face.

I grab Kimmie's hand and hold up her sparkly new ring to the light. "Where did you get this thing? It's killer! Wow. I mean, it almost looks real."

"Vic, I'm not kidding. DJ proposed last night."

"Yeah, right." I laugh.

"Vic . . ." Kimmie raises an eyebrow. "I'm serious."

What? How? "I . . . I don't understand. This is crazy." My thoughts fly all over the place. "Why would you do that?"

"I love him. What do you mean *why*?"

"How? You don't even know him!" I cry.

"Yes, I do." Kimmie narrows her green eyes. "Why are you acting like this?"

"Come on." I laugh. "You can't possibly know him after a few months. It's outrageous. And, well, stupid!"

Kimmie pulls a face. "*Stupid?* I can't believe you."

"*Me?*" I cry. "You're the one marrying someone you barely know."

"That's not true!" Kimmie shouts. "How can you say that?"

"Oh stop. You're settling. Admit it." Oops. I didn't mean for that to slip out.

"You're just jealous!" Kimmie hisses.

I snort, taking a few steps back. "That's ridiculous."

"Is it?" Kimmie yells.

"I don't have to stand here and listen to this," I say.

"Fine. Don't," Kimmie snaps. "But listen. *I love DJ*. He's part of my life now." She holds up her sparkly new engagement ring. "Permanently. You need to get used to the idea or maybe we can't be friends."

"Maybe we can't," I say, clutching my Hogan tightly and pushing past her. Hot tears stream down my cheeks as I race to the elevator. I punch the down button and start tapping my foot anxiously. Please don't let me run into Patrick. Please.

As I ride the elevator down, my head is whirling. What just happened? *Kimmie is engaged?* This is too unbelievable. I storm through the marble office lobby, throw open the doors, and run onto the sidewalk. I look right, then left down Wacker Drive, trying to figure out what to do next. That's when I see . . .

Aiden?

Sure enough. There he is in a rumpled white linen shirt, khaki shorts, and suede flip-flops, looking as hot as ever. He's standing in front of his platinum Porsche Boxster chatting on his cell phone and fiddling with his BlackBerry.

What a coincidence.

I haven't seen Aiden in forever. He called a couple times after the fashion show, but when I didn't return his calls, he dropped off the face of the earth.

Aiden flashes me a sexy grin and waves.

I just want to evaporate. Disappear. I feel like running back into the building or just running . . . somewhere. I mean, I can't see Aiden like this. I can't see anyone like this. I'm a mess.

It's too late, though. Aiden is clicking off his cell phone and walking this way.

"Long time, no see, doll." He pulls me in for a hug, holding me a little closer and longer than he needs to. I breathe in his sharp cologne. All the bad memories of him start flooding back and I pull away.

"What . . . what are you doing here?" I finally ask.

Aiden points to Lambert's office building. "This is one of my dad's properties. I'm meeting with an electrical contractor."

Right. Of course. His dad owns real estate on Wacker Drive. I rub my temples.

"Everything okay?" he asks, biting his lip playfully.

I nod, but my tears give me away.

"Hey, now. No need to cry, doll. Wanna go for a ride? Forget about things for a while?"

"No," I say, but for some reason I walk toward his car, anyway. He opens the door and I climb in. I'm completely in a daze. I don't know what I'm doing anymore. I feel so confused.

Aiden and I don't say a word. He veers onto Lake Shore Drive and guns his Boxster. I sink into the plush black leather seats and close my eyes as we fly up the hot, sandy lakefront. Wind whips my hair all around, and I try to forget everything. Kimmie. Patrick. Erase it all.

I must fall asleep for a bit, because the next thing I know, we're whizzing up Wacker Drive in front of the Lambert office building again.

"Feeling better?" Aiden asks.

I nod.

"Good." He grins mischievously, running his hand up my thigh. "Now why don't we make you feel even better?"

Chills prickle down my spine. "What are you doing?" I hiss.

"I've missed you," he whispers, nuzzling my ear.

I push him away. "Don't. Things are different now."

"What? You have a boyfriend?" He leans over, sliding the skirt up my leg. "We don't have to tell him. Come on. Let's go back to my place. It'll be our secret."

"I'm serious, Aiden. I'm not interested." I fling open the car door just as he's leaning toward me. I fall into the street, my skirt scrunched up around my waist.

I look up to see Patrick, walking out of Lambert's office building. And the next few moments play out in slo-ooow motion.

Patrick's mouth drops.

He says something, but I can't hear.

He looks so hurt . . .

So disappointed.

"It's over." I finally hear the words come out of Patrick's mouth. He shakes his head, turning and walking away.

"Patrick, wait!" I call after him, struggling to my feet. "It's not what it looks like. Swear."

He doesn't turn around.

And that's it. I officially ruined everything. Patrick. Kimmie. It couldn't get any worse now.

Aiden shrugs. "So you wanna go back to my place or what?"

"Just leave!" I shout at Aiden.

I slump down onto the curb, putting my head in my hands. What is going on? My entire world is crumbling. All my friends are leaving me. I've ruined things with a perfectly wonderful guy. My stupid job has taken over my life. I . . . I feel so alone. So lost. I feel like running away. Escaping.

But where should I go?

That's when it hits me . . . Barneys.

I need to go to Barneys. Everything is always better there. The next thing I know, I'm bursting into Barneys, the familiar scent of *new* washing over me. Rich luscious leather bags. Crisp citrusy summer perfumes. Fresh clean lotions. I usually love this smell—*new* everything, just waiting to be plucked up and purchased. But something's different today.

I wait for that first flicker of happiness, that giddy little rush, that sheer exhilaration that only shopping at Barneys brings me.

But it never comes. I still feel empty and numb inside. Why isn't this cheering me up? I scuffle past the jewelry counter, nodding to the Nicole look-alike, and drag myself upstairs to the women's department.

Why did I say all those awful things to Kimmie? She's my best friend. I should be happy for her! Who cares if her news surprised me? If she's happy, I'm happy. Right? I wish I could take everything back. Start over. Throw my arms around her, jump up and down, and tell her how exciting it is.

And Patrick? What a disaster. He looked so furious, so disappointed. He's never going to speak to me again. Ever. I ruined the best thing that ever happened to me. My life couldn't get any worse.

I am a terrible, terrible person.

I wipe away a stray tear with my fist. I don't even know what I'm doing anymore. My life is a mess. Everyone else seems so put together. Like they have a grand plan they're executing—getting married, moving to the suburbs (or New York!) . . . even having a baby. The trouble is, I don't seem to be fitting into their plans.

What's *my* plan?

Be a stupid wingwoman for the rest of my life?

Be single and broke?

I suddenly notice I'm standing in front of the bridal department. My eyes skim the long silky dresses. I just don't get it. What's all the fuss about? It's just a wedding. They're just dresses. I reach out and finger one of the shimmering floor-length gowns. I mean, what's so special . . .

Oh my God.

This gown feels amazing.

It's so soft. I pull the hanger off its hook and hold the dress up to my chin, letting the smooth gorgeous layers of silk flow down all around me.

"Wow," I sniffle.

It really is gorgeous.

I close my eyes, feeling the fabric swish all around me like a soft delicate hug.

"It would look divine on you," I hear a gentle, motherly voice say.

My eyes snap open to see a petite woman with silver hair dressed in head-to-toe St. John. She reminds me of my Gramms. "Um . . . I didn't mean . . ." I wobble with my words, trying feverishly to shove the dress back onto its hook.

She smiles warmly, holding out her hand. "I'm Francine."

"Um. Hi," I say, taking her hand. "I'm Victoria."

"Would you like to try it on?" Francine asks, nodding to the dress.

"Oh no!" I gush. "I couldn't. I'm just, you know, looking."

The older woman smiles knowingly, then winks. "Of course you are, dear."

I slide my fingers along the fine, lustrous fabric. "It's very pretty."

"Why don't you slip it on? See how it feels? It could be *the one.*"

I pull a guilty face. "I shouldn't." I eye the delicate beading along the hem longingly.

Oh well . . . it couldn't hurt. It's just a dress. Right?

No way! Stop this right now, Vic.

"I guess I could try it on," I hear myself say.

The next thing I know, I'm standing on a marble pedestal with creamy silk spilling all around me as I swoosh back and forth in front of a million glossy mirrors.

"Gorgeous," one woman says. "Simply made for you."

"Stunning," another woman gushes.

"Do you think?" I peep.

"Absolutely." Francine nods smartly.

I know. I know. It's so wrong of me, but the dress feels so

wonderful. And what's the harm in playing pretend for a few minutes? I mean, all the ladies in the bridal department are being so nice to me, listening to every word I say and telling me how amazing I look. And I do. I . . . I feel so pretty. Like a princess.

The funny thing is, as I stand here, I can actually picture myself walking down the aisle in this dress. A sharp unfamiliar feeling rises in my stomach. This dress was made for me . . .

Yes. It truly was! No one else can possibly wear this dress but me. *It's mine* . . .

That's it. I want this dress.

I need this dress.

"I'll take it," I say, before I can stop myself. Oh dear God. Why did I just say that?

"Fantastic!" The women clap in delight.

I smile nervously. I'm crazy. I've gone completely mad. I mean, I can't buy a wedding dress. I'm not even engaged! I . . . I don't even have a boyfriend. What kind of person does this sort of thing?

"When is your date, dear?" Francine asks, scribbling in a black leather-bound notepad.

"Date?" I squeak.

"Your wedding. When is it?"

"Oh right," I say, pulling anxiously at my ear. "We haven't . . . um . . . set a date yet."

"Okay. Then when would you like to schedule alterations?"

"Um. Not today. You know . . . my mom still needs to see the dress and everything," I say, grinning widely, praying these nice ladies won't see through me.

"I see," Francine says, looking slightly confused. "Shall I simply hold it for you then?"

"Um . . . yes. That would be great! Thanks."

"Just sign here," Francine says, handing me a pen. "Oh . . . and we'll need a $1,000 deposit."

Gulp. Oh, what the hell?

"Of course," I say, pulling out my credit card.

Chapter 34

FROM: gwynnie_pooh@girly.com
TO: victoria_hart@vongo.com
ATTACHMENT: wedding_details.doc
PRIORITY: *Super-Ultra-Mega Urgent*
SUBJECT: Da-da-dadum!

Eee! I'm getting married this Saturday! THIS SATUR-
DAY. Oh my God. My nerves are a total wreck. Mother is
driving me mad. Mrs. Goldstone and Kaitlyn are flying
in tomorrow. Yuck! If I make it through the next few
days without strangling someone, it'll be a miracle.
I swear. I'm so glad you're coming with me to pick up
the dresses on Friday. Fred Sander said he had a surprise. He's so brilliant. I'm sure it'll be amazing!

Anyway, Polo needs a few more things done. 'Kay?
See the attached.

Kisses,

Gwynnie

P.S. I still can't believe your wingwoman gig was
for Bryan's bachelor party! What a small world. Oh my
God. I feel so much better knowing that Kaitlyn never
showed up. Maybe that bitch finally got the hint.

WEDDING_DETAILS.DOC

Hello, sweet pea!

We're almost there. As always, thanks for your
help. *Merci, merci!* Toodles.

XOXO,
Polo

1. Call and confirm the DJ. Tell him to arrive at the Lincoln Park Zoo by the carousel at five o'clock sharp for setup. Make sure he received Gwynnie's playlist and tell him he'll be shot on-site if he plays the Macarena, the hokey pokey, the Electric Slide, or any other cheesy group dance-along. I mean it. Our wedding bonus depends on it.

2. Bring the following emergency items to the wedding: steamer, iron, ironing board, spray starch, lint roller, sewing kit, safety pins, bobby pins, cotton balls, Q-tips, Band-Aids, eye drops, mints, tampons, clear OPI nail polish, Kiehl's hand salve, red DiorKiss lip gloss (Gwynnie's fave!), DiorSkin light pressed powder, Aveda Air Control hair spray, and whatever else you can think of.

3. If you could call the zoo and see if they can get rid of all the animals near the carousel, that would be great. Gwynn hates the way the sea lions smell (and their annoying barking), and the lions scare her. They have cages. Right?

4. One last thing. Tell the wedding photographer to make Bryan look more like Jude Law. Maybe she can work some magic in Photoshop? Ooh. Come to think of it, can she paste Jude's picture over Bryan's face instead? It might be easier. Just a thought . . .

I hate myself. *My life is a total disaster.* I spend the next day in bed with my fluffy white duvet over my head, only sitting up long enough to scarf down an entire box of Fannie May pixies . . . and trinidads . . . and to call for two orders of cheese fries from Muskies (the best cheese fries in Chicago!). I call Kate at Chicago Wingwoman and cancel all my gigs. She's furious, but finally agrees . . . only after reminding me about the wedding gig a dozen times.

"You can't miss it. No excuses or you're fired," she snaps.

Whatever. Maybe it's time I found something more serious, anyway. More traditional. More like a desk job. I know. I know. I said I'd rather die than do a stuffy desk job again. But at least with that I wasn't blowing an ungodly amount of money on clothing and drinks. And I didn't get bombarded with crazy e-mails from wannabe clients. (Oh dear God. This one guy from Estonia e-mailed and said he'd fly me overseas if I promised to find him a wife in five days. What the . . . ?) And I wouldn't be meeting men like Aiden and Patrick, and I wouldn't be miserable like this . . .

I eventually drag myself out of the apartment and go for a drive. And to my surprise, I end up at Oakbrook Mall. It's where I shopped growing up in Naperville. I used to love Oakbrook. How it was open air with all the white brick stores. All the European-style coffee shops. Ooh. And that gelato stand with the cute red-and-white-striped awning in the summer. But most of all, I loved coming here with Mom. We spent most of the time at Sears, but every once in a while I'd drag her into the other shops. And *sometimes* I could talk her into a scoop of raspberry gelato. God. It feels so long ago.

I sit down on a white stone bench, near a grassy patch with a few yellow rose bushes, just watching people pass by. What am I doing here? I close my eyes. Honestly. I think I'm losing it. And the saddest part is, I don't even have anyone to call. *Not really.* Kimmie is furious with me. And, well, everyone else is busy with their own thing.

Ooh. Wait a minute. What about Everett? He picks up and

before I know it, I'm telling him everything. About Julia, New York, the baby. About Patrick and the credit card. The car ride with Aiden. The fight with Kimmie. How my wingwoman job is taking over my life. I just keep talking and talking. It spills out of me so fast, I can barely keep up. Everett stays quiet, just listening until I'm finished.

"What . . . what should I do?" I sniff. "Everything is so wrong."

"You already know what to do," Everett says at last. "You're just scared."

"I am," my voice wavers. "What if they never forgive me?"

"They might not," Everett says slowly. "Especially Patrick. It sounds like he's really angry with you. But if you love him, you have to go after him."

"I can't," I whisper. "He never wants to see me again."

"You have to do what you have to do. That's what you always tell me."

After we hang up, I sit on the cool stone bench in a daze. I see young blissful couples strolling by hand in hand. Proud moms pushing navy plaid strollers. Squealing toddlers waddling around with sticky red sippy cups. Teenage girls giggling in mobs and pointing to boys. And cute wrinkly grandmas speedwalking in their neon tracksuits. I watch as all these families, these generations pass me by. They look so happy. So full of life. Why am I so scared of growing up? Of getting older? Whether it's marriage, turning twenty-five, moving to new cities (or the suburbs!), having kids, whatever? I mean, these people seem completely content. Maybe I've been wrong this whole time?

I hop in my VW Bug and head home, watching the shimmering skyline grow larger and larger as I fly back into the city. I love this effect. I always have. As I drive into the heart of Chicago, it feels like the city is about to open its great mouth and swallow me up.

And to tell you the truth, today I kind of wish it would. That way, I could disappear forever and forget all about this great big mess I've created. My stomach tightens. How will I ever face Kimmie at the wedding? What will I ever say to Patrick? How could I have screwed up this terribly?

Ugh.

Well, I suppose I *should* drop by the drugstore on my way home to pick up those little emergency items for Gwynn. Hmm. Now what did I do with her latest to-do list?

CITY GIRLS

THE MUST-READ MAG FOR THE CHICAGO SINGLETINI

Leo

It's time for a face-off: you against your insecurities. No more complaining. No more drama queen. While you may feel like you're experiencing a midlife crisis, little singletini, you're not. The truth is, you're the one standing in the way. The sooner you figure this out, the happier you'll be.

YOUR WEEK AT A GLANCE

STRENGTHS: Strip-club stalking
WEAKNESSES: Alarm clock must die
CONQUESTS: Looks bleak . . .
TO DO: Let go of the past or you'll never fully move into the future. Great things are in store. What are you so afraid of?

(Stupid astrologers. Why do I even bother?)

Chapter 35

OH NO.

Something's wrong. Something's horribly, horribly wrong. I can feel it as soon as I poke my head into Fred Sander's studio Friday afternoon. The girl with the cute black pageboy haircut sitting behind the front desk looks frazzled.

"I'm meeting Gwynn Ericsson here today," I tell her.

The girl shoots me a fearful look. "She's back there." She winces. "Be careful."

"It's all wrong!" I suddenly hear Gwynn shriek.

Uh-oh.

"Fred will never work again!" she screams. "Father will make sure of it. You tell him he messed with the wrong bride! Fred—*he's so dead.*"

I run back to the dressing room and find Gwynn sitting in a heap of fine Italian silk. She lifts her head when I walk in. Her eyes are swollen.

"My dress," she howls, flicking her blond hair off her shoulders. "It's ruined!"

"Are you sure?" I ask, pulling her up so I can take a look.

"Yes, I'm sure!" she cries.

I take a few steps back to inspect the damage. To be totally honest, the dress looks fine. Gorgeous, actually. She looks exactly like, well, Cinderella.

"I give up. What's wrong?"

"Look!" she shrieks, turning to the side. "That idiot Fred thought he'd surprise me after my last fitting and add a few last-minute details. He calls it his special touch. I call it *the worst dress in the world.*"

"Stop!" I laugh. "I'm sure it's not that . . ."

She turns.

Oh dear God.

Her butt. It's so big! I lean in for a closer look. I can't believe this. I thought I'd never be able to say this but: *Gwynn looks fat.*

Really fat. By no fault of her own, though. It's the dress. There are mounds and mounds of ruffles flooding out from her rear. You can't tell from the front, but as soon as she turns to the side, her new big booty is revealed. It's one of the biggest butts I've ever seen!

I fight the urge to laugh. "We can fix this."

"How?" she wails. "It's ruined. My life is over."

"It's not over." I twirl her around and begin tugging at the ruffles. Yikes! There are hundreds of layers back here. We'll never get this thing looking presentable in twenty-four hours. Ever. What are we going to do?

"I bet Kaitlyn is behind this," Gwynn hisses.

I wriggle my nose. She very well could be. I mean, if Kaitlyn has the power to force me to wear pink sequined underwear with wings in front of hundreds of strangers, I'm sure she can ruin a wedding dress or two.

That's when it hits me. "Take it off," I order her.

"What?"

"You heard me. Take it off. I've got an idea."

Twenty minutes later, we're sprinting down Rush Street.

"Come on!" I yell over my shoulder at Gwynn. "Hurry!"

"I can't," she pants, suddenly stopping in the middle of the sidewalk and throwing her hands on her knees.

I run back and grab her arm, yanking her forward. "Let's go . . ."

"I can't believe everything is ruined! RUINED!" she whimpers.

"Everything'll be fine. Trust me."

Thank God. We're almost there. I can see the red awnings and the slick black letters that read: BARNEYS.

I push Gwynn through the glass doors and up to the second floor, desperately hoping this plan works. I mean, Gwynn and I are nearly the same size! Fingers crossed . . .

"What's going on? Why are we at Barneys?" Gwynn asks.

"You'll understand in a minute," I say, leading her up to the bridal department.

"Stay here," I say. "I'll be right back."

I race into the dressing room and I run smack into Francine. Her eyes light up.

"Victoria! Hello! What a pleasant surprise. Did you bring your mother to see the dress?"

"Um . . . kind of."

Francine looks confused.

"There's been a change of plans," I whisper.

"Oh dear. The wedding is still on, isn't it?"

"Of course it is," I lie. "But you see, my friend is getting married tomorrow and she *needs* to wear this dress. We're the same size and, well, this is an emergency."

Francine looks fearful. "But it's *your* dress. I don't think this is a good idea."

"I know. I know. *But she needs it.* You understand. Just go and get the dress. Okay?"

Francine huffs off, shaking her head and mumbling something about "crazy brides these days."

I run back and find Gwynn. "Okay," I say, pushing her toward the dressing room. "Everything's going to be fine."

Gwynn looks worried. "What's going on?"

I throw her a strapless bra and tights. "Put these on."

Francine brings in my dress, looking flustered. "Here's your dress, Victoria. Are you certain you want to do this?"

"Yes. Thank you," I say, gently leading Francine out of the dressing room before she blows my cover.

I grab the delicate dress off its hook and hold the hanger up for Gwynn to see. "Ta-da!" I sing, spinning the gown around like I'm dancing.

Gwynn's mouth drops. *"It's amazing!"* she breathes, reaching out and touching the shimmering silk. "I've never seen anything like it." She checks the label. "Ah! It's Donna Karan. I adore Donna Karan."

"It's yours," I say, holding it out to her.

"How? What do you mean?"

"Just try it on," I say.

"Are you serious? Oh my God!" Gwynn squeals, already throwing her clothes off and stepping into the gown.

"I can't believe this. It's incredible!" she cries, examining every inch of herself as she slowly turns right, then left. She smooths out the gorgeous layers of silk flowing down all around her.

"What do you think?" I grin.

"I love it! But . . . how did you know?"

"Long story," I say. "Let's just say, I had a feeling."

"You're the best! You saved the day, Vic," Gwynn says, throwing her arms around me.

Ha! Did you hear that? I'm brilliant. I am a Personal Attendant Queen. Seriously. Maybe I should consider doing this professionally? What do you think? I'll admit it, I had a few setbacks in the beginning. But no one's perfect. I have potential, though. Look at how happy Gwynn is. I'm, like, a guardian angel. A freaking bridal hero!

"This is just too fabulous!" Gwynn coos, then wrinkles her nose. "Make sure it gets pressed and messengered over to my condo by five o'clock. "Ooh! And my shoes will look dreadful with it! Pick up new ones. Size 7½. 'Kay?"

Um. On second thought. Scratch that.

There's a knock at the dressing room door. Francine sticks her head inside. "How is everything?"

"Fantastic!" Gwynn says brightly. "We'll take it."

"Now?" Francine asks incredulously. "It hasn't been altered."

"It's perfect the way it is," Gwynn says, swooshing back and forth on the marble pedestal just like I did.

"Victoria, are you absolutely certain this is okay with you? *It's yours.* Finding your wedding dress is truly a once-in-a-lifetime experience. I strongly advise you to reconsider."

Gwynn tilts her head, shooting me a funny look.

"I appreciate your concern," I say sweetly. "But I really don't mind. So if you'd just wrap up the dress, that would be great!"

"Vic, what's going on?" Gwynn asks slowly once Francine leaves the dressing room. "Why does she keep calling this *your* dress? Are you secretly engaged to Patrick or something?"

My heart sinks and I turn away, snatching up my Hogan. I should probably tell Gwynn that Patrick and I are through, but I don't have the energy. Not now.

"No," I say at last. "No chance of that."

Chapter 36

FROM: gwynnie_pooh@girly.com
TO: victoria_hart@vongo.com
PRIORITY: *E-M-E-R-G-E-N-C-Y*
SUBJECT: Aaaaaahhhhhhhh!
I'VE HAD IT. I hate Bryan's mother. I hate, hate,

hate her! Check out the message I found. A *nobody Chicago girl*? HA! Eliminating Bryan's manager position at the Goldstone Group? HA! I swear, this is the final straw. I'm going to give this woman a big fat piece of my mind at the rehearsal dinner—once and for all.

HAAAAAAAAATE HER.

Gwynnie

FROM: goldstone@thegoldstonegroup.com
TO: bryan_goldstone@thegoldstonegroup.com
PRIORITY: *Extremely Critical*
SUBJECT: FW: Call me immediately
Dearest Bryan,

Kaitlyn informed me that you're still planning to go through with the wedding. I demand you put a stop to this nonsense immediately.

There's still time. Break off the engagement! Do it now. I can't stand to see you with a nobody Chicago girl. You are a Goldstone! You deserve the best. I'm begging you, come back to New York, back to Kaitlyn, back to me. It's time.

And let me warn you, I've spoken with your father. If you choose to ignore this final plea, we will be forced to eliminate your position in Chicago. I hate that it's coming to this, but you leave me no other choice. It's for your own good.

Do the right thing . . .

Mother

"Oh my God, Vic! I've been worried sick about you." Julia races up and hugs me as soon as she arrives at Gwynn's rehearsal dinner. "Kimmie said you two had a super-crazy fight! And then you weren't returning any of my calls . . . and . . .

and . . ." Julia lets go of me and scans me up and down. "What's going on? Tell me this instant. Are you going through some weird quarter-life crisis?"

Wow. I've never seen Julia this upset.

"I don't know what happened," I say honestly. "I freaked."

"About Kimmie getting engaged?"

"I guess so. It was a bit of everything. Is Kimmie coming tonight?" I ask quietly.

"No. She has to work," Julia says, watching me carefully. Her fine porcelain-doll face is wrinkled deeply with concern. "How are you feeling?"

I shrug. "Better, I guess." Except for Patrick. Should I tell her the story? That we're through?

Kevin walks up and puts his arm around Julia. "There you are. You ran off so fast! Hi, Vic. Ready for the big day tomorrow?"

"You bet." I smile. "Listen. I'm going to grab a drink. Do you guys want anything?"

"I think we're all set. Thanks," Kevin says, holding up his frosty highball glass and a water bottle for Julia. I eye Julia's stomach to see if she's showing yet. (Hmm. Maybe there's a tiny bump?)

As I make my way over to the bar, I peer into the crowd. There's an eerie vibe. Everyone seems so ooey-gooey happy tonight. Almost too happy. Fake even.

Polo, Pierre, and Philip flit about gaily, wearing those tiny black headsets and yapping orders at one another every few minutes. Angel and Dawn proudly show off their engagement rings. Mom and Dad happily snap photos with their digital camera. Kevin and Julia laugh hysterically at something Gwynn's crazy old grandmother Birdie just said. (Looks like her red feathery friend stayed home. *Thank God.*) Even Gwynn's punk sister, Eva, has a smile plastered on her face.

My entire body tenses. Something is going down tonight. I

can feel it. Maybe it's because I know Gwynn is ready to unleash on Mrs. Goldstone. Or maybe it's because I know the truth: *Kaitlyn kissed Bryan in New York.*

I know. I know. I should have told Gwynn about the kiss. I'm a bad, bad friend. But what can I do now? I mean, I can't tell her the night before her wedding. Can I?

I glance over at the soon-to-be-married couple. Gwynn is tucked under Bryan's arm. They're holding champagne flutes and grinning enormously, almost freakishly. Bryan wipes beads of sweat off his forehead with a napkin, and Gwynn glares at Kaitlyn as she struts by in an outrageously short black dress and lime green snakeskin Dolce pumps.

Oh God. Kaitlyn is like that annoying fly you keep swatting at but can't seem to squash. All I can say is she better buzz far, far away, because Gwynn is liable to smash her into pieces tonight. Her *and* Mrs. Goldstone.

Hey, is that Jay Schmidt over there with his stupid camera? I forgot Polo said *City Girls* was doing a spread on Gwynn's wedding. (Apparently girls around the city are dying to know all the details.) A few months ago I would have loved to give Jay a piece of my mind, but I just don't have the energy tonight. And, well, he's not worth it.

I take a sip of champagne and let my mind drift back to Patrick. Sigh. I wonder what he's doing? Is he thinking about me? I just can't believe it's over. Why did I have to go and ruin everything? It all happened so fast.

My cell phone rings and for one blissful moment I actually convince myself it might be Patrick. I check the number.

My heart sinks. It's Everett.

"Hi," I say quietly, turning away from the crowd and cupping a hand over my mouth. "I can't talk. I'm at a rehearsal dinner."

"Oh, sorry!" Everett gushes. "I . . . I just wanted to see how everything is going."

"The same," I say sadly.

"Hang in there," Everett says. "Do what you . . ."

"I know. I know. I have to do what I have to do." I sigh. "What about you? How's your cowgirl?"

Everett is quiet for a few seconds. "I think I'm ready," he whispers.

"YOU ARE?" My face lights up. "That's great." And it is! It really, really is. I'm so happy for Everett. I hope he goes through with it, and I sincerely hope he ropes in his cowgirl. "Make sure to call and tell me the verdict. Okay?"

Right then, someone lets out a loud *"shh"* and the Toast and Roast begins. Mr. Ericsson toasts the couple, wishing them health, happiness, and all those other good things you're supposed to wish a soon-to-be-married couple. Crazy old Birdie wishes the couple a great life and even greater sex. (At least she left the condoms at home!) And then aunts and uncles all take turns toasting and telling cute stories about Gwynn and Bryan. Jay snaps pictures of it all.

Cute story.

Everyone applauds.

Another cute story.

More applause.

And then . . .

"I'd like to make a toast, or *roast,* if you will," one of Bryan's fraternity brothers says, swinging his pilsner glass around dangerously. (This frat boy is my client tomorrow night. He was a wild one in New York!)

Bryan moans.

"To the groom and his beautiful wife," frat boy begins.

Everyone applauds, and someone clinks a fork on their glass for the bride and groom to kiss.

Gwynn and Bryan lock lips for a long moment. Jay snaps a picture.

Everyone cheers. Everyone, that is, but Mrs. Goldstone and Kaitlyn. They're huddled together shaking their heads.

"Hey now, that wasn't the roast!" frat boy yells.

There are a few whistles and then a hush falls over the banquet room.

"I'd like to tell a story . . ."

Uh-oh. This doesn't sound good.

"Bryan wasn't always the straitlaced guy he is now. Oh no. There was a time—way before Gwynnie—when this guy was the *player* of all players. Let me tell ya!" Frat boy takes a swig of his drink.

This doesn't sound good *at all*.

"Bryan could bring the ladies home two at a time. And boy, he could talk 'em into doing all kinds of crazy-ass shit . . . ," he slurs.

There are a few gasps from the audience.

Oh dear God. Someone needs to stop this guy. *Now.* I look over at Gwynn. Her face is on fire and her lips are pulled into a tight angry line.

"It was AWESOME!" frat boy yells, lifting his glass violently, spilling on the floor.

Bryan stands up, his neck splotchy red.

"But hey, all that making out was before he met Gwynn. *Most* of it, anyway. Right, Kaitlyn?" Frat boy winks at Kaitlyn and Bryan.

OH. NO.

Gwynn's face flushes wildly. Her eyes dart from Bryan to Kaitlyn, then back again.

Kaitlyn smiles smugly.

Bryan rips the microphone out of frat boy's hand.

"Hey, I wasn't done!" frat boy yells.

"Oh, I think you were," Mr. Ericsson says, stepping up behind Bryan.

"Aw, man. Lighten up. I love this guy." Frat boy slaps Bryan on the back. "I was just about to say how great Gwynnie is for Bryan. She tamed him. I wish she'd tame me, too. *Grr-rrr.*" Frat boy flashes his teeth at Gwynn and grabs himself.

I cover my mouth in horror.

Gwynn jerks up from her seat, the chair falling backward with a *thunk*. She glares at Bryan, her nostrils flaring and her face on fire.

Jay crouches down and snaps picture after picture. (I could just kill him. Does he have no respect?)

"I can't believe you! I knew something was up with you two. I knew it. DID YOU MAKE OUT WITH HER?" Gwynn shrieks. "DID YOU HAVE SEX WITH HER, TOO? HMM? You make me sick." Gwynn yanks her purse off her chair and runs toward the bathroom.

"Come on. It was an accident! You don't even know the whole story," Bryan calls after her.

"*Emergency! Turn the music on. Oui.* I repeat. Turn the music on," Polo shrieks into his headset, already waddling over to the microphone to distract the crowd.

Julia and I race into the bathroom after Gwynn. I give Jay a don't-even-think-about-following-us look and to my surprise he stops dead in his tracks. (Hmm. Maybe he has some sense of decency after all?)

"What an asshole!" Gwynn screams, kicking the stall door. She sends the door slamming against the wall, and whooshing angrily back and forth, back and forth.

"I'm really sorry," Julia says, putting a hand on Gwynn's back. "He said it was an accident?"

"LIKE IT MATTERS." Gwynn juts out her chin angrily.

"You're absolutely right," Julia says, stepping back in fear. "It doesn't matter. Asshole. Yes. Totally."

There's a knock on the door.

Gwynn narrows her eyes. "Who is it?"

Bryan sticks his head inside. "It's me."

"Get out! GET OUT!" Gwynn shrieks, lunging for the door like a wild animal. "I never want to talk to you again. You cheating asshole! It's over. Do you hear me? *The wedding is off.*"

There's another knock on the door. Kaitlyn enters.

Here we go . . .

"You!" Gwynn shouts, her chest heaving, her hands balled into tight fists. "YOU BITCH."

"Me?" Kaitlyn says sweetly, taking a few steps back. "All I've been doing is helping you."

"HELPING?" Gwynn shrieks incredulously. "You call stealing my fiancé helping?"

Kaitlyn blinks innocently. "Hardly. All I did was help Bryan plan *your* honeymoon. I helped select the destination and comped your luxury suite at my family's hotel. I wouldn't exactly call that stealing your fiancé."

Aaack! That's right. Kaitlyn's family owns that ritzy hotel line—K Hotels. How could I have forgotten? That Bali brochure *must* have been the missing blue folder. And all the messages. *Hot. Too hot. I'm here for you.* It was all honeymoon related!

It's all making sense. Stupid, Vic. Stupid. It's so obvious now!

Hey! But wait a minute. What about Mrs. Goldstone's nasty e-mails? *What about the kiss?* I saw Kaitlyn . . . she was all over him!

"You're a liar!" I hear myself blurt. I immediately slap a hand to my mouth. Why did I just say that? Why?

All heads whip around to stare at me. Bryan groans. Kaitlyn's eyes narrow into two tiny dark slits. That's when Mrs. Goldstone pokes her happy little head into the bathroom, barely able to contain her glee at the sight of more fighting.

Arghh! Could this get any worse? I close my eyes, willing my mouth to speak. Gwynn is going to kill me, but I have to say it. It's now or never. *"I saw you kiss Bryan!"* I shout at Kaitlyn. "You may have helped plan the honeymoon, but you had your own agenda. Admit it. You wanted Bryan this entire time!" Oh God. Oh God. Who am I? Throwing out accusations like that? I could probably get sued. Or at least strangled.

I brace myself.

"So what if I did?" Kaitlyn says haughtily. "Bryan and I were meant for each other. Everyone knows that," her voice goes shrill. "Bryan belongs to me. HE'S MINE!"

Gwynn glares at me in disbelief. *"Vic? You knew* about this?"

I nod painfully. "I . . . I . . . it wasn't Bryan's fault. Swear. He told her no. I saw the whole thing."

Gwynn shakes her head furiously at me, then slowly turns toward Kaitlyn. I can actually see blood racing up her neck and into her cheeks.

"I HATE YOU!" Gwynn finally explodes. "Get out! GET OUT! I never want to see you again!"

Kaitlyn sniffs. She lifts her gorgeous blond head and looks from Bryan to Gwynn, then back again. "You know what? Fine. I don't have to take this," Kaitlyn huffs. "I'm sorry, Mrs. Goldstone. But I'm better than this, I . . ."

"Save the drama." Bryan rolls his eyes. "Just go."

"GO!" Gwynn screams hysterically.

"Look at this!" Mrs. Goldstone's voice ripples with anger. "Your fiancée is clearly crazy. She has no class. Do the right thing, Bryan. You're better than this . . . this trash."

"AND YOU!" Gwynn spats, jamming a red fingertip into Mrs. Goldstone's ivory Chanel suit. "I've read your e-mails. I know you hate me. And I know you're threatening to eliminate Bryan's position. But you know what? We love each other. And I have enough money, we don't *need* yours. How do you like that? We'll be just fine without it—and without you! You . . . you . . . cow."

Julia snickers and immediately coughs to cover it up. Bryan looks horrified and amused all at once. And Mrs. Goldstone looks like a volcano about to erupt. Her flushed cheeks shaking, her eyes bugging out.

"Oh, you little tramp!" she hisses. "You're nothing but new money trash. [*Hey, wait a minute!*] Kaitlyn and Bryan are the perfect New York couple. Perfect! Wealth. Family. Privilege. But *you* had to go and mess it all up. Didn't you? [*What the . . . ?*] Kaitlyn's job was to win him back once and for all. *She failed me.* But don't think I won't throw another well-bred New York girl his way. You wait. This isn't over. [*Ah!*] You're not elegant enough, witty enough, pretty enough [*The nerve!*], or intelligent enough for my son. You're a nothing. A nobody. [*Oh! That's it. No one talks to my friend like that. NO ONE!*] My son is a Goldstone. He deserves . . ."

And before I know what I'm doing, I'm picturing my enemy just like in kickboxing class. My right fist is balled up tight and . . . *whh-aaapp!*

I . . . oh dear God.

I just punched Mrs. Goldstone!

Okay, well, not exactly. *I tried.* I mean, we all saw what a disaster I was in kickboxing class. My slo-ooow motion gave Bryan time to leap in front of his mother, so my right hook only made a harmless jab at his left hand. (Hmph. She did stumble into the wall of hand dryers, though. That must have hurt a little bit?)

Jaws drop. Eyes are huge. Gwynn looks like she could throw her arms around me. And YOW! My knuckles are on fire. Ouch. Ouch. Ouch. MENTAL NOTE: ALWAYS WEAR BOXING GLOVES.

Mrs. Goldstone steadies herself, her red eyes brimming with

tears. "I only want the best for you, Bryan. For you to live close to your father and me. To marry someone we can be proud of."

"I love Gwynn. You know that," Bryan says firmly. (Doesn't his hand hurt *at all*?) "You need to leave."

Mrs. Goldstone lifts her chin high, drawing in a sharp breath. "I won't be attending the wedding tomorrow. Nor will your father." She puts a shaky hand on the bathroom door. She looks at her son for a long moment, then leaves.

Bryan slips out after her.

Gwynn collapses onto the floor in a sobbing mess. "It's over. My wedding, my life. Everything. It's over," she mumbles. Julia and I scoop Gwynn up and carry her out to my car.

"What's going on?" Mrs. Ericsson demands a few minutes later when I go inside to collect Gwynn's stuff. I quickly explain the situation, deleting the part where I tried to punch the future mother-in-law. (Well, wouldn't you?)

"You have to fix this," she says anxiously. "We can't cancel the wedding. The gossip columns would have a field day. You have to *do* something."

"Like what?" I ask helplessly.

"I don't know. *Think of something.*"

My mind races wildly as I jet out to the car to meet Julia and Gwynn. I throw Gwynn's purse and her oversized Gucci bag in the backseat, and that's when I see . . .

The Bali brochure.

"Where did you get this?" I ask Gwynn incredulously.

Gwynn shrugs. "Bryan gave it to me tonight. I already knew we were going to Bali, though. Some surprise. Hmph."

"I told you, Gwynn! *This is the brochure.* The missing blue folder," I spout.

"It can't be," Gwynn huffs indignantly. "That isn't blue. It's indigo."

Oh dear God. I knew I shouldn't have paid any attention to

Gwynn's ridiculous opinions on color. I'd strangle her if she hadn't been through so much already tonight.

We finally get Gwynn to sleep around three o'clock in the morning. Julia and I talk her into *maybe* marrying Bryan tomorrow. *Maybe.* The agreement is, she'll think about it. That's it. No promises.

Julia and I patter into the guest room. I set the alarm and fall into one of Gwynn's fluffy floral goose down beds. What a night . . .

·

I WAKE TO THE LOUD irritating *beep-beeping* sound of delivery trucks backing up in the alley below. I sit up slowly. What time is it? I twist around, squinting to see the alarm clock.

OH SHITTY.

I rub my eyes and check the time again.

I can't believe this.

It's eleven o'clock?! Gwynn was supposed to be at the spa over an hour ago.

Not again. *Why can't I ever be on time?*

Okay. Don't cry. Just think.

"Julia?" I whisper painfully. She doesn't stir.

"JULIA?" I say louder. "It's almost noon!"

Julia props herself up on an elbow, rubbing her eyes sleepily. "Hmm?"

"Look at the clock. We're late!" I whisper hysterically.

Julia's eyes grow wide. She bolts upright. *"What?"*

"You heard me—we're late!"

"Oh my God." Julia leaps to her feet, flies down the hallway, and throws the covers off Gwynn. "Get up! Get up!"

Gwynn sits up and yawns, looking utterly confused. "What's going on?"

"We're late!" Julia and I both yell.

"It's ruined. Everything's ruined," Gwynn sobs a few minutes later. She sits cross-legged on her bed as I phone Maxine.

"Tell the bride not to worry. We have a team of hairstylists and makeup artists armed and ready," the spa receptionist says.

"Okay. We're set. Let's go," I say to Julia and Gwynn, grabbing my Hogan.

Gwynn doesn't budge. "No. I'm not marrying him."

I glare at her incredulously.

"He doesn't deserve me." Gwynn juts out her chin indignantly.

"You're unbelievable." I snort. "Bryan loves you. Do you realize how lucky you are?"

"I don't care," she sniffs. "It's over."

"Oh stop!" I cry. "It was all Kaitlyn and you know it!"

"I don't care. I can't be with someone like that."

"Like what? Someone who loves you? Someone who's forfeiting his job and his family for you? Someone who professed his love for you to a mother who's done everything but try to murder you? GET OVER YOURSELF. I did not spend the last six months playing James Bond for nothing! Do you hear me? Bryan loves you. You love him. And you're getting married today. *The end.*"

Gwynn's mouth is gaping open. Julia looks scared.

"Are we clear?" I ask.

Silence.

"I said, are we clear?"

Gwynn nods.

"Good," I say, yanking Gwynn off the bed. "Because you're getting married this evening. We have a lot to do."

On the way over to Maxine I drop off the bridesmaid dresses and my ridiculous Buddhist monk robe at Happy Cleaners to get pressed.

"Shouldn't they already be pressed?" Gwynn peeps from the backseat.

I shoot her an evil look. "*They were*. They got wrinkled in my car."

"It's fine. Don't worry." Julia smiles, patting Gwynn on the knee. "The dresses will be starched and ready in less than an hour. We'll pick them up while you're getting your makeup done. Okay?"

Gwynn nods.

By the time we get to Maxine, Angel and Dawn are already propped up in big puffy black pedicure chairs, sipping mimosas and admiring their glossy pink toes. Those two are *incredible*. We're almost two hours late and they don't even think to call us?

"Hiii!" Angel coos, holding up her fizzy flute in cheers. "So is the wedding still on? Or do I need to return my shoes?"

"It's on," I say icily.

"Well done." Angel nods her approval. "So where's our bride-to-be?"

"Marco is doing her hair downstairs."

"Super," Angel says. "That's where Dawn and I are headed next, too. What about you two? Are you getting any treatments done today? Oh wait. You guys aren't bridesmaids. My bad."

"*What a bitch,*" I mutter to Julia.

Julia squeezes my hand as we walk down to Marco's hair station. "You're an awesome personal attendant," she says.

I smile. "The best."

Chapter 37

O KAY. STAY CALM. Stay very, very calm.

I can fix this. I'm just not sure how yet . . .

"What are we going to do?" Julia's voice crackles over my cell phone. "I made them search for twenty minutes. They even let me go in the back and sift through all the dresses. They're not here. I promise."

I close my eyes, setting a rose bouquet down on Gwynn's black granite countertop. (I had to run back to Gwynn's place to meet the florist. They delivered the bouquets early!)

"Let me get this straight. You're telling me that Happy Cleaners lost the dresses? Even my hideous Buddhist monk robe?"

"Yes," Julia squeaks.

"Put the manager on the phone," I say, taking a deep breath.

I can't believe this. How could Happy Cleaners misplace four garments in a little over an hour? Is that humanly possible? Thank God Gwynn's wedding gown is hanging from her closet door, safe and sound. Custom-pressed at Barneys and messengered right to her condo.

"Hello!" a chipper man says. "Happy Cleaners. We clean to make you happy. How can I help you?"

"Listen. Do I sound happy to you?"

What a disaster. It turns out our dresses got put in the wrong pile—the trash pile. The lady working the front counter got confused. The super-trendy peasant dresses and silly robe apparently looked so ripped and frayed, she thought they were old rags and dumped them.

Right. So. The whereabouts of Gwynn's hot designer threads by Fred Sander? Somewhere between Chicago and the closest landfill. We need four new dresses—ASAP.

"Okay. Grab a cab back to Maxine and stall Gwynn for as long as possible," I tell Julia. "Don't tell her a thing."

"The wedding is tonight! What are we going to do?" Julia sounds frantic.

"I don't know yet. But I'll think of something," I say. "Gotta go."

Okay. Think, Vic. Think. I need a miracle to happen here. And that's when it hits me. Sugar! They have the most amazing vintage dresses ever. I mean, they won't look like those horrific peasant and fairy godmother numbers (thank God!), but I'm sure they'll be gorgeous. And we can mix and match them a bit. Right?

I dial Polo's cell phone. "We have a slight problem. Here's what we need to do . . ."

•

My CELL PHONE RINGS about thirty minutes later. I'm pacing in one of Gwynn's guest bedrooms in a total panic.

"Honey bunny, it's Polo. I'm at Sugar. Cici is showing me the most sensational dresses. Oh my God. *Divine.* Don't you worry, my sweet. I'll be there soon."

"Don't forget shoes!" I say frantically.

I continue to pace back and forth, back and forth. My cell phone rings again. It's Kate from Chicago Wingwoman.

"Just calling to confirm your gig today," Kate says crisply. "I'm sure I don't need to remind you about our agreement. Hmm? If you flake on me today, you're fired. Got it? I don't care whose wedding this is. Don't test me."

Ugh. Great. Just great. That desk job is sounding more appealing by the minute. At least, with that, my butt never showed up on billboards! (Uh, didn't I mention that? No one else seems to realize the photos in the new Chicago Wing-woman ads are of me in the fashion show, so I'm trying Gwynn's "pretend" method and ignoring it altogether). This is just completely impossible. There's no way I can play wing-woman and personal attendant on the same night. And Gwynn is my good friend . . . even if she has turned into a monster the last few months. I can't do this to her. Can I?

Ooh. Wait. Maybe she never has to find out.

Yes. Yes. Just like that night at Zentra when I pulled one over on Kimmie and Julia! I can do that again. Right? No one will ever suspect a thing.

But this is Gwynn's wedding . . .

Arghh! What should I do? I can't handle this. Seriously. My chest hurts. Is that a sharp pain? Oh God. I'm having a heart attack. I really am this time.

Just then, the door to the guest bedroom flings open. It's Polo. THANK GOD. His arms are heaping full with delicate dresses in all different colors—nude, indigo, black, peach, white, mint green, fire red . . .

"I adore Sugar!" Polo sings, tottering into the room and dropping the dresses on the bed. "Fabulous. And I found the cutest ties!" He holds up three identical pale pink Armani ties. "For Pierre, Philip, and I. We'll look adorable. *Non?*" He smiles and rubs his bald head happily. "And look!" He pulls out a sil-ver shoebox. "The ties match these!" Polo slowly opens the sil-ver box to reveal the cutest pair of pale pink Manolos with tiny silk ribbons that tie in floppy bows around the ankles.

"For Gwynnie." Polo grins, absolutely delighted.

"They're adorable," I say, wrinkling my nose. "But they're pink. Shouldn't they match her white dress?"

"*Non, non, non! Pink is très better!* And they'll match our ties. I can't believe I didn't think of this sooner. Gwynnie-pooh will love it. Trust me."

"What about the dresses?" I ask, slightly frantic.

"Ah, yes." Polo's stubby fingers fly through all the dresses. "Red? Mint? Hmm. These four frocks pair up nicely." Polo holds up two ivory dresses and two black dresses with ivory accents.

"Wow. These are *amazing*." I finger the intricate beading on one of the short ivory frocks.

That's when Julia runs into the guest room in a wild tizzy. "They're coming. They're coming. I couldn't hold them off any longer at Maxine. I think they know something is up!"

"How? Did you tell them?" I blurt.

Julia bites her lip. "Maybe."

"Julia! How could you?"

"The wedding is in three hours! No one has a dress but Gwynn. They forced it out of me. And . . . and I'm pregnant." Julia pouts. "I can't take this pressure."

At that moment, Gwynn, Mrs. Ericsson, and the brides-maids all burst into the guest room.

"YOU LOST THEM?" Mrs. Ericsson shakes her head in fury. "How could you? I'll be the laughingstock. I told every-one, *everyone* that Gwynn's bridesmaids are wearing custom Fred Sander. What will I tell people? Hmm?"

"I'm sorry," I say, my hands shaking.

"Sorry? That's not good enough," Mrs. Ericsson says, point-ing a bony finger at me angrily. "What should I tell everyone?"

"Tell them the truth," Eva grumbles. "They were fucking ugly as sin."

I love Eva. I could hug Eva!

"That's enough of your mouth, young lady." Mrs. Ericsson glares at her daughter.

"Whatever. I like this dress," Eva says, holding up one of the sexy black frocks with intricate gathers around the waistline. "It's fucking hot."

Gwynn's eyes light up. "Wow. They look like Prada's new line."

"Stop it," Mrs. Ericsson seethes. "Don't encourage your sister."

"I'm not." Gwynn shrugs. "I like the dress. And I think it's 100 percent better than the stupid Fred Sander dresses. And he screwed up my wedding gown. He . . . he *fucking* sucks."

Eva grins wide, patting her big sister on the shoulder. "Right on."

"Ah—I can't deal with you two!" Mrs. Ericsson throws her hands up in surrender. "Do whatever you want."

I start spreading out the dresses and helping Polo choose. Two red ones. A divine peach frock. So many dresses! He's right, though—I love the four black and ivory Prada-like ones. They definitely don't match, but they'll coordinate . . . *sort of.*

"And look!" Polo says proudly, pulling out the pink Armani ties and matching Manolos. "The cutest!" he sings.

Gwynn's entire face lights up. She grabs one of the pink Manolos, then eyes the three matching ties. "I LOVE IT."

Chapter 38

I CAN'T BELIEVE IT. This is it. Gwynn is officially getting married. The white Rolls-Royce purrs up to the Lincoln Park Zoo entrance and we all pile out. Gwynn is wearing the pale pink Manolos and my Donna Karan wedding dress. (Our little secret! Okay. Fine. Polo knows about the dress, too. But only because he had to write me a check.) And then Angel, Dawn, Eva, and I have on the vintage Prada look-alikes from Sugar. (*Sooo* much better than my original Buddhist monk robe!)

It's a magnificent evening. Deep lavender sky. Shimmery golden sun. Sweet white roses bursting all around. I can already see the gigantic white tent set up by the sea lion tank. There are rows and rows of white-linen-covered chairs facing an ivy-covered trellis. And there are two snow-white trumpeter swans waddling about. How cute. (Did Polo rent them? Or wait. Are they the same ones I saw that sunny afternoon with Everett?)

As we make our way through the redbrick pavilion and over to the white tent, I watch Gwynn closely. I've never seen her like this before. She looks so vibrant, so alive, so breathtaking. Her shiny blond hair is swept up into a classic chignon with a tiny diamond leaf tucked just above the knot. And her soft silk white dress flows around her like a cloud. I'm afraid to touch her. She barely looks real.

It feels strange to see someone I've known for almost six years about to walk down the aisle. Commit herself to someone else. It's like this secret bond they're about to share. It's theirs and only theirs. I can feel myself tearing up. I always knew I wanted that someday. It's such a shame I screwed everything up with Patrick. Maybe we'd be doing this too someday . . .

Stop. Stop it right now, Vic. You need to put Patrick out of your mind. It's over.

Julia and Kevin walk up.

"I hear you two had quite a morning." Kevin grins.

"You could say that." I laugh.

That's when I spot Kimmie and DJ walking up the brick pavilion. Kimmie catches my eye, then looks away. My stomach tightens.

"Kimmie!" Julia says, running over and grabbing her arm. "Come say hi."

DJ smiles nervously and scratches his head, and Kimmie looks down at her feet. She's wearing a new pair of red alligator pumps. Very cute. (I wonder who they're by? I've never seen them before.)

Julia nudges us closer together encouragingly.

"Hi," I say at last.

Kimmie lifts her curly red head up and for a short awful moment I imagine her pouncing on me, hissing, scratching my face, kicking me with her sexy new red pumps. Instead, to my surprise, she smiles and says, "Hey."

"I am so stupid," I blurt. "Can you ever forgive me? I was just scared. I made a mistake. And . . . and have I mentioned that I'm stupid? So stupid. And . . ." I close my eyes and brace myself. "I'm just so sorry."

Silence.

I peel open an eye.

Kimmie is grinning back at me, shaking her head in amusement. "I forgive you, you big dope."

My eyes fly open. "Really?"

"But only on one condition," Kimmie says. "That you'll be my maid of honor."

"Are you serious?" I squeal, jumping up and down. "Of course I will!" Kimmie and I hug, and Julia claps like a proud mother.

We laugh and to my surprise, my laughing turns into sobbing. And for some terrible reason, I can't stop. The tears keep streaming down my cheeks.

"Oh my God. What's wrong?" Julia asks.

"Nothing," I sniffle. "I'm just so happy. Everyone's getting married. You're moving away . . . *and having a baby!*" I sob. "It's so great! Everything's . . . so great."

"You don't sound great," Julia says, putting her arm around me.

"What's going on?" Kimmie demands.

I wipe a few tears away with a tissue. "I feel so alone. And . . . I . . . I messed up with Patrick. We're over."

"*What?*" Kimmie gasps.

"I accidentally st-stole his credit card . . ." My voice wavers.

"And he sa-saw me with Aiden. But nothing happened! I sw-swear!"

Kimmie's jaw drops. "So that's why he's leaving . . ."

"Leaving?" I blow my nose.

"Vic . . ." Kimmie puts a hand on my forearm, wrinkling her nose. "I thought you knew. Patrick is moving to New York. His flight leaves today. Right after his big promo event at Wrigley Field. His Gatorade client is throwing the first pitch."

"What?" My heart stops. This doesn't make any sense.

"He said he was finally taking over his dad's agency," Kimmie says.

Oh dear God. This can't be true. Patrick doesn't want to move to New York. He doesn't want to take over his dad's agency. He . . . he told me. He doesn't.

Oh no. I sink to the ground in shock. I can't believe this. I saw him almost a week ago outside of Lambert Advertising. Did he know he was moving then? It all happened so . . . so fast . . .

"Quick. Julia, what time is it?" Kimmie asks.

"Um . . ." Julia checks her watch. "It's almost five. But Kimmie . . . what are you thinking? The wedding is at six thirty. Seriously. We can call Patrick. Let's not go crazy. New York is only a flight away. Vic can even stay with me. We don't need to do anything drastic."

"He can't leave Chicago. He can't get on that plane. It'll be over," Kimmie says.

"Oh no." Julia looks worried. "Here we go . . ."

"What's going on?" Gwynn floats over to us, smiling dreamily.

Kimmie pulls us into a huddle. "Okay. Here's the plan . . ."

"You have one hour," Gwynn says, handing us the keys to the Rolls-Royce. "I mean it. I will *kill* you if you're late to my wedding."

"Let's go!" Kimmie cries, shoving us toward the car.

"You guys, maybe Julia is right. Maybe I should call. I mean, what if we can't find him at Wrigley Field?" I say frantically. "There are thousands of people there and . . ."

Kimmie stops and stares me straight in the eye. "What are you so afraid of?"

"What?" I ask.

"I can tell you love him. What the hell is your problem?" Kimmie demands. "Go after him. Come on already!"

She's right. Kimmie is so right! What am I so afraid of? Patrick is the best thing that's ever happened to me. Am I really going to let him walk out of my life without a fight? No . . .

I'm a lover *and* a fighter!

"Who's driving?" I yell, diving into the backseat.

Gwynn looks over her bare shoulder at her perfect white wedding and takes a deep breath. "Oh . . . screw it. I am! Move over," she tells Kimmie.

"WHAT?" we all shriek.

"But your wedding?" I say, biting my lip.

"Like they'll start it without the bride. Besides, I have a short-cut." Gwynn grins.

Wow. I haven't seen that smile in months. It's the old Gwynn. The fun Gwynn! The Gwynn who used to fly us around the city in her red BMW.

Tears well up and I have this sudden urge to leap out of the car and throw my arms around Gwynn. Tell her . . .

"Well, *let's move it!*" Gwynn barks. "I have a wedding in an hour. Remember? Snap. Snap."

Okay. Fine. Maybe not *exactly* the same Gwynn. But close . . .

The four of us swerve through Lincoln Park and cut over to Sheridan Road. We fly like madwomen up to Addison Street. The windows are down and our hair whips around wildly.

"Shouldn't we slow down?" I yell over the wind.

"Be quiet," Gwynn snaps. "I'm concentrating."

Julia is buckled in tightly and holding on for dear life. "We're going to die. We're going to die."

I look at the speedometer in horror: 75. Oh dear God. *On a residential street?* Thank God there's a stop sign ahead. Gwynn squeals onto Addison and floors it again. Green light. Green light. God. We're getting so lucky with the lights! We're almost there.

We peel up to Clark and Addison and Gwynn slams on the brakes. There are Cubs fans swarming on the streets and I can feel myself starting to panic. I peer up at the giant red WRIGLEY FIELD: HOME OF THE CHICAGO CUBS sign and close my eyes. What am I doing?

"Get out!" Gwynn shouts, flipping on the hazards. "What are you waiting for? Go buy tickets. Run!"

The four of us stumble out of the Rolls-Royce in our full wedding gear and race up to the ticket booths. People are nudging their friends and pointing at Gwynn in her silky white wedding gown.

"Congratulations!" a Cubs fan calls over to Gwynn.

"Thank you so much," Gwynn gushes, twirling around to model her dress.

"Four tickets please," I gasp, slapping down my Visa.

I can hear Gwynn in the background. "Yes. Yes. I love it, too. It's Donna Karan. Did you notice the beading around . . ."

"Sorry. We're sold out," the cashier grunts.

Aaack!

I whip around frantically, but Kimmie is already shoving wads of cash at a ticket scalper. "Let's go!" She points to the park entrance.

As soon as we push our way through the ticket turnstile, Kimmie runs over to a green-vested usher.

"Excuse me, sir. I'm with Lambert Advertising," Kimmie says sweetly, batting her eyelashes. "Our Gatorade client is throwing the first pitch and I have an extremely important message for Patrick Lewis, the creative director. How would I find him?"

The usher eyes Gwynn's wedding gown and shoots us all a funny look, then shrugs. "Come with me," he says slowly.

And before I know what's going on, the usher is opening a small green gate and leading us onto the immaculately groomed field. (Oh dear God. We're actually stepping onto Wrigley Field. This is insane!) There are Cubs players in their blue-and-white pin-striped uniforms warming up on the field, throwing base-balls back and forth and stretching their calf muscles. I can't believe we're doing this . . .

I'm about to turn around and say we should leave when I see Patrick. He's standing on the pitcher's mound with about six other men in black Gatorade polos. My breath catches. And that's when I know it.

I have to do what I have to do. *No matter what.*

"What are you waiting for?" Kimmie shrieks.

"Go! Go! Go!" the girls cry.

And with that, I run onto the field, feeling my heels sink-ing into the grass. "Patrick!" I say breathlessly. My heart pounds wildly.

Patrick looks up in astonishment. "Victoria! *What are you doing here?*"

I can hear Kimmie, Julia, and Gwynn elbowing one another and whispering nervously.

"I heard about New York. You can't leave!" I blurt.

Patrick's jaw flexes. He pulls his black glasses off and props them on his head. "This is crazy! You need to go. I'm working."

Someone clicks on a microphone. "Testing. Testing one, two, three."

"I know. I know this is crazy." My lips quiver. "But I don't care. I . . . I want you to stay. I want to work things out. I'm so sorry about everything. Let me explain. *Please.*"

One of the Gatorade clients taps Patrick on the shoulder and hands him the microphone. "It's time. You need to announce us."

"Okay. One second." Patrick smiles tightly at his client, covering the microphone with his hand. "Listen. Just go." Patrick shakes his head. "I have to do this."

"No," I say, reaching for his arm, but accidentally grabbing the microphone. I can hear Gwynn, Kimmie, and Julia gasp as my voice fills the stadium, but I don't care. I'm here to win Patrick back. I have to do what I have to do. And if all of Wrigley Field has to hear it, well, fine.

"You can't get on that plane. It was a mistake," I plead. "The credit card. Getting in the car with Aiden. All of it."

A hush falls over the stadium and I can hear a few Cubs fans shouting:

"What the hell is going on?"
"Shh! I think she's proposing or something."
"Holy Jesus. I've seen everything now . . ."

"Victoria, this is insane. Give me the microphone!" Patrick stares at me in astonishment.

"No!" I step back, my hands shaking. "You have to forgive me first."

"Forgive her already. Let's start the game, for fuck's sake!" an angry fan shouts.

"How can I trust you? You lied about everything," Patrick says angrily. "For all I know, you've been dating Aiden this entire time."

"No!" I cry. "You know that's not true. You have to believe me. I don't even like him. I like you . . . *I love you.*"

"GO VICTORIA!" a familiar voice hoots. I look up to see my client Marty with his arm slung around his rosy-cheeked brunette. "Give him hell."

"I'm sorry," Patrick says, shaking his head. "I can't do this."

Well . . .

That's it.

I tried.

A few fans boo as I exit the field, my chin down, shoulders drooped.

I can't believe it. It's over. It's really over.

Chapter 39

AS I WATCH Gwynn walk down the aisle, birds chirping and the soft breeze blowing through the zoo, I cry for several reasons. I cry for myself. Because Patrick and I didn't work out. I cry because I know after today things will never be the same. *Not really.* We're officially stepping into a new stage of our lives. And, well, new beginnings are always a bit scary.

I cry for Gwynn. Because I'm so incredibly happy for her and Bryan. As they hold hands and say their vows under the ivy-covered trellis, I realize that all the hard work, crazy wedding lists, stalking, snooping, punching (oops!) . . . was worth it. They look so happy.

I guess that's what it's all about. Just finding that person. That one single person who makes you happy. And taking a leap with them.

I leaped today. And it didn't work out.

But as I peer out over all the wedding guests, and I see Kimmie and Julia grinning back at me, I know everything is going to be okay. I know that we'll always be here for one another—through everything—the jobs, the boyfriends, the weddings, all of it. Maybe change and growing up isn't so bad when you're surrounded by all the people you care about the most.

•

DURING THE COCKTAIL HOUR, I halfheartedly try to set up the drunk frat boy with a few single girls, but I quickly reach my limit. The frat boy is disgusting. He keeps groping the girls. Groping me. Slugging down more and more beer. And that's when I know it's over. I don't want to be a wing-woman anymore. I want to be with my friends. *This is Gwynn's wedding.* Something I want to remember. Not waste on some drunk frat boy. No. This is too important.

"I quit," I say at last.

"*What?* You can't quit. You're my wingwoman!" frat boy bellows, swinging his pilsner glass all around.

"Yes I can. And I am."

"But I hired you. I paid double. I'll . . . I'll tell Kate!" he slurs.

"Please do," I say icily, turning on a heel. "Because I'm through."

Wow. I can't believe I just did that. My entire body shakes as I head toward the bar. I'm no longer a wingwoman. Part of me is sad because I've always loved matching people up. But the other part of me knows this job was always temporary. I knew I had to grow up someday. Right?

I grab a flute of champagne and peer out onto the dance floor with its white twinkly lights dangling above everyone's heads. Gwynn and Bryan are dancing slowly, completely lost in their own world. Polo, Pierre, and Philip are busily barking orders into their headsets. (Polo was right. Their pale pink ties really do look adorable with Gwynn's matching Manolos!)

Mom and Dad are munching away on some of Gwynn's mocha truffle wedding cake. They look up and I wave. Birdie is clicking around with her red cane trying to hand out condoms to all the guests. (Good thing Gwynn isn't paying any attention.) Julia and Kevin are laughing hysterically as DJ attempts to throw Kimmie over his shoulder while she kicks and screams like mad. And the two white swans are touching their orange beaks together for a kiss. (Hmm. Did Polo teach them how to do that?)

Mr. and Mrs. Goldstone didn't show—to Gwynn's sheer delight. I feel bad for Bryan, but he seems to be taking it well. Maybe even expecting this sort of thing from his parents?

That's when my cell phone rings. It's Everett.

"SHE SAID YES. My cowgirl said yes!" he cries.

"Everett, that's wonderful!"

"I just called to say thanks, Vic. I mean it. You're the best wingwoman ever. You're like Cupid."

I smile happily, my cheeks flushing. "Too bad my arrows didn't work on Patrick."

"What's that?"

"Nothing," I say weakly. "I'll call you later this week. Okay?"

"Hey, real quick," Everett says. "I was talking to a buddy of mine. He could use a makeover. Like you did for me. Clothes. Hair. Dating tips. He'd pay you, of course. Would you be interested?"

My ears perk up. Makeovers! That's right. I L-O-V-E-D giving Everett a makeover. Could this be my next job?

"Sure! Give him my number," I bubble.

Even after we say good-bye, I'm still smiling. Everett sounded so happy. So confident. I feel like I really helped him. I'm glad I was a wingwoman for his sake . . . and for Oscar's. Oscar called me the other day. I guess he's getting along really well with Chiseled Girl. They're going rock climbing this weekend. (Ha! How funny is that?) Who knows. Maybe I'll keep doing a few wingwoman gigs on the side. Just for fun . . .

But what else? Could I really do makeovers full-time? Or should I settle down and find a desk job? I look up at all the glittering stars and try to picture myself sitting at a desk again. Staring at a computer all day. I don't know. I might not be ready for that again. Oh, what's the rush. I'll figure it out . . .

·

LATER ON, as I'm dashing off the dance floor to grab drinks for the girls (Singletinis, to be exact; we haven't had those yummy concoctions lately), I run smack into . . . Jay Schmidt. He flashes me a big toothy grin.

Good. Great. Just who I wanted . . .

Wait. Why is he smiling like that? He looks so pleased, so smug, so . . . oh God. Is there another photo I don't know about? Another . . . ?

"You're welcome," he says sweetly.

I blink. "Excuse me?"

"Your photo," Jay says, raising an eyebrow. "It's going national. Big campaign from what I hear. Huge! The whole *Got Wings* thing was brilliant and, well, *City Girls* did publish photos of your butt before anyone else. My photos, that is." He smiles expectantly.

What?

He's kidding, right?

Just then, my cell phone rings. I absently rummage through my bag.

"You could at least say thanks." Jay huffs, swinging his camera around his neck and walking onto the dance floor.

"Hello?" I say, rubbing my temples.

"Victoria, we need to chat," a voice explodes into my ear.

Oh shitty! It's Kate from Chicago Wingwoman. What do I do? Should . . . should I hang up?

"I understand you just quit," Kate barks, before I can utter a word. "This is very good news."

I scratch my head. "It is?"

"Absolutely. I need you for a different job. I want to bring you on as a spokesmodel."

A WHAT?!

"Our *Got Wings* campaign was such a hit, we're expanding it to every major metropolitan area in the country," Kate says excitedly. "It seems people are loving your ass. It's so real. So normal looking."

"Um . . . thanks. I think?"

"Anyway, we just hired Nine Communications to do the national campaign. Have you heard of them? New York agency. Very prestigious."

Wait a sec. Nine Communications? Isn't that Patrick's family's company?

"I'm thinking we'll need you in New York for a couple of months at least. Lots of events. Photo shoots. I don't suppose you could lose a few pounds? Hmm? Nothing drastic. Just five or ten. Your butt is fabulous, though. So obviously don't change that one bit."

Is this for real? I mean . . .

"No need to give me your answer right now," Kate continues. "Think about it. Maybe let me know by Monday or Tuesday? Nine Communications will be in touch to set up your travel arrangements. Sound good?"

"Um . . . sure. I guess so," I say dazedly.

I drop my cell phone into my bag and right as I glance up, I see . . .

Oh my God.

Patrick?

My mouth falls open. My heart races.

"What . . . what are you doing here?" I stammer as he squeezes through the crowd toward me.

"I can't stay long." Patrick glances at his watch. "I'm on my way to catch the red-eye, but I, well, I wanted to see you."

"You did?" I squeak.

"I got a few phone calls this evening." Patrick smiles. "From Kate . . . *and your friends.*"

"What?" I eye Kimmie, Julia, and Gwynn on the dance floor. They wave back at me excitedly.

"They all said you need to come to New York." Patrick grins.

"Oh, they did, did they?" I say, raising an eyebrow playfully.

"Yep." Patrick shakes his head. "Kate asked me to handle your travel. And so, I was thinking you could put all your expenses on my card." His dark eyes twinkle. "My corporate card, that is."

"Right. Of course." I nod, my entire body tingling with excitement.

Patrick takes a deep breath. "What I'm really trying to say is . . . I'm sorry. I really am, Vic. I wanted to say it earlier at Wrigley Field, but I wasn't expecting you and . . . it doesn't matter. I should have trusted you before. I'm sorry."

Ahhhhhh! *I can't believe it.*

Okay. Act cool. Breathe. "I don't know," I say, wriggling my nose. "What's the limit on your card again?"

"Vic!" Patrick laughs.

"I'm kidding!" I cry, throwing my arms around him. "I can't believe you're here."

"I'm glad I am." Patrick wraps his arms around my waist. "I've missed having my wingwoman around."

"Oh yeah?" I bite my lip. "Well, I have news. I'm hanging up my wings."

"*Really?*" Patrick's eyes grow wide. "I hope you aren't hanging them up for too long. I'm launching an entire campaign around your cute little butt."

"I haven't agreed to anything yet." I grin.

"What are you two doing?" Kimmie suddenly howls from the dance floor. "Get out here and dance!"

I gaze up into Patrick's warm dark eyes. "Want to?"

"You go." Patrick smiles, waving toward the girls. "I have a flight to catch. But I'll see you in New York?"

"We'll see," I say coyly. "We'll see."

As Patrick bends down and kisses me good-bye, I realize that I am officially the happiest, luckiest singletini in Chicago. And, well, maybe soon I'll be the happiest ex-singletini in Manhattan?

I mean, you never know.

New York might not be *sooo* bad . . .

Right?

(Pure bliss!)

P.S. Dying to Know
What's in a Singletini?

Okay. Okay. You twisted my arm. I'll tell you our super-secret recipe, but only if you promise to keep it quiet. You know . . . just between you and your best singletini pals. (I mean, we don't want everyone and her sister sipping on this sweet little cocktail, now do we?) Hope you like it as much as we do.

Cheers!

Vic

The Recipe

WHAT YOU NEED

Sugar

1½ ounces SKYY Melon vodka

½ ounce of cranberry juice

Ice

2 ounces of your favorite champagne

WHAT TO DO

Dip the rim of a frosty martini glass in sugar. Shake the vodka and cranberry juice with ice and strain into your glass. Top off with the champagne. Voilà!

(Ooh, I almost forgot! Drink smart—and slow. No one likes a sloppy singletini.)

SKYY VODKA.
www.skyy.com   www.singletini.com

Special Thanks

Writing this book was such a great experience and it would not have happened without the help of two truly amazing women:

Jenny Bent, my brilliant agent, who took a giant leap of faith in me. I will forever be grateful for her constant enthusiasm and invaluable guidance.

And Shana Drehs, my genius and ever-fabulous editor, whose sharp eye and hilarious ideas made this book a million times better. I feel incredibly lucky to have worked with her.

I'd also like to thank Selina Cicogna, Kim Dayman, Sibylle Kazeroid, Lauren Dong, Laura Duffy, Catherine Groat, and everyone at Three Rivers Press. I'd like to thank my friends and family, especially John, Sue, Sherri, J. D., Susan, and Caleb. And thank you to the entire Grimse and Ochab crew for all your support.

Thank you to my tough and insightful undergraduate and graduate writing instructors at the University of Illinois and DePaul University: Jean Thompson, Ted Anton, Craig Sirles, Anne Calcagno, and Larry Heinemann.

Thanks to all the folks at Landor, particularly Tyler Mallison, Rebecca Titcomb, Matt Irwin, Kimball Wilkins, Matt Gordon, Amanda "Gucky" Peterson, Anthony Shore, and Michael Friel.

Warmest thanks (and a million hugs!) to the girls and the original "singletinis," who inspired me and cheered for me every step of the way: Lauren Doughty, Jen Hodapp, Jen Hovey, Julie Lasser, Amy Miller, Liz Minster, Shannon O'Hare, Carrie Rodman, Kristine Speyer, and Holly Zar.

And finally, but most important, thank you to Ralph Grimse for your endless patience and encouragement . . . and, well, for letting me hog the couch and the computer for the past two years. (They're all yours now. Swear.)